POSTER GIRL

ALSO BY VERONICA ROTH

Chosen Ones

The End and Other Beginnings: Stories from the Future

CARVE THE MARK SERIES

Carve the Mark

The Fates Divide

DIVERGENT SERIES

Divergent

Insurgent

Allegiant

Four: A Divergent Collection

POSTER GIRL

VERONICA ROTH

wm

A John Joseph Adams Book

WILLIAM MORROW

An Imprint of HarperCollins*Publishers*

This is a work of fiction. Names, characters, places, and incidents are products of the author's imagination or are used fictitiously and are not to be construed as real. Any resemblance to actual events, locales, organizations, or persons, living or dead, is entirely coincidental.

HarperCollins books may be purchased for educational, business, or sales promotional use. For information, please email the Special Markets Department at SPsales@harpercollins.com.

FIRST EDITION

Designed by Emily Snyder
Title page photograph © magann/stock.adobe.com

Library of Congress Cataloging-in-Publication Data has been applied for.

ISBN 978-0-358-16409-8
ISBN 978-0-06-328202-5 (international edition)

22 23 24 25 26 LSC 10 9 8 7 6 5 4 3 2 1

To Tera and Trevor,
hosts of the pandemic oasis where I wrote this book
and dearest friends

POSTER GIRL

ONE

WHEN SHE THINKS of the time before, she thinks of the photo shoot. The woman who applied Sonya's makeup smelled of lilies of the valley and hair spray. When she leaned close to dust Sonya's cheeks with blush, or to cover up a blemish with a fingertip dotted beige, Sonya stared at the freckles on her collarbone. When she finished, the woman slicked her hands with oil and ran them through Sonya's hair to make it sleek.

Then she held up a mirror for Sonya to see herself, and Sonya's eyes went first to the woman's face, half-hidden by glass. Then, to the pale halo of her Insight, a circle of light around her right iris. It brightened in recognition of Sonya's own Insight.

Now, a decade later, she tries to remember what her reflection looked like in that moment, but all she can see is the final product: the poster. On it, her young face gazes out at an unseen horizon. One of the slogans of the Delegation embraces her from above:

WHAT'S RIGHT

And below:

IS RIGHT.

She remembers the camera flash, the photographer's hand as he reached to the side to show her where to look, the gentle piano music that played in the background. The feeling of being right at the heart of something.

SHE pinches a cherry tomato from the stem and drops it in the basket with the others.

"Yellow leaves means too much water," Nikhil says. He frowns at the book in his lap. "Wait—or too little. Well, which is it?"

Sonya kneels on the grit of Building 4's roof, surrounded by plant beds. Nikhil built them. Every time someone in the building died, he took the worst of their furniture and pried it apart, saving nails and screws and salvaging what he could of the wood. As a result, the beds are a patchwork of wood colors and textures, here a strip of polished mahogany, there a piece of unvarnished oak.

Beyond the roof is the city. She doesn't pay attention to it. It may as well be the backdrop of a school play, painted on a sheet.

"I told you, that book is useless," she says. "Trial and error is the only way to really learn anything, with plants."

"Perhaps you're right."

This is the last harvest of the year. Soon they will clear the beds of dead plants and cover them with tarps to protect the soil. They will move all the tools into the shed to keep them dry and carry the pots of mint down to Sonya's apartment so they can chew the leaves all winter. In January, after months of eating from cans, they will be desperate to taste something green.

He closes the book. Sonya picks up the basket.

"We'd better go," she says. "Or everything good will be gone."

It's Saturday. Market day.

"I've been eyeballing that broken radio for two months, and no one has shown an interest. It'll keep."

"You never know. Remember that time I waffled about that old sweater for three weeks and lost it at the last second to Mr. Nadir?"

"You did get it, in the end."

"Because Mr. Nadir *died.*"

Nikhil winks. "Every end is a new beginning."

Together they walk to the top of the staircase. They go at Nikhil's pace—his knees are not what they used to be, and it's a long descent to the courtyard. She takes a tomato from the basket and holds it to her nose.

She never gardened as a child. She learned everything she knows now through failure—and boredom. But she still associates the sweet, dusty smell with summer, and so she remembers the haze of heat above the sidewalk, and the tension in badminton racquet strings, and the purple-red of her mother's sangria, an infrequent indulgence.

"Don't eat our product," Nikhil says.

"Wasn't going to."

They reach the bottom of the stairs and walk across the courtyard. It's green and unkempt, the trees straining at the building that contains them, scratching the windows of those lucky enough to have a view. Sonya is jealous of the ones who do. They can pretend. The others, like Sonya, whose windows look out at the city beyond the Aperture, confront the fact that they're imprisoned daily. Three stories below Sonya's window is a coil of barbed wire. Across the way is a collapsing corner store offering five minutes with a pair of binoculars for a nominal fee. She tied a sheet across her windows ten years ago and hasn't drawn it back since.

On her knees at the edge of the garden path is Mrs. Pritchard, her graying hair in a chignon. She's digging a dandelion out by the root using a shovel made of a few kitchen spoons tied together. Her hands are bare and her wedding band still gleams on her finger, though Mr. Pritchard was executed a long time ago. She sits back on her heels.

"Good morning," she says. The Insight in her right eye brightens as she makes eye contact with Sonya, and again when she looks at Nikhil. It's a reminder that even though the Delegation has fallen, someone could still be watching them.

"Is it market day already?" she asks. "I keep losing track."

Despite kneeling in the dirt, Mrs. Pritchard looks perfect, her shirt free of creases and tucked into a pair of trousers. She has altered clothes for Sonya before, after Lainey Newman died and her things were redistributed within the Aperture.

"Good morning," Nikhil returns.

"Good morning," Sonya says. "Yes, Nikhil wants a broken radio, for some reason."

"A broken radio that Sonya will fix," Nikhil says.

"I don't know the first thing about radios."

"You'll work it out. You always do."

Mrs. Pritchard makes a strained sound behind pressed lips, and then says, "Those tomatoes are more valuable than a radio. What could you possibly want to hear from—" She gestures toward the outer wall of the Aperture. "Out there?"

"I'm not sure yet," he says. "I suppose I'll find out when I get a radio."

She changes the subject. "Have you spoken with Building 1 about assigning patrols for the visitation?"

"Anna assures me they're handling it."

"Because we can't have another *incident* like the one from three years ago."

"Of course not."

"We can't have them thinking we're a bunch of wild animals—"

Three years ago, when the three leaders of the government *out there* visited the Aperture, several drunk residents of Building 2 threw bottles at them. For weeks afterward, deliveries to the Aperture were halted. Some people went without food. It's in everyone's best interest to keep the peace when outsiders visit—but with the guards' policy of nonintervention, it's the prisoners' job to police themselves.

"Mary," Sonya says. "Please, don't let us interrupt your work."

She smiles. Mrs. Pritchard sniffs, and picks up her makeshift trowel. Sonya and Nikhil continue along.

They walk through the brick tunnel that leads them across the alley. There are names etched into the bricks, which Sonya runs her fingers over as she walks. There are no graves for the people they've lost; the names are all they have. The floor of the tunnel is covered in candle wax, remnants of mourners. She has often thought that the wax should be scraped off the ground and melted into new candles, but she doesn't do it. They're all used to practicality swallowing sentimentality in the Aperture, but these walls are untouchable.

"Thank you for that," Nikhil says. "She's been pestering me about that for weeks."

"It's always something. Last week she was mad about the trash bags piling up next to the dumpster. As if any of us have control over how often trash is collected here."

Before she exits the tunnel, Sonya reaches up to find the name she carved there herself, standing on a rickety stool with the head of a screwdriver in her fist. *David.* Her fingertips come away gritty.

There are two streets in the Aperture: Green Street and Gray Street, named for the colors of the Delegation. They divide the Aperture into quadrants, and in each quadrant is an identical apartment building. Theirs is Building 4, and it's full of widows, widowers, and Sonya.

The market is at the center of the Aperture, where the two streets cross. Sonya remembers what real markets looked like, rows of wooden stalls with canvas tops to protect against the weather. Here, everyone brings what they have to trade, and some lay their goods out on blankets, while others walk around making offers. Almost everything is junk, but junk can be useful, a bundle of spoons turning into a trowel, a rickety table becoming a garden bed.

She hasn't forgotten the feeling of fine things. The cold slide of silk on her bare arms. The snap of new shoes on wooden floors. Her fingernails pinching a crease into wrapping paper at Christmas. Her mother always bought gold and green.

As it turns out, time does not dull every edge.

She pulls closer to Nikhil as they pass a group of men closer to her age. She knows all their names—Logan, and Gabe, and Seby, and Dylan—and it's for that reason that she pretends she doesn't see them. They are a sprawling group, one leaning against Building 2, one in the middle of the street, one perched on the curb, one with a hand on the light pole.

"Poster *girl,*" Logan sings, as he turns around the pole, held up by his fingertips.

Even before she was in the Aperture, people called her that. They used to do it because they recognized her face but didn't know her name. It used to feel like a compliment, when she was sixteen and finally stepping out of her older sister's shadow. It's not a compliment anymore.

"Can't pretend not to know us in the Aperture, Sonya. Only so many fish in this fucking fishbowl," Gabe says, as he sidles up next to her. He slides his arm across Sonya's shoulders. "Why don't you hang out with us anymore?"

"Too good for us, probably," Seby says. He picks his teeth with a fingernail.

"Are you, then?" Gabe grins. He smells like moonshine and lavender soap. "Not how I remember it."

Sonya lifts his arm away from her shoulders and gives him a little shove. "Go find someone else to bother, Gabe."

All four of them laugh at her.

"Good afternoon, boys," Nikhil says then. "Hope you're staying out of trouble."

"Of course, Mr. Price. Just catching up with our old friend."

"I see," Nikhil says. "Well, as it happens, we are on an errand, so we'll be on our way."

"Sure thing, Mr. Price." Gabe wiggles his fingers at her, but doesn't follow them.

Building 2, where most of the younger people ended up after they were all locked in, is the most chaotic place in the Aperture. Logan was in school with Sonya once, a few grades above her. He almost burned down Building 2 last year while cooking a drug made out of cold medicine. And there are always fumes from tubs of moonshine wafting around the building's courtyard. There was a time when she could identify who made each batch by how it burned her nose and pinched her throat. All anyone wants in Building 2 is to grind time down like a molar.

Gray Street meets Green Street in a stretch of cracked pavement, covered now in old quilts and heaps of all manner of things: stained or ripped clothes piled high, stacks of cans with the labels scrubbed off, cords with frayed ends, folding chairs, split pillows, dented pots. For the most part, they're castoffs, donated by people outside the Aperture. The organization that collected them, Merciful Hands, comes every month with new offerings and apologetic smiles.

Sometimes people sell the new things they make from the old, a little broom made of a bundle of wire, sheets stitched together from fabric scraps, dining trays made from hardcover books. Those are Sonya's favorite things. They feel new, and so little here is.

"Look, just as I told you." Nikhil picks up an old radio alarm clock. It has a screen for a display, with two speakers framing it. Black and squat, chipped at the corners. Wires spraying out the back of it. Georgia, a resident of Building 1, is perched on an old crate behind the graveyard of old electronics.

"Doesn't work," she says.

It's not much of a sales pitch.

Sonya takes the radio from Nikhil and makes a show of peeking in the back to see the innards.

"I don't know," she says to Nikhil. "It may not be fixable."

Her education was not in service of repairing old radios. Nor did it teach her to grow tomatoes on the roof of a crumbling building, or to fend off idle men who were already drunk at noon. She has learned many lessons here in the Aperture that she had no interest in learning. But Nikhil looks hopeful, and he wants her to have a project, so she smiles.

"It's worth a try," she says.

"That's the spirit."

He negotiates with Georgia. Three tomatoes for a broken radio. No, Georgia says. Seven.

A few feet away, Charlotte Carter waves Sonya over.

She looks like something out of a story, in her gingham dress and her long braid and her skin dappled with freckles and age spots. Her eyes crease at the corners when she smiles at Sonya.

"Sonya, dear," she says. "Can you do me a favor?"

"Maybe. What do you need?"

"My brother, Graham—over in Building 1, do you know him?"

It's a silly question. Everyone knows everyone in the Aperture. "We've met."

"Yes, yes. Well, his last stove burner stopped working yesterday, and he hasn't been able to cook anything since then." She purses her lips. "He's been using the one in my apartment."

"I'll have to check to see if we've got any spare burners," Sonya says.

"Tonight?" Charlotte sounds eager. The tendons stand out in her throat. "I don't mean to rush you, it's just that he tends to cook and then . . . *stay.*"

Sonya suppresses a laugh. "I have a party tonight. But I can go in the morning."

"Oh yes," Charlotte says. "The goodbye party, I forgot."

Sonya ignores the sad tug at the corners of Charlotte's mouth. "Tomorrow morning?"

"Yes, that will be fine."

Nikhil and Georgia are still arguing. Sonya rejoins them just long enough to hear Georgia accuse Nikhil of giving her bad tomatoes the last time he bought something, and then she clears her throat.

"Five tomatoes," Sonya says. "It's a generous offer and I won't repeat it."

Georgia sighs, and agrees. Sonya hands over the tomatoes.

Nikhil stays in the market all day, sometimes, talking to everyone. But not her. She goes back to Building 4 with the clock radio under one arm, alone.

She takes the little tomato she stole and bites into it, the taste of summer breaking over her tongue.

Sonya owns one nice dress. It appeared in a heap of Merciful Hands donations two years ago, a shock of butter yellow. She saw the others pining for it, and she knew the generous thing to do—the thing that would have earned her DesCoin under the Delegation—would be to let one of the younger ones have it. But she couldn't let go of it. She folded it over her arm and took it home, where it hung in front of the tapestry for weeks, like a painted sun.

She keeps it under her bed now, in a cardboard box with the rest of her clothing. She takes it out and shakes it, sending dust into the air. It's creased at the waist, where she folded it, but there's not much she can do about that. Mrs. Pritchard is the only one in the building with an iron.

As she puts it on, she thinks of her mother. Julia Kantor went to parties all the time. To get ready, she sat on the tufted stool at her vanity to twist her hair into an updo. Tipped perfume onto her finger, and then dabbed it behind her ear. Poked at her drawer of jewelry to find just the right pair of earrings—the pearls, the diamonds, or the little gold hoops. Her hands were so elegant that everything looked like an elaborate pantomime.

Sonya touches the back of her neck—bare, because she cuts her hair with clippers now, but the habit is hard to break. She twists a hand behind her back to push up the zipper. The dress is a little off, too big in the waist, too tight in the shoulders. It floats to her knees.

The party is in the courtyard of Building 3. She'll have to walk past Building 2 to get there, so she tucks a short knife into her pocket.

But this time, Gray Street is empty. She can hear laughing and shouting from one of the apartments, the thrum of music, a glass shattering. The scrape of her own footsteps. She walks through the center of the Aperture, where the market has been cleared away. She hops over a crack and turns down the tunnel that leads to the courtyard of Building 3.

If Building 4 is a place of reminiscence and Building 2 is a place of chaos, Building 3 is a place of pretending. Not pretending that the outside world doesn't exist, but pretending that life in the Aperture can be just as good. Building 3 hosts weddings and dinner parties and poker nights; they teach classes; they do calisthenics in little groups, running back and forth down Green Street and then Gray Street, and marching up and down the building's stairs.

Sonya is bad at pretending.

The courtyard is not as well tended as the one in Building 4, but there are few weeds, and someone has pruned back the trees so they don't tickle the interior windows. A string of lights hangs from one side to the other; only a few have gone dead in their sockets. There's a little table set up on the right side, where candle stubs in glass jars flicker with light.

"Sonya!" A young woman sets a basket of bread down in front of the candles, dusts off her hands, and reaches for Sonya. Her name is Nicole.

Sonya hugs her, the can she brought digging into her ribs.

"Oh," Nicole says. "What did you bring?"

"Your favorite," Sonya says, holding up the can. The label is worn, but the picture on it is still intact: sliced peaches.

"Wow." Nicole holds the can in both hands, and it reminds Sonya of catching butterflies as a child, how she peered into the gap between her hands to see their wings. "I can't accept this! These come around, what, once a year?"

"I've been saving them for this exact occasion," Sonya says. "Ever since the Act passed."

Nicole's smile is crooked, half-pleased and half-sad. The Children of the Delegation Act passed months ago, allowing those residents of the Aperture who were children when they entered it to be released back into society. Nicole is one of the oldest who was cleared to leave. She was sixteen when she was locked away.

Sonya was seventeen. She won't be going anywhere.

"Let me get a can opener," Nicole says, but Sonya takes out her knife. She carves a neat circle into the top of the can, then taps it to pop it up on one side. Other people are arriving, but for a moment it's just Sonya and Nicole, standing shoulder to shoulder with their fingers stuck in syrup. Sonya slurps a peach slice, and it's sweet and fibrous and tart. She licks the syrup off her fingers. Nicole closes her eyes.

"They won't taste quite like that out there, will they?" she says. "I'll be able to get them anytime, and they'll stop seeming as good."

"Maybe," Sonya says. "But you can get other things, too. Better things."

"That's my point, though." Nicole pinches another peach slice between her fingers. "No matter what I get, nothing will ever taste as good as this does right now."

Sonya looks over Nicole's shoulder at those who have just arrived: Nicole's mother, Winnie, a doe-eyed woman who lives in Building 1; Winnie's friends, Sylvia and Karen, their hair in matching soda can curls; and a smattering of people from Building 3, including the others who were too old to qualify under the Act. Renee and Douglas, who were married two years ago in this courtyard, and Kevin and Marie, recently engaged. Marie wears Kevin's old class ring, stuffed with wax to make it fit on the right finger.

"That's quite a dress, Ms. Kantor," Douglas says to her. The last time she saw him, he was thinning on top, but his head is shaved now, his beard coming in thick. "Pilfer that from a widow?"

"No."

"Only joking," he says.

"I realize that."

"Okay." Douglas makes a face at Renee. "Tough crowd."

"Don't you know? Poster Girl's a fucking killjoy now," Marie says. She walks up to the table, sticks her fingers in the can of peaches. She's wearing a dress, too, made of a shirt and a skirt stitched together at the waist. On her wrist is a blurry tattoo of a sun. "Building 4 is where fun goes to die. Sometimes literally."

"Marie," Kevin says, in a hushed voice. "Don't—"

"Yes, I'm so sorry to be missing out on all the fun in Building 3," Sonya says. "That early morning calisthenics club you started sounds like a riot."

Marie's lips pucker, but Renee laughs.

Nicole looks up, then points overhead as an airplane passes over the Aperture. Everyone stops to watch it. It's a rare enough event that even those who don't care about leaving the Aperture make a note of it. Evidence of other sectors, other worlds beyond their own. Travel between sectors was almost unheard of under the Delegation, and it doesn't seem to be that much more common under the Triumvirate.

"Are you patrolling tomorrow?" Winnie asks Douglas. Her eyes are soft with concern. "I thought I saw your name on the volunteer list."

"Wouldn't want to miss all the excitement," Douglas says.

"Hopefully there isn't any excitement at all," Winnie says. "I don't like you boys having to take on that responsibility."

"Nonintervention policy," Douglas says with a shrug. "Guards're here to keep us in, not keep us well-behaved."

"It almost seems like they want us to eat each other alive in here."

"Better that than the alternative," Sonya says, a little too loudly. Everyone looks at her, and she straightens. "I don't think I want *them* to be the ones who decide what 'well-behaved' looks like, do you?"

Some in the Aperture still trust their old regime, the Delegation, to be the arbiter of good. Some don't bother with "good" at all. But regardless, their unspoken agreement is not to place any trust in the outside government, in the Triumvirate. No one who keeps them locked up here, who participated in the execution of so many of their loved ones, could be capable of goodness. Even when Sonya had no interest in following Delegation rules, she still hated the Triumvirate—the supposed righteous who killed her family, her friends, Aaron.

"Well." Winnie sniffs. "I suppose not."

Wind blows through the courtyard. The sky darkens, and the lights twinkle overhead. Sonya sneaks another peach, and asks Sylvia about her bad knee, and tells Douglas how to troubleshoot his broken box fan. Nicole drifts from person to person, and tells them about her new, government-assigned identity, and all the things she's planning to do in her first week outside. She won't be living nearby; she'll take the train to Portland, start over with a new name. Buy a pint of milk and sit near the bank of the river and drink every last drop. Go out dancing. Walk around all night, just to do it, just because she can.

At one point, Renee nudges Sonya with an elbow.

"A bunch of us are going to the roof for a cigarette. Want to come?" she says.

"I'm going to turn in early," Sonya says.

Renee shrugs and joins the others. Sylvia and Karen are leaving. The candles have all burned out. Nicole's cheeks shine with tears. Sonya hugs her again.

"I can't believe they won't let you out," Nicole says, her breath hot and fierce against Sonya's ear.

Sonya holds Nicole at arm's length and thinks this is a good way to remember her: dimly lit, hair tousled by the wind, eyes wet, angry on a friend's behalf.

"I'll miss you," she says.

Nicole gives her the peach syrup to drink. She sips it as she walks back to Building 4 slowly, savoring.

SHE wakes that night to a sharp, loud sound, like the crack of a whip. She sits up in bed, and by the glow of her Insight she can see that the trunk she drags across the doorjamb—the only "lock" she has been able to manage—is still in place.

Barefoot, she walks to the windows and pulls back the tapestry that covers them. The street below is empty. The wind blows a newspaper across the crumbling sidewalk. The metal shade covers the windows of the corner store like a closed eyelid.

She thinks of the video her father showed her when she was a child, beaming it from his Insight to hers. Footage from a smoky street embroiled in conflict. Cars parked askew, streetlights tipped over. And coming from every direction, the deep, sharp sound of gunshots.

He sat next to her on the couch as she played it again and again with the implant. *This is what the world was like,* he said, *before the Delegation.* Showing her cost him two hundred DesCoin—children weren't supposed to watch that sort of thing. But the sacrifice was worth it to him, to answer her questions.

The moon is high and waxing, almost full. Another month behind her. Time keeps marching forward.

She goes back to sleep.

AT first, when someone died in the Aperture, they were like bees absconding from the hive, leaving wax and honey—no one else took what they left behind. But soon the rules of propriety shifted out of necessity. Now when someone dies, everyone in the building swarms the space and picks at their possessions until only the graying honeycomb is left. Whenever Sonya needs a new part, she consults the building map by the south stairwell, where the empty apartments are marked with red Xs, to decide which apartment to check for remnants.

This one—apartment 2C, formerly Mr. Nadir's—smells like cooking smoke and cat. There are no cats in the Aperture, so it must be a scent Mr. Nadir brought with him. She's been here before. A few times, she came to fix his overhead lights—his wiring had always been faulty. Once, she came for dinner. And another time, after he died, she came to take his little refrigerator, dragging it up four flights of stairs by herself.

His stove is broken, but the burners, four cold coils of metal, still work. She removes one and tucks it into the bag at her side, then wanders into his bathroom. No one cleaned it after his death, so there are still toothpaste flecks dried up in the sink and fingerprint smudges on the mirror. She leans in close to see one—a thumbprint, maybe, with whorls and ridges unique to him.

Then she goes downstairs, to the courtyard, to meet Charlotte.

Today Charlotte is not in gingham but brown linen, cinched at the waist. The sky is clear, the air still holding on to a little of summer's warmth. Charlotte sweeps her long braid over one shoulder and smiles at Sonya.

"Good morning," she says. "How did you sleep?"

"Good morning," Sonya says. "Did you hear that noise last night?"

"I did," Charlotte says, and they start walking toward the tunnel together. "I'm not sure what reason they have to be setting off fireworks at this time of year, but you'd think they would be decent enough not to do it at night."

"It didn't sound like a firework to me," Sonya says.

"What else could it have been?"

Sonya shakes her head. "I don't know. Something else."

"Well, who knows what they have out there now," Charlotte says.

Out of habit, Sonya looks up to David's name as she passes through the tunnel. It was the fourth name she etched in brick in the Aperture, but her family's names are in the tunnel that leads to Building 2, where she used to live, so she never sees them. *August Kantor. Julia Kantor. Susanna Kantor.* All dead and gone.

"Graham worked in the Delegation morgue," Charlotte says. "He was a manager, actually—that little friend of yours, Marie, she worked for him. He was always a bit . . . odd. Even when we were children."

"You're not close?" Sonya says.

"Not particularly," Charlotte says. "That must sound terrible. I know I'm lucky to have him here at all."

Sometimes Sonya wonders what it would have been like to have her sister here with her, in the Aperture. Susanna was four years Sonya's senior, and she lived her life as if Sonya wasn't in it, an only child who just happened to have a sibling. It was more careless disregard than malice. Susanna didn't need anyone. Of all the qualities Sonya envied her sister for, she longed for that one the most.

As Sonya and Charlotte cross Green Street, Sonya looks toward the entrance to the Aperture. The gate is where the place gets its name. When it opens, interlocking plates pull away from a central point, and the effect is like a pupil dilating in the dark.

Standing right in front of that pupil now are Nicole and Winnie, embracing. Nicole's bag is at her feet. The guard at the gate, a sturdy man in a gray uniform, waits a few feet away for them to let each other go.

Nicole wipes her face, picks up her bag, and offers her mother a wave. She walks through the center of the gate, and the pupil contracts behind her. Winnie holds a hand over her mouth to muffle a sob.

Charlotte meets Sonya's eyes.

"Let's give her some privacy," she says, and Sonya turns away.

She has watched three friends walk through that gate: Ashley, Shona, and Nicole. Ashley and Shona were both fourteen when they were locked in the Aperture—shortly after it was formed, just after the uprising, a decade ago. They were from Portland, so she had never met them before, and she didn't befriend them until they were older, old enough to move out of their parents' Aperture apartments and into Building 2. She doesn't know what their first years there were like; she never asked. A person has to be careful what questions they ask here. Everyone's pasts are pockmarked with tragedy.

Now Sonya can add another one to her list: she's the youngest person left in the Aperture.

They pass through the tunnel and into Building 1's courtyard. She hasn't been to Building 1 often in the years she's been in here. Building 3's residents live in a state of denial, but Building 1's are in a state of acceptance. Of surrender. It's the part of the Aperture that feels the most like a prison.

She crushes overgrown weeds, now sagging under their own weight, to make it to the door. It squeals when Charlotte opens it. They walk in silence up to the third floor, where the hallway smells like cigarettes. There are trash bags piled up against one person's door, collapsed cardboard boxes against another's. The carpet is fraying on one side, pulling away from the baseboards.

Charlotte knocks on Apartment 3B. Somewhere, someone is yelling. Someone else is listening to morose guitar.

Graham answers the door. He is an unremarkable-looking man: only a little taller than Sonya, short gray hair that wraps around the crown of his head like a shawl, hooded eyes. The skin under his jaw has gone soft and fleshy with age.

"Ms. Kantor!" he says. "It's been a while. Hello, Charlotte. Come in, come in."

The apartment feels like a junkyard. Lining the walls are crates full of small things: one has doorknobs and handles; another, small cardboard boxes; a third, empty glass bottles. He sets up a blanket at the market every week with a selection of discarded objects, she recalls. The residents of Building 2 must find him useful enough, with their endless need for empty containers. For moonshine, naturally.

"I see introductions aren't necessary," Charlotte says.

"I knew Sonya's father," Graham says. "Don't you remember August? He was in my year at school. We were on the swim team together."

"My memory is not quite that long, I'm afraid," Charlotte says.

"He used to come have lunch with me sometimes, in the morgue. Well, not *in* the morgue. Always had a weak stomach, your father. Used to plug his nose when we walked past the dumpsters behind the market—all the boys made fun of him for it, August Kantor, so dainty—" He lifts his nose, pinches it with his thumb and index fingers, to show her.

She smiles.

"He would have described himself as *fastidious,*" she says. "But that sounds like him."

"How did he pass away? Was he executed?" Graham asks, and Sonya's smile fades.

"Graham!" Charlotte smacks him on the arm. "Don't ask her that."

"I didn't mean any harm by it, I just—"

"No, he wasn't," Sonya says. "Charlotte says you have a broken stove?"

Graham leads her into the kitchen, and Charlotte follows, her cheeks red. He shows her the faulty burners, one after another, their coils staying dark and cool despite any jiggling of the knobs. Sonya sets her bag down at her feet and walks to the far wall, where the circuit breaker is hidden behind a gray door. She finds the switch for the kitchen and turns it off.

"How did you learn how to do all this?" Graham says. "A good Delegation girl like you, I know you didn't get it in school."

"You'd be surprised what you can learn from a manual and some trial and error," Sonya says.

"She's young," Charlotte says. "Young people are always good at figuring these things out. Especially in a building full of old people where no one knows how to do anything."

"You are not an old person," Sonya says.

"I told her that when she decided to go to Building 4," Graham says. "But she insisted."

"I may not be old, but I am a widow," Charlotte says. "I feel at home there. The same as Sonya, after . . ."

She clears her throat.

"Well," she says. "We are all familiar with loss, in Building 4."

Sonya is only halfway listening. Replacing a coil is not difficult—the old one is unplugged, and the new one goes in its place. She's done it a dozen times, but she still likes the feeling of it, knowing where something goes, being the one to get it there.

She wasn't good at much, growing up, at least not compared to Susanna. Susanna was funny; she knew how to dance; she had an ear for music; she got good grades without apparent effort. Sonya was prettier, and there had been a time when that felt like everything that mattered. But beauty wasn't useful in the Aperture, and so she had found another use for herself. She wasn't gifted with wiring or technology or tools or anything that the residents of Building 4 routinely called upon her to do—but she was willing, and sometimes that was enough.

She did like to be useful.

"Who did you lose, Sonya?" Graham asks her, when Charlotte disappears into the bathroom. He's a lonely man. And he always has been, so loss fascinates him. After all, you need to have had something in order to truly know how it feels to lose it.

She turns on the power, and then tries the stove knob. She holds her hand over it to feel it heating.

She doesn't know why she answers him. She wasn't planning to, until she did.

"Everyone," she says to him.

She turns the burner off.

"All fixed. Thanks for the story about my father."

"Happy to oblige," he says.

ON the day she lost everyone:

They sit at the table in the cabin at their usual places: August at one end, Julia at the other, Susanna at their father's right, Sonya at his left. August pours each of them a glass of water. Julia hums as she tips the pills from the bottle: one, two, three, four.

Sonya recites the lyrics in her head.

Won't you keep an eye on me
And I'll keep an eye on you

Five, six, seven, eight. Julia passes a pill to Susanna, a pill to August, and a pill to Sonya, and keeps one for herself.

One step after another . . .
We'll make it through.

The pill is bright yellow against Sonya's palm.

TWO

There's a man in her apartment.

Sonya's hand goes to the knife in her pocket. She knows what it is to be caught unaware, to face the consequences of being on your own among people who have nothing to lose.

But there are no locks in the Aperture, so there's nothing she can do to keep her little apartment safe when she's not in it. Not that it matters much—there's nothing to steal. And he isn't here to steal anything.

He sits at her little table, in one of her folding chairs. It's a proper table, left in this apartment by whoever occupied it before the uprising. There's a name carved into the front of it, BABS, written in childish uppercase. She's invented a story about Babs in her mind—a girl, maybe eleven, unruly, scolded for swinging her legs when she sits, for never being able to stop moving. Desperate to be permanent, somehow; etching the letters with her steak knife when her parents weren't paying attention.

Sonya knows the man. His name is Alexander Price. Tall, his knees bumping the underside of the low table. His eyes so dark they look black. He has a beard, trim but not neat, creeping across his throat, uneven in places.

"Get out," she says to him.

She's holding Graham's useless stove burner against her stomach like a shield.

"Now, that," he says, "is not the Delegation hospitality I was raised to expect."

"I reserve that for guests, and you're an intruder," she says. "Get out."

"No."

"You think that just because I'm a prisoner here, you can walk into my home whenever you like?" She puts the burner coil down on the square of countertop where she prepares food. His eyes flick to her tight hands, and then to her face. He seems unbothered.

She searches automatically for the ring of light around his right iris. But there isn't one.

Everyone she ever saw before the uprising—and now after it, with a few exceptions—had an Insight. Its absence is like a missing finger, or a missing ear; he looks unbalanced without it. Or unfinished, like someone stopped drawing him too soon.

"You look the same," he says. "Except the hair. I'm surprised the old geezers in here let you cut it that short. That haircut wouldn't earn you any DesCoin."

She turns back to the apartment door and opens it wide. Cool air from the hallway wafts in. Her next-door neighbor Irene isn't home—she spends most of her time downstairs with Mrs. Pritchard and three of the other widows, the most proper ones. But Sonya wants him to know that if she screams, her voice won't be muffled by the door.

When she turns back to him, he's frowning a little. "I'm not going to hurt you. Do you really believe I'd do that?"

"I believe many things about you now," she says.

This is the man who told the uprising where to find her family when they tried to flee the city. Without him, they might have been able to escape. Without him, they might have lived. She wasn't ready for the pain of this, of seeing him again.

She waits, because she doesn't trust what will come out of her mouth if she opens it.

"Well," he says, after the silence has coiled tight between them. "I'll just get to the point, then."

He takes something out of his pocket. It's a device, rectangular, the right shape for a palm. An Elicit. She recognizes it, not from experience, but from lessons on the history of the Insight—it's an old piece of technology that predates it. Like the Insight, the Elicit was designed to go with a person everywhere, to augment their reality and communicate with a network about their behavior.

The system seems clumsy to her now—why carry something in your hand when you could carry it in your head, instead? If you spend all your time holding something, caring for it, feeling its warmth—it may as well be a part of your body, as integrated as an eye.

He holds the Elicit at the bottom right corner, careless. Though she doesn't know how to use it, she knows it's valuable; if she took it from him now, she could trade it for anything she wanted in the Aperture, just because of its rarity.

But there's nothing to want in the Aperture.

The Elicit lights up, and its reflection in his eyes almost makes it look like he does have an Insight. Almost makes him look like he used to, neat and tidy, his smile always reluctant. Alexander, the older brother who walked in his younger brother's wake.

She was betrothed to his little brother, Aaron, as a teenager. Aaron and Sonya were the perfect Delegation match, with the perfect Delegation future. But Aaron was killed in the uprising, in the street, along with hundreds of others.

Alexander shows her the screen. On it is an article she's seen before. Under the Delegation, there was just one news source that fed to everyone's Insight upon request; you could read it just by staring out the window on the train. But with the Delegation's fall, newspapers seem to be back in fashion—there are half a dozen of them competing, each with a different interpretation of the same data. This one is the *Chronicle,* she can tell by the elaborate *C* at the top, and this particular edition already turned up in the Aperture, months ago. CHILDREN OF THE DELEGATION, the article reads, in bold black letters across the top. *Rose Parker,* the byline says.

"I've seen it," Sonya says. "And?"

"You've seen it?" He raises his eyebrows. "I guess Rose smuggled some in here? Wouldn't want her great work to go unrecognized."

He puts the Elicit down on the table, still lit up.

"So you know, then, that we have this article to thank for the Children of the Delegation Act. Everyone who was a child when they were put in the Aperture, held accountable for their family's crimes, is now eligible for release. People like you." He tilts his head. "Well, not *exactly* like you. You were a little older, weren't you?"

"It's interesting that you're pretending not to know," she says.

She and Aaron had been the same age, after all.

Alexander's mouth twists.

"You have perhaps noticed that many of the younger people in the Aperture have been released lately. Given new identities and a chance to live a worthwhile life instead of . . ." He waves a hand. "This."

She sees her run-down studio apartment as if for the first time. The bed with its patched-up sheets, its fraying blanket. The scratched frying pan drying next to the sink on a ragged, stained towel. The things she has used to decorate the space: plants lined up on the sill above the kitchen sink, growing out of tin cans; the patterns she painted in black on the tapestry that covers her living room windows, shielding her from observers; the cluster of lamps with dim bulbs she put on a crate near the bed. Alexander, though, remembers where she lived before.

Fuck you, she thinks, one of many phrases she has never said aloud—in the past, because they would cost her DesCoin, and now, because they would be a sign that she is going backward, to the girl who lived in a pit of grief and knew the taste of moonshine. But she thinks it anyway, *Fuck you, I hate you, I hope you choke and die—*

Alexander waits, as if for a reaction. Finding none, he continues:

"You have presented a unique problem. Not young enough to be an easy candidate for release, but not old enough for us to forget about you."

"Is that what you've done with us, in here? Forgotten about us?"

"For the most part, yes. And you can't imagine what a relief it's been."

"Well, if you think I've spared a single thought for *you,*" she says, "you're mistaken."

"I'm heartbroken." He reaches into his pocket and takes out a piece of paper folded into fourths. "As I was saying. We came up with an idea for a trade—"

"We?"

"We will give you an opportunity to right one of the wrongs of the Delegation. If you succeed, you can have your freedom. If you fail, you will continue to rot in here."

The word *rot* makes her flinch. That was how David talked about it, near the end—like he was a piece of meat left on a countertop to spoil. She could never find the words to disagree with him. She wasn't sure she even did.

"I'm not some ant you can fry with a magnifying glass," she says. "I'm not going to squirm for your entertainment."

He pauses, the paper still half-folded. "You don't even want to hear what we want you to do?"

She's squeezing the edge of the counter so tightly she's lost feeling in her fingers.

"No," she says. "Get out."

Alexander puts his Elicit back into his pocket. He stands. Even though there is as much space between them as she can get, he feels too close.

"Have it your way, for now," he says. "But I'll be back in a few days. Hopefully by then you'll have come to your senses."

THE three representatives of the Triumvirate visit the Aperture once a year, accompanied by a small battalion of journalists and peace officers. The stated purpose of their visit is to meet with Aperture leaders—each building elects two—but Sonya knows better. The Triumvirate are here to prove they haven't forgotten. To make a show of mercy—but also to remind the public that the favored sons and daughters of the Delegation are still safely locked away.

David used to say that visitors to the Aperture made him feel like an animal in the zoo. Before he died, they spent visitation days drinking themselves into a stupor. Sometimes they put on old propaganda songs and sang them at the top of their lungs, in the hope that the

Triumvirate would hear them through the walls. But most of the time they just fell asleep in David's bed in the middle of the afternoon.

This year, a panicked Mrs. Pritchard finds Sonya right before the representatives arrive and asks her to change the dead lightbulbs in the maintenance hallway. The representatives will be touring the ground floor, and as Mrs. Pritchard says, "We don't want them to think we don't take care of ourselves." Mrs. Pritchard is eternally embarrassed, always aware of deviating from a norm that only she is keeping track of. It's easier to do as she says than to argue with her.

Sonya carries a stepladder and a bag of lightbulbs to the maintenance hallway. One by one, she unscrews the dark bulbs from their sockets and replaces them, then carries the ladder another few feet to do it again. She has made it to the end of the hallway when the door at the other end opens and the representatives of the Triumvirate walk in.

She doesn't know their faces, but there's no one else they could be, dressed like that. One wears a knee-length red dress, her hair sleek and almost as short as Sonya's. Another is in a blue pantsuit, her fingers adorned with green stones. They are Petra Novak and Amy Archer—she doesn't know which one is which.

The third, a tall man in a dove-gray suit, is the first to recognize her. His name is Easton Turner. He was elected sometime in the last few years. David heard about it on a radio.

"My, my," he says. "Isn't this unexpected."

Sonya finishes screwing in the lightbulb, and descends the ladder. Nikhil and Mrs. Pritchard are close behind the Triumvirate representatives, and a few feet behind them are journalists with microphones extended and Elicits raised, likely recording video. Sonya straightens. She wishes she was wearing something neater than a pair of loose trousers and an old T-shirt with an unraveling hem. She wishes she didn't look quite so much like the adolescent girl in everyone's memories.

Easton says, "Don't you recognize her, Petra? She's the girl from the propaganda posters."

"Wow," the woman in the red dress says. Her fingernails are long and filed almost to points at the ends—precise and sharp. "So she is. What is your name, anyway?"

"Kantor," Sonya says. "Sonya."

"I forgot you were in here, Sonya," Easton says. He's handsome in a way that suggests he looked too boyish and soft when he was young and has only just found his face. His hair is salt-and-pepper, thick, short, trim at the neck.

"*Why* are you in here?" the woman in the blue pantsuit—Amy Archer—asks Sonya. She sounds like a security guard who's caught someone trespassing. "Didn't the Children of the Delegation Act secure your release?"

"No," Sonya says. "I just missed the age cutoff."

"But we did approve something related to you, didn't we?" Easton says. He taps the side of his nose, and points at her. "Yes, yes. A special exception, if you perform an act of service."

"I heard something about that," Sonya says.

Petra smiles.

"Oh, did you?" She laughs. "And?"

"And," Sonya says, and she shoulders her bag of lightbulbs. "I wasn't sure what to make of it."

"What to make of it," Petra says.

"I'm under the impression it isn't compulsory," Sonya says. "There's a choice involved."

"Of course," Amy Archer says. "We simply assumed that you would jump at the chance."

"Unless, of course, you are . . ." Petra's eyes drop to the bag of lightbulbs at Sonya's side. "Satisfied with your current station."

Sonya clenches her jaw so hard her teeth squeak.

"Well," Easton says. "I hope you make the right choice."

Petra grins at Easton. "'What's right is right,' after all."

Everyone—Easton, Petra, Amy, all the journalists and security guards behind them, even Mrs. Pritchard—laughs.

Sonya reaches for a response and comes up empty-handed. She moves to the side with her stepladder as the group passes her, Nikhil squeezing her shoulder as he walks by. Journalists thrust Elicits in her direction. She recognizes one as Rose Parker, the one who wrote the Children of the Delegation article.

When the hallway is empty again, it's quiet except for her ragged breaths.

LATER that evening, she goes to Nikhil's apartment for dinner, and Nikhil is in his robe and slippers, holding a cup of tea. Mary Pritchard grows chamomile in her apartment and dries it on her kitchen counters. He must have traded tomatoes for the tea, or green beans.

She holds up the can of beans she brought, and he gestures to the kitchen, where a pot of rice waits on the stove, already cooked. Nikhil gets out another mug and pours half the chamomile tea into it.

"I heard you had a visitor this morning," he says, offering the mug to her.

She pours the beans into a pot and turns on the burner beneath them, then sits at Mr. Nadir's old dining room table. After Mr. Nadir died of heart failure, Nikhil went to his apartment to unscrew the legs and carry the tabletop up four flights of stairs to his living room. By that time, the apartment was already picked over and stripped bare. Sonya put the legs back on for him—facing the wrong direction, but Nikhil said he liked them that way, so they left it.

The underside of the table held a surprise: a picture of Mr. Nadir's daughter Priya as a teenager, taped right in the middle. During the uprising, Priya betrayed her father in exchange for her own freedom.

Nikhil and Sonya left the picture where it was.

"*Visitor* is a kind word for it. I would say I had an *intruder* this morning," she says. "How was your meeting?"

"Fine. Useless," Nikhil says. He leans back against the counter. "Tell me what happened with your intruder."

Despite the closeness between their families before, she saw Nikhil only occasionally after they were first locked in. But then David died, and one night she came home to a man waiting for her in their empty apartment. She knew him, but only in the distant way she knew many people in the Aperture. He attacked her, and she jammed her thumb in his eye socket. She didn't feel safe there afterward, so Nikhil persuaded the people of Building 4 to let her in.

She still sees the man sometimes. He wears an eye patch now.

Sonya shrugs. "Some resistance goon was just sitting in my apartment when I got back this morning."

"Some resistance goon."

She hesitates a little before answering. "Yes."

"And they offered you a way out."

"If I do their little dance, yes."

"But you didn't accept."

"No."

Nikhil gives her a long, searching look.

"Why not?" he says.

"You heard how those Triumvirate people talked to me," she says. "Even if I could complete whatever task they give me, what kind of life could I have out there? There was a time when my face was everywhere."

"And there will come a time when no one will remember it," Nikhil says. "You just have to endure until then."

"I'm tired of enduring things," Sonya says.

He replies, "I don't accept that."

Most of the time she forgets that she's not an old woman. If grief pares a person down, she is whittled just as slim as the rest of Building 4. She belongs with the widows, settled in for a long wait. But now she sees the shadows that have collected in the lines of Nikhil's face, and she remembers his age, and her own.

"This is a gift, Sonya," he says. He sets his hand on her arm, gently. "Just think about it."

SHE receives the notification the next morning. Her Insight's constant light pulses, once, and then a sentence unrolls before her like a banner. `Mandatory Medical Check.` For a moment the words are layered over what she sees, the suds in the sink, the sponge in her hand. And then they're gone.

It is a sensation at once familiar and strange. Her parents had the

Insight implanted in her brain when she was an infant, in accordance with both law and custom. It was a brutal procedure, in a sense—a thick needle stuck in the corner of a newborn's eye. But cultures have always embraced brutality in service of a greater good, sometimes long after it was still necessary. Immersive baptism. Circumcision. Initiation rites.

Under the Delegation, the Insight was active, granting a person access to all the information they could possibly need. As a child, she asked it all the questions she might otherwise have asked a parent who didn't know the answers: *Why is the sky blue? How fast does the fastest person run? How do cars work?* It supplied the answers visually, or auditorily, depending on her preference. And the Insight was more than that, too. It connected her to people—made it so she could watch an episode of *Cluefinder* with her friend Tana late at night when she was supposed to be sleeping, or listen to a new composition of her sister's just seconds after Susanna recorded it. The Insight walked through life with her.

And when the Delegation fell, it went silent.

The new government linked all the prisoners of the Aperture into a closed system, so the Triumvirate could still see through their eyes at any moment, if it wanted to. And the Triumvirate could send prisoners messages, like the one she just received. But there was no music, no videos, no television. No voice calls, or looking something up mid-conversation to verify it, or assurances of safety when you were lost or in trouble.

She blinks, and the message is gone. She finishes the dishes, leaving them to dry on a dish towel on the counter, and dries her hands. She checks herself in the mirror, heaves the trunk away from the doorjamb, and leaves her apartment.

Medical checks happen annually, unless you have a condition or submit a special request. Dr. Hull for the men, Dr. Shannon for the women. There were no offices for them in the Aperture for some time, but when Alan Dohr of Building 3 died of alcohol poisoning, they turned his apartment into one.

On her way out, she sees Mrs. Pritchard sitting on a bench in the courtyard with Mrs. Carter, both of them knitting. Yarn is in short supply, so most of the time, when Mrs. Pritchard and the others knit, they have to unravel something else they've made.

"Hello, Mary, Charlotte," she says, as she passes through the courtyard.

"Where are you headed?" Mrs. Pritchard asks. She likes to know things.

"My annual," she says.

Mrs. Pritchard shakes her head. "Terrible, terrible, what they do to you young ladies."

Sonya doesn't answer. She walks through the tunnel to Gray Street and turns right. In the center of the Aperture, a group of six is playing with an old soccer ball. They set up buckets for goals on either end of Green Street. Gabe and the others are standing near the outer wall, smoking cigarettes, talking to one of the guards above. Probably making a deal, she thinks, though she's not sure what Gabe has to offer an Aperture guard other than subpar moonshine.

When she passes through the tunnel to Building 3, she sees Renee, Douglas, and Jack, a graying writer who lives on the second floor, gathered around something. When she draws closer, she sees that it's a newspaper, spread out on a low table in the corner of the courtyard.

"Sonya!" Renee says. "Come look at this. Yesterday's news."

Sonya draws closer, leaning over Renee's shoulder to see the front-page headline. THE ANALOG ARMY CLAIMS RESPONSIBILITY FOR MURDER. There are two pictures beneath it, side by side: in one, a young man with a swoop of brown hair grins. The caption: *Sean Armstrong, 32, found dead in his apartment on Tuesday night.* The other picture is a close-up of a note scribbled on a slip of paper, with a safety pin through the top of it. The caption: *A note signed with the Analog Army insignia, found pinned to the victim's chest.* The picture is too blurry to read most of the writing. Sonya catches a few stray phrases: *designed implant technology . . . reestablish cloud-saving structure* . . .

"It's a list of his supposed 'crimes,'" Jack says, following her gaze.

"The Analog Army," Sonya says. "This is the terrorist group that bombed that tech manufacturer last year?"

For a time, they had consistent access to newspapers because of that journalist, Rose Parker, who was working on the Children of the Delegation piece. She brought only one copy, most of the time, but people passed each one around the Aperture like it was fine china or gold leaf. Nikhil read them aloud in the evenings to Building 4—to those who cared to listen, anyway. Plenty of people, like Mrs. Pritchard, didn't want to know what was going on outside the Aperture. Sonya didn't blame them. After all, it had nothing to do with them anymore. With any of them.

"The very same," Jack says. "Wish I could get a copy of their manifesto."

"They're a bunch of psychos who hate technology," Douglas says. "What more is there to know?"

Jack gives Douglas a blank look, like he doesn't even know where to begin.

"Just because you completely lack curiosity doesn't mean the rest of us do," Renee says, flipping to the next page of the paper. "I wonder who designs the logo for a terrorist organization. You think they hired someone for that?"

"That logo?" Sonya says, looking at the two *A*s layered over each other. "No, that's definitely the work of an amateur."

"An Amateur Analog Army Artist," Renee says, laughing.

"Where'd you get this, anyway?" Sonya says.

"Rose Parker came with that big pack of journalists yesterday," Jack says. "She handed it over. Apparently those 'fireworks' we heard a couple nights ago were actually gunshots."

"Gunshots," Renee says. "How did the Analog Army get their hands on a gun?"

"No idea."

"Can you bring this to Building 4 later?" Sonya says. "I'm sure Nikhil will want to do a public reading."

"Sure thing," Jack says. "I'll bring it by his place."

"Thanks," Sonya says. "Gotta go. Doc's waiting."

Renee's face contorts. None of them like the doctor.

THE apartment looks just like every other apartment in the Aperture: one big room with kitchen and bathroom attached to it like a boil. Instead of a bed dominating the small space, there's medical equipment: an exam table, a cabinet full of supplies, a few machines in a row. This is the only room in the Aperture that is allowed a lock, or people would have stolen all the supplies ages ago.

Dr. Shannon is an older woman, stern, her hair worn as short as Sonya's but white as snow. Her hands sometimes shake when she uses her stethoscope. She can never find Sonya's veins when she draws blood, which she observes each time with an accusatory air, as if Sonya is making her veins small on purpose. She checks her watch when Sonya walks in.

"I got the message at an inconvenient time," Sonya says. "I came when I could."

"Well, fine, I suppose you don't normally need much time anyway," Dr. Shannon says. "Sit on the table and let me take your blood pressure."

Sonya goes through the ritual of it: stripping off her cardigan, rolling up her sleeves, sitting on the cold metal table that Dr. Shannon sanitizes after each visit, putting her arm out for the blood pressure cuff that squeezes her, stepping on the scale that pronounces her weight "healthy enough," eyeing the paper folder Dr. Shannon flips through to remind herself of Sonya's medical history.

"You seem fine," Dr. Shannon says. "Time for your shot."

Sonya turns her arm out.

The injection lasts for a year, though Sonya hasn't needed it to prevent pregnancy since David died. It's mandatory for every person in the Aperture with the capacity to bear children.

She knew David from her life before, but only as a name and a face at the back of a classroom, nothing more. One night early in her Aperture sentence, she danced with him at a party—he was the only one there who knew the foxtrot. Later, her lips burning with moonshine, she went back to his apartment and took off all her clothes to let him look at her. He was just a body, then. And she just wanted someone to touch her.

He wasn't Aaron, and that wasn't difficult in the way that she had expected. Aaron had been an inevitability, and she had wanted him in the same way she wanted childhood to end and the rest of her life to begin. Under the Delegation, though, being with David would have cost her DesCoin—and that was all she wanted, right after she was locked in the Aperture: to shed as much DesCoin as possible, now that the Delegation was gone. She drank and smoked and swore and stripped herself bare and let herself want, and she expected it to mean something, to *change* something.

And then David died of his own volition. She hosted his funeral in a black dress in the center of the Aperture, where she said little, just laid a dandelion seed head on the pavement to watch its seeds split off into the wind.

"Is there a way to just eliminate the possibility of pregnancy forever?" Sonya says, as Dr. Shannon prepares the syringe. "Without surgery, I mean?"

"Technically, yes," the doctor replies. She dabs the inside of Sonya's arm with a square of gauze soaked with antiseptic. "But I wouldn't recommend it."

"Why not?"

"You're still young. Something could change—"

Sonya laughs. "In here? No, it can't."

"The Triumvirate already released some of you," the doctor says. "Someday, they may release all of you. And you might want to have a child when that happens."

The needle is sharp and then over. The table doesn't warm beneath her legs. The air stinks of mildew and dirt. Maybe whoever lived here before—not Alan Dohr, but the person who lived here before this part of the city was seized by the Triumvirate and converted into the Aperture—kept gardening equipment in it. Shovels leaning into the corner. Bags of earth piled near the door. A place for making things new instead of tending to the dying.

Probably not.

Dr. Shannon presses a cotton ball to the injection site and tapes it in place with her free hand.

"Mood rating for the last week?" she asks, as she always does.

"Out of one hundred?"

Every time, out of one hundred. One hundred, a delirium of happiness. Zero, a soul-crushing sorrow.

"Fifty," she says, without waiting for the doctor to answer.

"You've never given me any other rating."

"That's because I always feel fine."

Dr. Shannon strips off her gloves, and throws them in the trash.

"Most people don't always feel fine, Sonya," she says. "Particularly when they've experienced some of the things you have."

"How is this relevant to my health?"

Dr. Shannon takes a flashlight out of her pocket. Sonya knows this ritual, too. She sits up straighter as Dr. Shannon shines the light into her right eye to look at the Insight.

"Many people in the Aperture are on medication to help them stabilize their moods," Dr. Shannon says. "Your lot in life is difficult, and you should have the tools to manage it."

Sonya unrolls her sleeves.

"You know what might help us all manage it?" Sonya says. "Fresh produce. More than one set of sheets. Some way to pass the time that isn't kicking a half-deflated soccer ball around on some asphalt."

Dr. Shannon sighs.

"Unfortunately, I am not authorized to offer any of those things. Medication, however . . ."

"Do I seem like I have unstable moods to you?" Sonya says.

"No," Dr. Shannon replies. "You are very much under control, Ms. Kantor, and you always have been."

Sonya puts her cardigan back on.

"Then what's the problem?" she says, and she stands to leave.

THREE

HE'S BACK.

Standing in her kitchen with a glass of water in hand, which means he went through her cupboard to find it. His big hand outstretched to touch the thyme growing behind the sink, in the patch of light that comes in from the emergency stairwell. He's wearing a chain around his neck. At the end of it, a ring with a purple stone that she recognizes as his mother's.

When he sees her looking at it, he tucks it under his T-shirt collar.

"I think I made myself perfectly clear," she says. "You're not welcome here. Which means you're also not welcome to rifle through my things."

She leaves the door open behind her.

"Not much to rifle through," he says. "But if I needed a bunch of old fraying wires, you're the first person I'd come to."

She looks at her row of wooden crates, like a garden path leading to her bed. She has a collection of things, just like Graham Carter. A crate for tools—even old, rusty ones have their uses—and one for wires; one for nails and screws of all sizes and shapes; one for bits of things, plugs and jacks, small speakers with no boxes, antennae, switches, and splice caps. And on a low table near the bed, her soldering iron, one of the greatest finds of the last decade.

"They must be pretty desperate if they're relying on you for tech support," he says. "Before the Delegation fell, you couldn't even hang a picture frame."

"Before the Delegation fell, you hadn't betrayed your entire family," she says. "Things change."

His jaw works like he's chewing on something. He sets the glass down on the kitchen counter and takes a folded piece of paper out of his pocket.

"I'm here to give you another chance at earning your freedom," he says.

It's only the memory of Nikhil's worn face that keeps her from telling him to go fuck himself.

"There's a girl," he says. "She was an illegal second child under the Delegation. Illegal second children were, when discovered, removed from their birth families and placed with upstanding members of the community who couldn't have a child of their own."

His voice sours at that. *It's for the good of us all,* Sonya thinks automatically, one of the Delegation's key phrases. Replying to him with that phrase would have earned her at least thirty DesCoin. Enough for lunch at Al's—closed now, of course.

He continues: "The Delegation was in power for thirty years, so unfortunately not everyone can experience any restoration. But we've been locating the children who are still minors now, and so far, we have returned all but one to their birth parents. This girl is the last one. She was three years old when she was taken from her parents, but we can't figure out where she was placed. The others, we just matched the parents' account with the adoption records. We put pictures of Grace in all the newspapers, asking for information, but no one has come forward with any. It's very strange."

He unfolds the paper as he speaks. He handles it with careful fingers, as if it's tissue and might rip at the slightest pressure.

"Our offer is simple," he says. "Find her—or find out what happened to her—and earn your ticket out of here."

Sonya gestures widely to encompass the apartment. "You may have noticed I'm a prisoner here. Not exactly in a good position to find anyone."

"You will be given a pass to move in and out of the Aperture while you conduct your investigation," he says. "We will monitor you, of course, via your Insight."

"How convenient that you never let us remove them," she says. "Even though you made them illegal for everyone else."

"It is, isn't it?"

"You're the *government,* and you couldn't find her," she says. "What makes you think I can?"

"I'm an administrator, not an investigator," he says. "I wasn't authorized to dedicate that much time to this. You, however . . . have all the time in the world."

She hears a door opening down the hallway—Mr. Teed leaving for his afternoon walk. He tips his hat to her and ambles toward the stairwell.

Nikhil said this was a gift. Nicole saw it that way. She was so relieved when she was approved for release that she burst into tears. She debated her new alias for days. *Do I look more like a Victoria or a Rebecca?* She talked about how she'd always wanted to live in Portland, anyway; how she didn't mind working at the new Phillips factory at all, better to do menial labor than wear away at time in the Aperture.

But Sonya's future feels blank. A wall of white light.

"Tell me," she says. "Why should I want what you have?"

"Excuse me?"

"You come in here in secondhand clothes"—she's only guessing by the uneven stitching on his shirt, mended by unskilled fingers—"with a thankless job as a Triumvirate lackey, and no wedding ring on your finger, and you tell me I should want to be free of this place. Well—for what? What will I get out there? Heckled in the street by people who recognize me from a decade-old poster? A job at a factory? What?"

He presses the paper flat to the countertop between them.

"You are . . ." He laughs a little. "You are a fucking piece of work, you know that? You want to stay here and eat cold beans out of a can and watch some old people die one by one? Be my guest."

He picks up his glass and drinks the last of his water. Sonya looks down at the paper on the countertop.

Written at the top of it is a name:

Grace Ward

Beneath it is a photograph of the Wards, black-and-white and grainy. They stand shoulder to shoulder in front of a white wall. Mr. Ward is tall and thin, and Mrs. Ward is small and stout. Both look like people who smile easily, the lines in their faces still shaped by mirth, though neither is smiling here. There's no photograph of Grace.

Alexander slams his glass down, and walks around the countertop, toward Sonya and the door.

"All right," Sonya says.

She stares at the name at the top of the page.

"All right *what?*" he says, scowling at her.

"I'll do it." Grace's address, her date of birth, a description of her appearance, are all written on the paper. Sonya folds it in half and tucks it into her back pocket, then steps to the side to clear a path for Alexander to leave.

"Are you . . . What?"

"I'm not sure how to make it much clearer for you. I accept your offer."

"Okay," he says, drawing out the word. "I'll . . . leave your pass at the guard station. You can pick it up tomorrow morning."

His fingers skim the wall on his way to the door, tracing faint lines in the whitewash. There's powder on his fingertips when he pulls them away. He turns back to her once he's in the hallway.

"What changed your mind?" he says.

"Well," she says, "do they still make those butter cookies? You know, the ones that come in that red packaging with the little dog on it? They were shaped like bones."

"Arf's. Packaging's blue now," he says.

"Yeah, those. God, I miss those," she says.

She closes the door between them.

SHE has to weave through a crowd to get to the gate the next day. News is contagious in the Aperture, and this is bigger, somehow, than the release of the youngest prisoners—because Sonya will be coming back at the end of the day. She steps around the sleepy-eyed men of Building 2, then Jack with his little notebook; Renee in a negligee and robe, smoking a cigarette; Graham with his thumbs hooked in his belt loops.

The guard who sits in the security office positioned right next to the gate is familiar, though she doesn't know his name. He's worked here for a long time, but she never goes near any of the guards. She didn't need to be warned about them. Plenty of women in the Aperture warned her anyway.

The guard—Williams is the name on his name tag—compares her face to the picture on her security pass. It's from a decade ago, from when she was seventeen. In it, her hair hangs limp over her shoulders, and there are dark circles under her eyes like bruises. But it still looks like her. He hands it to her, and she puts it in her jacket pocket.

"You have to check in within twelve hours of leaving," he says, "or we'll suspend your privileges until you can cooperate better."

"Fine," she says, and she goes to stand in front of the Aperture's aperture.

She's shaking. For over a decade, Green Street and Gray Street, Buildings 1 through 4, the market, the courtyards—they've been her entire world. A planet shrunk down to a snow globe. No choices, no strangers, no wide-open spaces. But now she remembers the largeness of the world, and it feels as oppressive as the air inside a closet.

Loops of barbed wire stand rigid atop the gate, which is wide enough for a truck to pass through. The guard pushes a lever, and the metal plates in front of her screech as they pull away from each other. She stands, for a moment, in the center of that dilating pupil. Just a few feet beyond the gate, held at bay by peace officers, is a crowd of people holding signs.

And behind her, a crowd of prisoners straining to get a look at the outside world.

She steps through the gate and into a wall of sound: clicking camera shutters and shouts, and everywhere, everywhere, her name:

Ms. Kantor, how does it feel to be outside for the first time in—

Sonya, what do you think about the Children of the Delegation Act that—

Poster Girl! Over here!

There are signs attached to broom handles and rulers and branches. Some are friendly:

WELCOME BACK, CHILD OF THE DELEGATION

Some are not:

DON'T SHOW MERCY? DON'T SEE MERCY!

For the most part, the signs all display the same image: her face, on the same poster the Delegation once plastered across the city, but with a single word struck out and supplanted.

WHAT'S ~~RIGHT~~ WRONG
IS ~~RIGHT~~ WRONG

Her own eyes, rendered light gray by the black-and-white, stare back at her from between the words. She doesn't know which direction to go, doesn't know which direction she's facing. She wants to shout; she remembers the knife-sharp sound of her own voice when she dug her thumb into that man's eye in her apartment, but this is not the dark void of Building 2, this is *out* and it's *everywhere* and she can only press forward.

A hand closes around her elbow, and she jerks it back. But the woman's face has that look about it, the gentle urgency of someone who is helping. Sonya recognizes her as Rose Parker. When Rose's arm slips across her shoulders, she allows it. She ducks her head into the embrace and watches their shoes moving in tandem.

Her shoes are so worn she can feel each pebble through the soles. Rose's are pink sneakers, the color of unripe watermelon. They walk away from the crowd so fast they're almost running. Sonya is breathless by the time the noise fades. She breaks away from Rose and leans back against a brick wall.

They are in an alley across from an overflowing dumpster. The alley itself seems to be overflowing, full of chairs with busted seats, shredded plastic bags, sagging couches with the stuffing spilling out, balled-up newspapers, rotting cardboard boxes. The smell is pungent. Across from her, graffiti tangles together on the brick in every color.

FUCK THE DELEGATION catches her attention, but there are other phrases she doesn't understand.

ANALOG ARMY
UNMEDICATION FOR ALL
BUST THE BORDERS

"You all right?" Rose says, and there's flint in her voice.

When she came into the Aperture to conduct her interviews for the Children of the Delegation article, her hair was in dozens of tight braids, but now it is a tumult of tight curls held back by a floral scarf.

"Yes," Sonya says, and she adds, "Thank you," because she is supposed to. Her Insight glows in its perpetual halo; someone—probably Alexander Price—is watching.

"I don't know if you remember me," Rose begins. "I never got to speak with you, before."

"I remember."

Rose wanted to interview her along with the others. She was in the market, a recording device in hand, calling out to every young person she could find in the Aperture. She was a magnet with the same polarity, a repulsive force surrounding her. She had spoken to Sonya by name. *Ms. Kantor, if you have a moment to talk about—*

Sonya hadn't had a moment.

"Well," Rose says. "Mr. Price said I could maybe buy your cooperation with these."

She reaches into a bag hanging at her side and takes out a slim blue box that says ARF's with a cartoon dalmatian perched on top of the *F.* Butter cookies.

Sonya frowns. She doesn't take them, even though she wants them. She can already feel them crumbling over her tongue.

"My cooperation," she says.

Rose takes out a black device with a fuzzy microphone about the size of a walnut at the end of it. "I was hoping to write a piece about you, one of the Delegation's famous faces, and—"

"No," Sonya says.

"I could tell everyone about your mission, let them know that you're trying to do good—"

Sonya laughs.

"Playing puppet for your new government on an impossible errand is not 'trying to do good,'" Sonya says. "If you'll excuse me, please."

She moves toward the end of the alley. She doesn't know where she is, her thoughts too scattered to remember the geography of the city. But she has to get away.

"Wait." Rose offers her a business card. Her name, phone number, and address are written on it. "Just in case you change your mind."

Sonya's mind often feels, to her, like clay hardened by the sun, left out too long to take a new shape. But she takes the card anyway.

THE city is loud. Everywhere is the shriek of the HiTrain over rails, the honking of buses telling pedestrians to scatter, bike bells tinkling behind her, beside her, in front of her, and voices—shouting, chattering, laughing, ranting voices. It takes her a half hour to understand that she is listening for something else: the shush of car tires, personal vehicles allocated only to those with the highest Desirability scores. They are nowhere in sight.

She climbs the steps to a HiTrain platform, not to ride it, but to look at one of the maps. The HiTrain was built during a push for public transportation, long before she was born. It's not as fast as the Flicker, a vacuum tube train that connects each segment of the megalopolis, but it's better for short distances. She pulls her hood low over her right eye. The Insight's glow stands out here.

Looking at the map, she begins to remember where she is. The Aperture is in the middle of the Seattle branch of the megalopolis, where the jagged line of skyscrapers tapers off to more moderate buildings. Nearby, all along the seawall that contains the waterfront, are the neighborhoods people used to clamor to live in. It was a privilege to move away from the noise of the city center, a mark of loyalty and service.

She is just a few neighborhoods away from Washington Park, where her family lived. The piece of paper with Grace Ward's name on it is in her pocket, folded into fourths. She stands on the platform and watches the next HiTrain come in, its wheels whistling on the rails. A crowd waits near the edge of the platform. Their clothes are a full spectrum of color, from neon bright to drab beige. One girl, a teenager, wears a tight bodysuit splattered with paint. Her hair is stained pink. Sonya can't stop staring at her as she snaps gum between her teeth and bounces on her toes, eager for the train doors to open. An outfit like that used to cost a person at least five hundred DesCoin for the day—a penalty for being disruptive. Most people didn't bother.

When the doors open, everyone piles on. They have no Insights to scan at the door, and Sonya begins to wonder if *she* can ride the HiTrain. It used to cost DesCoin. It doesn't seem to cost anything anymore.

She waits for the next train to come, standing beside a woman with a shopping bag between her feet. Pinched between her thumb and forefinger is a paperback book. Sonya reads it over her shoulder. It's poetry:

Do you recall that feeling
of steering your eyes away—
of steering your mind away?

The woman sees Sonya looking; she picks up her bag and moves away. The HiTrain coasts into the station, and Sonya follows the others on, half expecting an alarm to go off when she passes through the doors. But they only close behind her with a snap, and the train lurches away from the station, swaying like a boat in a wake.

Sonya stays on her feet, near the door. The other passengers settle into stained, cracked seats. A boy no older than twelve slurps Coca-Cola from the can; Sonya resists the urge to scold him for breaking the rules, to add a few DesCoin to her count. A man jostles an older woman for more space; she scowls at him, but pulls her arm tighter to her body. A woman in ragged clothing walks the aisle on unsteady feet. Sonya stares at the map on the HiTrain wall. There are only two stops separating her from Thirty-Fourth, where she needs to get off.

Outside, the city is shrouded in fog—not the heavy fog of pollution, but the mist of a typical morning. The streets are busy and there are signs of disrepair everywhere, as if nothing has been mended since the day she stepped into the Aperture. Perhaps nothing has. A stoplight dangles from a pole, precarious, its light flickering. A crack in the road has grown so wide it could swallow a man; a woman steers her child around it. The Delegation was good at keeping things tidy, but the Triumvirate, it seems, is not.

The train brakes, and a robotic voice calls out Sonya's stop. She steps onto the sagging platform alone. She's been here so many times—she took the HiTrain to school every morning, and to Aaron's every other day, and to her friend Tana's on Saturday afternoons to see C-rated movies at the theater near her house. It made her feel grown up, riding the train alone; she pretended she was on her way to work, or to pick up her kids from school.

Now she feels ancient. A specter haunting a graveyard.

She descends the steps to street level. Everywhere else, the disarray of the city seemed to be the result of bad behavior; here, it's due to neglect. The stores—once a row of charming boutiques and coffeehouses—are boarded up. The grass in the parkways is wild and tall; the tree branches tangle in the power lines and hang heavy over the street. She steps over a fallen streetlight, bits of glass crunching under her feet.

She remembers children in strollers, wearing hats to protect their faces from the sun; she remembers couples walking shoulder to shoulder, their knuckles brushing as their arms swung; she remembers dogs sniffing at front gates and the corners of fences. But this is no longer a place for those ordinary things. She turns at the next intersection and walks down the street where her family lived.

There's debris here, too, but a different kind. She steps over a broken fishing pole, a knitting bag with shiny needles poking out of it, a children's bicycle with no tires. She recognizes the tattered frame of a brocade sofa from the Perez house, turned upside down on their front lawn, now obviously a home for small mammals. She stops in the middle of the street to look at the front doors torn off their hinges on each side, the broken windows, the charred remains of second stories.

Her family fled early in the uprising. Her father came to them late at night and told them to pack a change of clothes and a toothbrush. They drove down the street with the headlights off, only the car dashboard and their Insights glowing—

Sonya keeps walking.

The Kantor house is made of red brick. Two stories high, with fir trees at the edges of the property. The right side of the house is half-collapsed, the second floor tumbling into the first. Sonya's room and the guest room fold in on themselves.

Two white pillars frame the front door, which rests against the side of the house, where the lilac bushes used to be. Broken furniture is strewn over the lawn, like entrails spilling from an animal carcass. She stands on her tiptoes near the front door to feel along the frame for the spare key. It's there, covered in dirt, paint from the frame sticking to it. She slides it into her pocket.

The rugs are gone, the walls cracking and flaking, the furniture absent or broken. She doesn't trust the steps that lead upstairs. She wanders into the formal dining room, to the left, where the tabletop has shattered, leaving beads of glass all over the wood floor. The metal frame stands unaffected.

All the drawers in the built-in cabinet along the far wall are open. But something in one of them catches the light—one of the napkin rings her mother saved from her first dinner party, a simple yellow loop made of plastic. It looks like something for a baby to teethe on. Her mother always talked about how determined she was to make things "nice" even when they were young and poor—plastic napkin rings, polyester napkins instead of paper, matching melamine plates. *There's no excuse for a lack of effort,* she liked to say, one of the phrases Sonya repeated to herself when she saw unkempt or disruptive people.

She keeps moving until she reaches the threshold of her father's office. She wasn't allowed to go in, even as a teenager. But it's only wreckage now. There are books everywhere, left to rot on the hardwood. His desk has been ripped apart, files everywhere, shelves broken, keepsakes smashed. The clay dish she made him in primary school, a cradle of leaves painted deep green to match his walls, is in pieces on the floor. She crouches to pick them up, one by one.

Near the edge of the desk is the poster, encased in glass. WHAT'S RIGHT IS RIGHT. He kept it hanging right in front of him so she could watch him work—that's what he said, anyway. She stays for a long time in a crouch, the pieces of the dish in her hands, her adolescent face glaring back at her in grayscale. Someone sprayed a red X on the glass, but she can still see through it.

Her father was the one who asked her to sit for the poster. Susanna didn't like it. She grumbled about it for days. But Sonya had squealed with excitement at the thought of her face being all over the city.

She stands and leaves the office. The rooms are arranged in a square, connected by hallways, so she walks right through the kitchen, with its broken tiles and collapsed cabinets, to the laundry room, half-buried in rubble, the washing machine unperturbed.

She collects things as she goes: a spoon from the wreck of the kitchen, one of Susanna's guitar picks wedged between the floorboards, a bottle cap her father saved from his first date with her mother. She notes the big homescreen—a wide glass panel designed to sync with all their Insights—in the living room, bashed in repeatedly with a blunt object, and the spray paint on the wall in the foyer that reads DELEGATION SCUM. That, she looks at for a long time.

All the little keepsakes in her pockets clatter together as she walks back down the street, away from her family's home.

THE piece of paper with Grace Ward's name on it gives the Wards' address, but Sonya doesn't go there. Instead she rides the HiTrain toward the Seattle downtown, where pillars of buildings crowd together along the waterfront. There, perched unevenly on a downward slope, is a blocky, asymmetrical glass structure once used as a public library, in the time when print books were more abundant, and now used as one again. The Delegation used it as a community gathering space, the books locked away behind glass, like museum relics.

Sonya has been there before, though she only ever read books projected into her eye via the Insight display. The library is where the Delegation records are kept. That much she knows from Rose Parker's article.

She follows a line of people into the blue glow of the lobby. She feels the way she did when she was a child, like a small fish in a large fishbowl, the angular glass panes above her refracting light. To her right are seats that descend into the ground, a lecture hall; ahead are bright yellow escalators. She goes to a nearby desk, where a middle-aged man wears a name tag. JOHN.

"Hello," she says to him. "Would you please tell me where to find the Delegation records?"

John's eyes fix on her Insight. He hesitates with his stylus over an Elicit screen; he seems so startled by the sight of her that he has forgotten his task. But Sonya knows there are different kinds of surprise, with and without delight. This is the latter.

"For what purpose?" he says.

"Pardon me?"

"For what purpose," he repeats, slowly this time. "Do you need the Delegation records."

"Is that a standard question?" she says. "Or are you only asking *me?*"

He has a scar near his hairline. It is not the first one she's seen, though it's more obvious than many, because his hair is thinning, gray sprinkled among the brown. She assumes it's from the surgery to remove the Insight. It's an inch long, paler than the rest of his skin.

She takes the Grace Ward paper out of her pocket, unfolds it, and presses it flat to the desk in front of him.

"I'm not here to reminisce," she says. "I'm here to find information about this missing girl. Okay?"

John looks at the name at the top of the paper. His posture sags a little.

"It's on the top floor," he says. "You'll need a pass. Hold on."

He gets her a square of bright paper laminated in plastic. *DELEGATION RECORDS* is written on it in permanent marker.

"Thank you," she says. She tucks the Grace Ward paper back into her pocket, and walks toward the escalators.

As she travels up to the top floor, someone going the opposite direction points at Sonya and elbows her friend, excited. They both wave, and for a second Sonya wonders if she knows them, before she hears them shout, "Poster Girl!"

THE Delegation records take up most of the top floor. Rows and rows of taupe bookshelves with a slim file for each person who lived in the Seattle–Portland–South Vancouver megalopolis. She stands among them with the laminated pass in hand, unsure where to go. Above her, the diamond-patterned glass ceiling slants to its apex. Through it, she sees the stone and glass structures that crowd around the library, blocking some of its light.

By instinct, she focuses on the ceiling to learn more about the building—the architect, the year it was built, the style. But the Insight display is, of course, inert; it presents her with nothing. She wonders if Alexander Price is watching and mocking her for the old habit.

At the top of the escalator is a sign explaining the records room:

It may strike us as odd that the Delegation—with its reliance on the Insight to track, reward, and punish its citizens—would keep paper records. Indeed, they kept both digital and analog files on their citizens when they were in power, with the analog files containing only the information that the Delegation deemed most pertinent. The more expansive digital records were purged by an unknown government official during the uprising, but freedom fighters were able to recover the entirety of the paper records from Seattle's City Hall, which we make freely available to our patrons here. We believe that staying in touch with our history empowers us to avoid its worst mistakes.

Sonya reads it with her mouth curled into a sneer, lingering on the phrase "freedom fighters." She thinks of her father covering her mouth with his hand on the way to the car as they made their escape, his palm smelling of lemon soap; of the red lines on her wrist from the zip ties after her arrest; of the three black body bags arranged on the moss outside the cabin—

She plucks a file off one of the shelves and reads the name at the top. TREVOR QUINN. She puts it back and pulls a file off the next shelf down. REBECCA RAND. She's alone in this section, unsupervised. She could get lost here, burying herself in the stories of what was. The objects she took from her family's home jingle in her pocket as she walks down to the end of the room, where she finds the *W*s.

There is a row of Wards, not all of them related. They're arranged alphabetically. Alexander, Anna, Anthony, Arthur. All the way to George, Gertrude, Gloria, Grant, Greg. No Grace. An illegal girl doesn't have a Delegation file.

But Grace's parents' names were on the paper Alexander gave her: Roger and Eugenia Ward. So she picks up Eugenia's file and sits on the floor between the shelves. The pages are dense with text. PREFERRED LOCATIONS is the heading on one; FREQUENT PURCHASES is the heading on another, a DesCoin amount assigned to each item. Trash bags, zero DesCoin; tampons, four DesCoin; a six-pack of beer, fifty DesCoin. Sonya's parents had argued about the tampon amount once, with her mother demanding to know why tampons were not a zero-tier item when they were so necessary, and her father arguing that not everyone used them, and not everything could be zero tier, she could buy sanitary napkins instead at two DesCoin—

She scans the list of the Wards' earnings—highlighted yellow and labeled AVERAGE. Roger seemed to take in very little DesCoin, period, suggesting a failure to participate in society, and Eugenia lost hers through carelessness, little things like crossing the street outside of approved zones, entering the train before others had exited, cursing in front of her child. But there's nothing notable. Sonya moves to recent purchases, looking for a sign that they were housing an illegal second child, but they had been careful. They must have planned ahead for a second child, put aside diapers, food, toys from their first daughter to provide for the second. It was an elaborate undertaking.

Sonya chews her fingernail. There are a few oddities noted in the report, namely that Eugenia Ward favored certain luxury shelf-stable goods, such as nuts, specialty candy, and mustard—not common for someone of her status, and out of line with her other purchases. But even that is not helpful to Sonya—she can't track down the teenage Grace Ward by following mustard purchases.

She puts Eugenia's file back where it belongs, and she's retracing her steps down the center aisle to the entrance when she sees the label for *K*, and veers off course.

Her fingers drift over August and Julia, uncertain, before she plucks SONYA KANTOR from the shelf.

She skips the early pages—BASIC INFORMATION, PREFERRED LOCATIONS, RECENT PURCHASES. She was young then, with few purchases to speak of. Movie tickets, snacks at the corner store, school supplies. Her DesCoin history brings a smile to her face—she always had a high number, for someone her age, which means she earned plenty of DesCoin with her behavior and bought only items with a high Desirability score—tickets to C-rated movies, healthy snacks, modest clothing. Each entry is highlighted in green—according to the key, green means ABOVE AVERAGE.

Near the back is a page titled CONTRIBUTION ASSESSMENT:

Sonya Kantor is a legal second child (Permit #20692) of August and Julia Kantor. She does not show signs of mental illness beyond the norm, though she has a propensity for moodiness greater than the average for her age. She exhibits moderate intelligence, below the level of the rest of her family. That said, her average school performance can be attributed to a lack of interest as well as a lack of ability—she is bored by difficult texts and appears to achieve acceptable grades only to earn DesCoin. Her extracurricular interests are relatively shallow, and though she is competent at piano and voice, she does not possess a particular talent in either. She is compliant with Delegation protocols, with a strong desire to please and a good memory for rules and regulations. She trusts easily and does not possess a great deal of curiosity. Though she occasionally demonstrates furtive interest in the same gender, she appears to be demonstratively heterosexual and will be a suitable partner for a promising Delegation employee. However, she is not a viable option for Delegation employment herself.

Sonya stops reading. She closes her folder and puts it back on the shelf, between her mother's and her sister's—there was only one Kantor family in the megalopolis, so there are no other names to sort through. As she walks out of the library, the laminated pass left behind on the carpet, she presses her palms to her cheeks to cool them.

She rides the escalators down, running her fingers over the objects in her pockets—the bottle cap, the fragments of the dish she made, the guitar pick. Then she puts up her hood, shielding her right eye from view, and walks back to the HiTrain.

FOUR

ALEXANDER PRICE STANDS at her window, where the tapestry blocks her view of the street beyond the Aperture. He's holding the tapestry back so he can look down at the corner store where she has seen people with binoculars, peering into the windows of Building 4 like birders. His hair, now that it's long, is wavy and thick, oil dark. When he turns toward her, a curl falls over his forehead and he doesn't seem as threatening. He more closely resembles the boy she used to sneak looks at across the kitchen island when she was supposed to be listening to Aaron.

She still leaves the door open behind her.

There was a crowd at the entrance when she returned, waiting for her. She had no choice but to elbow people aside. One of them shouted in her face, his breath stale and hot. One of them spat on her coat; she wiped it away once she was inside with a handkerchief she had tucked into her sleeve. A few others tried to get pictures of her with their Elicits, or her signature on little slips of paper. She was steady as she walked away from the guard station, and then slumped against the outer wall of Building 4 to catch her breath.

She thinks, now, of the wall in her parents' house that says DELEGATION SCUM.

"Why are you here?" she says to Alexander, in a tone that would have lost her two DesCoin, if it still existed.

"Seems like you had quite a day," he says. He turns his head to the side. There's a scar on his temple, a shade darker than the rest of his light brown skin, jagged, like the surgeon who removed his Insight slipped a little with the scalpel.

"I've been going over your footage," he says.

"Then you saw that there's no way for me to find that girl," she says. "I have nothing to go on. Not even a mention in her parents' files."

"I saw that you have no particular interest in finding her." He lets go of the tapestry and steps away from the window. "Judging by the first thing you did when you left the Aperture."

"Are you telling me you never went back to your old house?" she says. "I doubt Grace Ward's parents will notice the extra hour I spent there."

"This isn't about the time; it's about your priorities. There's a family out there that hasn't seen their daughter in a decade. If you think it's okay to—"

"What I think is that your Triumvirate doesn't expect me to find her," Sonya says. "So I'd better take all the time I can get outside the Aperture."

"Fucking typical. You never even considered trying to help these people, did you?"

"Of course I did. But I also considered that the person who gave me a decade-old cold case to solve in exchange for my freedom wasn't really interested in me *getting* my freedom, he just wanted a publicity stunt that makes the Triumvirate look merciful."

Alexander steps closer to her, and stares at her for a long moment before he speaks again.

"Empty your pockets."

Eat shit, she thinks. *You fucking asshole, you—*

"No," she says. "Get out of my apartment."

"This is not *your apartment,* this is a cell that belongs to the citizens of this sector, funded by their tax dollars, and they generously permit you to live in it instead of in the maximum security prison." He moves closer to her, and this time, she doesn't back away. She thinks of the knife in the kitchen drawer, with its taped-up handle.

"Empty your pockets," he says again.

She used to think she had nothing to lose. That's the philosophy of the crowd she and David used to hang out with, too. And they're right—they have life sentences in the Aperture, after all; no more severe consequences await them for whatever they do to each other. They could be moved to the prison along with the Triumvirate's murderers and thieves, perhaps, but that's never happened, and so they think, *Go ahead and watch,* as they defy the rules of their imprisonment. *Go ahead and stop me.* And no one does, no one has.

Sonya has something to lose now. So she gathers up the bits of things that are in her pockets. The pieces of the dish she made her father, Susanna's guitar pick, Julia's napkin ring, the spare key to the house, August's bottle cap. She drops them all on the kitchen counter beside her with a clatter.

Seeing those things through his eyes, now, they look like garbage. She could have found them in an alley.

He sneers a little, sweeps them into his hand, and drops them in his coat pocket.

"You shouldn't pine for your old life," he says. "Everything you enjoyed about it came at someone else's expense."

"I didn't do anything. I didn't do anything to anyone."

He snorts.

"I have nothing left of my family," she says. "That's all I have left of them."

"It's a pile of *junk,* Sonya." He scowls at her. "You want to know whether I ever went back to my family's house? Sure I did. But I didn't take anything they bought with other people's suffering."

He's close. He smells like mint gum. His teeth are white and gritted.

"I helped the uprising burn it down," he says.

"I . . ." She tries not to choke. She looks up at him. "I used to wish you had died instead of him." She laughs a little. "God, I used to fantasize about it every night . . . inventing a whole world where he was alive instead of you. Where we were together in the Aperture, or where he had been spared somehow, and he was free, married to some other woman, two kids, a little house . . ."

She remembers the glow of the Insight against the cracked ceiling in her first Aperture apartment, a light that never went out, though power in the Aperture cut off at ten p.m.

She goes on: "Now, though, I hope you keep living for a long time. I hope you think of him every minute. I hope you inhale the pain of missing him and exhale the guilt of betraying him."

He and Aaron had the same dark eyes. Long eyelashes. He blinks at her, and then he steps around her. The bits and pieces of her old life clack together in his pocket as he walks.

She turns to watch him go. Over his shoulder, she sees Nikhil, pausing mid-step in the hallway, a handful of tomatoes clutched to his stomach.

The two men are still, staring at each other. Then Alexander shoves open the door to the staircase and disappears.

THEY eat the tomatoes raw, whole, no question of cooking them. Cooking them would mean not feeling the tension of the skin giving way, and that's half the joy of eating a tomato. They're not the only plants ready for eating—there's cabbage and green beans, now, and carrots and radishes, for the colder months. They tried to grow bell peppers one year, and the plants withered in the sun.

Sonya heats up rice and beans, cooked the other night and kept cold in her little refrigerator, one of the only ones in Building 4. Sonya had wondered, as she dragged the refrigerator upstairs from Mr. Nadir's apartment, whether such an act would have earned her DesCoin—for recycling—or lost them—for pilfering from the dead. As with so many things these days, it was hard to say.

She left the paper with Grace Ward's name on it on the table. Nikhil unfolds it and looks it over.

"Who is she?" he says.

"So you don't know her, then," she says. "I thought maybe you would know her name. Her parents would have passed through your office once they were caught."

Before the uprising, Nikhil worked for the Delegation, like Sonya's father. He determined sentencing for people guilty of serious violations of Delegation protocol—people who had more than one child without a permit, or who tampered with their Insights, or smuggled Undesirable or illegal goods into the underground markets. It was a miracle he escaped the fall of the Delegation with his life. Plenty of the unlawful people who had passed through his office to receive their punishments became dissidents in the uprising.

It helped, perhaps, that he didn't run.

"Too many people passed through my office," Nikhil says. "Too many for me to recognize all their names. Though I did always feel sorry for the ones in violation of Protocol 18A. Of all the crimes a person could commit, wanting a second child is not so terrible."

Sonya raises an eyebrow.

"But it was a supremely selfish act," she says. "Protocol 18A was put in place to ensure that we had enough resources for every child. Your desire to replicate your genetic material shouldn't supersede the common good—"

"I can't believe you still have all that memorized," he replies, with a wry smile.

"I don't have it *memorized,* I just . . ." She thinks about the assessment in her file, the one that said she had a good memory for rules and regulations.

"Grace didn't have a file," Sonya says, tapping the paper. It's rumpled and worn already, from how many times she's folded and unfolded it. "I was surprised by that, because I assumed the Delegation would keep a record, even if she was illegal."

"The Delegation would." Nikhil frowns at the paper. "Maybe it was only digital."

Sonya sighs.

"Did you ever read that fairy tale—about Vasilisa the fair?" she says. "My father read it to me, once. Vasilisa's stepmother hates her, because she's beautiful, because she's not *hers.* So she sends Vasilisa into the woods to get fire from Baba Yaga, a witch who boils people and eats them." She stares at her hands, clasped loosely on the table, her fingers curled. "She doesn't expect Vasilisa to come back. She expects her to die. Giving her that task . . . it's just a way to get rid of her." She smiles a little.

"You believe they have sent you to get fire." Nikhil picks up the wrinkled paper and chews a tomato. "Well, perhaps you're right. The Triumvirate capitulated to public demand with the Children of the Delegation Act, but they are likely not excited about the idea of freeing a *symbol* of the Delegation. But if you can't find anything in the official record . . . you might consider consulting with the unofficial one."

Nikhil puts the paper down, and folds his hands on the table. His hands are spotted now, shriveling like figs in the sun. He still has hair, feather-light and white. It reminds her of dandelion seeds, standing high in hope of a breeze.

"Many of the people I sentenced had committed Evasion, which meant they paid someone to temporarily suspend their Insight's feed—making them invisible, essentially, just for a few hours at a time," he says.

"I didn't know that was even possible."

He nods. "Difficult, yes, and expensive . . . but possible. Most of them used that time to indulge their worst impulses. Everything you can imagine, and more."

"Who?"

Nikhil waves a hand vaguely at the city beyond her wall tapestry. "Anyone, everyone. Delegation insiders and outsiders. There are depraved people everywhere, but some are better at masking it than others."

She thinks the Aperture has made this obvious. The polished young men and women of the Delegation now cook euphoric poison in their basement, fight in the street, and steal from each other's unlocked apartments, among other things. Even Mr. Nadir had kept his small refrigerator behind plywood so no one else knew about it.

"What does this have to do with Grace Ward?" she says.

"Ah," Nikhil says. "In the last few days before the uprising, I met a remarkable woman who had facilitated many of these Evasions. Emily Knox was her name—though she was known only as Knox. I don't know that she will know your girl, but if I had to look for *unofficial* information of any kind, I would go to her."

Sonya nods.

"What sentence did you give her?"

"I don't remember," Nikhil says, with a sigh. "But I did not often show leniency to the focal points of Undesirable activity."

The tomatoes are gone, their wiry stems in a pile on the table. Shouts echo from the street beyond the Aperture, as they do every night at sundown, when it's easier to peer into the windows of Building 4. The crowds are thinner on this corner than near Buildings 1 and 2, where the Aperture residents frequently throw trash at onlookers from their windows. Tonight, at the corner store across the way, it's just a loud, laughing conversation. Sonya feels—and suppresses—the urge to crack open the window so she can hear what they're saying.

Nikhil clears his throat.

"You didn't tell me Alexander was your Triumvirate contact." He says it like he's setting down something heavy, and she realizes he's been waiting the whole conversation to bring it up.

"You asked me if it was some resistance goon," she says. "And that's what he is."

Nikhil nods.

"You don't need to protect me from my son," Nikhil says.

"I don't think of him as your son." Sonya sweeps the tomato stems from the table and into her palm.

"How is he?"

Nikhil has Alexander's and Aaron's eyes, though his are watery, like he's always on the verge of tears. She has only ever seen him cry on the anniversary of Aaron's and Nora's deaths. He was devoted to her, to Nora; he even took her name when they got married, a rare thing.

She thinks all the time about why Alexander turned on them, on all of them. It certainly wasn't because his parents didn't love him enough.

"The same," Sonya says. "He's the same."

She gets up and throws the tomato stems in the trash.

Later they sit in silence, Sonya in the kitchen and Nikhil in the chair beside his bed, a pile of socks in his lap. He mends them for everyone in the building; he says it's good for an old man to have responsibilities.

The radio is on the table in front of her. She took the plastic case off the back, so its parts are visible, like she's doing a dissection for a science class. She has removed the worn wires and is trying to find replacements in a second radio, this one broken beyond repair, that she found in the late Mr. Wu's apartment on the second floor.

She has her soldering iron and an array of screwdrivers she traded for a quilt five years ago. She doesn't know what she's doing, but trial and error has worked for her before.

Sonya stares hard at the tangled wires inside the radio, a habit from a lifetime of using the Insight at its full capacity. In times past, that kind of stare would have prompted the implant to present information in the ocular display. The Insight would have taught her how to fix the radio.

But the Insight only watches her now, it doesn't help her. She pries the plastic casing away from the end of the wire, exposing the twisted metal strands beneath it. She begins the delicate process of reattaching it to the newer radio, strand by strand, with the soldering iron.

Nikhil starts to whistle. The first few notes have Sonya drawing up straight, her spine rigid. Her hands freeze over the wires.

The song is "The Narrow Way," a Delegation song.

"Nikhil," she says.

He looks up.

"Don't."

He looks at her for a long moment, and then nods, returning to his work in silence.

It was the song her mother hummed, right before.

WAIT, wait, I have a good one," Sonya said to David once, as they sat on the floor in his apartment. Tokens carved out of wood litter the ground between them. Lined up between their knees are five small teacups from a child's tea set, and a bottle of cloudy moonshine that tastes like glue.

She reaches out and taps his nose and recites:

Four Delegationers sit as the world blows up.
Four pills in hand and four water cups
Count down from four and it's bottoms up
One Delegationer sits as the world blows up.

The way they joke, sometimes, is like digging a hole. Who can go deeper, who can go darker. If you can laugh while you're drowning, David says, who's to say you're not going for a swim?

This time, her eyes burn with tears. She tries to laugh, and her chest heaves instead. David reaches for her, pulls her against him. A wooden token digs into her hip. She buries her face in his T-shirt, and breathes in the smell of his soap until she steadies again.

FIVE

THE NEXT DAY, Renee waits for her at the gate before she leaves. Her hair is piled on top of her head and knotted with a strip of old towel. She still wears the creases of a pillowcase on her cheek.

"Hey," she says.

"Good morning," Sonya says. "You all right?"

"Yeah, fine. I was just wondering . . ." She looks at the gate. "Can you buy things out there?"

"No," Sonya says. "They're not giving me a stipend or anything. I'm not even sure what they use for currency now."

Renee sighs.

"Well, if you find a newspaper lying around," she says. "Grab it, would you?"

Most of what she knows about Renee, she learned in a haze of cigarette smoke at a party. She worked for the Delegation; she has a little sister outside the Aperture. She always wanted a big wedding in the garden at her parents' house, and two kids, if she could get a permit for the second. Girls. She wanted girls. She's always trying to get the Aperture leaders to demand the end of mandatory birth control, and Nikhil says the request always gets tacked on to the bottom of the list. Hard to get people to rally behind birth control, he says, when they still aren't eating enough.

"Sure," Sonya says. "I'll keep an eye out."

Renee stands back as the gate opens.

There are fewer protesters at the entrance today. They part for Sonya like water around a stone, but their eyes, following her down the street, are hungry. Once she's far enough away from the crowd, she puts up her hood to shade the Insight.

She hears scuffling behind her, but when she turns to look, there's no one.

Pinched between her thumb and forefinger is the card Rose Parker gave her the day before. The address printed at the bottom is a long walk from the Aperture, but Sonya decides not to take the HiTrain. She feels the pebbles poking through the worn soles of her shoes, the grit of the sidewalk. She walks in the street, her hands in her pockets and the misty air wetting her face.

She takes a detour through the park, following the edge of the concrete-lined reservoir, the art museum with the rippling stone face, the angular metalwork on its windows. The grass is unkempt, spilling over onto the sidewalk, and little white flowers are in bloom everywhere—weeds, but still she thinks of pulling them up by their roots so she can plant them in the courtyard. Mrs. Pritchard might not approve.

She hears the scuffling again, and looks over her shoulder. There's a man walking behind her, his hands in the pockets of his blue jacket, his face turned up to the sky, as if he's relishing the mist. She walks faster, choosing a path that will take her back to busier streets. Her hand flexes, empty. She didn't even try to bring her knife out of the Aperture.

Rose Parker's office is in a small, plain building with a security guard near the elevators and a woman in a prim suit at the reception desk. She holds a book in one hand and an apple in the other, so she turns the pages of the book with sticky fingers. The book is not one Sonya recognizes. Its glossy cover reads *The Artistry of Thieves,* and there's a ship on the cover, drawn cresting green and purple waves.

Sonya takes off her hood just as the woman looks up. The apple falls out of her hand as she takes in Sonya's face. Before Sonya has to explain herself, someone taps on the glass separating them from the office beyond—Rose Parker, in a blue, geometrically patterned dress. She beckons to Sonya to come in, and neither the receptionist nor the security guard objects as Sonya passes through the doors to the office.

It's an open space, bright from the windows along each wall, and the lights in the center of the room, which hover together like bubbles at the top of a glass of milk. The sight seems dated to Sonya—that kind of fixture, with free-floating, glowing spheres, was common when she was a child, but in her teenage years it fell out of fashion. Between that and the paper books and the Elicits, she wonders if it's possible for time to run backward.

She wonders if Alexander is watching her now.

"I'm surprised to see you," Rose says to her. "I thought you would probably light my business card on fire right after we spoke."

"I didn't have matches," Sonya says, surprising a laugh out of Rose.

"Wow. A joke, from the poster girl." She touches her chest. "Come on, my desk is over here."

All the desks are at long tables with low shelves serving as dividers. Most are filled with stacks of paper—old articles, competing newspapers, pamphlets with staples at the corners. At the far end of the room are several wall screens, not unlike the one Sonya saw smashed in her family's home. They play what appears to be a news feed.

Under the Delegation there was one news feed: Channel 3. Sonya knew the anchors like they were old friends, Elisabeth with the morning report, Abby with the evening, Michael with the weather forecast. On the screens in Rose Parker's office, there are four different feeds running simultaneously, the faces unfamiliar, the headlines unintelligible: *The Analog Army Claims Responsibility for Murder of Tech Magnate. Triumvirate Representative Petra Novak Promises Continued Aid to Victims of Phillips Bombing. Flu Vaccine Delayed Due to Syringe Shortages.* They're headlines for another world.

"So you've changed your mind about doing an interview, then?" Rose smiles like she already knows the answer. She drags a metal chair over from one of the other desks and puts it beside her own.

When they sit, their knees almost brush together. Sonya crosses her legs at the ankle and folds her hands in her lap. Rose stares at her like she's done something strange.

"No," Sonya says. Scattered across Rose's desk are scraps of paper with scribbled notes on them. *Seemed skittish; follow up with neighbor* is on the one closest to her, with a box around the word *neighbor. This seems like bullshit* is written on another one, with an arrow pointing at something written in shorthand.

"I needed help with something," Sonya continues.

"So, just to remind you where you and I stand," Rose says. "You refused to participate in my Children of the Delegation interviews. You refused another interview after I saved you from that crowd. And now you want my help." She tilts her head, a diamond-shaped earring catching the light. "Why should I give it to you?"

Sonya frowns. "Do you know why I've been granted permission to leave the Aperture?" she says.

"I might," Rose says. "But I'd love to hear how *you* choose to explain it."

Sonya senses she's about to walk into a trap, but there's no way to avoid it. "I'm supposed to find a girl. She's a teenager now, I guess. The Delegation rehomed her because her parents violated reproductive legislation—"

"What a fascinating word, *rehomed,*" Rose says, leaning forward so Sonya can see the tangle of capillaries at the corner of one of her eyes. "Because what it means is that a child was ripped from her parents because they weren't quite indoctrinated enough to the Delegation to find favor. A cruel euphemism, don't you think?"

Sonya straightens in her chair. Even after all this time, she still waits for the alert that her DesCoin levels have dropped, their conversation deemed Undesirable. But though the glow of the Insight continues unabated, the display remains dark.

"Have I offended you?" Rose asks, again with that head tilt.

"I went to look at the Delegation records." Sonya's throat is tight. "There's no record of her existence in the old files."

"Ah, so you've been there already," Rose says. "Did you look at your own?"

Sonya thinks of the wiry carpet beneath her, the cold shelf behind her, the weight of the file in her lap. The paragraph that declared her to be docile but mediocre. She thinks of her father's file, her mother's, her sister's, all lined up in alphabetical order—

All lined up in black bags on the moss—

"So you did," Rose says, her voice softening a little. "We've all done it, you know—"

"I think it's odd there's no record of Grace Ward at all, not even a mention in her parents' files," Sonya says. "I know you probably don't know anything about Grace, but I thought of someone who might. Emily Knox."

Rose sighs.

"Yeah, I know her," Rose says. "Pretty sure every journalist in the city does; she's not shy."

"Can you tell me where to find her?"

"*Can* I? Yes." Rose smiles. "But I'd like a trade of my own."

Under the Delegation, everything was quantified; everything that a person said or did warranted either a positive or negative quantity of DesCoin. But that trade was conducted with the Delegation, not between users of the Insight system. If you did something good, you were rewarded by the Delegation, not by the person you did it for; your gift had intrinsic value whether the receiver appreciated it or not. The Delegation was a straightforward intermediary, the arbiter of worth.

In her first days in the Aperture, it was confusing to barter—to get something you wanted only if the other person believed you had given them what you promised. It required, among other things, trust—that if you gave first, you would receive. Rose expects that trust now, and Sonya is not sure she can give it.

"A trade for what?"

"An interview. Just five questions, nothing big."

Rose opens a drawer and takes out the recording device Sonya saw her with in the Aperture, a black box with a microphone at the end of it, covered in foam. She sets it upright on the desk, between them.

"Two questions," Sonya says.

"Okay, but no one-word answers. I want complete sentences."

Sonya clenches her hands. She nods. She wonders how much of herself she will have to give away to find Grace Ward, if it will be worth it in the end. Rose presses a button on the recorder, and it lights up from within, blue shining from the holes in the black casing.

"Okay, first: tell me how it feels to be back in the world again, after so long away from it."

"How it *feels?* How is that newsworthy?"

"I'm the one who gets to decide what's newsworthy," Rose says. "Answer the question."

Sonya feels hot. She touches a cool palm to one of her cheeks. She moves to tuck a strand of hair behind her ear before realizing her hair is too short for that now, and has been for years.

"It feels confusing," she says. Rose gestures for her to go on, and she sighs. "It's like everyone is speaking a different language. I understand the words, but I don't know what they mean anymore. Triumvirate this and Analog that and—none of the books are the same, the stores, the brands, the *packaging,* the—You say I'm 'back in the world' . . . but it's not my world, is it?" She swallows hard. "My world is gone."

Rose writes on one of the little scraps of paper on her desk. Her writing is too tight, too slanted for Sonya to read it from where she sits, not without leaning closer, which she doesn't do.

"Second question," Rose says. "Something I've wondered since I first saw you in the Aperture. You were getting a lot of attention there; you get a lot of attention here. You don't seem to enjoy it. So why did you even agree to do that propaganda poster to begin with?"

"First, I want the address," Sonya says. "Emily Knox's address."

"You don't trust me?"

Sonya stares at her, hard, Insight aglow, the way she would have in the time before, to find out Rose's Desirability score, the level to which she was trusted by the government. No number presents itself.

"No," Sonya says. "I don't know why I would."

Rose smiles a little. She tears off the bottom of her scrap of paper and writes something on it. But she keeps it pinched between thumb and forefinger, waiting.

"My father asked me if I wanted to do it," Sonya says. "My sister, Susanna, she was always better at everything—better at math, better at history. At dancing. At talking to people. Everything. So when he asked me . . ." Sonya sighs. "It was my chance to have something that she didn't have. I was sixteen. I just wanted . . . something that was mine."

She plucks the paper from Rose Parker's grasp.

"It backfired," she adds.

She stands and walks across the room, toward the glass door where she can see the receptionist with an apple core balanced on the edge of her desk, her book still in hand, the security guard still slumped against the wall near the elevators. Her face, her ears, are warm. She's dizzy.

She thinks of the guitar pick Alexander took from her. She found it wedged between the floorboards in the living room, where Susanna liked to practice. Susanna was a competent musician, nothing special. What Sonya had liked more than the songs she played was the sound of her fingers slipping along the frets, a sticky slide.

FOR a moment, outside the office building where Rose Parker works, Sonya can't remember which direction she came from. All the buildings look the same. All the people who pass are loud and sharp, wrinkled brows and nylon-covered elbows, boots splashing through puddles and splattering her trousers. She unfolds the scrap of paper, and doesn't recognize the address. She isn't sure if the street names have changed, or if she just doesn't remember them.

She stands at the edge of the sidewalk, where curb meets road. Behind her is the Aperture, a rooftop garden in pots, a broken radio, a roof that leaks every time her upstairs neighbor, Laura, takes a shower. In front of her is the HiTrain, a churning sea of people moving in all different directions, a criminal named Emily Knox. She wonders if it's as good as they say, to take out the Insight, to be all alone.

A body rushes toward her, and she flinches before realizing it's Alexander, his collar turned up against the chill, his cheeks dotted with mist.

"There you are," he says. "Something happened, come on."

He puts a hand on her elbow, and she jerks it free. He doesn't seem to notice, leading her to an alley with an open dumpster. A mangled wooden chair stands beside it, the legs twisting in all directions, splintering.

"Are you following me?" she says.

"I told you we would monitor your Insight," he says, fumbling in his pocket for something. "The Wards got in touch with me this morning."

"The Wards?"

"Yes, you know, the Wards, the people whose daughter you're trying to find by consulting with a notorious criminal?" He takes a tangle of wire out of his pocket with a silver device at the end of it. "They reached out to me and they sent me this audio file—"

At the other end of the tangle of wire is a headband with two foam pads at either end, folded in half. He straightens the headband and claps the foam pads over her ears with a snap. She winces.

The cord stretches taut between them. She notices for the first time that his eyes are wild, his hair piled on one side of his head, curling into the air.

He presses a button on the device, and she remembers standing across the HiTrain platform from Aaron after school, her on her way home and him on his way to his father's office, how he liked to beam songs directly to her Insight. The prompt would come up on the display, `Aaron Price would like to share a song, do you accept?` And she would nod, and the song would play, the deep connectors of the Insight translating sound into electricity in her brain, as if it was whispering into her ears. They listened together on separate trains, moving in opposite directions.

The sound in her ears now is faint. She covers the earpieces with her palms, pressing the voice closer.

". . . reached the voicemail of Eugenia Ward, please leave your name and a way to contact you and I will get back to you as soon as possible . . ." Eugenia's voice is low and even, a voice accustomed to soothing. Sonya looks up at Alexander, frowning, as the beep sounds, and a new voice crackles to life.

"Hello?"

It is low, too, for a woman's voice, and unsteady, breaking—

"This is . . . this is your Alice."

Sonya's hands tighten around the earpieces, around her ears.

"They told me you were gone, they told me you were dead and I believed them, I believed them, but I saw you in the paper and I—" The voice whispers, urgent now in its quiet. *"What kind of a person says that if it isn't true, says that to a child? What kind of a person—"* In the background, a door slams. *"I'm scared. I don't know—I don't know what to do, I can't—I have to go. I have to go."*

Scuffling, a crackle against the mouthpiece.

The sound cuts off. Sonya releases the earpieces, but doesn't take them off.

"Rose Parker ran an article after you were released from the Aperture. About you, about what you're doing," Alexander says. "She thought it might help you. Apparently she was right."

Sonya shakes her head.

"That's Grace? She called herself Alice," she says.

"As in Wonderland," he replies. "The Wards used to call her their Alice. You know—down the rabbit hole." His mouth twists. "Because she lived in a secret room in their house."

She removes the headphones and folds them in half again, but doesn't hand them back to him. She hears that croaky voice again, the voice of a girl who suddenly sounds like a woman and isn't used to it—Grace Ward would be about thirteen, all sprouted now, with skinny legs and spiderwebs of stretch marks on her thighs and a halting, unsteady walk.

"She's somewhere in the reach of the *Chronicle,*" Sonya says.

"The *Chronicle* distributes to the entire megalopolis," he says. "Doesn't exactly narrow things down."

"The point is, she's alive," Sonya says, and she reaches for the silver device still clasped in his hand, ignoring the prickle of strangeness as she touches him—this man she wishes were dead, this man she told so in no uncertain terms—"I need to take this with me."

"Take it where?" he says. "You're not going to see Emily Knox—"

"Why not? Maybe there's some way to find out where this message came from—"

"Like I said, she's a *criminal*—"

"And what am I, exactly?"

She tries, again, to take the device from Alexander. He holds on to it.

"Ten years hanging around with some Delegation lowlifes and you think you're tough now?" he says. "Emily Knox has spent time in an actual prison. The list of crimes she's suspected of could fill an encyclopedia."

"Oh, so you have a better idea?"

"You could talk to the Wards."

"The Wards are a nice, wholesome family with a welcome mat and a swing set," she says. "They're not going to know any more than they needed to know to keep their daughter hidden."

He frowns at her.

"Like you know them all of a sudden?" he says. "You haven't even walked past their apartment. How do you know?"

"I know," she says. "And I'm going to talk to Emily Knox. Now."

"Fine, then I'm going with you," he says, and she gives up, and walks toward the HiTrain.

SIX

As they wait for the HiTrain to arrive, Alexander takes a pair of sunglasses from the inside pocket of his coat and offers them to her. They're too large for her face, but they're dark enough to disguise her Insight.

The HiTrain coasts into the platform. It's a newer one than the one she rode to her old neighborhood the day before. The clouds covering the sun are hazy, like smoke swirling across a lit cigarette. In the moment before the glass doors open, she sees her reflection in the train's chrome-plated side.

Her hair needs a trim. Its color is darker now than it was in the posters, dirty blond, a fringe around her face. Her mouth is drawn into a tight line. She can barely see the light of the Insight through the lenses of the sunglasses.

She only comes up to Alexander's shoulder. He was an oddity in his family, in more ways than one; Nikhil, Nora, and Aaron were all small, careful, graceful. And then, Alexander—ungainly Alexander, loping like a wolf. Hunched over his desk with a pen between his teeth, his nose inches from the page.

The train car is relatively empty, except for an old lady in orthopedic sneakers with a shopping bag between her feet, and a father humming to the infant child balanced on his hip. They sit across the car from the other passengers, and then across the aisle from each other. Alexander's knees spread wide when he sits, taking up more space than he needs to. Sonya draws up straight and folds her hands in her lap.

Alexander rolls his eyes a little.

"You do know that there's no DesCoin anymore, right? You're not still waiting for the Delegation to come back and tally up all your good manners?"

She used to check her total ten times a day, hungry to see it increase. She lived her life eager to be noticed, sitting on the edge of every seat, every script of courtesy memorized down to the inflection. If Susanna was going to be brilliant, then Sonya would be immaculate, a perfect Delegation girl.

She leans forward.

"Do *you* know there's no DesCoin anymore?"

"Excuse me?"

"It seems to me," she says, "that if your every choice is in defiance of a system, you are as much a servant of that system as someone who obeys it."

Alexander stares at her. She watches the man and his son at the other end of the train, the little boy grabbing the man's shirt collar with a tiny hand, the man guiding it away, pointing at something out the window. *Look, a bus!*

"You told me you reunited some of the other children—the displaced children, like Grace Ward—with their birth parents, after the Delegation fell," she says. "How did you find them?"

"The Delegation did keep records of adoptions, in general," he says. "Not all the adoptions were displaced children—some were abandoned, or voluntarily surrendered. But I cross-referenced physical descriptions and birth dates from the birth parents with the adoption records. There were a few older ones, like Grace, who there was no record of anywhere—and of those, Grace is the only one who would still be a minor. We're leaving all the ones who are adults now alone. Seemed kinder."

The brakes squeal. The old lady picks up the bag at her feet, heaves it into her arms, and limps out of the train car. The man is sitting now, bouncing his child on his knee.

Sonya says, "I'd be curious to know how Grace's parents managed to hide a second child for as long as they did."

"That's the thing. Most of them only made it a few days after the child was born before they were discovered. For some it was months. But Grace . . ." He shrugs. "She's old enough to remember them, at least a little."

Sonya frowns. It wasn't like the Delegation not to keep records. Data meant optimization—a better algorithm for purchases, better reminders from your Insight to correct your bad habits, better information in your display as you moved through the world.

Alexander goes on: "We think there's no record of those adoptions on purpose. Taking an infant child is bad enough, but taking an older child who's already bonded with her parents is especially cruel. The Delegation likely didn't want a record of that cruelty to exist. It wouldn't be the first thing they failed to log."

"Have you considered that the adoption records were in the digital files that were purged in the uprising?" she says.

He scowls at her.

"We have a saying, when it comes to the Delegation," he says. "'Never ascribe to carelessness that which can be adequately explained by shame.'"

The train stops again, and this time, Alexander gets to his feet. Out the window, Sonya sees sunlight on water, a boat coasting over the waves. The robotic voice of the HiTrain announces that they are at the Pike Place Market stop. Sonya gets up and follows Alexander to the platform.

"I'd like to speak to some of the birth parents," she says. "They might have information that would help me."

"Speak to the Wards," Alexander says. "I thought that would be the first place you'd go, actually."

The Wards live in the first-floor apartment of a small complex not far from the Aperture. Twelve units. Sonya knows.

"I will," she says, "but more information is better."

He wheels around to face her.

"You hear these people were reunited with their kids and you think, *Well, they're fine now, no harm done*?" He rakes a hand through his hair so hard he tears a few strands loose. "Getting your kid back after losing their entire childhood is better than nothing, but it's also worse than nothing. Every day is a reminder of what you didn't see, of time you didn't get. So no, I'm not going to re-traumatize these parents by letting the face of the goddamn Delegation interrogate them."

"Don't call me that."

She takes off the sunglasses he loaned her, folds them, and presses them to his chest. Then she puts her hood up and walks down the steps to the street. She hears him following, that uneven gait, his from birth.

Pike Place Market is the smallest building in the area, full as it now is with skyscrapers, all vying for the same view of Elliott Bay. It bears a glowing red sign, PUBLIC MARKET CENTER, with a clock beside it—a faithful copy of the original, Sonya's Insight once told her, when she came with the other Delegation volunteers to scrape gum from the wall behind Market Theater. She was disgusted by it at the time, and not just because of the gum—because of the defiance that led people to revive the old tradition despite the Delegation outlawing it. Now, though, it reminds her of how stubbornly some people in the Aperture cling to Delegation rules that no longer have meaning—the widows separating their compost from the rest of their trash even though it all goes to the same dumpster, the rules about serving the oldest first at the dinner table, even though they're all gray and wrinkled except Sonya. People love their small rebellions. She knows what that feels like, though she's since lost her taste for them.

The oblong building boasts a grid of square windows, and beyond them, lights and bustle and bodies, bundles of fresh flowers, whole crabs piled together on beds of ice, displays of jam and mustard in tiny jars that remind Sonya of the Wards, the odd charges in their purchase history.

The building that houses Emily Knox is one in a cluster of glass pillars, a few blocks from the cracked cobblestones that surround the market. The street name is Triumvirate, a substitution for its former name, Delegation, as though even the word is now a crime, all symbols of the past doomed to be locked up in the Aperture.

Alexander raises a long arm to point out the right building, the glass tinted smoky orange instead of blue or green, like the ones around it.

It's flat and squared off at the edges on one side, and curved on the other, a steep arc like a diving bird. It doesn't hold a place in Sonya's memory. She stares at it for just a moment too long, waiting for the Insight display to provide her with its history.

"Old habits die hard, huh?" Alexander says.

Fuck you, she thinks.

They walk past a man holding a stack of pamphlets; he thrusts one in Sonya's face as she passes him. It reads *The Dangers of Digital: Why Elicits Are a Slippery Slope That Leads Back to the Insight.* Stamped at the bottom are the words CITIZENS AGAINST DIGITAL TAKEOVER. Sonya looks back at the man. His thick beard obscures his face, but his eyes lock on hers, taking in the glow of the Insight. He opens his mouth, as if to speak, and she hurries along.

"CAD nutjobs. They're a feeder organization for the Army, you know," Alexander says, plucking the pamphlet from her hand. "'Slippery slope.' That's like saying that alcohol leads directly to Blitz." He pauses. "Blitz is a recreational drug. A stimulant."

"I know." Her voice sounds so hard it's almost tinny. "Plenty of people have died of overdoses in the Aperture."

Sonya never took Blitz. There was no reason to want an excess of energy in the Aperture. Nothing to occupy your busy hands, your busy brain. Better to dull everything, to mute it, like a T-shirt worn soft by countless washings. But David took it sometimes and stayed awake all night teeming over with ideas. Escape, revenge, home improvement projects, everything.

David also took it to die.

Alexander frowns. "I didn't know."

"Why would you?"

David would have been released with the other Children of the Delegation, had he lived. Nikhil had pointed that out to Sonya when the first few younger ones were released, and it kept her up at night for a week, the thought of the little blue pills in David's palm, so like the little yellow one in hers, a long time ago.

Vines crawl up the side of Knox's building, a curved, organic shape layered over the building's strict geometry. Beneath the tangle of leaves is the entrance, two doors framed with grand ironwork. She walks into the building, where security guards stand at either end of the lobby, guarding each elevator bank. A screen greets her, the robotic voice saying, liquid smooth, *Welcome to Artemis Tower, please sign in.*

Alexander nudges her aside, taking her place at the screen. He types her name, and Emily Knox's, and hesitates over the line that asks for a reason for his visit: `Social Call, Celebration, Business, Other.` "Other" is his final selection.

Sonya wonders how, in a world without DesCoin, a person comes to live in a place like this. There's another form of currency, now simply called "credits," but she doesn't know how a person like Knox earns it. Nikhil said she flourished under the Delegation, but without Insights to hack, how does she flourish now? Someone who is useful to two opposing regimes, Sonya thinks, can't be decent.

`Now requesting access from your guest, Emily KNOX,` the screen reports.

"She's not here," one of the guards says, from the far end of the lobby. Behind him is a fountain, just a heavy tray on the ground with a bubble of spray in the center.

"Do you know where she is?" Alexander says.

"Ordinarily I wouldn't say," the man replies. "But given *her* . . ." He gestures to Sonya. "I'm sure she'd love to know what you want, Poster Girl. She's at the bar across the street, the Midnight Room."

Sonya shivers at the way he looks at her, eager, like she's something he wants to unwrap. She's already passing through the doorway by the time Alexander thanks the man.

"Nice of him," Alexander says.

"Was it?" Sonya replies.

The Midnight Room occupies the ground floor of the building across the street—with the glass tinted dark blue—and its facade is as dark as its name. Sonya hesitates before opening the door. She thinks of the people who spat at her as she left the Aperture that morning. DELEGATION SCUM painted on the wall of her living room.

She could go talk to the Wards, instead.

The interior of the Midnight Room is pure black at first, in contrast to the daylight. Shapes materialize from the dim, dark leaves covering the walls, hanging from the ceiling. Low lamps shine here and there. All along the bar, there are orbs full of artificial insects—small drones, buzzing mechanically against the glass. The plants must be artificial too, convincing fakes. Someone plays light, gentle piano in the corner.

A woman sits at the bar, a black boot braced against the chair next to her. Even sitting, it's clear she's tall, her shoulders broad. Her long black hair is tied back, and she holds a glass of dark liquor in one hand, an Elicit in the other.

"You must be Sonya Kantor," the woman says, her eyes still on the Elicit in her hand. "We've never met and you want to come into my apartment? I usually like to go out for a drink first." She sets the Elicit down and sips from her glass. "Maybe that's why you're here now."

Everyone else in the bar—a small scattering of people buried in the foliage—is silent as she speaks.

"You know the hood's not really doing much to disguise that thing in here, right?" the woman—Emily Knox, obviously—says.

Sonya tugs the hood down. The Insight is a perfect white circle around her iris, an eclipsed sun. Knox pushes the chair beside her back with the toe of her boot, and gestures to it.

Sonya sits, her knees together. Knox hugs a knee to her chest, balancing her glass on top of it, and stares at Sonya.

"I came to ask for your help," Sonya says.

Knox laughs.

"Ice princess," she says. "Poster Girl. Descending from her kingdom on high—" Light laughter ripples through the other people in the bar, their faces hidden. "All right, maybe ascending from the shithole to which we've exiled her—to ask for *my* help? Little old moi?"

She sips her liquor.

"I never thought I would see the day," she says.

"Well," Sonya says. "Neither did I."

Knox laughs again. "Get the Delegation girl a drink, on me. Who's that?" She gestures at Alexander, lingering a few feet away.

"My minder," Sonya says.

"Nobody likes a babysitter," Knox says. "Sit down and stop looming, Minder."

The bartender sets a glass in front of Sonya, the drink clear, the glass frosty.

"I don't drink alcohol," Sonya says.

"Oh, you do today," Knox says. "I'm not talking to you until you spend some DesCoin for me." She smirks. "Figuratively speaking, of course."

She's older, but there is no sign of it in her face, her skin smooth, her dark eyes lively with scrutiny.

Sonya feels like a puppet dangling by Knox's strings. She sips from the glass. It tastes like pine and citrus, and burns her tongue. Another thing she has to trade away, she thinks, to find Grace Ward.

"There's someone I need to find," Sonya says. "Her name is Grace Ward. She was rehomed—"

"Rehomed." Knox snorts. "No. Try again, without the Delegation-speak."

Sonya sets her jaw. She hears Alexander laugh a little, beside her.

"Oh, let's not pretend you're not a former Delegation henchman yourself, Alexander Price," Knox says. "Alexander Price, with his father's face and his mother's name. Just because you figured out which way the wind was blowing faster than your girl here doesn't mean you're not still Delegation scum." She raises her glass to him in a toast. "Lucky for you, scum drinks free today, on me."

"Did you memorize some kind of Delegation leadership database?" Alexander says, his brow furrowing.

"I have a stellar memory for the people who tried to put me away for life—and their families, just in case I needed to do some blackmailing," she says. "My arrest was ordered by August Kantor, and I was sentenced by Nikhil Price. What a pair. Cheers, to my narrow yet somehow inevitable escape."

Little pinpricks of light shine all around them as people raise their glasses to Knox. She looks expectantly at Sonya.

"Well?" Knox says. "You want my help but you don't want to toast my freedom?"

Sonya raises her glass. Knox touches it with her own.

"Let's hear it again, Ms. Kantor," Knox says. "And say it right this time."

"I need to find a girl named Grace Ward," Sonya says. "She was taken from her parents—"

"By whom, pray tell?"

"By the *Delegation,*" Sonya says. "She was placed with adoptive parents and given a new name. I need to find her and reunite her with her parents."

"And what's in it for you?"

Sonya hesitates.

"Freedom," she says.

"Ah, freedom. Freedom for the Children of the Delegation, I hear that's all the rage these days." Knox drains her glass and drops it on the bar top. "There was a very straightforward sense of justice when you were sentenced. For decades, the Delegation held people accountable for the actions of the people around them. It saved us all money on police, you see. You don't need *nearly* as many 'peace officers' if you turn your own citizens into them. I bet . . ."

She leans closer. Her eyes are straight at the top, single-lidded, irises so dark they are indistinguishable from the pupil.

"I bet you were great at that," she says. "I bet you would have shushed your own mother at the dinner table if she dipped even a toe into sedition." Knox frowns, sits back. "Well, maybe not. I bet you at least did the cost-benefit analysis—negative DesCoin for disrespecting your elders versus positive DesCoin for defending the state."

Sonya never scolded her mother—she never had to, as Julia was more careful to respect the Delegation than even August had been. But she remembers the mental math. She still does it all the time.

"Anyway," Knox says. "It seemed so nice, so clean, to put you Delegation children in the Aperture—to do the same damn thing to you that the Delegation did to us, hold you responsible for your family. Heap their crimes on your head. Only . . ."

Knox tilts her head.

"It's still not really justice, is it? Because all of you fucks living in the Aperture get to just remake your little kingdom in there," she says. "Which brings me to an interesting cost-benefit analysis of my own—because I don't want to help you earn any freedom, Sonya Kantor. But I also think it would be more of a punishment for you to reenter the real world than to spend the rest of your life in that birdcage."

Sonya's drink has lost its frost; water beads on the bowl of the glass and runs down the stem. She came here empty-handed, with nothing to trade.

"Maybe it would be simpler," Sonya says, "if you considered Grace Ward's parents."

"Nothing simple about them, either," Knox says. "Reuniting them forces a new awareness of all those years stolen from them, in retaliation for something that's not even a crime anymore. That wasn't a crime for everyone even then—weren't you a second child?" She clicks her tongue. "But your parents *earned* you."

They had showed her the permit once. *Exception to Protocol 18A,* it read at the top. The blanks were full of her parents' information, her sister's. DesCoin amounts at time of application. Height, weight, existing health issues. All the right criteria met.

Alexander takes the silver device from his pocket, along with the length of cord and the headphones, folded up neatly. He puts them on the bar top and slides them toward Knox.

"She called them yesterday," he says. "So I'm pretty sure they want to find her, and she wants to be found. There's a recording of it on this thing."

For the first time since Sonya walked into the bar, Knox hesitates. She picks up the silver device and looks at it, the cord still stretching across the sticky bar top.

"Mr. Price," Knox says, after a moment, wagging a finger at him. "You've got a point, clever man. You ought to thank him, Sonya, he's a better negotiator than you are."

Knox expects her to actually thank him, Sonya knows—to prove that she will be obedient. Knox is her puppeteer in earnest now, a performer with a captive audience.

"Thank you," Sonya says, terse.

Alexander looks down at the glass that the bartender put in front of him. He doesn't respond.

"All right, then, let's settle up your bill," Knox says. "I require that my Delegation clients pay in advance, you see. In your case, you're going to finish that drink . . ." She slides Sonya's glass closer to the edge of the bar. "And then you're going to sing me a song." She smiles. "A Delegation song."

She glances at Alexander.

"They're illegal now, of course," she says. "But God, I miss that good old-fashioned propaganda, don't you?"

Every song on the radio had once been approved by the Delegation, for the most part a perfunctory process as long as there was nothing scandalous in the lyrics. But there were a few commissioned by the government to promote good values—five, maybe.

Knox went on: "Which one do I miss most? Probably 'The Narrow Way,' what a catchy little dirge it was."

It's possible Sonya's mother wasn't humming "The Narrow Way" on that last day, that it was one of the others, and she has just heard them all so many times that they are stuck together in her mind like a box of birthday candles melting on a stovetop.

Sonya wonders if Knox knows how this song haunts her. Could she know?

"Screw you," Sonya says.

Knox laughs again, but there is flint in it, this time.

"That's the price," Knox says. "Pay it, or fuck off."

Alexander, now employed by the government, could object to the illegality of performing the song—but he doesn't, and Sonya doesn't expect him to. She thinks again about Vasilisa, sent again and again into the woods by the stepmother that wanted her dead. That story ended in fire. There's no reason to expect there won't be fire in this one.

Sonya tips the entire drink into her mouth at once. It scalds her throat on the way down. She's glad for the muddle it brings to her mind when she steps away from the bar and faces the room. It's still too dark to see anything concrete—instead, she gets impressions of people, the flutter of fingers, the white of an eye, the flash of a leg.

Won't you come with me
Along the harder road?

Sonya's voice is reedy and thin and coasts just under the right pitch. Her face flushes with heat and she is glad, then, of the darkness in the bar, hiding her humiliation.

Won't you walk with me?
The path is one I know.

People hoot and raise their glasses. Knox puts her head on her hand, and watches.

Five, six, seven, eight. Sonya feels like she's back at that table with her family. It wasn't vibrato shaking her mother's voice as she sang. Sonya looked at the water her father poured for her, at the way it rippled despite all the Kantors being still, like the earth itself was trembling in anticipation of what they were about to do—

I've been down that other road
And it's as easy as they said.

Some people are swaying along with the lilting melody, lifting their hands in the air and laughing. Sonya remembers Susanna's guitar, her fingers stumbling over the strings, her mother's rich voice chiming in from the kitchen. *Mom, stop! I need to focus,* Susanna says, and Sonya thinks of it as Susanna stares into her water glass, pill in hand, cheeks shining with tears—

But wide and flat though it was then

Sonya trembles, and her voice trembles, but she presses on.

I didn't much like where it led.

A group in the corner holds up their Elicits, screens lit, and sways back and forth.

Everyone laughs.

Won't you set aside
The lies that you've held dear
Don't you know that
What's better is right here?

As a child it was her favorite line, *what's better is right here,* because her father used to pat his knee whenever he sang it, and when she went to sit on his lap, he squeezed her tight and kissed her cheek with a loud smack. And she could always believe *here* was good, was right, was better than whatever else was out there.

This walk is narrow and it's steep
It'll surely test your heart
But it'll fill all those hollow places
You've had since the start.

"Hey, Deb," someone calls out. "Want to go get 'filled'?"

"Don't threaten me with a good time!" someone—presumably Deb—calls back.

Won't you keep an eye on me
And I'll keep an eye on you
One step after another . . .
We'll make it through.

Everyone joins her for the last few words: *"Make it through."*

Knox applauds. Sonya sits on the stool, her face hot, her hands cold. She tries to steady herself.

Then Knox's eyes glitter strangely, and she drags the headphones toward her, gathering the cord in her palm as she leans in to say—quiet enough to make their conversation private at last—"You know what I've never told anyone?"

She straightens the headband of the headphones, and drapes them over the back of her neck.

"I actually miss it sometimes, the Delegation," she says. "Well, not the Delegation exactly, but the Insights. I was so good at Insights. I'm good at a lot of things, but they were such lovely little toys, so difficult to misdirect."

"Misdirect?" Sonya says. She's still trembling from the song.

"Yeah, you can't turn them off, once they're on," Knox says. "It's an extremely resilient technology. Mine is still on right now, taking in data. It's just not connected to the rest of me; same with everyone else's in this city." She runs a fingertip over her temple, right on top of the scar along her hairline. "But it emits a signal. They all do. I've tried to tell people, but they all think I'm a little nuts. Or—a 'radical.'" She performs quotations on either side of her face. "I think it's more that they don't *want* to believe it."

Sonya doesn't know whether to believe her or not either. If she's right, the Triumvirate is lying to everyone in the megalopolis about their Insights. But she could just as easily be toying with Sonya.

"Why don't they just remove them?" Sonya says.

"By the time you reach adulthood, your brain has developed around the implant," Knox says. "You can't remove it without doing serious damage. At least that's what Naomi said."

"Naomi."

"Naomi Proctor," Knox says. "My former teacher."

If Sonya's Insight had been fully functional, it would have given her information about Naomi Proctor, but it would have been unnecessary; every person brought up by the Delegation knew that name. She was hailed in all the history books as the one who made paradise possible, who made great strides in improving public safety, who brought them the order and safety of the Insight. She never worked for the Delegation—instead, she taught at the university.

She died when Sonya was a child. Sonya's mother took them to the public procession, the slow march of the coffin through the streets. Sonya gave her handkerchief to an old woman with tears streaming down her cheeks—an act that earned her one hundred DesCoin, just as she knew it would.

Naomi's death cemented her legacy, made her famous in a way that slowly fading away couldn't have. The great inventor, a brilliant light who gave her all to the Delegation.

"I was told people came to you to have their Insights temporarily disabled," Sonya says. "But you're saying that's not possible?"

"Insights can't be killed, but they can be deceived," Knox says. "When people came to me, I redirected their feeds for a few hours—looping, we called it. The Delegation would receive some repurposed footage, which I pulled from the person's history—a night at home with spouse and child, usually. But the person's actual feed would pour into my own servers."

"I'm sure that was useful to you."

Knox grins.

"It certainly was." She puts the headphones on, and presses the power button with her thumb. Her fingernails are bitten down to the quick.

Sonya watches her as she listens. Her eyes narrow, at first, and then drop to her glass, the ice melting at the bottom. Knox listens to the message once, then begins it again, her head tilting. Sonya can hear the door slamming in the background of the recording through the earpieces, and she remembers how Grace's voice broke on the words *I'm scared.* Finally Knox takes the headphones off, folding them.

"What's the name of this kid again?" she asks Alexander, the playful quality gone from her voice.

"Grace Ward," Sonya says. "Alice is just a nickname."

"*Grace Ward,*" Knox says. "An exemplary name. Worth one thousand DesCoin at least." At Sonya's blank expression, she continues. "Oh, you didn't know that different names could earn different DesCoin amounts? Your parents could have bettered their scores considerably if they had chosen something less Russian and more common."

She points at Alexander with her thumb. "Like that one over there. *Alexander.*"

Sonya thinks of her parents arguing about tampons in the kitchen. Some things, her father had insisted, were just arbitrary, the result of little forethought on the part of the Delegation.

"I don't understand," Sonya says finally.

"Of course you don't." Knox rolls her eyes. "A name suggests an *origin.* The Delegation wanted all those origins to be disguised by homogeneity. Which means that the most highly rewarded names were common ones . . . for a particular subset of the population, anyway." She smirks. "Which is why your brown-skinned friend over there has his *mother's* name, Price, instead of his father's, which was Mishra, and why I"—she waves a hand over her face to indicate the epicanthic fold of her eyes—"am walking around with a name like *Emily Knox.*"

Knox had told Alexander he had his father's face and his mother's name. Nora Price had been a diminutive woman with thick red hair worn in a braid that trailed over one shoulder; she had played with the end of it when she was daydreaming, which was often. Alexander looked more like her than Aaron had, though both of her sons resembled their father more: light brown skin, black hair, dark eyes.

Sonya remembers something she overheard at a dinner party once, about Nikhil taking his wife's name when they got married. *A good choice,* their neighbor, Ms. Perez, said. *It'll save him a lot of trouble.*

"So Grace Ward," Sonya says.

"Not sure why they bothered naming her that, if she was an illegal second child," Knox says. "They didn't earn anything by having her. They must be boring by accident, and not on purpose. How old was she when she was taken?"

"Three," Alexander replies.

"Three." Knox lets out a low whistle. "Now, that's impressive. Shouldn't be possible, really, with how Insights register each other."

"But she probably didn't have an Insight if she was illegal."

"Oh, she must have had an Insight," Knox says. "When Insights lock on each other, they register each other's presence—but they are also designed to search out human faces, and to detect human voices.

Even if you can tend to an infant blindfolded, you can't keep them silent for three years."

Knox's glass has a layer of water in it now, from the melted ice cube. She tips it back, swallows.

"It's time for you to go, Ms. Kantor," Knox says. "I'd like to have another drink without the phrase 'The Narrow Way' rattling around in my head, thanks. I'll get in touch with you if I find anything on this."

She doesn't say how, and Sonya doesn't ask. Knox tucks the silver device into her pocket, unplugs the headphones, and tosses them at Sonya. It's a dismissal.

EVERYTHING inside the HiTrain car is bathed in greenish light. Most of the seats are occupied, but the car is quiet, full of people with heads bowed toward their Elicits; people leaning against the glass barriers with eyes closed; people with books held between thumb and pinkie; people with slumped posture and scarred hairlines. The only two seats available are side by side, so Sonya and Alexander sit with their shoulders brushing together every time the car sways, and she pulls her arms in, squeezing her hands between her knees.

He taps his fingers, pinkie, then ring finger, middle, index, and thumb, in a ripple.

She always got to the Price house early on Wednesdays, before Aaron got home from soccer practice. When she did, she went straight upstairs to wait in his room for him—usually posed on his bed, her head angled just so, so he'd tell her she looked like a painting. But she could never stop herself from slowing down as she passed Alexander's door, where he inevitably sat at his desk, hunched over his homework. One night, though, she saw him with photo negatives. Each strip of them, acquired at vintage stores and donation centers, cost fifty DesCoin—the Delegation didn't reward nostalgia. Alexander had stacked them on his desk, and one by one he held them up to his task lamp.

He noticed her standing there, watching. *Want to see,* he asked her, almost like it wasn't a question. She stepped into his room, over the soft blue carpet. It smelled like orange—there was a peel in the trash can. She took one of the negatives from him and held it up to the light, closing her right eye so the Insight's light wouldn't interfere. She saw a collection of aluminum cans in one, a man and woman with their arms wrapped around each other in another, a dog with its tongue curled around its nose in the third. And beside her, Alexander sat with his fingers tapping, waiting to hear what she said.

Each one's a world, she said, because it sounded like it might be profound. She wanted to steady his hands.

When she thinks of it now, after everything he did, she feels uneasy, like she might be sick. She tries not to bump him with her knee.

No one on the train speaks to her, but everyone looks at her, their attention drawn by the glow in her right eye, the glow that once assigned value to every choice. Now those small choices—posture, the length of a stare, the activity one chooses to pass the time on the train—are empty of value, and the people are ruled by whim instead.

She never wanted to be rid of the Insight, before. Before the uprising, it was like a friend, one who kept her from getting too lonely. She spoke to it sometimes, knowing it couldn't read her thoughts; told it benign secrets, like how much she loved the smell of pipe tobacco and how stupid Aaron made her feel when he talked politics and which people at school she sometimes thought about kissing. She told herself it understood her private indiscretions, the way she cursed to herself when she was alone in her house and made a mistake, the urge to touch herself when she couldn't fall asleep, the smug feeling of seeing the billboard of her own face on the way to school every morning. It knew her during a time when she was desperate to be known.

But now all it does is watch in silence. All the Insight does is make people stare at her.

The car empties as they go. As soon as another seat opens up, Sonya comes to her feet, rearranges her coat around her, and moves away from Alexander. She thinks it will be a clear enough sign. But when her stop comes, he gets off the train with her.

"I didn't realize you lived so close to the Aperture," she says.

She doesn't move toward the stairs.

"I don't," he says. "But it's dark, so I'm going to walk you there."

"Go home, Alexander."

"You don't have to be so—"

"How many times do you want me to debase myself in front of you?" she demands. "How many times will be enough?"

His hands are tucked in his pockets. His skin glows orange under the lights on the platform, which flicker a little as she waits for his answer. He seems stunned.

Finally, he clears his throat and speaks:

"I'll get you the contact information of one of the families that's been reunited with their child. I'll leave it for you at the gate."

She's tempted to ask what changed his mind, what made him think that her face will no longer be a torment inflicted on people who have already suffered enough, as he suggested earlier. But she doesn't. She leaves instead, turning toward the steps and descending, cold air rushing into the worn spots in her shoes. Her socks are damp, and she makes a plan: leave her shoes by the door, hang her socks on the clothesline in the bathroom, wrap herself in the quilt that covers her bed, sleep until morning. Maybe she'll be lucky and Nikhil will have left food in her kitchen; maybe tonight is the night he decided it was time to open a can of chicken soup instead of beans or corn or peas.

The streets are empty and dark on the way to the Aperture, and her Insight lights the way.

SEVEN

Sonya sits at Mr. Nadir's table with the radio again. Charlotte is playing cards with Nikhil, a slow, sedate game that requires a firm grasp of strategy. Sometimes minutes go by without either of them taking a turn. Sonya lines up the wires she's ripped from the radio and stripped of their plastic casings. Charlotte is humming, but it's not a Delegation song—it's something older, probably classical.

Everyone in the building has something that everyone else wants, and Charlotte's is a music player. It plays digital files, stored on little devices like the one Alexander played Grace Ward's voicemail on earlier. Charlotte has spent years acquiring as many of them as she can, and every month the other residents gather in her little apartment and make requests. Each of the old devices has a name—Johnny, Margot, Belinda, Pete, the list goes on. Charlotte's favorite is Margot, which holds an impressive collection of orchestral music recorded by the Sea-Port Symphonic. Sonya's favorite is Katherine, an eclectic collection of genres, most of them harder-edged. No one else ever wants to listen to Katherine, but Charlotte lets her in sometimes to listen to it by herself.

"I wonder if there's anyone in the Aperture that could help you," Nikhil says. "Someone who worked in Insight assignation, perhaps—maybe they sold Insights on the sly."

"You think someone who broke Delegation laws would end up in the Aperture?" Sonya says. "This place is full of loyalists. That's why they're in here."

"Not necessarily," Nikhil says.

"I think Kevin worked in assignations," Charlotte says. "Even if he didn't do anything illegal, perhaps he knows who did."

Sonya nods, and runs her fingertips over the wires laid out in front of her.

"It troubles you, then," Nikhil says, giving Sonya a sideways look over the top of his cards.

"The radio?" she says.

"Obviously not," Charlotte remarks. "Quiet, I'm on the verge of something."

"You've been on the verge of something for three minutes," Nikhil says.

Charlotte makes a face at him, and lays down a card. Nikhil is ready with his own, matching her just a few seconds later. Charlotte scowls and returns to staring at her hand.

"It troubles you," Nikhil says, "that Grace is alive."

"What an awful thing to say," Charlotte says. "Of course it doesn't trouble her that the girl is alive."

"I'm not saying she wanted Grace to be dead," he says, "just that she believed it was a fool's errand, and now it isn't."

"Better not to be the fool," Charlotte says, laying down her card.

Sonya selects a wire that looks right, and clamps it to the connector on the old radio, on each end, two sets of needle-nose pliers sticking out of the back. Chewing on her lip, she flips the power switch.

The radio crackles to life.

"Is it?" Sonya replies.

THE guard at the entrance—Williams—is ready for her the next morning, a business card pinched between his first two fingers.

"Someone left this for you," he says. "Gangly fellow."

The front of the card reads ALEXANDER PRICE, DEPARTMENT OF RESTORATION. Beneath it is an address and phone number. She stares at "Department of Restoration" for a moment, and then flips the card over. *Ray and Cara Eliot.* The address is in Olympia, which means she'll have to take the Flicker instead of the HiTrain. She's never ridden the Flicker alone.

A note at the bottom of the card reads—in cramped writing—*I let her know you would be coming.* She remembers him washing the dishes after weekly dinners, leaned up against the counter with his sleeves bunched around his elbows, whistling under his breath, like even the song in his head was something he wanted to keep for himself. She remembers how she watched him when no one was looking, and it eats at her now, the thought of that past longing.

"He told me he would," she says to the guard. "Can you tell me where the nearest Flicker station is?"

"Downtown," Williams says. "Near the Beaver Building."

Her face heats as she asks, "Do I need credits for it?"

"Not unless you want a fancy seat," he says. "You can thank the Triumvirate for making public transportation free for all."

Sonya tucks the business card into her pocket. "Thank you."

She thanks him every time he opens the gate for her, and he scowls every time.

There are only a few people waiting for her outside the gates today, none of them holding signs. One is a woman with rosy cheeks, who asks her for a picture together. Sonya is too startled to refuse. She watches the woman's hands shake as she holds up a small camera secured to her wrist with a strap. The woman smells like baby powder. Sonya doesn't remember to smile.

One of the others tries to talk to her, calls her Poster Girl, asks her if she's lonely, and she just keeps walking. He follows her, at first, but she doesn't turn to look at him, and eventually, his footsteps fade, and there's just the crunch of gravel and paper under her feet.

It's bright today, the sun gleaming on the pavement and shining on the chrome side of the HiTrain as it pulls up to the platform. She finds a seat alone at the back of the car and leans her head against the glass to watch the city pass by. The buildings shift from low and crumbling brick to towers of metal and glass. When she was a child, she thought of them as giants from old legends, titans and nephilim, Svyatogor atop his massive steed. But the wonder of youth has faded. Now she knows how many people are stuffed inside every building. The more there are, the less any one of them matters. Who cares about a single blade of grass when you're standing in a field?

She gets off the train at Rainier Square. The Beaver Building, as Williams called it, stands across the street from the station, a seamless concrete pedestal that arches up to a rectangular shaft, nicknamed so because the bottom looks like it was chewed by a beaver. A sign points her toward Freeway Station, just two blocks east, and she remembers where she's going.

Her father took her on the Flicker when she was ten years old. He signed her out of school for it, telling her it was worth the DesCoin to spend some time with her alone. They walked to the station together, hand in hand, and rode the Flicker south, to Tacoma, where her grandmother lived. He sat next to her on the way, and instead of working, as he normally would have, he ignored the occasional flutter of his Insight—notifications from work—to point out different parts of the city on a map for her. The smell of pipe tobacco and soap enveloped her every time he shifted in his seat. He showed her how to make a comb into a harmonica by laying a piece of paper on top of it and making it flutter as he sang.

It's an hour before the train will arrive, but instead of waiting inside, surrounded by people reading newspapers, she goes outside to the platform. The train tracks are straight, surrounded on all sides by concrete. *The Flicker tracks were built under an old road,* her father told her on their way to the station, and she can see it now, the wide stretch of land carved into the city as if by the point of a knife, the same way Babs drew her name on the side of the table in her apartment, working her name into the wood.

She takes the business card out of her pocket and looks at it again, *Alexander Price, Department of Restoration.* It's a strange job for someone so intent on leaving the old world behind, a job that wraps itself around the past. She wonders if he chose it or if it was given to him as a kind of punishment, the way the Aperture was given to her. He betrayed the Delegation, but maybe, in the eyes of the uprising, he didn't betray it thoroughly enough.

She descends to the train when the gate springs open, automatically, at its arrival. She's one of the first to board, so she chooses a forward-facing seat near the front of the car and folds her hands in her lap, spine straight, ankles together. People move into the car and settle in. It's a late-morning train, so it isn't packed with commuters—there are two solo parents pushing their respective strollers, three university students with backpacks in their laps, two old men with a magnetic chess set.

The vacuum tube doesn't allow for windows, so along each side of the train are screens for advertisements, lit up in brilliant colors. A woman tosses her hair over her shoulder, holding up a shampoo bottle the size of a finger. *Just one drop does the trick!* A child holds a bright blue camera up to his eye and points it at his dog. *The Memory Keeper: all the feeling of analog with the convenience of digital.* A man stares at a heap of dishes in his sink and heaves a sigh. *Tired of doing dishes?* In the next frame, his sink is empty, and he's holding up a pill the size of a fingernail. *Nourishment can be dish free with NutriNeat Meal Replacer.*

A voice announces that the train will be leaving soon, and encourages Sonya to buckle herself in, as a precaution. She does, tightening the belt over her lap. She remembers the sudden acceleration from her childhood, throwing her back against the seat and making her ears pop. The acceleration is more gradual now, but she still feels the pressure against the sides of her head, the force that fights her every movement.

She looks over at the university students, taking books out of their backpacks and laughing. They aren't paying attention to her, and neither are the chatty parents a few rows behind her, a woman with a shaved head and a man with a lip ring. She loosens her seat belt, and, watching the advertisements shift to some kind of luminous vodka, slumps down and stretches her legs out, her ankles cracking.

No one looks at her.

An hour later, Sonya is in Olympia, on Union Mills Road, a set of old, rusted train tracks behind her and a dilapidated apartment building across the road from her. The number on the building, 2501, matches the one Alexander wrote on the business card. Ray and Cara Eliot. And Cara is expecting her.

She crosses the street. The Eliots live in unit 1A. Their name is written on a sticker on their mailbox, so she knows she's at the right place. In the side yard is a clothesline with sheets hanging from it, and a boy sitting in an old sandbox. He is too old for playing in sand—his limbs too long and too skinny, maybe eleven years old. One of the containing walls has collapsed, so sand spills into the sparse grass of the yard, wet and dark where it mingles with the dirt. The boy holds a stick and stabs repeatedly at the sand with it, poking holes over and over. She knocks on the door.

A woman answers. She wears loose jeans and a green men's work shirt with a collar. Cara Eliot.

"Hello, Ms. Eliot," Sonya says, her Delegation manners filling the space for her. "My name is—"

Cara Eliot gives a mirthless hiccup of a laugh.

"Oh, I know," she says. "I used to stare at your face every morning on the way to work. Come in."

She walks away from the door, leaving it open. Sonya opens the screen door and follows her into a cramped living room with a pea-green sofa in it, sagging in the middle where the springs have worn out over time. A homescreen the size of a textbook stands on a beat-up coffee table across from the couch. The carpet is beige and stained here and there, red and brown and blue. Cara has moved into the kitchen, adjacent to the living room, which teems over with plastic bowls and cups, pots with cooked food burned into the bottom of them, cereal boxes and cracker boxes and boxes of dried noodles.

"Ignore the mess. Have a seat," Cara says, gesturing to the little table that stands between living room and kitchen, the rooms all bleeding together. She busies herself at the stove, where a pot of water is heating. "Gosh, I don't know what to offer someone like you. Tea?"

"Yes, please," Sonya says.

"It's nothing fancy," Cara warns her, and the words seem to encompass not just the tea, but the entire apartment, worn and stained and collapsing.

"I live in the Aperture," Sonya says. "I haven't had tea in years."

"Right." Cara laughs a little. "Almost forgot."

Across from where Sonya sits is the door that opens up to the side yard. Through the window beside it, she can see the boy in the sandbox, still stabbing at the ground with his stick.

"Yeah, that's him," Cara says, when she sees Sonya looking. "Sam. We got him back last year, thanks to your friend Mr. Price."

Sonya thinks of Nikhil when she hears "Mr. Price."

"It's still strange to hear someone call him that," she says.

"Well, whatever you call him, he asked me if I would talk to you. I was pretty surprised." Cara pours hot water from the kettle on the stove into two mugs, and carries them over to the table, setting one down in front of Sonya. "Delegation's poster girl, in *my* house?"

"Alexander told you I'm trying to find a girl?" Sonya remembers Knox's insistence on avoiding Delegation euphemisms. "A girl who was taken, like your son."

"He did," Cara says, settling back in her chair. "He didn't say what you needed to know, though."

"I'm curious about how you hide someone when Insights make that impossible."

"Well, we didn't do such a good job of it." Cara looks out the window at her son, blurred by the distortion of the glass. "Only made it a couple weeks before they took him." The corners of her mouth pull down. "We didn't get pregnant on purpose. There's no infallible birth control. And we knew if I went to the doctor, they would tell me to terminate. I didn't want to."

"Why not?" Sonya says, and the look Cara gives her is all edges.

"He warned me about you, you know," she says. "Said you might be a little insensitive. Still stuck in an old pattern."

Sonya sets her jaw. She wraps her hands around the warm mug.

"If Sam wasn't planned," Sonya says, "and having him was dangerous for both of you—I just don't understand."

Cara touches her hands to her stomach, still staring out the window.

"Like I said, I didn't want to," Cara says, firmly. "I was . . . *happy.* I was scared, but I was happy. That should be enough, shouldn't it?" She meets Sonya's eyes. "Aren't you a second child, Ms. Kantor?"

"Yes," Sonya says.

"Your parents wanted you, too, didn't they? They dreamed about you, and planned for you, and imagined what you might be like." Cara's skin is freckled, even her eyelids. She closes them now, for a moment. "I did that, too. In the days after I figured out I was pregnant, I thought about all the things he could be, and I *wanted him.* The difference is that nobody told me I was worthy of him."

Sonya thinks of the petition her parents showed her, the one asking for permission for her to exist. The one with all their credentials—justifying their desire, arguing for it. A promise that her life would be worth something. And now . . . the most she's accomplished in her life is a few crops of tomatoes, a mended radio, and a refusal to die. There's no way to guarantee a worthwhile life.

Cara moves on: "So I stopped going to the doctor. But we couldn't start spending DesCoin on supplies—our daughter, she was four, she didn't need diapers or any of that stuff—so for a while we were just confused, but then my mom said there was a whole currency for people who couldn't spend DesCoin freely."

"What was it?"

"Mustard." Cara laughs, a little too loud. "All luxury nonperishables, you could sell them back to retailers, and buying and selling them was DesCoin-neutral. So if we bought mustard or . . . jars of pickles, or whatever, we could go to the black market to swap them for the stuff we needed. The other parents would bring their extra supplies to the market and trade them for mustard, then they could sell the mustard back and get DesCoin. It was a network—everyone working in small enough quantities that the Delegation didn't notice. And even if they did notice, were they really going to investigate a bunch of mustard?"

Sonya sits still, the cup of tea steaming in front of her. The Wards' purchase records had luxury nonperishables in them—jellies and jams, mustard, jars of cornichons and pickled onions.

"That's how we got diapers for a while," Cara says. "Sounds stupid now."

"Not really," Sonya says. "Is that how you bought an Insight for Sam?"

"Oh, we never got an Insight for him," Cara says. "That's how they found us. Someone told us if we stayed blindfolded when we were with him, we would be okay—but they were wrong." She flinches a little and sips her tea. "I heard that there was somebody working in the Insight office who would mark new Insights as faulty and sell them to people like us—we never got the DesCoin together for that, though."

Sonya sips her tea, too. It tastes like smoke and seaweed. She wants to ask for sugar, but she doesn't.

"The people who adopted him," she says, and she feels like someone walking across a newly frozen puddle, hoping the ice will hold. "They got him an Insight? Through the usual means?"

Cara nods, and stares at the light in Sonya's right eye.

"The earliest they'll remove Insights now is ten," she says. "He'd just had the surgery when we got him back. His adoptive mother—the parents split after the uprising, how ironic—she saved up a long time to get it taken out. Seemed strange to me that she was so determined. The system was good to her, wasn't it?"

"So you met her," Sonya says. "Did she ever say how she was chosen?"

Cara shrugs.

"They submitted an application for adoption," she says. "She had some medical issue, she couldn't get pregnant. They got approved, and one day they were informed that the Delegation had a child for them." She shrugs again, too fast, compulsive. "She isn't a bad person. She was good to him. We have monthly visits, you know. So he can still see her."

Sonya can tell it costs her something to admit the woman who raised her son—the woman who stole his first steps, first laughs, first scraped elbows, all his beginnings—is not a villain. She can't quite imagine it. The feeling of being a parent is alien to her.

"I can tell he misses her, though," she says. "Even though he doesn't say so. But then, he doesn't say much of anything, really."

She sips her tea.

"How did Alexander find him?" Sonya says, quiet again.

"He matched up adoption records with the date Sam was taken," she says. "That wasn't the name we gave him—we called him Andrew—but he was raised as Sam so it seemed easier to . . . Anyway, in our case, there was only one couple that adopted around the same time that he was taken, so it was easy enough. It's not like we recognized him." She laughs, and it's so bitter Sonya has to look away. "Maybe he looks like us, and maybe he doesn't. He looked like her, too. His mom. Close enough for her to pretend, if she wanted."

The boy in the yard has set the stick down now, and is walking across the yard, his hands in his pockets.

Deep lines frame Cara's mouth when she frowns.

"What's it been like, having him home?" Sonya asks.

Cara sighs.

"Hard, sometimes," she says, and she brings her mug up to her lips again. "He's angry. Hates us, sometimes. Hates us less, other times."

She smiles down into her empty mug. "But it's like . . . I had something wrapped around my chest that whole time, keeping me from breathing." Her lip wobbles, just a little. "I can breathe now."

The boy is smaller in the window now, just a red smudge on the glass. Sonya drains the mug of tea.

WHEN Sonya sets out for the train station, Sam is outside, kicking rocks ahead of him in the road. She keeps her head down as she passes him. His jeans are too short, his white socks showing above his ankles. He has his hands stuffed into his pockets.

"What did you want with my mom?" he says, and she stops.

His eyes go straight to the Insight, and then skip to the rest of her face, her clothes, her shoes.

"I needed some help with something," she says. "Something your mom knows about."

"Oh." He taps his right temple. He has a scar there, darker, almost purple. Newer than most. "You haven't gotten it taken out yet?"

"No," she says.

"Why not?"

"I'm not allowed to."

He frowns. "I thought they were bad."

"I think that's the point."

"So . . . you're being punished?" he says, and she nods. "For what?"

Sonya doesn't answer.

"She told me to stay out of the house while you were there," Sam says. "I figured it was because she wanted to talk about me. Sometimes I wonder if she wants to get rid of me."

"She doesn't," Sonya says, frowning. "Why would you think that?"

He shrugs. "We fight a lot."

"You're getting to know each other."

"Yeah, I guess."

"She doesn't want to get rid of you," Sonya says again. "She loves you."

"She doesn't know me."

"You don't need to know someone to love them," Sonya says.

He narrows his eyes at her.

"It's true," she says, and she keeps walking toward the train station.

LATER Sonya stands at the Aperture gate with a newspaper tucked under one arm. She found it left behind on the HiTrain and grabbed it, though she doesn't remember much else about the journey. She can't stop picturing Sam in the road, kicking rocks. *Sometimes I wonder if she wants to get rid of me.* What a thing for a child to think about his mother, she thinks, and she realizes she's been waiting for a few minutes now without having scanned her badge.

Behind her, a group of men at the corner store drink from dark bottles. They haven't noticed her yet. She takes her security pass from her pocket and holds it up to the scanner.

The pupil of the gate dilates large enough for her to walk through. She hurries through it, and she's just past the guard station when she hears her name.

"Ms. Kantor!"

It's Williams. He's never said her name; she's surprised he even knows it. His hat is askew on his head, and he's holding an envelope with her name scrawled across it in unfamiliar writing—cursive, slanted in the opposite direction to Alexander's.

"Somebody left this for you," Williams says. His eyes drop to the newspaper under her arm. "Reading the paper, are you?"

Sonya looks him over carefully. She wonders if he'll take it from her.

"Maybe," Sonya says. "Is that a problem?"

Williams shrugs, and offers her the envelope. It's already torn open.

In the early days of the Aperture, the guards were more involved. They patrolled Green Street and Gray Street. Every time Sonya went anywhere, they walked alongside her, asking her what she liked, what she would do. No one went anywhere alone. Then one of the young men turned restless, and a guard beat him so badly he died. After that the Triumvirate came up with the nonintervention policy: the Aperture would police itself, for better or worse, and the guards would keep their distance.

"What?" he says. "You're not technically supposed to get messages, you can't blame me for taking a peek."

"I suppose not," she says. "Thank you for passing it along."

She slips it into her pocket and walks toward Building 4. A group lingers at the gate end of Gray Street—Marie, Douglas, and Renee, passing a hand-rolled cigarette around. Marie blows smoke rings; Douglas and Renee are arm in arm.

Sonya went to their wedding, two years ago, in the courtyard of Building 3. Nicole opened one of the stairwell windows and they leaned out of it together, shoulder to shoulder, to watch the ceremony from above.

She could take the Flicker to visit Nicole. No one would stop her. But she won't.

"Hey there, Detective Kantor," Douglas says to her, as she approaches. "Any news from the outside?"

Just a boy shuttled from one family to another and back again, she thinks. But she only shrugs. "Same old."

"Now, that just can't be true," Marie says, the cigarette pinched between two fingers. She takes a long drag from it. "Come on, Poster Girl, give us something to work with."

Sonya passes the rolled-up newspaper under her arm to Renee, whose eyes widen at the sight of it.

"Thank you," she says, as if a discarded newspaper is a precious thing. She unrolls it. It's one of the newspapers that competes with the *Chronicle*—the *Megalopolis Gazette.* The front-page headline is RELAXED TRAVEL RESTRICTIONS ON THE HORIZON? And the subheading: *Representative Archer Meets with Sector 3 Leaders to Discuss Easing of Delegation-Era Travel Restrictions, Citing Stabilization of Triumvirate Government.*

"You know, if you called me by my actual name, I might be inclined to do you a favor," Sonya says to Marie.

"Oh, fuck you," Marie says, but there's no heat in it. She offers Sonya the cigarette. "Want some?"

"No, thank you," Sonya says. "Where's Kevin?"

"He's got a cold, so he's lying in bed with a washcloth on his face like a fainting Victorian maiden," Marie says. "Why?"

"Just need to ask him about something."

Marie shrugs. "So ask him. It's not like our door's locked."

"Can you bring back another newspaper?" Douglas says.

"Depends on what you'll give me."

"My good favor?" Douglas says, grinning.

"What do you want?" Marie says.

Sonya considers this.

"Save me a cigarette," she says.

Renee snorts a little, but as Sonya passes through the tunnel, she hears "Deal!" behind her. She reaches up to touch the brick with David's name on it, crunching dried wax from other mourners' candles beneath her soles. No one is in the courtyard today; it's too cold for that. She steps into the stairwell and leans against the concrete wall, taking the envelope from her pocket to read the letter inside it.

Ms. Kantor,

Audio file was a dead end, but I have another idea. Come by my apartment tomorrow and we'll negotiate. Don't bring your minder; he's a drag.

—Knox

EIGHT

THE LOBBY OF Knox's apartment building is empty and quiet, except for the bubbling of the fountain. Sonya stands in the center of the room, before the screen, waiting.

Emily Knox's apartment is a lion's den.

The screen glows green. "Access granted," the cool feminine voice says, and the security guard on the right side of the lobby beckons to Sonya, then gestures to the elevator bank.

"Thirteenth floor," the guard says, her eyes lingering on Sonya's Insight.

"Thank you."

The only sign that the elevator is moving is the changing numbers on the screen above the doors, and the shifting pressure around Sonya's ears. It eases to a stop at the thirteenth floor, and Sonya steps out into a white hallway with a white marble floor. A plant—devil's ivy—spills over a pedestal near one of the apartment doors.

Sonya moves toward it. She doesn't know the number of Knox's apartment, but there are only three options to choose from, and set into the middle of one of the doors is a mechanical eyeball. When she stands in front of it, a ring of white light appears around its artificial pupil, a mockery of an Insight. The eye blinks, and the door opens.

"Guest: Kantor, Sonya," a computerized voice announces.

Her name crawls in red light across the ceiling. There is still no sign of Knox, but Sonya walks into the apartment anyway.

The living space has the look of a place that was meant to be elegant and simple—a wall of windows opposite the door, looking out over the bay; a floor of huge stone tiles; airy, high ceilings—but Knox has filled it with wires and screens, keyboards and lamps, fans and tools. It puts Sonya's collection of bits and pieces to shame.

A desk arcs around the middle of the living space, a grid of computer screens dangling above it, of all different sizes and shapes. Cords hang in bundles across the ceiling, moving in different directions; tags dangle from them, labels that Sonya can't decipher. A strip of pink LED lights wraps around the edge of the desk. A small army of figurines, cobbled together from old computer parts, stands on the kitchen counter. There are bowls stacked high in the sink.

Before the door closes behind her, Sonya grabs a screwdriver from the table near the door and sticks it in the doorjamb, so the door stays open.

Knox sits in a desk chair in an oversized T-shirt and no pants, wool socks up to her knees, her black hair hanging loose over her shoulders. Perched on her nose is a pair of glasses meant for a larger face than her own. She holds an apple against her chest, half-eaten, with one hand, as she types with the other.

"How does your apartment know my name?" Sonya says to her.

"I taught it to log your Insight upon your arrival," Knox says, without looking up. "Now you're in the system. I'm surprised your minder let you come."

"He didn't 'let' me," Sonya says. "But he's probably listening in."

"Not for long." Knox reaches under the desk into a little metal drawer unit. She fumbles around in one, swearing under her breath, and then another, finally coming up with a curved metal band that looks like a headband or a broken crown. She presses something on the side, and Sonya hears a sound like a bulb dying. Knox gets to her feet, and reaches for Sonya; Sonya steps back.

"Relax," Knox says. "Just put it on, would you?"

Sonya takes the headband from her and slides it into place over the crown of her head. It buzzes against her skin.

"I thought you said you couldn't disable Insights," she says.

"I didn't," Knox says. "I created an audio disturbance, that's all."

She sits down again and lays her hands over the keys of one of her keyboards. She does it with the grace of a pianist, long fingers fluttering as she types.

"Oh." Sonya touches the humming metal. "Thanks."

She looks at Knox's grid of screens. She can't tell what she's looking at exactly, except a series of open terminals full of white text. Beneath them is Knox's desktop wallpaper, a desert landscape with rocky red mountains and a cluster of cacti.

"A girl can dream," Knox says, when she catches Sonya staring. "Travel permits between regulated zones are not much easier to come by now than they were under the Delegation's control, if you can imagine it. Apparently our current government is too unstable to be trustworthy."

"You can't make a counterfeit permit?"

"Believe it or not, skill with computers doesn't translate to falsifying paper documents," Knox says. "Though I'm sure if I asked the right person, with the right leverage . . ."

Knox is different here, Sonya thinks, in her own space, without an audience. She brings her knee up to her chest, and Sonya sees her underwear, black, pinching at the top of her pale thigh.

"You must be desperate," Knox says. "You know very bad things could happen to you in this apartment and no one would ever hear you scream, right?"

"I know I wedged your front door open."

Knox laughs.

"All right," she says. She closes down the open terminals on her screens, one by one, until all that's left is the desert. Knox picks up the silver audio device from among the knickknacks scattered across her desk—spare keycaps for her keyboards, magnetic dishes full of tiny screws, espresso mugs with coffee dried around the rim—and offers it to Sonya.

"That's basically useless," she says. "No location data whatsoever." She picks at a thread on her sock. "However, as I mentioned, I have another idea."

Sonya looks around for a place to sit, and doesn't find one.

"There is a surefire way to find your girl," Knox says, "and it's with her UIA."

"UIA."

"Unique Identification Address," Knox says. "Every Insight has one, and it can't be changed or fooled. It's not something her parents would have; only the Delegation had access to them, it's how they kept track of everyone. I never needed them myself, because my clients were always right in front of me—but if I had Grace Ward's . . ." She tilts her head. "I could find her exact location."

In the light of day, Sonya sees gray hairs mixed with Knox's black ones, and creases at the corners of her eyes. A woman like a sheet of hammered steel, worn by the world but never capitulating to it.

"How do I find it?" Sonya says.

Knox's eyes glint, and it isn't reassuring.

"You'll need access to the UIA database, which was on the Delegation's server. Only problem is . . ."

"The server was purged right before the uprising," Sonya says.

"Was it?" Knox smiles. "The prevailing theory is that some well-meaning Delegation pinhead saw the writing on the wall and did all the Delegation employees one hell of a favor by deleting all evidence of their misdeeds. But in the various back channels to which I am attuned, someone else has claimed responsibility. Someone from a little extremist group known as the Analog Army."

Sonya thinks of the murder on the front page of the newspaper, the smiling young man and the list of his crimes, safety-pinned to his chest. The double *A* stamped at the bottom.

"They killed that man a few days ago," she says. "I saw the headline."

"I keep forgetting you barely get news in your little birdcage," Knox says. "They've killed a lot more than that. Plus a couple explosions for good measure. They want to force us to revert to the pre-digital age *by any means necessary.* They started off light, with some Elicit hacks, some empty threats. Sent a death threat to one of the Triumvirate last year. And then they escalated to actual murder. It's all been downplayed by government officials, but those who know, know." She smiles. "And I always know."

"If that's the case, why would they want to eliminate all the Delegation records?" Sonya says. "If they hate Insights, you would think they would want to reveal as much about the people who benefited from Insights as possible."

"You are assuming they actually did eliminate the Delegation records," Knox says. "The thing about zealots is how much hypocrisy they can justify."

Sonya frowns.

"I don't really understand why those records are so powerful."

The question doesn't cost her as much as she expected it to. Knox probably already thinks she's stupid. Sonya spent most of her life hoping she wasn't, and then pretending it didn't matter if she was. Now it feels irrelevant.

"Then you don't really understand how much you can find out about a person just based on where they go and when," Knox says. "That data includes not just where a person went under the Delegation—records of their indiscretions, of their unsavory connections, of their *extracurricular activities*—but the ability to trace any person in this entire city *now.*"

"So the Analog Army wants to control that data," she says. "Because they think 'by any means necessary' means using technology to destroy technology, hypocrisy be damned."

"Smarter than you look, aren't you?" Knox gets up, her oversized shirt draping over her body like a ball gown. She sets her apple down on the desk. "That's not as much of a compliment as it sounds; don't get too excited."

"I wouldn't dream of it," Sonya replies flatly. "If the Analog Army has the UIA database somewhere, why haven't you gone to get it yourself?"

Knox runs a fingertip along the edge of the desk, pink light playing over her fingers.

"Given their loathing for digital anything, you won't be surprised to hear that whatever data they've stored is on its own independent server, and I would have to physically walk into their headquarters to gain access to it," she says. "And they are particularly attuned to me, as someone who profits from all things digital no matter what regime we are living under."

"And you think they won't be attuned to *me?*" Sonya says, laughing a little. "I'm carrying around a still-functioning model of their most hated technology in my skull."

"True," Knox says. "But you are also investigating the disappearance of a child and have a plausible explanation for why you might want to speak to them."

"So I should just, what? Go in there and ask them to give me the UIA database?"

"Yes," Knox says. "They'll laugh you right out of their little clubhouse. But all I need you to do is get through the door." She shrugs. "And place a copying device on their server."

"You just told me they're dangerous."

"And you've spent the past decade in a prison," Knox says. "You seem determined to have it both ways. You can't be both the pretty Delegation princess and the hardened prisoner of the Aperture at the same time."

"Aw," Sonya says. "So you think I'm pretty?"

Knox sneers at her.

"What am I supposed to do, just walk up to wherever they keep their hideout and knock on the door?" Sonya says.

"I have a plan for you, obviously," Knox says. "I just need to know whether you're up for it or not."

Sonya considers Emily Knox, of a height with her, barefoot on the cold tile floor, her breath sharp with apple. It seems she's been given a series of impossible tasks now; tasks she's not suited for. But there's a feeling of inevitability in each of them, that whatever path she walks now, it's the only path that leads forward instead of back.

"Just so we're clear," Sonya says. "What you want in return for handing me Grace Ward's location . . . is a database full of UIAs that you have already told me you can use to track anyone who ever had an Insight, regardless of whether it's been disabled or not. Meaning that I am going to risk my life to give you the ability to blackmail everyone in the Sea-Port megalopolis."

Knox grins, a dimple forming in her cheek.

"Seriously, poster girl," she says. "Smarter than you look."

Sonya sighs, and remembers Cara Eliot looking out her window at the son she barely knows. That's the gift she would be giving Eugenia Ward, if she succeeds. It feels like a pale thing, really, but it's the only thing.

"You have to help me hide from my minder," Sonya says.

"Easy," Knox says, and when she smiles, it's a little too gleeful.

ALEXANDER is standing in the lobby when she exits the elevator, looking unkempt, as usual. He wears a blue moth-eaten sweater with a worn hem. Shoes that have seen better days, cracking at the places where his feet bend when he walks. The pocket flap on his coat is falling off. Nikhil could mend it, she thinks, the way he mends everyone's socks, one eye squinting as he threads the needle with careful fingers, his tongue poking into his cheek.

When he sees her, he says, "Come on, I need to talk to you." He glances at one of the security guards. "Um—outside, maybe."

Sonya follows him to the courtyard in front of the building, where the vines stretch across the copper-tinted glass. An evergreen with sagging branches looms over them. The rain has subsided to a mist.

She looks up at him and waits. Knox's device distorted their conversation, but if Alexander is here, he still knows that she went to meet with Emily Knox alone.

"I assume she gave the recording back," he says.

Sonya takes the device with Grace Ward's voicemail on it out of her pocket and offers it to him. He takes it, sliding it into his own pocket.

"Nothing useful on it?"

"No," Sonya says, and he nods.

"I keep waiting for you to yell at me for consorting with a known deviant," she says, after a moment.

"You've made it pretty clear that you would prefer that I leave you to your own devices," he says. "So that's what I've been doing."

She keeps her face passive.

"What are you doing here, then?" she says.

He looks around—at the ivy on the building, at the evergreen behind her, at the street beside them.

"Something weird happened," he says. "Someone came to my office today—from the Triumvirate."

"You work for the government. Aren't all of you 'from the Triumvirate'?"

"Technically. But I mean someone higher up."

Sonya sighs a little. "You're going to have to connect the dots for me here, Price."

"My office is a shithole," he says. "It's in the very back of the old, mildewy administration building where Suza was an intern, remember that place?"

The summer after she graduated secondary school, Susanna had come home every day complaining about the musty smell and dim interior of the administration building—about the stained carpeting and the peeling paint on the walls and the fact that she was working with all the people the Delegation forgot, as she put it. And their father didn't correct her, which meant she was probably right.

"No one has ever taken an interest in what we're doing," Alexander says. "I've been investigating restoration claims since the Delegation fell, basically, and it's never mattered to anyone. But today, this guy John Clark shows up in his fucking fancy shoes and tells me it's time to let the last case die."

"He told you to give up?"

"Not specifically." He shakes his head. "It was the same kind of rhetoric people have been spouting about our office a lot lately . . . that the only way to heal is to leave some things in the past. So he framed it like—like he was trying to have compassion for Grace. As in, it's been ten years, and maybe it's better to just leave her where she is—that kind of thing. But . . ."

"But why now?" Sonya says. "Why not earlier?"

"Yes," he says. "And coming down to tell me himself instead of just talking to my boss . . . kinda seems like overkill."

Sonya nods. The wind blows mist onto her cheek, onto Alexander's hair.

"And you came all the way here to tell me this," Sonya says.

"Right now, they're just asking me to drop this. Pretty soon, they could be telling me." He takes a step back. "I just thought you should know."

A NEWSPAPER—A COPY of that day's *Chronicle*—is rolled up and tucked into the lapel pocket of her coat. Williams doesn't give her a second look as she passes through the entrance to the Aperture. She walks down Green Street, her hands in her pockets, and down the tunnel that leads to Building 3's courtyard.

The courtyard is a maze of sheets hanging on the laundry lines. Jack sits among them, at a small table with moss growing on the legs, a notebook in his lap. He nods to her.

"Hey," she says, "do you know which apartment is Marie and Kevin's?"

"Right next to Renee and Douglas, third floor," he says. "Can't pry those four away from each other."

"Thanks," she says.

Sonya climbs two flights of stairs, unzipping her coat at the top to cool off. She knocks on the second door on the left and unrolls the newspaper to look at the front page. REPRESENTATIVE TURNER PROPOSES RELAXING RESTRICTIONS ON ELICIT NETWORKS. The grainy photograph beneath it is of Easton Turner shaking hands with the president of one of the top Elicit manufacturers, Auriga, according to the text. Sonya has never seen a picture of Easton Turner where he wasn't smiling. Standing at his shoulder is a man wearing a suit with sharp shoulders. *John Clark,* the text reads, *assistant to Representative Turner.* The man who visited Alexander.

The door opens, revealing Renee in an old negligee the color of champagne, the lace fraying along the low neckline. It goes down to her knees. There are snags in the fabric that stretches across her belly. She isn't wearing a bra. The smell of burned food wafts into the hallway, and a radio crackles. Behind Renee is an apartment the same size and shape as Sonya's own, a big room with a kitchen spilling into it. Renee's and Douglas's clothes are piled here and there, along with unwashed plates and glasses, cigarette butts stabbed into them. Renee raises an eyebrow at Sonya, who holds up the newspaper.

"You must have really wanted that cigarette," Renee says. "Come on in, I'll find you one."

Sonya follows her in, but only a few steps. She doesn't close the door behind her. The radio plays an advertisement for a signal interrupter, brand name Your Space. *Don't let intrusive signals eat away at your privacy! Build yourself a fifth wall with Your Space! Setup is quick and easy, and for just three payments of*—the signal fades, crackles. Renee digs in a plastic crate she's set up next to her bed, as a bedside table.

"Anything new out there?" Renee asks her.

"The other day I saw an ad for glowing vodka," Sonya says. "Does that count?"

"Not really," Renee says. "Any idiot with a glow stick can make that a reality."

Sonya sets the newspaper down on the kitchen counter, next to a cutting board with papery garlic peels sitting on top of it. They look like feather down.

Renee crosses the room with a cigarette pinched between two fingers. She offers it to Sonya, who reaches for it, only to have Renee pull it back, her eyes narrowed.

"You sure you remember how?"

"Oh, shut up."

Renee snorts a little and drops the cigarette in Sonya's palm.

Their Insights meet, flash a little brighter in recognition of each other. Sonya tries to imagine Renee without one, her right eye dim, a sliver of a scar at her temple. Her eyes drop to the swell of Renee's stomach—not a pregnancy, because no one can get pregnant in the Aperture, but time, shifting her body into a new shape.

"I should have gone to David's funeral," Renee says.

"Wasn't really a funeral."

"Yeah, but I should have gone."

Sonya tucks the cigarette into her pocket.

"I get it, you know," she says. "He was hard to be around, in the end."

"He was like some kind of prophet," Renee says. "Only nobody wants to hear about the future in here."

David was always preoccupied with the pointlessness of it all. That with no children, no newcomers, time was just paring the Aperture down to the bone. One day there would just be a few of them left, he said, the youngest ones, and what would they do, among all those hollowed-out apartments, empty streets, bare courtyards? He didn't want to be around to find out.

He didn't leave a note.

"Are Kevin and Marie home?" she says.

"Probably," Renee says. "Why?"

Sonya stands in Renee's door frame and points one hand right, one hand left, in a question.

"Right," Renee says.

She follows Sonya to the right, in her champagne negligee and bare feet. Marie is the one who answers Sonya's knock, her short dark hair piled on top of her head in a half-knot, her body swimming in an oversized gray sweatshirt. Her apartment, unlike Renee's, is spartan—no mess and no excess, nothing that doesn't have a purpose. Kevin is sprawled on the bed that takes up most of the living space, holding a book over his head.

"Yes?" Marie says.

"I need to talk to Kevin."

Marie sighs, and steps back to let her in.

Kevin closes his book with a snap and sits up, his long legs dangling over the edge of the bed. The sheets have crisp corners.

"Hey there, Sonya," Kevin says. He puts special emphasis on her name. He's always been difficult to read, his soft, sleepy eyes at odds with his occasional sharp remark. Renee once told Sonya that he was a bully in high school, but a few years ago Sonya saw him coaxing an injured mouse into a shoebox in the courtyard below, cooing at it under his breath. The inconsistencies make her nervous.

She says, "Charlotte told me you used to work in Insight assignations."

"Yeah," Kevin says. "Mostly a data entry job, though, not the exciting stuff."

"I'm trying to find out how a person would get an Insight for her illegal daughter," Sonya says. "I wondered if you knew anything about that."

Over in the kitchen, Marie stops scrubbing the countertop.

"A person," Kevin says. "You mean the parents of that girl you're looking for."

"Her name is Grace."

"Have you considered that maybe *Grace* is better off where she is, wherever she is?" Marie says.

This is your Alice, Grace Ward says, in Sonya's head.

"She remembers her parents," Sonya says. "So, no. She's not better off."

Marie's posture relaxes by a fraction. She resumes scrubbing.

"I never had access to the Insights, they were in a secure room at the hospital," Kevin says. "My job was to make sure supply was good, make sure the logs were accurate."

"And when they weren't?"

"Dunno. I would submit a report to my bosses and move on."

Marie clears her throat.

"I might know something." She wipes her hands off on her sweatshirt, leaving streaky handprints. "I worked in the morgue. You know—with that freak Graham Carter, the reason I'm in here."

Sonya remembers Charlotte mentioning that. The morgue is the right place to put someone like Marie—the daughter of important Delegation members, her mother the head of Education, her father a prominent speech writer, but Marie herself, unrefined, all edges.

"Met your dad a couple times, too. He used to *stare* a lot, just like you. Like there's nothing going on upstairs." Marie whistles and gestures in front of her forehead. "Couldn't bear to look at the corpses, like he thought they would leap up and bite him."

"Most people wouldn't consider it odd to be uncomfortable around corpses," Sonya says.

"Yeah, well. Most people who are weird about corpses wouldn't go to the goddamn morgue that often. To see *Graham,* no less."

Sonya knew her father's friends. They came over once a month to play backgammon; they brought their wives with them for dinner parties; they greeted her when she walked past their houses on her way to school. She doesn't remember Graham Carter being one of them. It's strange to think of her father with a life she didn't know anything about.

She says, "You're here just because you worked for Graham?"

"No, plenty of his peons escaped unscathed," Marie says. "But I was higher status than they were. He told me to keep quiet about some autopsy results. Delegation sweethearts who died by suicide or overdose or whatever. Can't have the general public find out that model citizens are anything other than perfect, right?"

"Well," Sonya says, "you didn't have to do as he said."

"What a peach you are." Marie's mouth puckers. "You didn't have to pose for that poster, either."

"No, I guess I didn't."

"Anyway, I'm pretty sure I saw him sneak Insights out of the storage area a couple times, creepy bastard." She tosses her sponge into the sink and hoists herself onto the counter. "Insights grow, did you know that? We inject them when they're tiny, and they expand and wrap around the brain."

Renee wrinkles her nose. "God, I really don't want to know this."

Marie snorts and continues: "You have to extract them within twenty-four hours of dying, because they shrink into themselves, like they're aging backward. Then they can be wiped and reimplanted—they're recyclable. Part of the marvel of them."

She wiggles her fingers theatrically.

"But taking them out is a delicate operation, because they're so embedded in the brain," she says. "Still not sure how the Triumvirate figured out how to remove them."

Sonya thinks of Knox telling her that every person on the outside who thinks they're free of their Insight is deluding themselves. Maybe she's telling the truth.

"Sometimes the shrunken ones would get lost," Marie says. "Nobody paid much attention to that, because they're so goddamn small at that point, who wouldn't lose track of a few of them? Except, you know, Graham was a real nickel-and-dimer, never lost track of a single minute of my break time, was always hassling me about putting equipment back *right* where I found it. Can't see him losing track of anything."

"So you think he took them to sell them?"

"Either that, or he was running some weird experiments in his basement," Marie says. "If that man didn't have a bunch of brains in jars somewhere before the uprising, I'd be shocked."

Kevin laughs.

"Thank you," Sonya says. "That's useful."

"I think I need to burn that knowledge from my brain with alcohol," Renee says. "Who else wants a drink?"

As Sonya descends the steps to the ground floor a few minutes later, she thinks of her father, and whether he really had such a blank stare. Whether she has it, too. August took his time with things. Sometimes she stood by the front door on her way out just to watch him tie his shoes with only his fingertips, like he was plucking harp strings. When he helped her mother in the kitchen, she complained about how long it took him to chop vegetables, but they were always in perfect cubes. Perfect rows.

The memories buoy her all the way home. She stops in her apartment to light the end of the cigarette, and then climbs with it pinched between thumb and index finger to the roof, where the garden she shares with Nikhil sags under the weight of that morning's rain. She checks the radish leaves to make sure bugs haven't gotten to them, then goes to the edge of the roof and leans into the half wall. Below her is the same view she gets from her apartment. The corner store with its voyeurs; the dirty street.

She sticks the cigarette between her lips and takes a tentative drag. Fire surges into her lungs and she coughs, coughs until tears spring into her eyes. Her mouth tastes like ash.

She does it again. She closes her eyes, and envisions the red flash of her DesCoin count as it diminishes. Maybe she hasn't lost her taste for small rebellions after all.

NINE

Sonya is in a dressing room, flanked on both sides by mirrors. Hanging on a hook beside her is a black dress with a full skirt, not unlike one she might have worn to Friday dinner at the Price household to prove that she was worthy of Aaron, her spine flat against the high back of the chair and her mind attuned to the differences between the forks. She started going weekly after the Delegation suggested the match. She and Aaron had been friends for most of their lives, but the promise of the Delegation's approval—and of the DesCoin that would accompany the wedding, like a dowry—had cemented their relationship, and the Prices had folded her into their family, as the Kantors had embraced Aaron in return.

And she had learned not to look at Alexander, the bundle of disorganized energy and ungainly limbs at the other end of the table. Her eyes tended to get caught on him.

A faint hum fills her head, Knox's headband disrupting the audio of her Insight. Alexander seemed not to notice it last time, too distracted by the visit from John Clark, but he might notice it after this, and she's ready to lie to him if she has to.

"Not sure why this is necessary!" Sonya calls out to Knox, who's waiting for her in the shop.

"You have expectations to meet," Knox says. "Be a good little princess and put it on."

The Insight's constant monitoring meant constant vulnerability, something she trained herself out of thinking about as a child. Her parents assured her the Insight was safe, it wouldn't watch her change or shower, but that reassurance was empty after the uprising, locked away by enemies who had no reason to exercise restraint. At first, in the Aperture, she changed in the dark and showered without looking at her body, but that level of vigilance couldn't be sustained for long. She hasn't thought about it in a long time, but it's different now, knowing there's one specific person who could be watching her. Knowing it's Alexander.

She takes off her coat and her sweater—pilling everywhere and mended half a dozen times—and her pants—dotted orange at the knee from a bleach mishap. She stands in just her underwear, as worn as the rest of the clothes she wears, the elastic rippling at the waist. Gravity is already beginning to catch her, tugging at her forehead, her breasts, her hips, her thighs—just enough for her to notice. She dares him to look at her. She makes herself pause before stepping into the dress to convince herself she's not afraid of being seen.

When she steps into the dress, though, she steps backward in time. The skirt reaches just past her knees; the waist is snug.

"You decent?" Knox calls out. She steps into the dressing room without waiting for an answer. "Never mind, I don't care. Let me zip you."

Knox's hands are cold, and she's not gentle with the zipper.

"Looks right," Knox says. "I'll get you some shoes. What size?"

"Eight."

She leaves again, and Sonya feels the ghost of hair on her shoulders, what she would have felt the last time she wore something like this. But it hasn't been that long in a decade.

Sonya's mother helped her get ready for the graduation dance just a month before the uprising. They went to pick out a new dress together, a stark white sheath, an echo of a wedding gown. Susanna joked it looked like a towel wrapped around her, because Susanna never could say anything nice to Sonya about how she looked. But their mother had whispered, as she zipped Sonya into it, that she looked beautiful. And Sonya had believed her.

Later, in a stolen moment, Aaron's mouth against her throat, he told her she looked obscene, and she thought it was worth the DesCoin it cost her to hear it.

The choreography of getting dressed is the same now. Knox's hands on the zipper. Standing barefoot on the cold floor. The tickle of nervousness in her throat. People say history repeats, Sonya thinks, but they don't mention that it warps every time.

She runs her fingers over the skirt. The fabric is thick and smooth; it falls just right. Knox walks in again while she does it and meets her eyes in the mirror.

"Here," she says, thrusting a pair of shoes at her. They are matte black, like the dress, and have a low heel.

"Didn't take you for someone who cared about fashion," Sonya says. Knox is wearing black pants and a white T-shirt. There is a thin gold chain around her wrist with a silver locket at the end of it.

"I know what's nice," Knox says. "Meet you out there. We need to find somewhere to discuss the plan."

Sonya folds the clothes she was wearing and carries the stack out of the dressing room. The woman at the register stared at her when she first came in, her eyes following Sonya around the shop as Knox picked out a few dresses, and she stares now, too.

"Excuse me," Sonya says, "do you have a bag I can put my clothes in?"

"Oh—of course," the woman says, and she ducks under the counter to search.

The light above her flickers out, leaving them in semidarkness. The clerk curses, and bumps her head on the counter as she straightens.

"That's the third time this week," she says, pointing up at the light fixture. "Sorry about that."

She rings up the dress and shoes in the half-light. Sonya looks up at the fixture. She steps back into the dressing room to pick up the stool in the corner and carries it to the front of the shop, where Knox is holding her Elicit over a sensor near the counter to pay.

Sonya puts the stool down under the light fixture. "Can you turn off the power for a second?"

The clerk frowns at her, but Knox, eyebrow raised, walks to the back of the store where the door to the circuit breaker has been painted with little yellow flowers to disguise it. She flips the switch as Sonya climbs up on the stool and unscrews the lightbulb.

She peers into the socket, her Insight casting a white circle on the ceiling. She reaches in, the metal grooves scraping her knuckles, and pulls up on the metal tab in the center of the socket. Then she screws in the bulb again and nods to Knox.

Knox flips the switch again, and the light turns on.

"Wow," the clerk says. "How'd you do that?"

"It's a common problem with these old fixtures," Sonya says.

"Well . . . thank you," the clerk says.

Sonya carries the stool back into the dressing room. When she comes out, the clerk offers Sonya a bag, and as she takes it, says, "You're even prettier in person, by the way."

Sonya pauses in the middle of shoving her clothes into the bag. Knox snorts.

"Thank you," Sonya says, and she walks out, Knox at her heels.

"Wow," Knox says. "She was *starstruck*. Doesn't that just warm your cold little Delegation heart?"

"No. It doesn't. Where are we going?"

"A little spot I like. You look like you could use some lunch."

"What happened, you woke up and decided to play dolls?" Sonya says. "Dress me up and now we're going to a tea party?"

"Something like that." Knox smiles. "How'd you get to be so handy?"

As always with Knox, Sonya isn't sure whether she's being mocked or not.

"Everything's always breaking in the Aperture," Sonya says. "And I got tired of doing nothing."

They turn down a narrow street that smells like wet cardboard and spray paint, and Knox stops in front of a small cafe. There are two round tables on the sidewalk with metal chairs around them, and one wilting bush next to the door with a few cigarette butts stabbed into the dirt.

Inside the place is dark, the floor faintly sticky. The walls are painted in bright colors above the wood paneling, one royal blue, one magenta, one orange, and the tables each have a layer of plastic over them. A man behind the counter greets them.

"Knoxy," he says. "Long time no see."

"Sammy," she says. "No more mustache?"

He shrugs.

Sonya is looking up at the menu, written in chalk next to the counter.

"Black coffee, and my friend will have . . ." Knox gestures to Sonya.

Sammy sees Sonya over Knox's shoulder, but his smile doesn't falter.

"Hot chocolate," Sonya says. "And a grilled cheese."

Knox pulls a face.

"Coming right up," Sammy says.

There are a few other people there, faces buried in books, sipping from multicolored mugs, scribbling in notebooks. Electronic music plays over the speakers, the beats at odds with Sonya's heart.

Sonya fills a glass of water at a station in the corner and carries it to the table in the back where Knox sits waiting. She drinks the entire thing. She doesn't usually get much to eat or drink outside the Aperture, unless she brings it with her.

"I keep forgetting it's not like they're paying you for this gig," Knox says. "Is it strange not to get paid just for following rules?"

"No," Sonya says. "It's been a decade for me, same as you."

The silver locket dangling from Knox's bracelet hits the edge of the table. Knox catches Sonya looking at it.

"You don't really ask questions, do you?" she says.

"I was raised not to be nosy."

Knox sighs, and props her elbows up on the table to open the locket. Inside is a picture of a young man. He has Knox's upturned lip, her high cheekbones.

"Twin brother," she says. "Dead now."

"I'm sorry."

"You're not, but that's fine, I'm not sorry for you either." Knox smirks. "My parents were Delegation loyalists, but not important ones. They obeyed, obeyed, obeyed. Mark didn't much like that. Mark was also an idiot, had no idea how to cover his tracks." She rolls her eyes. "So when the Delegation busted up the little resistance movement he joined, they not only locked him up, but they completely devastated my parents' DesCoin stores. They were destitute. Almost starved, ostracized from the community, lost their house, the whole thing."

Her bitterness is so potent Sonya can almost taste it at the back of her tongue.

"But we're all even now. Delegation cut out our eyes, and we cut out yours. That's how it works, right?"

Sonya doesn't remember the speech the Triumvirate gave the day she was locked in the Aperture. The representatives were different then, just interim leaders, and she thinks they must have said something about making things even. But when she tries to think of those days, they evade her. She remembers that she had no desire to be in the world outside, that she felt like the cat in the hypothetical box, both alive and dead—or perhaps neither. And it was easier to be that way in the Aperture, where no one would be opening the box to force an outcome through observation.

She's still not sure she wants anything different. But she has to find Grace Ward.

"What, nothing?" Knox says. "You're not going to tell me how unfair it all is, how you didn't do anything wrong?"

Sammy comes by with a tray in hand. He sets a mug of black coffee in front of Knox, and the hot chocolate and grilled cheese in front of Sonya. Knox's gaze is fixed on her, waiting.

"Why should I?" Sonya says. "You clearly have both parts of this little play memorized."

The smell of the grilled cheese makes her mouth water. Her father used to make them on Saturdays. He always made sure the cheese spilled over into the pan so it would crisp against the bread. He wore her mother's floral apron when he did it, to protect his clothes from the splatter, and he whistled, even though whistling meant two lost DesCoin. He knew how to make the sound flutter.

She bites into it, and closes her eyes. She wishes she knew how to whistle.

Sonya tries not to rush through it, tries to savor it, but now that she's started, it's impossible to stop. She licks her fingertips, one by one, and if she hadn't been with Knox, she would have licked the plate. She feels warm and sated.

Knox watches her with a knitted brow, like she's trying to solve an equation.

"Let's go over the plan again," Knox says. "You'll be meeting a woman named Eleanor, an Analog Army lieutenant, at a nightclub—"

"For some reason," Sonya says. She holds the mug in both hands, letting it warm her fingers.

"The reason is that a nightclub is loud and chaotic, easier to go unnoticed. I sent the request for the meeting through one of my unsavory contacts, whose name is . . . ?"

"Bob, who used to smuggle bits of tech from other districts when the Delegation was in power," Sonya says. "And I want to speak to a grown man who calls himself Myth, which is utterly ridiculous—"

"I wouldn't give that commentary in the moment."

"Obviously," Sonya says. "I tell Eleanor that I'm only going to talk to Myth about what I want, and no one else. And I argue with her until she agrees to arrange a meeting."

Knox has already finished her coffee. She runs a finger around the rim.

"She might use a device called a Veil. It'll make it so you can't see her face. More tech from the people who supposedly hate tech." Knox snorts a little. "And listen . . ."

She leans forward over the table.

"You need to act like someone who is completely harmless," Knox says, and for once, there is no mischief in her eyes. "That is very important. Smiling, wide-eyed innocence, Kantor. That's what's going to get you what you want."

"You spend half your time calling me 'princess,' I'm not sure what's wrong with the way I usually act."

"You're like . . . a piece of paper," Knox says, shrugging. "Looks blank and pale and boring, but if you handle it wrong, it'll cut the shit out of you. It'll make them suspicious if they notice it—so don't let them notice it."

"What if something goes wrong?" Sonya says, and Knox shrugs.

"Take off the audio disruptor and pray to whatever god you believe in that Alexander is listening in," she says. "I sure as hell can't do anything for you."

"You're a real peach," Sonya says, repeating what Marie told her the day before.

"Aren't I?" Knox grins. "You know, you ordered like a five-year-old. It's embarrassing."

"You would too, if you hadn't had cheese or chocolate in a decade."

Knox tips the last drops of coffee into her mouth, and sighs.

"Careful," she says. "You're almost making me feel bad for you."

THE nightclub is called the Loop. The name is a cheeky reference to Delegation evasion, Sonya is certain—as Knox told her, the only way to manipulate the Insight was to loop harmless footage for an hour or two. Loops meant gaps in the Delegation's attention, which for them meant safety. But an aperture is a gap, too, and Sonya has only ever experienced it as disappearing. As ceasing to matter.

Though it's getting dark, she wears sunglasses as she approaches the entrance, so her Insight doesn't attract attention. The thick man at the door stops her, a hand on her arm.

"Glasses off," he says.

She sighs and slides them off her nose. He stares at the Insight glow around her right iris, a beacon in the dark. Then he smiles in the way that some men smile when they catch a woman in a mistake.

"Go on in, Ms. Kantor," he says. "Someone's expecting you."

Sonya jerks her arm away from him, and walks in. A hall of fractured mirrors greets her, each one offering a jagged reflection. She stumbles, unable to discern depth, or shape. There are just bits of her everywhere, here a dark eye, there a soft chin, there a tight fist at her side. Then a woman walks around the bend in the mosaic, laughing, another woman trailing behind her; both wear tight dresses and high boots and wide grins. They don't pay Sonya any attention, but they show her a path.

On the other side of the mirrored hallway is an expansive space, two stories high. Everything is lit from beneath—white one moment, blue another, pink the next—and everything is mirrored. Mirrors hang from the ceiling above a wide dance floor tiled with mirrors; mirrors wrap around the circular bar in the center of the room; mirrors form curved partitions between chrome booths on the raised platform along the right side of the room. A circular bar stands in the middle of the space, and there's a glass dance floor on one side. Sonya stands, blinking, at the sight of herself a thousand times over, a pale woman in a dark dress that no longer looks right on her.

The light in her eye, though strange, is not the only glow in the room. Some of the dancers have it in their arms, rectangles of light, Elicits buried under their skin. Illegal tech, Sonya realizes—all implanted technology is illegal under the Triumvirate. There are others wearing circlets in their hair that look almost like crowns from behind, but when they turn toward her, she sees that there is a sheen of light projected over their faces, as iridescent as a bubble. They don't want to be recognized here.

Sonya moves toward the tables on the right side of the room. Once her eyes adjust to the light, they find a lone woman at one of the high tables near the back, a glass in hand. Her face is blurred, warped by a layer of shifting light. The rest of her looks out of place, in a gray sweater that climbs all the way up to her chin, her limp, dark hair pulled back in a knot. Sonya's head buzzes, a reminder that the headband is doing its work, as she weaves between the tables. The idea that the Insight wouldn't attract attention in a dark nightclub is proving incorrect; everyone she passes stares at her, and keeps staring at her after she's gone.

"Eleanor?" she says to the woman.

The woman's featureless face shifts up, and then down, as if she's looking Sonya over, and Sonya remembers to be what she's expected to be instead of who she is.

"Yes," Eleanor says.

"It's a pleasure to meet you, Ms. Lowry," Sonya says, as she eases herself into the chair opposite Eleanor. She crosses her legs at the ankle, and folds her hands in her lap. "Thank you for agreeing to this."

"You really do look the same," Eleanor says to her.

"Should I take that as a compliment?" Sonya says, light as air. She smiles, as if she's decided that it is. "Maybe time moves more slowly in the Aperture. So much has changed out here."

"Not enough, *some* would say," Eleanor replies. Her voice is toneless.

"Right, that's your organization's whole . . ." Sonya flaps her hand at Eleanor. "*Thing*, right? I read a manifesto the other day. Something about Elicits, maybe."

"Yes, it's our *thing*," Eleanor says. "If you weren't sure what our *thing* was, why did you arrange a meeting?"

"Oh, that was because of Bob," Sonya replies.

"Bob."

"Yes, Bob." Sonya looks around the room, eyes lingering on the Elicits that glow in some people's arms, like a window to their muscle and bone. "I wonder why you chose this place, if it's so full of people who are not . . . like-minded." She turns back to Eleanor. "Surely you do not approve of those." She touches her forearm.

"Sometimes we must keep company with those who do not share our worldview," Eleanor says. "Not that you would know anything about that, living in the Aperture."

Sonya laughs. A fluttering thing.

"Sometimes we do disagree," she says. "Just the other day I had a polite disagreement with Mrs. Pritchard about how frequently to dispose of my trash bags."

The lights shift colors. As they do, they show different parts of Eleanor's face—the edge of her jaw, square; the corner of her thin eyebrow; the curve of her nostril. Sonya tries to piece the features together, and can't. She wonders how a woman who wears a turtleneck to a nightclub fell in with extremists. Or found fervor in herself for anything.

"What did you do before?" Sonya asks.

"Before?"

"Before the Delegation fell."

Eleanor taps her fingers on the edge of the table.

"I worked for a company that analyzed Insight data," she says. "One of *many* that analyzed Insight data."

"Oh," Sonya says. "I didn't realize that work was done by companies."

"You didn't think the Delegation had enough manpower to watch every single person at every single moment of their lives, did you?" Eleanor laughs a little. "They outsourced. My job was to write programs that would recognize furtive movement."

"Furtive movement."

"Yes, people tend to move a particular way when they are trying to get away with something," Eleanor says. "I analyzed thousands of hours of footage, consulted with dozens of behavioral psychologists employed by the Delegation, and taught the computers to recognize that movement. The more automated the Insights became, the fewer people were needed to watch the footage. The programs could simply recognize wrongdoing on their own."

The lights—suddenly red—disguise Sonya's flush. All those years, and she never thought about who she was speaking to when she spoke to the Insight in her head.

As it turns out, she thinks, *you were speaking to no one.*

"And yet these people who despise Insights . . . they've welcomed you?" she says.

"I fed a lot of information to the uprising over a period of many years," Eleanor replies. "I thought we were going to have a true revolution. A brand-new society. But most of them were content to disable the Insights and give themselves comfortable government jobs and keep everything the same. So I sought out the people who would give me the change I was promised."

Eleanor sits forward and folds her hands on the table in front of her.

"So you see . . . if it had been up to me," she says, "you and all your little friends in the Aperture would have been killed in the street instead of locked away to bicker about garbage day."

Sonya flinches.

Aaron died in the street. He was found facedown, a few yards away from his house, a knife in his back, and a frying pan just out of reach.

"Tell me, Ms. Kantor," Eleanor says, sitting back in her chair. "What do you want from us, and why should we give it to you?"

"I was introduced to Bob because I'm investigating the missing girl, Grace Ward," Sonya says, the unctuous quality gone from her voice. She squeezes her hands together in her lap as the lights shift from red to purple.

"Introduced by whom?"

"Surely you don't expect me to remember everyone I've encountered during this investigation," Sonya says. "Anyway, something Bob said about your little organization made me think you could help me."

"And that was?"

Sonya smiles. "I'm not going to give myself away that easily, Eleanor. I have but a humble existence in the Aperture. I have nothing to offer anyone except for information. So I'm going to be careful about who I give it to. And if I give it to you, there's no guarantee it will get where it needs to go. Which is to Myth."

Eleanor waits for a few moments before speaking again.

"You don't trust me?" she asks.

"Why would I trust you?" Sonya says, eyebrows raised. "I don't even know what you look like."

"Yet you're asking me to trust you by letting you know the identity of our leader," Eleanor says. "And not just you, but whoever is watching you with that . . . thing."

"We both know there are ways around my Insight *and* ways to disguise your leader's identity," Sonya says. "As for trusting me, well, this comes down to risk. It's a great risk for me to trust you. It was a risk for me to even come here alone. There is no risk at all for you, in trusting me. All I want is to find the girl, get my freedom, and disappear from everyone's notice."

"Why should I care about that?" Eleanor says. "Why does your little mission have anything to do with us?"

"Because you want to know what's floating around about you, don't you? You want to know what Bob told me that made me come to you?

Because if it's something that someone like me can find out, then there are plenty of scarier, more dangerous people who can find out, too." Sonya tilts her head. "And maybe they'll do worse than I can."

"You think I'll decide to help you because I want to know a rumor?"

"Maybe, maybe not," Sonya says. "Or maybe you'll decide to help me because there's a girl out there who was taken from her parents by the same government you fought to dismantle, and she needs help. Or maybe you'll help me because you're curious, or because you think Myth will want to play with a little doll of the Delegation for a couple hours."

She leans forward, the edge of the table digging into her stomach.

"Or maybe," she says, "you're interested in what Emily Knox told me when I met with her."

The featureless face turns toward her sharply at Knox's name.

"I don't really care why you're going to help me . . . but you are," Sonya says. "Aren't you?"

For a while, Eleanor is still.

"I will ask Myth if he'll meet with you," she says. "And we will get in touch with you if he agrees."

"Thank you," Sonya says. She stands. "Have a nice day."

When she walks away from the table, her hands are shaking.

TEN

THIS TIME, ALEXANDER is waiting at her door. His tall, ungainly form leaning against the wall next to it. He wears the same wool coat, the same black shoes that haven't been polished in too long. As she approaches, he pushes his hands through his unkempt black hair and looks at her.

"May I come in?" he says. His breath is sharp with alcohol.

"Not if you're here to scold me," she says. "Have you been drinking?"

"It was trivia night," he says. "I do actually have a life beyond paper-pushing, you know. Friends. Hobbies. The whole rigmarole."

She pushes the door open with her shoulder, then takes off her coat and hangs it on the hook screwed to the wall just inside the living room. She doesn't understand why he's staring at her until she remembers Knox's dress, Knox's shoes. In the dressing room they were elegant, but in the Aperture, they're a costume.

"She insisted," she says, cheeks warming.

"I believe you," he replies. "So I went back over the last few days' footage—I haven't been watching you, I only scroll through the highlights."

"Oh," Sonya says. "Why?"

"I'm giving you space," he says. "But I still need to do my job."

"And?"

"And yesterday you were wearing a device that interfered with the Insight's audio receptors," he says. "Courtesy of Emily Knox."

Sonya walks into the kitchen and takes a glass out of the cupboard. She turns on the faucet and lets the water run for a few seconds before filling it. Sometimes the pipes spit rust-colored water at first.

"Yes," she says. "I was."

He braces himself on the edge of the counter, leaning into his hands so his shoulders bunch up by his ears. Again she gets the feeling that he's too close, even though there's a counter between them.

"You know, this isn't your job. This is an offer generously extended to you by the Triumvirate," he says. "It can be revoked just as easily as it was given."

She puts the glass down on the counter. Some of the water splashes over the edge. "Are you threatening me?"

"No." He closes his eyes. "God, you really do think the worst of me, don't you?"

She thinks of the boy with the photo negatives pinched between his long fingers, his knee jiggling under the desk.

"I am not *threatening* you, I am reminding you that I'm not the only one watching," he says. "Emily Knox has as many enemies in the Triumvirate as she has friends. She made a lot of bad behavior possible under the Delegation. She blackmailed a lot of people. When I tell you she's dangerous, I'm not kidding. She obviously wants something from you now, but if you don't give it to her . . ." He shakes his head. "To her, you're disposable."

"And you think I am unfamiliar," Sonya says, "with being disposable."

Alexander raises his eyes to hers.

"You think I don't know about people who only want to take," she goes on. "Here in this place where there are no locks and there's nothing to lose."

She drinks the entire glass of water in one long swallow and puts it back down again.

"There's a one-eyed man in the Aperture," she says. "Ask him where the other one went."

When they were younger, Sonya and Aaron, twelve, occasionally teamed up against Alexander, then fourteen, in games of checkers.

Aaron hated to lose, so when he did, he often stormed out of the room, and Sonya stayed behind to play again, just her against Alexander. Their games were quieter, slower. Sonya never touched a piece unless she knew where it would go, and Alexander took his time to think things through. Whenever either of them made a move, their eyes would lock over the board, and he was so focused, like he was staring at her through a pinhole.

He looks at her like that now.

"Grace Ward is out there, lost and afraid," Sonya says. "Don't tell me you don't hear her voice in your head, saying *it's your Alice.*"

"Of course I do," he says, his voice softening a little. "I guess I'm surprised to hear that you do."

She's never been aware of her own expressions—on the day of the photo shoot, she thought she looked soft and contemplative, but the result, on the poster, was a cold declaration. *What's right is right,* the text mirrored in her expression. Even after over a decade, she's still startled by the discrepancy between her insides and her outsides, how no one can see the tumult of her.

"You couldn't find her through conventional means," she says. "So I'm going to find her through unconventional ones. And you're not going to stand in my way."

He frowns, and for a moment the only sound is the drip of the faucet, the distant conversation of people at the market across the street, Laura's footsteps in the apartment above hers, preparing dinner. Sonya looks at the apartment behind him, quantifying DesCoin right away, minus twenty-five for leaving the bed unmade, minus one hundred for the cigarette butt in the trash can, minus ten for the empty fingerprint-marked glass on the coffee table made of crates.

"Do you really care about getting out of here?" he asks. "Sometimes I wonder if you don't have a different reason for doing all this."

Laura is tapping her toes. Sonya can't hear her singing right now, but she knows she must be; Laura always sings when she's alone.

Sonya flaps an arm at the rest of the apartment. "Wouldn't *you* want to get out of here?"

He's still frowning.

"Whatever you're doing, get it done quickly," he says, finally. "Before someone with a grievance against Emily Knox notices."

"I have no interest in dragging it out."

He nods. Buttons his coat. Turns up the collar at the back, to protect his neck from the cold. Pushes a hand through his hair to keep it off his forehead.

"I looked up my file after the uprising, too, you know," he says. "There wasn't much in there that I liked. We have that in common, I think."

He moves toward the door, but he stops with his hand on the knob. Sonya didn't realize he had closed it behind him when he came in.

"We don't have to believe what they said about us," he says.

He goes. In the silence he leaves behind, Sonya can finally hear Laura singing in a warbling soprano.

THE next morning, there's a note waiting for her at the guard station on plain white card stock:

Tonight at 7 at the Loop. Don't be late. Come alone.

"Didn't read that one, see?" Williams says to her.

"I noticed," she says. "Any particular reason you've decided to respect my privacy?"

He shrugs.

"Figured nobody cares what any of you are saying or not saying," he says, "so why should I?"

She gives him a grim smile, and tucks the note into her pocket.

SONYA carries the watering can up to the roof, where Nikhil is doing the planting. Earlier they turned the soil together, so it was no longer packed tight into the planters, and there's still dirt under her fingernails. Now he'll press the seeds into the little pots they use to get a head start on spring growth, as recommended by the book Nikhil read ten years ago when the library cart still came through the Aperture every two weeks. Now they see it every month, if that. The world outside has remembered them recently, but it's also forgotten them.

Her back aches as she opens the door to the little greenhouse. It was some kind of maintenance shed before, but they replaced some of the wall panels with glass, so now it's lit in uneven stripes. She sets the watering can down on the worktable next to Nikhil. He drags it over and tips it just enough to sprinkle the first row of seeds.

"Spinach and peas," he says. "Rose Parker made it happen, you know. I asked Nicole to tell Ms. Parker that we needed seeds, when she agreed to do the interview."

Sonya sits on the dusty trunk where they keep the tools and old pots. She slides her thumbnail under her other nails, one by one, to scrape away dirt.

"Speaking of Nicole," Nikhil says. "You might consider visiting her, on one of your excursions. See how she's adapting to her new life."

"She's starting over. She doesn't need someone from the Aperture coming back to haunt her."

"You're not a ghost, Sonya. She would be happy to see an old friend," Nikhil says. "And she might be able to give you an idea of what to expect when you leave here."

"Nikhil . . ." Sonya sighs. "You don't really think they'll let me leave, do you?"

"I think they made a public promise, and if they fail to keep it, you should make that failure public," he says. "You still have Ms. Parker's contact information, don't you?"

In the crate by the side of her bed is a tin box where she keeps small things: Spare pencils; a pencil sharpener. A paintbrush. An envelope the size of her palm with a pill in it. A packet of seeds for spring planting. Rose Parker's business card.

Sonya reaches into her pocket and takes out the note from the Analog Army. She's allowed to be away from the Aperture for twelve hours. If she leaves in fifteen minutes, Williams will register her lateness fifteen minutes into her meeting with Myth. At that point Williams will likely notify Alexander, who will then know to check her Insight feed.

She's ready to leave. The lunch she packed herself waits for her on her kitchen ledge, along with a handkerchief and the card with Alexander's office address on it.

"Listen," she says to Nikhil. He turns toward her. Dirt fills the creases in his palms. He dusts it off, lets it scatter across the floor.

"I'm doing something dangerous tonight," she says. "It might pay off. It might not."

"Dangerous," Nikhil says. He brings the cuff of his sleeve up to his eye to dab at the excess tears there.

"A meeting," she says. "With people who are capable of harm. If I succeed, I can find Grace Ward."

"And if you fail?"

"I'm not sure. But it won't be good."

He leans back against the worktable.

"And this is worth it to you, this risk?"

She so often thinks of that word, *worth.* Dark moments in front of her reflection, thinking that perhaps she was not worth the effort it took to acquire the permit that made her. Darker moments in the Aperture, after the lights went out, wondering just what the point of doing anything was if it stayed trapped there, unseen and unknown. The worth of a polite word versus a rude one, of self-control versus surrender to impulse, of lying to be kind versus hurting to be honest. All of life, an endless series of columns, this versus that, action versus inaction. It's all subjective. It's all math.

Still, she knows the answer.

"Yes," she says.

Nikhil's eyes sparkle, but that's nothing new. He nods.

"Take care of yourself," he says. "Live to struggle another day, yes?"

"As you always say: projects keep people sane."

SHE'S on her way to the entrance when she sees Graham Carter ducking into the tunnel that leads to Building 1's courtyard. Before she can stop herself, she's chasing him down.

"Mr. Carter!"

He turns at the entrance to the courtyard, eyes wide.

"Ms. Kantor," he says. "How are you?"

"Can I talk to you for a second?"

Graham nods, and gestures for her to follow him to a small table in Building 1's courtyard. She gets moss on her fingers when she pulls out one of the chairs, which is little more than a metal frame, the wood rotted away. A few empty bottles crusted with dirt rest in a pile nearby; there's crumpled paper and decaying fabric scraps here and there in the untamed greenery.

Graham seems not to notice it. He looks up at her, expectant.

"I don't know if you've heard," she says, "but I've been given a . . . project. I'm trying to find a missing girl. She was an unauthorized second child who wasn't found until she was three years old—which means she must have had a black market Insight."

Graham's face falls. He looks away.

"I heard you might know something about how that all worked," Sonya says.

"Been talking to Marie, have you?" Graham's mouth twitches into a frown. "I thought perhaps, eventually . . . eventually we might all be permitted to let go of our past weaknesses . . . I see now that was foolish."

"I don't relish dredging up the past, Mr. Carter," Sonya says. "But I had no one else to ask."

He sighs, and taps his fingers on the edge of the table. There is a flower carved into the top—a rose—covered in a film of algae.

"My mother—Charlotte's and mine—wasn't well," he says. "She wasn't ill, mind you, not really—she thought she was ill, all the time. Charlotte didn't understand, she just wanted Mom to snap out of it, stop worrying—but I had always been a little more like her, a little more . . . sensitive."

She has no trouble believing that. Graham is reactive, twitching and jerking with every movement, every sound. Birdcalls and slammed doors and the snaps of someone shaking out their wet clothes. The morgue must have been a good place for him, a place of deep quiet and soothing monotony.

"The thing is, under the Delegation, when you visited a doctor with insufficient justification—there was a penalty." He shrugs. "Sometimes Mom needed DesCoin. So when the bodies came in fresh, the Insights still viable—I would sell them. There was a network for it. Coded, so it was more likely to escape the Delegation's algorithms."

"What kind of code?"

"They named things after card games," he says. "Insights were hearts, Blitz was gin rummy—it got darker and grimmer, but I stayed on the surface of it. But with the code, if you wanted to meet, you could just say, 'Want to play hearts on Friday?' and no one was the wiser, see?"

Sonya nods.

"So," she says, "how did that work? The Insight part, I mean, not the market—you said you only did this when the bodies came in fresh."

"An Insight's hardware recognizes death right away, but its software takes time to adjust. If you take it out quick, you can put it in someone else so the Insight doesn't register the gap—so buyers would be on high alert the second an Insight became available. They'd get a doctor to do the insertion, which is a big needle right under the eye, here—" He touches his lower eyelid, pulling it down so she can see the red capillaries. "And then the system registers their unauthorized child under whatever name the Insight was associated with before. Only that name belongs to someone who's dead, so they're not in the system anymore. It's a loophole, see?"

"So if the Wards looked at their daughter, Grace," Sonya says, "the data would show them interacting with a dead person . . . but because the person was dead . . ."

"It would dump the data automatically," Graham supplies. "Smart little trick."

She thinks again of confiding in her Insight when she was alone. The more she learns about how automated the system was, the more foolish she feels. Alone in her house, alone in her head, telling a computer her deepest secrets—and of *course* that was all it was, but it felt like something grander, at the time.

"Do you happen to remember selling to the Ward family?"

Graham sighs. "Ten years is a long time for an old man to remember, my dear."

"I know," she says. "Thank you, though." She stands. "I have to go, I'm afraid. Have a good day, Mr. Carter."

She leaves him sitting there, slumped over the little table. She can feel him staring at her until she's out of sight.

THE night they fled the uprising, Sonya's mother told her not to bring anything with her. Her math book was open on her desk, the task light shining on it. Her sync screen, marked with fingerprints, was lit up on the desk, waiting for her to scan it with her Insight and transmit to the school's system. Her school clothes hung over the closet door. She left them all behind, only putting on her shoes before running down the stairs to the front door.

Her mother waited there with her coat, holding it out the way she had when Sonya was a child and wanted to play in the snow. Sonya plunged one arm into a sleeve. The front door was already open, and Susanna was crossing the lawn to get in the car, which hummed in the driveway, their father's face lit from beneath by the dashboard. Julia's hand inched along Sonya's shoulders as she moved around her younger daughter, and then she did up the zipper. It didn't occur to Sonya to tell her that she could do it herself. In that moment she was a child. She felt like a child.

Her mother's breaths came in short bursts. She looked up at Sonya. They had the same eyes, everyone always said, so Sonya saw her own fear reflected back to her in perfect symmetry.

She thinks of it, standing before Emily Knox in her bedroom. It's a bare space with only a bed in it—as if, when Knox isn't being confronted with the technological, her mind goes blank, and she can only think of what's necessary for survival. She stands right at the edge of Knox's white bed with its white sheets and the white walls enclosing them, Knox zipping the jacket she is loaning Sonya for the occasion, leather, black, a little too big. A thick strip of tech disguised as a bracelet is wrapped around Sonya's wrist. Knox's eyes lift to Sonya's. They're fierce, not afraid.

There's symmetry here, too.

SHE walks back to the Loop empty-handed. The tech hidden in her wrist cuff is a Remote Magnetic Resonance Duplicator—or "a leech," as Knox calls it. When Sonya finds the server that houses the Delegation's data—and Knox assures her it will be obvious, because the power supply required to maintain it will be conspicuous—she'll unbutton the wrist cuff, and press it flat to part of the server. Once it's in place, it will take days, perhaps weeks, to transmit everything—but if she's stealthy enough, the Army won't know anything about it until it's too late.

She bided some time in Knox's apartment, and some wandering the city streets, walking down the aisles of grocery stores to look at the things she couldn't buy, wandering through an Elicit shop to see all the flat screens with their multicolored cases, some iridescent, some glittery, some studded with metal. The world is full of new things that look old: printed books and piles of newspapers, the Insight's functions fragmented into half a dozen devices, cameras and keyboards and music players.

On the way to the Loop, she listens. To the distant blare of train horns. To the snap of shoes on wet pavement. To the dry screech of bicycle brakes. To a low voice humming somewhere behind her. She stuffs her hands into the pockets of the jacket and feels something in the right one. A slim, papery thing. She takes it out, lets the light of her Insight wrap around it. A cigarette. An old one, stored in the pocket for safekeeping.

She stands in front of the nightclub. The sign is in pink neon, a strip of light meant to look like a thread curling around itself—a literal loophole. It disappears around the edge of the building. It's seven o'clock, which means it will take an hour before the guard at the Aperture realizes she hasn't checked in after twelve hours, as she's supposed to, and contacts Alexander. She takes her hands out of her pockets and waits.

She recognizes Eleanor only by the incongruity of her conservative clothes and the Veil shimmering across her face. She's with two others—men, judging by their build, their clothing nondescript, their faces also shielded. Eleanor doesn't greet her, she just shoves a circlet into Sonya's hands and says, "Put it on."

Sonya crowns herself with the circlet, and when her hands leave it, it activates automatically, the Veil draping across her face. It is not the same gossamer as the one that covers Eleanor and the others; it is opaque, a wall of darkness that obscures her vision. She puts her hands up to her head to remove it, and Eleanor grabs her wrists instead.

"Did you think we were just going to let you see where our headquarters are?" Eleanor's breath is sharp with alcohol. "Leave it on, or the meeting is off."

Sonya takes her hands away from the circlet. Eleanor grabs her by the elbow and turns her, once, twice, like they're dancing. Sonya tries to hold fast to the layout of the street in her mind, the pink glow of the Loop's sign, the dark warehouses that surround it. Eleanor tugs her to the right, and she stumbles along, splashing through a puddle. The chatter of people outside the nightclub fades into echoes. She feels the heat of the two men behind her, their footsteps hounding hers. The sounds of the city are muted here, the HiTrain just a whisper, the bicycles and footsteps and tinkling of opening shop doors absent.

"Curb," Eleanor says, and Sonya trips over it. They're on a sidewalk. Eleanor's hand is firm around her arm. The leech squeezes Sonya's wrist. She tries to steady her breath—it's too loud, coming in sharp bursts. A betrayal of her body, the ferocity of an hour ago lost behind the Veil.

They walk through a doorway. Sonya hears the door open, feels the air change as she moves into a building. As Eleanor takes the circlet from Sonya's head, she looks over her shoulder and sees a sliver of the street as the door closes, the moon high, the city skyline muddy against the ever-darkening sky. She's in a wide hallway with a cement floor. The walls are rough brick, crumbling, with sloppy mortar. The windows behind her are blacked out by paint.

There's a light above them, a single bulb hanging from a high ceiling, and far ahead of them, lines of light outlining a doorway, but between the two is darkness. Eleanor turns to her.

"Feet apart, arms out," she says. When Sonya just stares at her, she makes an impatient noise. "I'm not risking you bringing weapons in here."

Sonya stretches out her arms and Eleanor runs her hands over Sonya's body, kneeling first to feel around her ankles and up her legs. Sonya feels her heartbeat in her throat, in her cheeks; the leech is right there on her wrist, pressing into the bones. Eleanor skims Sonya's sides, her arms, and feels the pockets over Sonya's belly. When she gets to the wrist cuff, she runs her fingers over it, but doesn't give it another look.

Eleanor gestures for Sonya to follow her, and she does, with the feeling of plunging into a void. The silent men behind her walk just a little too close, within reach. A thick bundle of cable runs along the side of the hallway, and Sonya thinks of what Knox told her about the server's power supply. The bundle of cables disappears into a room just off the hallway, but she can't follow it and she isn't sure why she ever thought she would be able to; she's hemmed in on all sides; she was a fool to think that years living in the chaos of Building 2 had prepared her for this.

Eleanor opens the door at the end of the hallway, and what lies behind it isn't what Sonya expects. It's a wide, cavernous space with the same brick walls as the hallway behind her, but it's stuffed full of *things.* Stacks of books; tables full of old record players, which Sonya recognizes only from history texts; television sets with busted screens as thick as her torso; piles of calculators, bowls of car keys, crates full of hair dryers, vacuum cleaner tubes, headphones that are more like helmets. Almost everything still looks grayish, speckled with dust too caked on to clean. In the corner of the room is a rug made of animal skin with a head at one end—a bear with a snarling snout. On top of it are sofas clustered around a heater. If Knox's apartment is a shrine to her love of recent technology, this place is a shrine of the opposite—every inch of it betrays a reverence for what came before.

It looks like Sonya's apartment.

Perched in the center of one of the sofas is a slim man, Veiled, his legs crossed. His socks are bright yellow tartan. She can hear the smile in his voice as he speaks.

"Miss Kantor! Welcome. Please, come and sit."

He gestures to the sofa opposite him. Its cushions are oversized and limp, all the life gone out of them, and patterned in sky-blue brocade. Eleanor steps away from Sonya, leaving her path clear. The man—Myth, obviously, or at least that's what she's meant to believe—sits casually, his arm stretched along the back of the sofa, his head cocked to the side. She sees hints of him through the Veil, not enough to know anything about him. His hands, however, betray him, creased and dotted with age spots.

Sonya sits on the edge of the cushion, her legs folded to the side. The heater in front of her is on, and a wave of warmth washes over her.

"Won't you stay awhile?" Myth asks. His voice is almost musical, like a performer rather than the leader of an organization that regularly plants explosives. Sonya recognizes the cue to remove her jacket. For a moment she considers protesting. She feels Eleanor at her back. She worries that taking the jacket off will draw attention to the bracelet, but refusing will draw more. She unzips it, and drapes it over her lap.

"I have heard so much about you," Myth says. "As you have undoubtedly heard about me."

Sonya has heard almost nothing. Myth is the leader of the Analog Army, feared, but not understood. Some people seem to be unconvinced that he actually exists, and she wonders if he does, or if the members of the organization take turns playing him, each one donning the Veil and taking on a different personality. She knows that demanding to speak with him was the only way to be admitted into this warehouse. That's all Knox told her, and she spares a moment to resent her for it, Knox preying on her ineffectuality, aware that she was unprepared for this.

"Of course," Sonya says, and she remembers the advice to be what Myth expects her to be. "I'm surprised you even agreed to meet with me."

"And why should I object to a visit from such a special guest?"

Despite his warmth, his lively voice, there's an edge to the question, as if he's testing her.

"Oh, just—because I'm carrying an Insight into your building,"

Sonya says, with a careless wave of her hand. Her fingers are trembling. "It causes a stir everywhere I go these days, so I thought it would only be worse here."

"You have my sympathy," he says. "Everyone else in this city has the option of getting that thing removed, free of charge. But you don't." His head tilts. "I suppose I shouldn't assume that you would, if you could."

He folds his hands over his knee.

"Would you?"

Sonya doesn't know how to answer. She doesn't know what he's trying to do, what he's getting at, what he wants.

"I don't know," she says. "It used to speak to me. Now it's just there."

"And you liked it," he supplies. "When it spoke to you?"

"Yes."

"Why?"

"Why?" Heat rushes into her cheeks as she searches for the words. "Because, it . . . it made the world feel—richer. Everything I looked at had history and complexity that was in my grasp. Everything I did had meaning."

"No," he says, softly. "Everything you did was *quantified.* There's a difference."

"They felt the same to me," she says.

"You were a child," he says. "You're no longer a child, but you're still using a child's logic. If it *feels* a certain way, it must *be* that way."

His voice is gentle. She feels like he's only seeing the girl on the poster, and there's nothing she can say to convince him there's anything more to her. She's just a black-and-white filter and a Delegation slogan to him.

"Why don't you help me with my logic, then?" she says. "I saw one of those CAD pamphlets the other day, about the Elicit being a slippery slope back to the Insight. It is, I assume, just the next in a long line of technologies you want to carve out of existence."

Myth's Veil ripples imperceptibly. It's just a random fluctuation in the iridescence, but for a moment it seems almost expressive.

"The Insight wasn't some aberration or anomaly," he says. "It is the symptom of a disease that still infects our population—the desire to make everything *easy,* to sacrifice autonomy and privacy for convenience. That's what technology is, Ms. Kantor. A concession to laziness and the devaluing of human effort."

"Forgive me, but . . ." She leans a little closer. "This room is a shrine to technology."

"Not all technology is the same. I encourage you not to get tripped up by semantics," he says. "A device that you carry with you everywhere you go, a device that monitors and watches you, is not the same as one that sits in your house and plays music or dries your hair."

"So where does your organization think we should have stopped?" she says. "Or are you just going to hack away at everything that makes life easier until it feels right?"

"We would never be so imprudent," he replies. "We have indeed pinpointed the historical origin of our present woes: the cloud."

"The cloud," she says.

"It almost sounds as if you haven't read *any* of the Citizens Against Digital Takeover literature," he says.

"Forgive me," she says. "I don't have access to a lot of it in my birdcage."

He pauses, for a moment, his hands clenching around his knee.

"Yes," he says, "the cloud: the invisible web that surrounds us all, saturating our very air with data that we cannot see or touch or even access, for the most part. Most people are not even aware of the term anymore; it has been lost to time. But before the cloud, if you had a piece of information—a document, perhaps, or a picture, you would store it on a device to which only you had access. The problem with this was that that device was a physical thing; it was subject to all the vagaries of a tangible object, it could be broken, or harmed, or stolen, or lost. It deteriorated with time, like a body. It was, in other words, finite."

He leans forward, and she catches a glimpse, through the Veil, of a single honey-brown eye.

"The cloud made everything infinite," Myth says. "And it facilitated the acquisition of massive amounts of data. And just who was the font of data, the endless source from which to draw, to profit, to distract, to control?" He taps his chest with his index finger. "We were. We were, and still are, an endlessly renewable resource of information. The more we know about each other, the more power is within our grasp to maneuver each other. Because the cloud is not, strictly speaking, real. Every byte of data that exists must still be stored in a physical location, even if it is not one you have access to independently. We have simply ceded those locations to others for our own convenience. At first, we gave them to companies, and that was bad enough. But then we made a catastrophic mistake. Can you guess what it was?"

Sonya stays quiet, and still.

"We gave it," he says, "to our government."

He sits back, uncrossing his legs and stretching his arms wide, to take up the whole width of the couch. His body is like a bundle of wire. If he stood, they might be the same height, but there is something grand about him, and something unsteady, the rabbit heart of a fanatic tapping away in his chest.

She thinks of the rows and rows of files in the library, a mausoleum for the Delegation. She's always thought of the records that were purged during the uprising as comparable to that library—some things were lost, perhaps, but for the most part, everything the Delegation knew was there in those file folders. It strikes her as foolish now. The Insight logged everything she ever looked at, everyone she ever spoke to, everything she ever did. The library could not contain all of that even for one person, let alone everyone in the entire megalopolis.

And all of that data now lives somewhere in this building.

"Which returns us to the reason why you are here," he says. "You believe we now have this data, and there is someone else in this city—outside of the Triumvirate—who very much wants access to it."

Sonya's hand squeezes the leech on her wrist so hard she thinks it could crack under the pressure.

"What has Emily Knox asked you to do, exactly?" he says.

She's small and young again.

"You're mistaken," she says. "I mean—yes, I heard a rumor that you have the Delegation data, and yes, that's why I'm here, but I—all I want to do is find Grace Ward."

"I am not mistaken," Myth says. "We know you are working for Knox; it is the entire reason you are in this building. Do you really think I would agree to meet with someone who simply wanted to find a missing girl from ten years ago?"

"Have you been following me?" Sonya says. "I may have met with Emily Knox once, recently, as part of my investigation, but—"

"If you wanted to convince me of that," Myth says, quietly, "you would have avoided referring to the Aperture as a 'birdcage,' as I know only one person who uses that sobriquet, and you wouldn't have picked it up if you'd only met her once."

Sonya falls silent. She can feel Eleanor at her back, the two men who escorted her here near the door. There's nowhere to run.

Myth says, "It's all right. Like I said, it's the reason you're here. I want to offer you a deal."

Trades again, Sonya thinks. She trades all the time, in the Aperture market, salvaged radiator knobs for wires, Nikhil's mended socks for buttons, patched-up tech for cans of chicken soup. And outside of the Aperture, too—Rose Parker's questions for Emily Knox's address; a Delegation song for Knox's help; Grace Ward for Sonya's freedom. Trades rely on trust, the belief that if you give what you agree to give, you will receive what is promised. Try as you might to secure a trade, someone still has to go first, someone still has to have that weightless moment where they give without receiving.

Myth won't be going first. That much is certain.

"If you truly only care about finding Grace Ward," Myth says, "then we will do everything in our power to help you. In return, I simply ask that you tell me Emily Knox's intentions, for this meeting and for the future."

Sonya's Delegation-trained brain makes columns and starts comparing them. She's already in the middle of a deal with Knox in which she went first, in which she trusted the most. Risk herself by going, unprepared and unqualified, to the Analog Army's headquarters, and she *maybe may might* have Knox's help, using Grace's UIA. But now her chances of meeting her end of the deal are next to zero. She won't be able to attach the leech, no matter what she does. If she betrays Knox, it's possible Myth won't follow through on his end—but there's a chance, at least, that he will.

In one direction, she thinks, there is certain failure. In the other, possible success. It's not a difficult comparison to make. But there's another one at work in her mind, harder to quantify—the cost of giving information to a bunch of extremists, the danger it could pose to Knox, the weight of that guilt. Heavier than a loss of DesCoin.

"You want me to betray her," Sonya says, not because she needs clarification on that point, but because she wants to buy herself some time to think.

"What did she do to win your loyalty?" Myth says, cocking his head to the side. The Veil ripples again, and again Sonya sees that warm brown eye.

There is no answer to that. Knox humiliated her in the Midnight Room; she was full of scorn and derision; she offered no help, no exit plan.

"She saw me," Sonya says. "Instead of the poster."

"And you think I don't?"

"I think I have no reason to believe any of you will actually help me," Sonya says. "And even if I tell you what Knox wants, you'll have no way of verifying whether it's true or not."

"Maybe it's your best chance."

"Maybe." Sonya sighs. She runs her fingertip along the edge of the leech cuff, thinks about taking it off and showing him the underside, meant to drain and duplicate his data. Her heart races. She stares at the rippling Veil.

"She sent me to get a look at this place," Sonya says. "My Insight has recorded its layout. My contact at the Triumvirate has agreed to hand over the footage if Knox helps me."

"Oh really," Myth says. "And for what purpose does Emily Knox wish to know the layout of this building?"

"It's your base of operations," Sonya says, shrugging. "Maybe she wants to rob you. Maybe she wants to spy on you. I didn't ask."

Myth's head tilts. His arm creeps along the back of the sofa.

"Is it?" he says.

"Is it what?"

"Is this"—Myth gestures to the room around them—"our base of operations?"

Sonya's hands go limp in her lap.

"I suppose I don't know," she says, and her voice feels like it's coming from someone else.

"We would never invite someone there," he says. "Just how naive are you?"

He lifts his head and nods, not to Sonya, but to Eleanor, still standing behind her.

"Please escort our guest to the holding area," he says. "Let's put her to good use."

Fear prickles in her throat. In her hands. Sonya gets to her feet, and starts toward the door. The guards stand in her way, two inhuman hulks, faces hidden, clothing identical. She stares up at them, each one in turn.

"Let me through," she says.

"Come, now," Myth says. He's closer than she expected; he's standing right behind her. "This is unbecoming of a daughter of the Delegation."

He puts his hands on her shoulders, and his dry, gentle touch makes her shudder. She doesn't think to scream. She twists and drives her elbow toward the Veil that shields him. It is just a projection, an illusion; her blow moves right through it, hitting some hard part of his face. He yells, and one of the guards hurls Sonya to the ground. Her head smacks into the cement; she drags herself to her feet, feeling the cold trickle of blood down her temple. She is surrounded, outnumbered, overpowered, but she loses her grasp on rationality. She claws at the guard who tries to pick her up from the ground, digging her fingernails as deep into his flesh as she can manage. He brings his fist down on her face, and everything goes soft at the edges.

They drag her out into the dark hallway she walked down on her way in, and then they follow the bundle of wires into the room where she thought she might find the server. They're holding her tightly enough to bruise. The bundle of wires ends at a generator, buzzing like a beehive in the corner of an alcove. Across from it is a door, a room; the guards muscle her into it, and shut it behind her.

The room is small and empty except for a steel table. It looks like it used to be a storage closet; there are bolt holes, faded lines on the walls where shelves were. It smells like mildew. There's broken glass swept into the corner in a pile of dust. A cloudy window no larger than Sonya's head lets in yellow light from the street. She left her jacket behind on the sofa, so she's cold, trembling.

Once the shaking starts, it overtakes her, arms, chest, legs shuddering with terror. She doesn't know what they'll do to her here, but she knows it will be bad, she knows it won't end with Grace Ward's UIA and the relative comfort of the Aperture. She curses Knox, ripping off the cuff and hurling it at the wall before sinking into the corner, her hand against her throbbing jaw.

"Price," she says, out loud, hoping he'll somehow hear her, that he's listening at this exact moment. "Alexander, if you're listening, please help me."

But even if he's listening, he won't know how to find her.

ELEVEN

THE CHILL HASN'T yet settled into her skin by the time they return: both guards, as indistinguishable from each other now as they were before, Eleanor, and Myth. All with their Veils in place, the same iridescent sheen four times over. Sonya stands, still wedged into the corner.

"You don't have to keep me here," she says. "I haven't seen anything important, I'm nobody, you can just let me go and nothing will come of it, you don't—"

"Please." Myth holds up a hand. His palm is bright pink. "I am not here to listen to you plead your case. I am here to find out how we can contact Emily Knox and let her know that you are here. Perhaps she will agree to a trade."

Sonya doesn't expect to feel hope. She knows Knox, knows the disdain she has for Sonya, for everyone in the Aperture. And she knows people, too; knows enough to have stopped believing in them a long time ago, knows the allure of comfort and safety is like a fishing hook through the lip, dragging a person through life. But as it turns out, hope lives inside her, a pilot light not yet gone out. Maybe Knox is more than Sonya assumes, maybe she's grown to like Sonya more than she thought, maybe—

"She lives in Artemis Tower," Sonya says. "Near the market."

"Very good," Myth says, his voice soft, soothing. "Now, I know Ms. Knox well enough to understand that she needs more than the mere awareness of you being here. She needs that awareness to become concrete. Which is why we will be sending her your eye."

"My eye," Sonya repeats.

"Well, we can't fully remove your Insight here without causing significant brain damage, but your eye is symbolic enough," Myth says. "Don't worry, there will be a sedative."

Myth walks out of the room, followed by the guards, one by one. Eleanor pauses before passing through the door and drops something on the concrete, almost like she's tossing it out the window. It's a metal canister about the size of an apple.

She leaves, and closes the door behind her. The canister springs open, and white vapor spills into the room like the early morning fog. Sonya stares down at it for a moment. She feels her heartbeat in her throat, so fast and strong she feels for a mad moment like she might taste it, and then she covers her mouth and nose to keep herself from breathing in whatever this gas is.

Her lungs burn, her eyes burn. She's desperate to scream but has to keep herself silent. She sinks to her knees on the cement floor, in pain, in terror, desperate for air and desperate to stop needing it.

In the end, she drops her hands with a strangled cry and gulps fog into her lungs.

The effects are immediate. Sonya's mind empties. Her muscles go slack. She stares at the opposite wall and sees the bright halo of the Insight. When the door opens again, she's transfixed by the luminous Veil on Myth's face. It reminds her of a soap bubble. She knows—distantly, as if in a dream—that she should feel something. But she's a drained water glass, a well gone dry.

"Sonya?" Myth says. "How do you feel?"

She just looks up at him. Nothing comes to mind.

Only one of the guards enters this time. He takes her arm, gentle, and she stands at his urging. He steers her toward the edge of the steel table, and she sits. He presses her back, and she lies down, her heels at the edge of the table, her hands at her sides.

It's then that something trickles in. Her eye. Something about her eye.

She sees the Insight's glow, so constant it has become just a single thread in the weaving of everything she sees. She sees her father crouching in front of her to tie her shoe when she was a child, the white circle around his iris lighting up brighter when he meets Sonya's eyes. *See? It loves you as much as I do.*

She watches Myth pull on a pair of rubber gloves. There's a metal tray somewhere near her feet with a scalpel on it.

Her eye. Something about her eye.

She sees Aaron bending over her as she lies on the couch in his living room, his hair spilling over his forehead and the white light that greets her at the touch of his gaze, so like a physical touch—*Worth the DesCoin,* she thinks, as his lips draw closer to hers—

Myth picks up the scalpel in his steady, wrinkled hand. She knows the feeling of that hand on her, soft, dry. One of the guards appears in the doorway, his face shielded by its shimmer, breathless.

"Someone from the Triumvirate," he says, his voice rough. "Outside."

"How did they find us?" Myth demands.

Maybe it's the scalpel, or the familiar light of the Insight, or the mention of the Triumvirate. Maybe it's just that she's empty and to be empty is unreasonable, untenable. Whatever the reason, Sonya screams.

Into the void around her, inside her. She screams, and Myth's hand presses to her mouth, and she bites, feeling tendon and bone and skin between her teeth.

Myth swipes with the scalpel, cutting her cheek, and she flails, her body spilling over the edge of the table. She hits the ground hard, and the tray clatters beside her, and there are voices in the hallway, voices in her head, voices all around her.

The scalpel glints on the floor, in the dust. She grabs it by the blade, and it cuts into her hand; she fumbles for the handle and stabs it into the hand that reaches for her, the hand that belongs to the guard. The guard screams, and for just a second she can see his mouth through the Veil, a red yawn, a red wound, and a floor spattered red.

Over Myth's shoulder, over the man's hunched spine, Sonya sees Alexander Price.

He's breathless and windblown, his hair wild around his head. He holds an Elicit in one hand, outstretched, and a knife in the other, his hands crossed at the wrist.

"Peace officers are on their way," he says. "You can either waste your own time giving me a problem, or you can get a head start. Either way, they're going to get this recording."

Myth puts his hand on the guard's back and steers him into the hallway and out, away. The guard's feet leave bloody smears on the cement. Sonya drops to her knees, gasping. Something warm runs down her cheek. At first she thinks it's tears, and she's surprised by that, because it's been years since she's cried. Then she remembers the cut on her face.

Alexander crouches in front of her, folding up long legs like he's collapsing an umbrella. He puts his hands on her shoulders and squeezes, firm, warm.

"You're all right," he says. "Shit." He reaches into his pocket, takes out a handkerchief, and presses it to her cheek.

All at once, she thinks of the strip of photo negatives, his fingers pinching one end and hers pinching the other; the checkerboard between them, Alexander always playing red and her, black; the kitchen counter that kept him away from her, but not quite enough.

"Why's there always so much between us?" she says.

Sonya drops the scalpel between them and leans forward, until her forehead is on his shoulder. He smells like wet wool. Like rain.

THE peace officers arrive, flooding the warehouse space in their white uniforms, pants, shirt, jacket, and boots all matching. They put on gloves, and start to sort through the items in the room where she met Myth. They stand around the generator across the hall and talk about pulling the data from the power grid. They crowd the sidewalk outside. Sonya is sitting on the metal table, sagging back against the wall, when they come in to ask her questions. She blinks at them in response.

A woman comes in, her bright red jumpsuit signaling that she's a paramedic. She shoos the peace officers from the room, and Alexander, though he stays in the doorway where Sonya can see him. Judging by the oblong stain on his chest, she got blood on his already worn coat.

The woman's name is Therese. It's written on her lapel. She sets her bag down next to Sonya on the table.

"I assume by that look you're giving me that you were given some kind of sedative," Therese says. "Can you describe it to me?"

Sonya clears her throat.

"It was an aerosol," she says. Her throat aches; she sounds hoarse. "White vapor. I feel . . ." She frowns. "Empty."

"Sounds like Placatia to me," Therese says. "Delegation developed it for civil unrest, much good it did them. I thought the uprising destroyed it all—guess not. I'm going to inject you with something to counter its effects. Okay?"

Sonya nods. She thinks—she isn't sure. But soon enough Therese is dabbing the inside of her elbow with gauze soaked in sour-smelling antiseptic and piercing her skin with a needle. Cold spreads through Sonya's arm and clutches her heart. Her head clears. What spills into the emptiness inside her isn't something she likes. It feels a lot like a scream.

"Better?" Therese asks her, and she's not sure how to answer.

"She's better," Alexander says. He has his arms crossed. "Wouldn't be looking at me that way unless she was."

Sonya raises an eyebrow at him. He rubs the back of his neck and looks away.

Therese cleans the cut on her hand and the one on her cheek. She glues both shut, and bandages them. She offers Sonya an ice pack for her swollen jaw, presses a few doses of a painkiller into her hand, and leaves. In the quiet before the peace officers return, Sonya looks at the metal tray on the ground. There's a cautery pen beside it—for flesh, not for wires like the soldering iron in her apartment. A pile of gauze. A small jar.

She brings a shaking hand up to her forehead.

"How did you find me?" she says to him. "Using my Insight?"

"Can't track you without your UIA," he says. "But when you didn't check in at the Aperture, I was alerted. Right in the middle of developing some negatives, by the way, which is why I probably smell like rotten eggs—anyway, I watched your feed. There was a moment, before the door closed behind you—you looked at the moon." He takes the Elicit out of his pocket, taps it a few times, and shows her an image. It's a still from her Insight feed. A narrow view of the street, the moon, the skyline fading into the sky.

"I went to the club you were at," he says, "and I tried to recreate this angle. Took me a while."

Sonya laughs a little, the narrowness of her escape sinking in. She brings both hands to her face and leans back against the gritty wall.

"Awfully nice of you to save my life, Price," she says.

"Anytime," he says, shifting a little.

She nods, and tears open one of the packets of painkillers. Her head is starting to throb.

ONE of the peace officers takes them back to the Aperture. The last time she was in a personal-use vehicle was after her arrest. After the uprising found her surrounded by bodies in a cabin in the woods, they zip-tied her wrists together a little too tightly and put her in the back of a beige sedan. She doesn't remember much about the journey, just trees turning into houses and houses turning into buildings, just a few images of bodies in the streets and broken glass and smoke, the aftermath of the Delegation's overthrow.

She forgot how odd it is to move through a city teeming with footsteps and voices and trains and bicycles in a bubble of silence. She stares out the window, her nose almost pressed to the cold glass, until the car pulls up to the Aperture gate.

She feels heavy with what happened, like she came in from a storm with soaked clothes. Alexander gets out with her, and she doesn't argue like she did last time he tried to walk her home. He doesn't touch her, but she can feel his hand hovering at her back as they pass through the Aperture gate, as if its shadow has substance.

Renee and Douglas are standing just inside with Jack, passing around a bottle of moonshine. Jack has his notebook tucked under his arm. They all go silent as she steps into the tunnel that takes her to Building 4's courtyard.

Mrs. Pritchard's floral print dresses—there are three of them—hang in the courtyard, drying on the clothesline. Alexander sidesteps one to get to the door, folding his body around it.

He says, "Where does he live?"

She knows who he means. "Fourth floor."

Her injuries are on her face, her hand, but the rest of her feels sore, too. Fear is hard on the body. She climbs the stairs slowly. His hand really does touch her then, his palm steady at the middle of her back. She smells his shampoo, grassy and fresh. They reach the fourth-floor landing, and she keeps expecting him to turn back, to avoid the awkward reunion with his father, but he doesn't. He stands at the door with her and waits for Nikhil to answer.

Nikhil is wearing his favorite cardigan, gray with the brown buttons, and his reading glasses, which magnify his watery brown eyes. For a moment, he doesn't even see her. He just stares at his son. They may not have spoken in years, she thinks, but Alexander is still the thing that reoriented Nikhil's entire universe, when he came into being. Nikhil sags; he looks old and gray and tired. Then he looks at her.

"Oh my," he says. "Come in, come in."

He ushers her into his apartment. He's listening to her radio. She still hasn't finished repairing it—the wires are spilling out the back. There's a worn book facedown on the bed. Alexander stays in the doorway, his hands on either side of the door frame, like it's threatening to buckle and crush him.

"I didn't think she should be alone," he says. "That's all."

"Good." Nikhil doesn't look at him. "Thank you."

Alexander says, to Sonya this time, "I'll come by in a couple days to make sure you're okay."

"I'll be fine." It comes out colder than she means it to. Something like hurt passes over his face, only for a moment.

Impulse drives her toward him. She reaches for his hand. Loops her fingers around his strict knuckles. Squeezes. Lets go.

She never touched him, before. Every time she went over to his house, she hugged Nora, she hugged Nikhil, she kissed Aaron's cheek, but she never touched Alexander, not in greeting, not to squeeze past him in the kitchen, not ever. It felt like something bad would happen if she did.

And maybe it will.

He seems almost dazed. He nods to her, to Nikhil, and leaves.

Sonya closes the door and then leans against it, sighing. Nikhil is busy in the kitchen already, reheating a pot of—something. Lentils and tomatoes—canned, this time. A hunk of bread the size of her fist.

"What happened?" Nikhil says.

"I got in over my head." She doesn't want to tell him how, or why. She'll only feel stupid. She already feels stupid. "He helped me."

"Good," Nikhil says, and he sets her place at the table.

She doesn't know she's hungry until she lifts a spoon to her mouth. Then she eats fast, to soothe the ache of emptiness. Placatia. An evil drug, she thinks, and she wonders how she never heard of it before. Maybe because she didn't attend any demonstrations—just saw them come up in her Insight's newsfeed from time to time, or heard her mother scoff at them over the dinner table. *Freedom fighters, they call themselves. Freedom from* what, *I'd like to know.*

She uses the bread to wipe the bowl clean. Nikhil sits across from her, his glasses now folded in front of him.

"Do you ever . . ." She shakes her head. "Never mind."

"Do I ever what?"

She swallows the last bite of bread, and carries the empty bowl to the sink. She stands there without turning on the water. "Do you think the Delegation was good?"

"No government is perfect," he says. "But overall . . . yes. I do."

She looks up at the glass above the sink: eight blocks arranged in a rectangular grid. The red light from an emergency breaker bounces around inside them.

"The Analog Army drugged me and tried to cut out my Insight," she says. "The drug they used, it was developed by the Delegation. Placatia."

"Well, that was intended for use in extreme situations, dear."

"It's not just that." She braces herself on the edge of the sink. "It's . . . the DesCoin value of tampons, or the penalty of naming your child after your family instead of Nora's, or draining the parents' accounts of DesCoin because their kid rebels—points for posture, points for listening to their music, points for *sleeping with your spouse*—" She chokes back a laugh.

"Those are such little things—"

"The *children,* Nikhil!" She slaps the edge of the counter, hard. "The fucking children, taken from their parents."

She chokes again, not on a laugh this time. She closes her eyes.

"Sonya," he says. He moves closer to her, leaning into the counter beside her. "You've had a hard day—"

"This has nothing to do with the day I've had." She scowls down at her hands. "I keep finding out things I don't like."

"Then perhaps you should ask yourself: is the Triumvirate better?"

"The Triumvirate has nothing to do with whether or not the Delegation was good."

"In an ideal world, maybe not. But we are not talking about ideals, we are talking about practicality, we are talking about *reality.*" There's a light in his eyes she doesn't recognize. A tear leaks from the corner of his eye and spills down his cheek. He wipes it away. "If perfect systems are impossible, we must look at possible systems instead. And I would rather live under the Delegation than under . . . *that.*" He waves at the outside wall of the apartment, where the megalopolis is hidden behind a curtain made out of a bedsheet.

"The Delegation was good to us," she says.

He smiles. "It was."

"But it wasn't good to everyone."

"The Delegation wasn't good to people who worked to destroy order and safety, or people who flouted society's rules with no purpose," Nikhil says. "Forgive me for not being particularly concerned with those people."

"You had Aaron just because. Because you wanted a second child," she says. "So did the woman I talked to the other day, the one whose son was taken from her."

"The difference is that Nora and I went through the proper *channels*—"

"The difference is that those channels were open to you, Nikhil. They weren't open to everyone."

The look he gives her now takes her back in time, to the night she stayed out too late with Aaron and he tried to sneak into his house after curfew. Nikhil was awake, in his robe and slippers, and he turned on the porch light. He didn't shout at them, just looked at Sonya, watching from the curb, and Aaron, frozen on the front steps, with such profound disappointment that Sonya wanted to wither and die.

They didn't stay out late again, after that.

"You are changing," he says, "just because the world wants you to."

He turns away and moves into the living room. Sonya, face hot, turns on the faucet and sticks her uninjured hand into the cold water. She scrubs her bowl and leaves it to dry on a towel. She walks out of the apartment without thanking him.

TWELVE

THE NEXT MORNING Sonya wakes to aches and pains and panic. She doesn't remember dreaming anything, but her heart races anyway; she puts her head between her knees and steadies her breaths. Then she sticks her head under the kitchen faucet.

She dresses, and cooks some oatmeal, and boils water for coffee. As she eats, she looks at the sunlight glowing through the tapestry, the shapes of the buildings beyond it casting faint shadows. She scrapes the bottom of the bowl to get the last of the oats, then pulls back the tapestry and opens one of her windows.

The windows don't open all the way, but they open enough to let in a stream of cold air. She stares down at the street below, empty now, too early for spectators or corner store customers. She grabs her knife with the taped-up handle, wraps it in a dishcloth, and tosses it out the window, aiming a few inches beyond the curl of barbed wire a few stories below her.

It lands on the broken sidewalk just outside the Aperture wall. She closes her window and pulls the tapestry across it again.

She picks it up a few minutes later, her Aperture exit pass in hand. She holds the knife in her pocket as she walks to the train station, her shoulders tense, her body wary and ready. She keeps her hood up. She stands on the train with her back to the wall. The city smears past, one building melting into another.

She gets off near the market and as she nears Artemis Tower, she's more aware of her heart than before. The CAD proselytizer on the corner thrusts a pamphlet at her as she passes; she doesn't take it, and it falls at her feet. She slips on it, a little, in her haste to get away.

Artemis Tower glints in the sun like a gold filling in the back of someone's mouth. She ducks under a vine that has fallen across the entryway, and steps into the lobby. The guard recognizes her, and waves her through.

Sonya's hand is sweaty around the knife handle. She steps into the elevator. The leech Knox gave her is in her pocket. She pounds on Knox's door with it clenched in her fist. The mechanical eyeball in the middle of the door swivels toward her. It blinks, and the door opens. "Guest: Kantor, Sonya. Clearance level two," the computerized voice announces, as Sonya's name creeps across the ceiling in red light.

Knox's black hair is piled high on her head, and she's standing at the window in a pair of gray sweatpants. She glances back at Sonya, and stiffens. Her eyes skip from the bruise along her jaw to the cut on her cheek to the leech in her hand.

"Oh good," she says. "You made it."

"I did," Sonya says. "Thanks ever so much for the help."

Knox smiles a little, and wheels around. Her feet are bare, and leave sticky footprints on the polished tile.

"I did tell you that you would be on your own, didn't I? Did you think I was bluffing?"

"Why don't you tell me what this does?" Sonya tosses the leech at her. "The truth this time."

"What do you mean, 'what it does'?" Knox opens the band and stretches it flat, looking at the flexible tech inside it. "It copies and transmits data. I didn't lie to you about that."

"Then what *did* you lie to me about?"

Knox gives her that little smile again, and Sonya surges forward, taking the knife out of her pocket and holding it up to Knox's throat, the blade just beneath her jaw. She backs up against the window, showing her palms, and Sonya follows her, knife still high.

"Don't fucking smile at me," Sonya says.

"Calm down, okay? God, I didn't think they would even let you out of the Aperture with that thing." She sounds steady enough, but her next swallow is labored.

"Not sure why I should calm down," Sonya says. "You've been playing with me this whole time."

"I haven't," Knox says. "All right, maybe I have, a little—but if you kill me, you won't get the information you need, and that was really the point of all this, wasn't it?"

"You've all but ensured that I won't get that information!" Sonya says. "You knew that wasn't the Army's headquarters, didn't you? You knew there would be no server, you knew it was a fool's errand, so why did you send me in there? Just for fun? Make the Delegation girl dance, now that you've made her sing?"

"Get that fucking knife away from my neck and I'll tell you."

Sonya stares at the place where skin and blade meet, and wonders if she could do it. It's the feeling of standing on top of a building: all that separates her from an ending is a moment and a choice. Like when she didn't swallow the pill. Like when she stuck her thumb in that man's eye. She can know herself backward and forward, but in moments like those, she's still a surprise.

She lowers her hand, and steps back. Knox rubs her throat, pulling away from the window. She looks like a cat recovering from some small indignity, picking her way across the tile and perching on the edge of her desk.

"I've known where the Army's headquarters are for months," she says. "It's hard to hide that kind of power consumption in a city that monitors its resources the way ours does. They just don't know quite what to look for, and I do." She smiles a little. "Have you ever seen a magic act?"

"Get to the point," Sonya says. She squeezes the knife handle.

"The point is: misdirection," Knox says. "They already knew I was going to make a move. I just needed to convince them that it was a different one than the one I was actually making. So while you were there drawing all their focus . . . I did exactly what I sent you in there to do, at the same time I sent you to do it. I attached a leech to their server."

She touches one of the keys on her keyboard, waking up the screen that hangs above them. An array of windows confronts them, but in the center is a green progress bar, ticking up and down with the flow of data. Knox gestures to it broadly, sweeping her hand across the screen.

"In a little while," she says, "I'll have access to the UIAs, just like we planned."

Sonya grits her teeth so hard they squeak. "I guess it's a good thing I survived, then."

"If you hadn't, I still would have tried to find Grace Ward," Knox says. "I'm not a monster."

"Oh?" Sonya tilts her head. "You could have told me what was really going on."

"I wasn't sure you could lie adequately."

"I did," Sonya says. "I lied for you. Just so you know."

"I never asked you to," Knox says, quietly.

"I did it anyway," Sonya says. She puts her knife back in her pocket and moves toward the door.

"Hey," Knox says. "You still need to find out the name registered to Grace Ward's Insight. I assume the Wards didn't register it to the name Grace."

"Yeah," Sonya says. "I know."

She looks back at Knox, still sitting on the edge of her desk, arms crossed, hair lank around her shoulders. Knox has a point: she never promised decency. From the beginning, she communicated nothing but disdain for Sonya and the people in the Aperture. There's no reason to feel betrayed. She got exactly what she expected to get.

But there is something humiliating about hope laid bare.

She walks out, shutting the door behind her.

SHE sits on the curb across the street from the Wards' apartment building for the better part of an hour, chewing on the inside of her cheek until it aches.

The building is a block of red brick with twelve units and a side yard hemmed in by a chain-link fence. The Wards live in the street-level apartment closest to the train tracks. The one with the wreath of wheat hanging from a nail in the door. The one with the worn red welcome mat.

Sonya rode the HiTrain past this building every day on her way to and from school. The train stalled right next to it half a dozen times while she was riding, waiting for signal clearance. She once watched Mr. Ward disassemble a rusted swing set in the side yard for twenty minutes, getting tangled in the swing chains, stomping on a joint to get the bolt to detach.

Someone puts a grocery bag down next to her on the curb and heaves a sigh. Sonya looks up to see a girl in her late teens, maybe, with curly brown hair and full cheeks. She's wearing a yellow rain jacket.

"You can just knock on the door, you know," the girl says, nodding to the apartment across the street. "No one's gonna bite you."

Her voice has a familiar rasp.

"I'm Trudie," the girl says. "Ward. What happened to your face?"

"Oh," Sonya says. Trudie—Gertrude Ward—is the Wards' oldest daughter, the one who made Grace illegal. She is thick through the waist and pink-cheeked. Her teeth have the too-straight look of someone whose bite was corrected.

Sonya stands, brushing flecks of rock from the back of her coat. Good Delegation manners carry her when her own brain doesn't—she sticks out her hand for Trudie to shake. "Sonya Kantor."

She doesn't explain what happened to her face.

Trudie shakes it, and picks up her bag. Sonya spots a bunch of grapes inside it, and her mouth waters. She hasn't had grapes in a long time.

"Coming?" Trudie says, and she starts crossing the street.

Sonya follows her to the red welcome mat and into a bright kitchen. The room feels worn, but in a way that suggests warmth, and use, and fullness at the end of a meal. The floor tiles are cracked, the oven door splattered with grease on the inside. The cabinets are white, painted so thick Sonya can see the brush lines from where she stands in the entryway. A short, stout woman wearing oven mitts takes a loaf of bread out of the oven and sets it on the stove.

"Mom, Sonya's here," Trudie says, and it's like Sonya is a friend Trudie brought home from school; it's like she's young and welcome.

Eugenia Ward straightens, eyes wide, the oven door still open at her feet. Her oven mitts are shaped like lobster claws. She stares at Sonya. She's pretty, eyes big and warm, her hair a neat, curly bob pinned behind one ear.

"Oh," she says. "Oh. Hello, Ms. Kantor."

"I'm sorry to disrupt your afternoon," Sonya says, and all at once, Eugenia Ward remembers herself. She takes off her oven mitts and closes the oven door. She turns the oven off. Her fingernails are neatly trimmed.

"We've been wondering when you would show up," Trudie says. She's unloading groceries: grapes and apples, a bag of flour, a carton of milk. Sonya used to look into this kitchen—a different color then, she thinks—and feel the disparity between her home's gleaming white counters and the Wards' cracked Formica. Now she feels that disparity again, but from the other angle. The abundance of food here, of space, so unlike Sonya's bare cupboards in the Aperture. Even the extra weight around Mrs. Ward's middle looks like a luxury to her now. A sign of comfort and stability, to be soft.

"Trudie, don't be rude," Eugenia says. "I'm sure Ms. Kantor has been hard at work."

Trudie rolls her eyes.

"I just . . . didn't want to bother you until I had to," Sonya says. It's technically the truth, though perhaps not in the sense that Eugenia receives it, like a courtesy and not for Sonya's own comfort. Sonya's throat feels tight and dry. She clasps her hands in front of her.

"Oh! Please, sit," Eugenia says, gesturing to one of the high stools pushed under the kitchen island. "Can I get you anything? Orange juice? Water?"

Sonya can't help the way she brightens at the thought of a glass of orange juice. Eugenia smiles a little, and opens the refrigerator. Stuck to it with magnets are images of the Wards with Trudie, of a dog that Sonya sees curled up in the hallway, its tail next to its nose. A dog cost three thousand DesCoin, Sonya recalls. A big purchase for a family like the Wards, not favored by the Delegation, not working important jobs.

Eugenia puts the glass of juice down in front of Sonya as she eases herself onto the stool, still wearing her coat.

"You're hurt?" Eugenia says.

"It's nothing."

"You look just like the posters," Eugenia says, and in her mouth, it sounds like a compliment. "I wasn't sure if you would."

"Most people don't seem to think that's a good thing," Sonya says, and she sips the juice. She is shocked, for a moment, by how *sweet* it is. It feels grainy. Her teeth ache.

"But you were so beautiful," Eugenia says. "I mean, you are. And you were just a girl. No older than Trudie."

Trudie folds the paper bag and shoves it under the sink. "Old enough to refuse to be on a propaganda poster."

"Trudie!" Eugenia says, and Trudie walks out of the kitchen, popping a grape into her mouth on her way out. Sonya can hear it crack between her teeth.

"I'm sorry," Eugenia says.

"It's all right," Sonya says. "You're very kind, thank you." She sips the orange juice again. "I came here to ask you about Grace, Mrs. Ward."

The soft smile disappears from Eugenia's lips, but she nods. "I assumed as much."

Sonya clears her throat. "I know that because Grace was three years old when she was discovered . . ." She pauses. She begins again. "When she was *taken from you,*" she says. There's no sense in using euphemisms with this woman, who has aged a lifetime in the last decade, her forehead creased and the skin under her eyes, dark as a bruise.

"Which means," Sonya presses on. "Which means she had a black market Insight, likely provided by someone who worked in a Delegation morgue."

Eugenia flinches a little.

"I don't need to know the details of that . . . exchange," Sonya says. "But my best chance of finding Grace is if I know the name of the person that her Insight was actually registered to. The . . . dead person."

Eugenia smooths the front of her floral apron down. She licks her lips.

"I don't feel proud of that," Eugenia says, and her voice wobbles. She's crying, Sonya realizes. She sits up straighter.

"I'm not . . ." Sonya shakes her head. "I'm not in a position to judge anyone, Mrs. Ward."

"It's not what I did to keep my daughter that I'm not proud of," Eugenia says, and something like sharpness comes into her voice as she lifts her eyes to Sonya's again. "Why do you need to know?"

"I'm afraid I can't explain," Sonya says. "This investigation has taken me to some unexpected places. Places you probably don't want to know about."

Eugenia sighs. She wipes beneath one eye, and then the other.

"You listened to the voicemail we received a few weeks ago?"

Sonya nods.

"Then you'll understand what I mean soon enough," Eugenia says. "The name of the dead woman was Alice Gleissner."

Sonya hears the croak of the voice on the recording. *This is your Alice.* Alexander told her it was a reference to Alice in Wonderland.

"A ghoulish joke, perhaps, between my husband and me," Eugenia says. "We called her our Alice because we didn't want to trigger an alert from our Insights by calling her by a different name. We were assured that wouldn't happen, that the loophole would take care of that—do you know about the loophole? Yes, of course you do, you've done your investigating—but we never felt sure of it. So we gave her the nickname, and we told her it was because of the girl in the story, Alice in Wonderland."

"Oh," Sonya says. "Um—do you have a piece of paper for me to write the name down?"

Eugenia looks her over for a moment as if unsure of her. She opens a drawer at the end of the island and takes out a notepad and pen. Sonya scribbles a message for Knox on it—*here's the name Grace's Insight was registered under*—and asks Eugenia to spell *Alice Gleissner* as she copies it down.

"You're different than I thought you would be," Eugenia says to her, as she tears the sheet away from the notepad and folds it. "More serious."

"Yes. Well." Sonya tucks the paper into her pocket and pulls away from the island. Suddenly she needs to be gone, like she's been underwater for too long and is becoming desperate for air. She leaves the half-finished glass of orange juice on the counter and moves toward the door. "Thank you for your time, Mrs. Ward."

She's made it to the door when Mrs. Ward stops her.

"Sonya."

She looks back.

"Thank you so much," she says, "for working so hard to find our daughter."

Sonya draws a sudden, sharp breath.

"Don't," Sonya says, as she opens the door. "Don't thank me, please."

She leaves the house, forgetting to close the door behind her, and spills into the street, dodging a cyclist who screams an obscenity at her, stumbling toward the train station, taking deep gulps of air like she's never tasted it before.

She rides the train back to Knox's apartment, leaves the note at her front desk, and returns to the Aperture.

That night, she dreams of sitting at the table in the cabin as someone hums "The Narrow Way" right behind her, right into her ear. She stares down at the yellow pill in her hand, and when she lifts her head, she sees that the Wards, not her own family, are sitting all around her: Trudie, Eugenia, and Roger. They tip their heads back in unison, to swallow.

When she wakes, startled, she realizes she was the one humming.

THIRTEEN

SHE CAN'T GET the song out of her head. She keeps moving to its rhythm, chewing on its words. *Won't you set aside the lies that you've held dear.* She thinks of Sam in the sandbox, poking holes with a stick. The fog of Placatia inching toward her. The unobserved hours people bought from Knox. *Don't you know that what's better is right here?* When she got older, she thought of Aaron when she heard that. It would be good, she thought, to marry him, to have a nice little house and weekly dinner parties and two children—with a permit for the second, as the law required. No use resisting it, and no reason to. It was good, because it earned her DesCoin; DesCoin put everything in order, measured and ranked by desirability.

It felt easy.

She goes up to the roof, to the little greenhouse where the seedlings are growing. She knows enough about plants now to know they are best left unfussed with, so she just sits on the stool and watches them and hums the birthday song, to banish "The Narrow Way." Her hands are shaking and she sits on them.

She hears footsteps on the roof, and sighs. She hasn't spoken to Nikhil in two days, not since he told her that the world was changing her. She nudges the door open with her toe, expecting to find him there. But Alexander is there instead.

"Mrs. Pritchard told me you might be up here," he says. "She hasn't changed at all, has she?"

"No," Sonya says. "Did she scold you for something?"

"She commented on the length of my hair." Alexander steps into the greenhouse and makes it feel smaller than it already did. "She never liked me. One time I picked all her irises and gave them to my mom like I'd bought them."

There's trouble in his eyes. He's always shifty, but there is something desperate in the way he sticks a hand in his hair, tugs it. She doesn't want to ask about it yet.

"You were never good with small talk, either," she says.

"I'm still not," he says. "I tried to be a photographer for a while, you know—didn't really want to work for the Triumvirate. But a key component of being a photographer is dealing with clients. And nobody wants a sullen weirdo at their wedding."

She suppresses a smile.

"So," she says. "What's wrong?"

He closes the door behind him and uses the toe of his shoe to drag the other stool out from under the workbench. He sits across from her, his hands clasped between his knees.

"Emily Knox is dead," he says.

The song plays in her head, not hummed in the rich voice of her mother, but sung in a reedy voice to a bar full of strangers.

"Dead," she repeats.

Alexander nods. He looks at the seedlings, even now tilting toward the windows, toward the light. It's cold enough now to see his breaths.

"Peace officers found her body last night," he says. "In the water. There was . . . evidence of foul play. An investigator came to talk to me this morning; he knew I'd seen her recently. He might want to speak to you, too."

"I don't . . . I don't understand." Sonya closes her eyes. She can't take the sight of him anymore, brow furrowed in concern—can't take the way she can hear it in his voice, either, but there's nothing she can do about that—"I just saw her yesterday."

"You saw her yesterday?"

Sonya nods. The last sight of her—sweatpants, bare feet, arms crossed, hair unkempt, watching Sonya leave the apartment. She doesn't know how to feel now. Knox sent her into the meeting with

Myth with no regard for her life. Knox helped her, too, understood that finding Grace was what really mattered.

And now she's dead.

"It must have been the Army," Sonya says. "She sent me to them as a decoy so she could break into their actual headquarters and copy their data while they were distracted. They knew she sent me. They must have found out about what she did, and come after her."

"Their *data,*" he says.

"The Delegation data," she says. "They have it. That's why I was—that's why I *thought* I was going there, to steal it."

Alexander's fingers creep across his wrist, like he's remembering the leech cuff.

For a while they sit facing each other, their knees a few inches apart.

"Do you know what time it happened?" she says.

"Late last night," he says. "But they don't know where. No one can get into her apartment."

"They can't get *in?*"

"She has an impenetrable security system," he says. "Are you surprised?"

Sonya shakes her head. She hasn't thought about it. The mechanical eyeball in the door seemed too cheeky to be a real obstacle, but it can't be the only measure someone like Knox has in place.

A line appears between Alexander's eyebrows.

"There's something . . . not right," he says. "When the Army killed in the past, they claimed it. There were . . . *theatrics.*"

Sonya remembers. "The list of a person's crimes pinned to their chest."

"Yes, exactly. But this time—one of the most well-known people in the tech world, the infamous *Emily Knox,* and they kill her in the street and dump her in the water? You don't think this is something they would have proudly claimed?"

"Maybe they were desperate. They didn't have time to plan."

"Maybe," he says. "But why? What was she working on that made it time sensitive? She already had their data—if it was just about retaliation, why not wait until they could make a huge headline?"

"She didn't have all the data yet, the leech transmits slowly," Sonya says. "Maybe there was something they didn't want her to find."

"If she hadn't found it yet, they would have disabled the leech, and then there would be no time pressure," he says. "It has to be something she *already found.*"

Sonya frowns.

"She had the UIAs," she says. "I got her the name associated with Grace Ward's Insight yesterday. She told me once I did that, she could find her. You think someone killed Emily Knox over a missing girl?"

"I don't know," he says. "But I know John Clark came by my office to ask me to let this go. I know Grace Ward is being held against her will. And now the only person who was able to help us find her is dead, and no one is claiming responsibility."

He sounds tense, almost excited. But Sonya feels heavy. Deflated.

"Someone wanted to stop me," she says, "and they've succeeded. You realize that, right? There's nowhere for me to go from here."

"There has to be," he says. "You can't give up now, Sonya."

"Why not?"

"Your *freedom.*"

"Fuck my freedom, Sasha!" she snaps. "What am I supposed to do out there? I don't have any family, or friends. I don't have any skills. I don't have any dreams. I'm just wearing away at the time I have left, wondering why I didn't swallow that Sol ten years ago."

His face contorts.

"If that's really how you feel, why did you ever agree to do this?" he says, quietly. "I keep wondering."

"That . . ." She closes her eyes. "Is none of your business."

"Fine." He stands, and moves toward the door. Stops, looks back. "You just called me Sasha, you know."

She does know. She can still feel the name in her mouth, the wrong shape. The name she called him as a child, because it was what her mother called him. Back before Sonya hated him.

He hesitates with his hand on the door frame, then turns around, and touches her shoulder, gently, where it joins with her neck. She looks up at him.

"I'm glad you're still alive," he says. "If that counts for anything."

He leaves. She puts her hand on her neck, where his fingers touched bare skin.

WITHOUT Nikhil to remind her, Sonya forgot that today is the anniversary of the uprising. She remembers in the late afternoon, when someone in the city beyond the Aperture sets off fireworks. She pulls back the tapestry in her apartment to look at them. Sprays of blue and green and purple dot the sky above the buildings in the distance. Outside, this is a holiday. The day the people triumphed over the Delegation, at last, and freed themselves from the tyranny of the Insight.

Inside the Aperture, it's not a holiday.

She puts on her warmest sweater and her coat, grabs her flashlight, and makes her way downstairs. The widows are meeting in the courtyard. Mrs. Pritchard wears her pearls. She only has them in the Aperture because she was wearing them when the uprising arrested her and her husband. She could have sold them to a guard, gotten herself some luxuries—a down comforter, a rug, a refrigerator—but she refused. Sonya respects her for it.

Sonya greets the widows and walks through the tunnel. She pauses at David's name and turns on her flashlight to see it, carved in neat uppercase. Then she keeps walking, crossing Gray Street and walking straight into the tunnel that leads to Building 2. She hasn't been there in years. She ignores Gabe and Seby, sharing a lighter in the courtyard, and points the flashlight up at her family's names.

Julia Kantor

August Kantor

Susanna Kantor

She tries to remember their faces, but they're just smears in her memory. She doesn't have any pictures of them, just the vivid memory of them slumped over at the table, glassy-eyed, as Sonya sat frozen, pill in hand. She assumes the uprising cremated their bodies along with all the others, and discarded the ashes . . . somewhere. Some people in the Aperture treat these names like grave sites, they come here and talk to the dead. David always said that was stupid, they were just names on a fucking wall.

She turns off the flashlight, and walks down Gray Street. The others have gathered where Gray Street and Green Street cross. Instead of the market, there's a line of four people standing in the exact center, papers in hand. A representative for each building, to read the names of the family members who died in the uprising. Sonya forgot to submit hers, this year, but Nikhil won't forget.

She stands in the crowd. The first year in the Aperture, they did this ceremony with candles, but candles are a precious commodity now. Flashlights, however, are something everyone has access to. They're part of the first aid and safety kits the Triumvirate issues to the Aperture every year. Someone at the front of the crowd bangs a pot with a spoon to get everyone to quiet down, and silence moves through the crowd fast. Everyone turns off their flashlights, leaving the Aperture in total darkness. Sonya holds her flashlight at her sternum, like a vigil candle, her thumb poised over the button.

In years past, people gave speeches. Four years ago, someone decided to read a poem—that was a nightmare. But this year no one seems inclined. The representative from Building 1—Kathleen—just starts reading from her list of names. As she says the first one, "Michael Andrews," a flashlight goes on in their midst, a woman buried in the Building 1 section of the crowd. More lights go on in that section as Kathleen continues.

Fireworks go off in the city, *pop pop pop.* Sonya hears distant singing. Her feet go numb as she waits through the names for Buildings 1 and 2 and 3. She flexes her hands around the flashlight. Nikhil begins his list, his voice deep enough to carry. He doesn't forget her family. "August, Julia, and Susanna Kantor," he says, and Sonya turns on her flashlight, sending the beam up to the indifferent sky.

His voice wavers only once, on "Aaron and Nora Price," as he fumbles with his flashlight to turn it on. When he finishes, they stand in silence, all their flashlights turned on, casting an eerie glow on every face, so they look ghostly. Appropriate, since they're remnants of the ones they lost, incomplete, hollowed out.

Someone turns off their flashlight, and everyone else soon follows. She thinks about trying to find Nikhil in the crowd, but she doesn't want to tell him that all hope is lost, that the impossible task she believed she had been assigned at the beginning really is impossible now. Instead she finds herself moving toward Renee, standing nearby with Douglas and the others from Building 3.

"What happened to your face?" Renee asks.

Sonya almost forgot about the cut on her cheek, the bruise on her jaw. She shrugs.

"Fell in with some bad people out there," she says.

Renee frowns.

"Well, we're going to the roof to get drunk," she says. "Want to come?"

"Yeah," Sonya says. "I do."

MARIE, Kevin, and Douglas are trying to sing a round, a song from the school they all attended as children, but Kevin keeps missing the moment. He throws off the rhythm, and Marie stumbles over her words, and then all three of them collapse into laughter. It's happened a handful of times, but every time it makes them laugh harder.

Renee passes the bottle to Sonya. Sonya takes it, and sips. She recognizes the shape of the bottle—it used to hold flavored iced tea. It still has the ridges from the label, and the logo at the bottom.

The moonshine tastes like melted plastic. It burns Sonya's chapped lips. She licks them clean, and tastes the air, wet and cool.

"How many did you have today?" Renee says. Her eyes are unfocused and dull. She rolls her flashlight between her palms, pressing the button each time. On, then off. On, then off.

"Sips? I don't know, I haven't been keeping track," Sonya says. Her mouth is getting clumsy, the sounds running together. "Why, you gonna charge me a newspaper for each one?"

"No, no." Renee snorts a little. "People. How many people did they read for you today?"

"Oh, dead family, you mean?" Sonya sets the bottle down between them. She doesn't remember who makes this liquor. It might be made out of potatoes, or apples. Both are more common in the Aperture than other ingredients. "Three. Mom, Dad, sister. You?"

"One. My brother. My dad died when I was a kid, and my mom's still out there." Renee gestures to the city beyond them. It's the same view Sonya has from her windows. The fireworks are finished now, for the most part. Every now and then there's a pop, a whizz of light through the air. "Pretending she *tried* to help her misguided children, but they just wouldn't *listen* . . ."

"They didn't drag her in here anyway?"

"No, she helped the uprising, apparently. No idea how."

"Nice of her to bring you into it."

"It was, wasn't it." Renee smiles. "Still, I guess I'm glad she's not dead."

She picks up the bottle and holds it out to Sonya.

"To your lost trio," she says, and she drinks.

"To your brother," Sonya says.

Sonya lost more than three. She lost Aaron and Nora, too. Her closest friend from school, Tana, tried to flee with her family, and they didn't even make it out of the city. The people she saw every day, sat with at lunch, traded notes with in classes—some of them are in the Aperture, some are outside of it, but a handful of them are dead. And then there's David. Not killed in the uprising, of course, but crushed by the Aperture, its permanence.

Sonya takes the bottle out of Renee's hand, and shrugs off her coat. She's hot now, though the air is cold. She wants to feel the air on her skin, so she climbs up on the ledge of the building and starts to walk like it's a tightrope, her arms out to the sides.

"You know what I can't forget?" she says.

"What the hell are you doing?" Renee says. She sounds afraid. "Get down, you'll fall off!"

"Will I?" Sonya looks at her, and picks up one of her feet. Renee is on her feet, reaching for her. Sonya takes a swig of moonshine and dances back, so she's out of reach. "Like I was saying—I can't forget the steps. You know, to all those dances they made us memorize." She steps forward and back, holding her arms up in a pantomime of a partnered waltz.

"Yeah, I remember those, too," Douglas says. He's on his feet now, and the others have stopped singing. "Come down here, let's show everyone."

"Aaron wasn't a good dancer. He didn't know how to lead, so I had to do it half the time, at those practice sessions," she says. "It was odd, because he *loved* to tell people what to do. He *loved* it. And nobody thought I could do much of anything." She laughs. "Guess they weren't wrong."

"Aaron, huh?" Douglas says. "Your friend, from before?"

"Friend? Hard to say," Sonya says. "Assigned Life Partner, more like."

She turns to face the city. The grid of lights blurs in front of her. The air is cold.

"Fuck you!" she yells. She holds the cold bottle against her cheek, and it comes away wet with a tear. She touches her face. She hasn't cried in years. She licks the side of the bottle to see if it's salty. All she tastes is dust.

It would be easy to fall forward. Easier in some ways than swallowing Sol. In the moments before she almost died with her family, she worried that the pill would get stuck in her throat. That she would spill water down her front, like she sometimes did when she was nervous. It had mattered, to die without a wet sweater. To die upright and without difficulty. They said Sol was painless, but how could they be sure?

I'm glad you're still alive, Alexander Price said, and she wonders if it's him she's saying "fuck you" to, or if it's Emily Knox, or the three family members she got to say goodbye to but never quite forgave for dying, or David, because he didn't even leave a fucking note.

Regardless, she steps down, and Douglas wraps her in her coat. Marie takes the moonshine. Renee puts an arm across her shoulders, and pulls her in close.

THE next morning, she's still dizzy from the alcohol, though all the edges it softened are sharp again. She drags herself through her morning routine, achy and nervous, and before too long she's on the Hi-Train again, coasting to a stop near Emily Knox's apartment.

She's here on a hunch. A memory of Knox in her kitchen, eating a bowl of cereal when the door admitted Sonya—she hadn't let Sonya in; the door knew her, the way one Insight flashed in recognition of another.

There's also no other place to pay her respects. Sonya doesn't usually have bodies to grieve, so this isn't new.

She stands outside Knox's building, under the vines, and digs her fingers into her eye sockets to relieve some of the pressure. Her stomach threatens rebellion, but the cold air helps to calm it. She walks into the lobby, and the security guard raises an eyebrow.

"You heard?" he says.

Sonya nods.

"It's a fucking shame," he says. "Brilliant mind like that, gone."

"It is."

"Her door's not gonna open, you know."

"The door itself is good enough."

He doesn't stop her from walking past him to the elevator. She leans against the back wall to steady herself as the elevator lifts from the ground. The pressure change almost makes her vomit. The doors open again, and she trips into the hallway, swearing off moonshine.

Her heart races as she approaches the door. She pauses with her hand on the frame, sucks down a breath, then steps in front of the mechanical eye. A ring of white light around the pupil glows. The lock clicks, and the door springs open.

"Guest: Kantor, Sonya. Clearance level four."

Sonya stands still, her hands trembling.

She steps inside.

Part of her expects to find the woman herself inside, barefoot and drinking espresso, having faked her own death by planting a bloated corpse in the water.

She walks from room to room, kitchen to living space to bedroom to bathroom, and finds them all empty. There are plates and bowls and mugs here and there, bits of food still on them. Knox didn't make her bed; the blankets are still rumpled from her body, the pillow still scattered with long black hair.

Sonya picks up the bar of soap in her shower. There are pink flowers pressed into it. Her shampoo is apple-scented. She's out of toilet paper, and left the cardboard roll on the holder. A bottle of pills in the medicine cabinet reads "Uptiq," a common antidepressant. A container for contact lenses sits on the edge of the sink.

She wanders into the living area, with its wide desk and array of screens, dark now. Sonya doesn't have much computer knowledge. Everything she knew how to do, before, was done with the Insight. She sits in Knox's chair, anyway, and feels along the edge of the desk for the button to turn on the pink lights.

At last, she dares to touch the keyboard. She taps the space bar, and waits. Hope is a gnat. Hard as she tries to kill it, it always evades her. She hates it, and hates that it buzzes around her now as the screens flicker to life and she stares at the black expanse of Knox's terminal.

Then her name appears in the terminal box. Well, not her name, exactly.

```
Hello, Poster Girl.
C:\FortKnox\directory>cd
C:\FortKnox\PosterGirl
C:\FortKnox\PosterGirl>"justincase.avi"
```

Something hums. An image of Knox fills the screen—no, a video.

She sits in the same chair Sonya is sitting in, in the sweatpants and loose shirt she wore the last time Sonya saw her. She brings a knee up to her chest, and starts to speak. Her voice comes from everywhere—ahead of Sonya, behind her, on either side, the apartment full of her voice.

"Well, if you're watching this, things went sour in a big way," Knox says. "Which was always a possibility. I've spent my entire life poking different bears with different sticks, and one of them was bound to get homicidal at one point or another. Still, I hope this program never triggers. Maybe one day I'll show it to you, and we can have a nice laugh together. Do you think you and I are capable of laughing together, Sonya? I'm not entirely convinced you know how to laugh anymore."

She reaches out of frame and picks up a mug of espresso. She holds it against her chest as she goes on.

"There are a few things you should probably know, if I've given up the ghost," she says. "The first is that there's something I didn't tell you about stealing the Army's data—I didn't just steal it. I deleted it. My leech was . . . more like a screwworm. It attached to their systems, copied their data, and then devoured the original. Once the Army discovers that, they're going to be . . ." She smiles, but it's unsteady. "Incandescent with rage."

Behind her, the sun is setting over the water. She must have recorded this right after Sonya left.

"I did this because I don't think anyone should have this data," she says. "Because I believe in creating stable systems. The Delegation used location data to root out their detractors. After the uprising, the very things that made a person favored by the Delegation made them a criminal to the Triumvirate, and vice versa. Just because you're not committing a crime now, by going where you go, by seeing who you see, doesn't mean that another government, another set of people with another set of priorities, won't come along and call you a criminal one day. The players change, the rules change, that's an inevitability . . . The most we can do is build a board that restricts what's possible. We can create *limits to power.* Understand?"

Sonya leans forward, because Knox is leaning forward, all traces of humor gone from her face, her eyes glinting. She is a zealot, too, Sonya realizes, just like Myth and the people of the Analog Army. But there's less danger in this kind of zeal.

"My intention is to use the UIA database to help you find Grace Ward, and then delete it," she says. "If I'm dead, I won't be able to do that—but you can. I can't guarantee that you will. I simply have to believe it. I have to believe in you." She laughs. "It's difficult to believe in you, Sonya Kantor. Do you know how many teenagers were in the uprising? People who were raised to obey the Delegation, but saw it for what it was anyway, and were willing to die to dismantle it. People who *did* die to dismantle it. You weren't one of them. You don't get a free pass, Poster Girl, just for being young. But God, I don't know, I think I have to believe that you're not trapped in amber. I fucking hope so."

She sits back, and clears her throat.

"In the bottom drawer, on your right, are two sets of instructions. Printed out." She smirks. "The first will tell you how to use the UIA database to locate Ms. Ward. The second will tell you how to wipe my computer system. I wouldn't recommend doing the second until you have actually laid eyes on Ms. Ward, just in case."

Sonya rolls closer to the drawer unit under the desk and tugs the bottom one open. Two pieces of paper rest on top, one labeled UIA DATABASE and one labeled ENDGAME. Sonya folds Endgame and slides it into the inner pocket of her coat. She presses UIA Database flat, hands trembling. She starts to type.

Knox's notes are a jumble, her handwriting cramped and difficult to read unless it's describing code. Sonya types in nonsense sequences, her fingers unused to finding the forward slash, the carat, the brackets. She presses "enter," and a new window opens on one of the other screens. It displays a huge, detailed map of the megalopolis, a web of fine lines that, for a moment, Sonya doesn't even recognize.

Knox's instructions tell her how to open the side panel and search for a name.

TYPE IN WHATEVER NAME YOU GOT FROM THE WARDS, SURNAME FIRST, they say. Sonya thinks of her note, waiting with the security guard downstairs the other night. The one that just missed Knox. She types in `Gleissner, Alice.`

Nothing appears.

Sonya folds into herself a little. The map is moving, shifting, the lines redrawing. The grid of roads disappears in favor of wobbly lines layered over each other, odd shapes, shading and numbers. Topography. The signal isn't coming from the city; it's coming from the land *beyond* it.

In the center of the map is a blinking blue dot. A white square appears beside it, along with some text:

```
UIA #291-8467-587-382, "Gleissner, Alice
  Elisabeth"
47° 27′ 01.3″ N
121° 28′ 26.5″ W
Status: Online
```

FOURTEEN

THE HITRAIN CREEPS from stop to stop. Somewhere, a baby shrieks, and she feels an irrational desire to scream back.

`Status: Online.` The words pulse inside Sonya like another heart. Grace Ward is being held in the wilderness beyond the megalopolis; no wonder she was never found.

She fidgets. She doesn't have a plan beyond going. She'll go to the Aperture; she'll pack what she has for the journey. She'll find a map—somewhere. The library. The corner store. Possibilities unfold before her like she's fanning the pages of a book, passing too quickly for her to acknowledge them all.

`Status: Online.`

She's standing by the door when the train pulls into her station. She flies down the stairs to the street, and jogs in hard-soled, worn shoes to the Aperture entrance. Standing in front of the metal eye of the gate is Alexander Price, and he has that look about him like he's about to give her a revelation and it's not one she wants to hear. She stops a few feet away from him.

He doesn't actually look that much like Aaron, she thinks, and maybe she only thinks that because it's been so long since she's seen Aaron's face. His features are harsher, longer. Time has sharpened him—sharpened her and Alexander both.

He moves closer, and so does she. The street is empty except for the guard at the Aperture gate and the man working the counter at the corner store. They're in a pocket of silence.

"The Triumvirate," he says, "has officially revoked their offer."

The words settle inside her. Not heavy, exactly, but strange. "Oh."

"They've commanded you to return to the Aperture now," he says, "where you're to stay for as long as it exists."

"Did they give you a reason?"

"They said it's time to move on. They'll be eliminating my department entirely, and reassigning everyone," he says. "I think it's pretty clear now that whoever wants to stop us from finding Grace Ward is working for them."

She nods. She looks at the gate, the interlocking segments closed now. She hears what he said again, and it sounds new this time.

"Working for *them.*" She looks up at him. "Not *us?* Didn't they reassign you?"

"No, I've been fired, actually."

"Fired."

"Well, I argued with them," he says, "and I may have become insubordinate. And I may have purged all your Insight data from the system so they can't use it against you later." He tilts his head. "Don't worry, I kept a copy."

She thinks this should scare her, or upset her. The hope of freedom is gone. Knox is dead. Whoever wants her to stop, to leave Grace Ward alone, is desperate and powerful.

But she feels steady. She knows what she's doing. She knows where she's going.

"Do you have a map?" she says. "Of our entire district, woods and all?"

One of his thick eyebrows pops up. "Yes."

"Good," she says.

"Are you—you know where she is?"

She likes the light in his eyes when it dawns on him. She nods.

"Knox held up her end of the deal," she says. "I'd understand if you don't want to come, if you just want to be done with all this and go back to your life, but—"

"I'm coming," he says. "I'm not done, Sonya."

She likes, too, the way his voice softens over her name. She smiles a little, and together they walk away from the Aperture gate, and toward the HiTrain.

ALEXANDER'S apartment, located just one stop away from hers, is a cramped place full of objects. He collects things: chess pieces litter his bookshelf, little glass figurines decorate the table by the door, a cluster of bud vases with dried flowers sticking out of them populates the middle of his dining room table. Picture frames cover his walls, but the photographs are all buildings: grids of windows, the hexagon-within-diamond-patterned face of the King County Administration Building, where he worked, the stacked stripes of the Space Needle's squat belly. His bookshelves are full of cameras, old and dusty, new and polished, some in-between.

She stands still while he busies himself grabbing two empty backpacks from his hall closet, full of hangers with no coats on them; going into the kitchen to collect a loaf of bread and a jar of peanut butter; burying his head in his chest of drawers in pursuit of sweaters. While he packs, Sonya wanders into the kitchen, which has the grimy feeling of a place that will never be clean, no matter how many times a person scrubs it. The countertops are white Formica, with circles burnt into it here and there from hot pans. There are photographs on the refrigerator, too: groups of people laughing, or smiling at the camera with their arms around each other; a woman at the water's edge, in sunglasses; a baby holding a dog's tail in his fat little hand. She never thinks about Alexander Price having friends, or a girlfriend. She spends her time at odds with him instead.

She came into the kitchen for a reason. Sonya opens one of his drawers and finds measuring cups and spoons, a spatula, a garlic press. She opens another one and finds a paring knife in a plastic sheath. She slips it into her pocket.

Knox is dead. It doesn't hurt to have a knife.

Alexander walks in and offers her a backpack. It's full, but not stuffed. She settles it over her shoulders, and he hands her a hat, a pair of gloves, and a pair of sunglasses that slant up at the corners.

"Cat eyes, huh?" she says.

"Old girlfriend left them here," he says. "As well as a couple bras I don't have a use for, aside from maybe—slingshots?"

"Interesting idea," she says, as she puts the sunglasses on her nose. "Do you need to let anyone know you'll be gone?"

"No," he says, looking confused. "Like who?"

"I don't know." Sonya taps the woman in the photograph, the one next to the water. "Her?"

"Just a friend. Ryan is her name," he says. "That's her baby grabbing the dog, actually."

Sonya nods.

"I wasn't always alone," he says. "Mostly I haven't been. But—no one serious."

Alexander is still for a moment before holding up the map, folded up now so it's only as big as his hand. He unfolds it, and lays it flat on the kitchen table, knocking over one of the bud vases. It shows their sector, the megalopolis that stretches from the water to the very edge of the forest preserve, the wilderness beyond it, the river on the other side of it that separates them from the next sector over, ruled by some other group of politicians, some other system.

She takes the slip of paper with Grace Ward's coordinates written on it out of her pocket, and she finds the latitude while he finds the longitude. Their knuckles knock together when they find the point where latitude and longitude meet. It's a place in the forest, near a lake, in the shadow of a peak. Alexander draws a red dot there with a pen, and folds the map so that part is facing out.

"Looks like we can take the Flicker eastbound, to the end of the line," he says. "And then we're in for a long walk. If we go right now, they might not be looking for us yet."

Sonya doesn't know who "they" are exactly. But they're in the Triumvirate, which means if they access her Insight feed, they can piece together where she is, wherever she is. So she and Alexander need to get there first.

An hour later she sits on the Flicker in the seat next to Alexander. He stretches his legs long, under the seats in front of them. His backpack is between his knees. Together they stare at the advertisements on the bright screen in front of them. The pixels coalesce into a woman's face. *Live life without limits,* she says, her smile wide and white. The pixels spray apart, and then realign into the words `Focusil: for those who strive.`

Alexander makes a face.

"Do they always do that?" she says. "Advertise a product without saying what it is?"

"It's a medicine," he says. "But it's for the healthy, not the sick. Which is in fashion lately."

She remembers the graffiti she saw when she first left the Aperture: *Unmedication for All.* She wonders if the two are related.

"Are you on any?" she says.

"I'm on one for the sick," he says, tapping the side of his head. "Uptiq."

"Wouldn't describe you as 'sick,'" she says.

He glances at her.

"Do I seem well?" he says.

She thinks of the mood score Dr. Shannon always asks her for—her constant "fifty," the number for "fine." *Most people aren't fine all the time, Sonya.* But she is—she has to be. When she wasn't fine, she was trying as hard as she could to make time pass as quickly as possible, and it scared her. She scared herself.

Alexander—perpetually unkempt, uneasy in his own body—doesn't scare her like that. But there's a lot she doesn't know about him. Where he's been. What he's seen. What he wants.

"I'm all right, mostly. I've got friends, a job—well, up until a couple hours ago, anyway. I go on dates. Take pictures. Go on runs." He shrugs. "But for a long time, I'd see certain things, hear certain things, and—I couldn't breathe. Couldn't think." He clears his throat. Shrugs again. "It may not seem right to you, that I would be affected by what happened to them. But I am."

He stares ahead at the next advertisement, which is for synthetic trees that grow without light. `Bring life to your gloomy apartment!`

She doesn't answer. All her words have dried up. She rests a hand on his arm instead. A moment's touch, and then she opens the backpack at her feet to see what's in it, just to cover the awkwardness.

When she straightens, she feels heat at the back of her neck, and it's not embarrassment. She looks over her shoulder at the train car behind her. There are clusters of teenagers, an older couple sharing a meal bar, a few men in starched shirts, typing away on Elicits. No one is paying attention to them.

Still, she touches the knife in her pocket, to make sure it's still there.

By the time they get off the Flicker, their car is empty. An announcement informs them that all passengers must exit here, at Gilman. It's a sleepy place, a sprawl of low buildings, half of which were once occupied by little stores and fast-food restaurants, before the Delegation pushed for centralization in the megalopolis. Now their windows are covered with plywood. A peace officer cruises past on a motorbike, patrolling the empty buildings to make sure no one is squatting.

Two people get off the train behind them: a man in a wide-brimmed hat and a woman in shoes that snap. All of them move down the same road. Sonya feels them at her back, though they seem to be walking toward Gilman's only neighborhood, a little cluster of houses near the tree line.

Alexander takes the map out of his backpack and unfolds it enough to pinpoint their location. He points to the wide road bisecting Gilman—six lanes across, with a gap in the middle for grass and trees that are now overgrown, splitting the pavement where their roots are too thick.

"We take this," he says, of the road. "For a while. A day's worth of walking, at least. Then we'll have to make camp. Hope it doesn't rain."

They go to a little shop for water, sleeping bags that buckle to the front of their backpacks, and NeverFail, a brand of campfire fuel that lights even when damp. The man at the counter stares at Sonya. She stares back.

The backpack is heavy on her shoulders. It bumps against the small of her back every time she takes a step. They start toward the tree line. Low hills rise up in the distance, rippling green clothed in mist.

His strides are longer than hers, and she has to grab his elbow to get him to slow down, breathless already and they're only at the beginning. He obliges. He carries most of the weight in his bag, stuffed to the brim. She holds the map tight in her left hand, so tight her fingertips turn white from the pressure.

They walk for a long time in silence, until Gilman disappears from view behind them, until sweat builds up under Sonya's arms and she unzips her coat. The mist in the air is cool against her cheeks.

"When did you join the uprising?" she says.

He gives her a startled look. "I'm not sure we should talk about this."

"It's just sitting here between us all the time. You want to keep pretending it isn't?"

He sighs. Adjusts the straps on his shoulders.

"Late," he says. "I joined it late. Just a few months before the Delegation was overthrown. I got them access to Nikhil's work records. Everything that was stored on the Insight servers was also stored separately, in the department heads' offices. It was easy, really. He wasn't on guard with me."

"Well," she says, quietly, "you were his son."

"Is that how he talks about me?" he says, bitterly. "Like I *was* his son?"

She frowns at him. She sees a flicker of movement in the trees, but when she looks at it, there's nothing. A deer, she thinks, or a squirrel.

"No, he doesn't say that," she says. "I used to, though."

"And now?"

"Now," she says, "I wonder how you ever knew that what your family was doing was wrong, when everything around you said it was right."

His arm brushes against hers as they walk. She twitches away. Her jaw aches from clenching it.

His eyes soften.

"I just felt it," he says. "I would look up the people he sentenced, afterward. He called them criminals . . . but all I could see was desperation. And I was desperate, too." He sighs in a cloud of vapor. "I tried to ignore it. But I couldn't."

"I never felt anything like that."

"You did," he says, and he pauses, touching her arm to stop her. He stands a little too close. She doesn't move away. She should, though; she knows she should. Just like she knew that she shouldn't go into his room, all those years ago, and breathe in the scent of orange peel, and let him show her glimpses into other worlds. Just like she knew that she should never, ever touch him. He betrayed his family. And hers.

"I know you did," he says, his hand slipping away. "You think I didn't see you, then? The way you listened. The faces you made when Aaron talked, sometimes. Like you didn't like what he said. I saw that. You felt it, but you taught yourself to ignore it, because it was everywhere, because you didn't trust yourself. Because they *told you not to* trust yourself. 'Set aside the lies that you've held dear,' right?"

He frowns, his dark brow creasing in the middle. There are lines around his eyes already. He's not a teenager playing at revolution anymore. He's a Triumvirate lackey, a shabby thirtysomething with bits and pieces of relationships scattered behind him. She tries, *tries* to see him that way.

"You knew what your father was," he says, softly. "He gave poison to his own wife, his own daughters. Do you ever think about what kind of man that made him?" His voice shakes. "Do you ever think about why you didn't swallow it?"

She feels an answer rising like bile in her throat. But she doesn't give it.

They keep walking.

AFTER a few hours, they stop for a bathroom break. Alexander disappears into the woods to the right; Sonya goes into the woods on the left. She sets her backpack down and opens one of the water bottles to sip from it. It's not quiet in the forest, or still. Everywhere, the wind rushes through the trees, making leaves flutter like confetti, and squirrels scramble from branch to branch, and birds launch into the sky.

Alexander's question tugs at her mind. She thinks of her father passing out the pills, one yellow capsule for each of them. In her memory, it glows against her palm. He tells her he loves her. She knows the uprising is coming, knows it's a wave that will overtake them all. Her mother squeezes her hand, one last time. She knows what the pills are, what they'll do. The painless end they offer.

At what point does she decide not to take it?

She leans back against a tree and pulls her pants down to relieve herself. The bark scrapes at the back of her coat. When she's pulling up her zipper, she frowns. She hasn't heard Alexander's footsteps in a long time.

"Sasha?" she calls out, and she moves back into the road. She creeps closer to the trees, aware that she left her backpack behind her, along with the water. "Are you decent?"

A strangled yell breaks the silence. She sprints into the trees. Twigs scrape her cheek and the undergrowth tangles around her legs. Alexander is on the ground, a big, broad man on top of him, strangling him. On the ground nearby is something black and L-shaped, formed just so, just for the shape of fingers. A gun.

Alexander's arms flail. He wheezes, thrashes. The man pulls him off the ground and then slams him back into it. Alexander's head snaps back.

Sonya kicks the gun deeper into the woods, then dives at the man's shoulder. Startled, he topples over. She fumbles in her pocket for the knife, and then the man is on top of her. She thinks of her finger digging into her attacker's eye socket in the dark of her old apartment. She flails, wild. Screams. And then turns her head and bites hard into his hand. She feels the yield of skin and tastes copper.

The man yells, and punches. Sonya turns her head. She reaches up, fumbling along the ground for the knife handle. He's against her, heavy, his breath sour and hot. So heavy she can't breathe. She digs into the dirt above her with her fingertips. The blade bites into her fingers; she grabs the handle and swings, stabbing up, in.

Into the man's neck. He lets out a sickening gurgle. His blood is warm and it's all over her. She's looking into his eyes as they go glassy.

She squirms beneath him, chest heaving, desperate to get away from him. The weight lifts away and the man falls to the side; Alexander stands above her, one hand on the back of his head, his eyes wide enough that she can see the whites of them. Everything is quiet except for her breaths, shuddering in and out of her. They sound like they belong to someone else.

Alexander holds out his hand to help her up. She lifts her own, and the red streaking it startles her. Alexander takes it anyway. Her legs feel unsteady. Her body aches. Alexander tugs her toward the road, and she resists him. She wants to be away from those trees, that knife, the too-still form of the man in the dirt—but she has to see.

His throat is red gore. A Veil covers his face. She reaches behind his ear to deactivate it. His face is familiar, but so unremarkable she wonders if he looks familiar to everyone. He's older than she is, his eyes creased at the corners, but still young. His arms are splayed in front of him, his fingers curled, relaxed now in death. There's a bandage on one of his hands.

Frowning, Sonya crouches beside him, and peels the edge of the bandage back. On his hand is a neat cut, scabbed over now but still fresh.

"I think I did this," she says. "I think I gave him this cut. He's with the Army."

"He had a gun." Alexander scrubs at his face with his clean hand. "How did he get a gun?"

"I don't know."

"I don't get it," Alexander says. "I don't understand why they would follow us all the way out here like this. It can't just be that they want revenge for what Knox did."

"Maybe it is," Sonya says. "Maybe it isn't. But we can't ask him now, can we?"

She tests herself, taking one step, and then another, toward the road. She rubs the grit out of her hair.

"Sonya . . ." Alexander follows her. She dropped her bag at the edge of the tree line; she goes to it, and her hands tremble as she tries to open the bottle of water. Blood streaks the plastic. She can't get the cap to open.

"Sonya." He covers her hand with his own, stopping her. "Hey, hey. Look at me."

Frustrated, she throws the water bottle at the ground. He touches her shoulders, turns her toward him. Touches her face. His hands are cool on her neck, her jaw. She looks up at him, into his eyes, brown as a deep, clear lake in summer.

"You saved my life," he says.

Her throat is tight. She nods.

"Thank you," he says.

Her hands have come to rest against his wool coat, heedless of the stain they will leave behind. She bunches the fabric into her fists, and then pulls him against her, hard, her nose coming to rest at the base of his throat. His arms loop around her. They stand for a long time.

As she walks, she tries not to think about it—the man, the knife, the nearness of the end.

She's felt it before. At the table with her family, four chairs, four glasses of water, a yellow pill in her hand. A tablet, not a capsule, stamped with the letters *SOL.*

SOL. Short for Solace, a drug prescribed for terminal patients who sought lasting relief from pain. It induced a feeling of euphoria and connectedness, and then a heavy sleep that culminated in cardiac arrest. *Go gently into that good night,* the advertisements said, a nod to the old poem that revealed no one in Solace marketing had actually read it.

SOL. It was short for "shit outta luck," too, which is how Sonya felt at the table in the cabin, her mother humming and her sister weeping and her father pouring water. Four eyes aglow, four paths converging. The end is inevitable. Inexorable.

Four heads tip back to swallow. Then she watches them all die.

FIFTEEN

THEY WALK UNTIL dark. At one point they take a break so they can rinse the blood from their hands and scrape it from beneath their fingernails. Alexander is the one to suggest they stop for the night. They make camp in the trees, but still in view of the road. Sonya finds some almost-dry branches heaped in the undergrowth, and comes back to find Alexander struggling with the NeverFail log. She crouches next to him, and nudges him aside to take over.

She knows how to clear a space for it, how to unwrap the complicated packaging to expose the artificial log within without stripping it of the paper—the paper acts as kindling. She lights it with steady hands, and then kneels beside it with hands outstretched. There are cuts under her fingernails from when she dug into the earth. Her body aches from the struggle, from the walking.

Alexander gives her an appraising look.

"What?" she says.

"I didn't expect you to have any survival skills," he says. "I certainly don't."

She smiles a little.

"My father taught me," she says. "We used to camp when we were kids, just Susanna and me and Dad. Pretty sure I could catch us a rabbit if I had to."

She piles the branches she gathered next to the NeverFail, to feed the fire later. Alexander unrolls his sleeping bag. There are shadows on his throat from being strangled, shadows in the shape of fingers. He sits with the bread and peanut butter and starts making them both sandwiches. She stares at him through the flames as he does it.

"You know that song I had to sing for Knox?" she says.

He nods, without looking at her. "'The Narrow Way,' right?"

"Yeah," she says. "My mom was singing that right before . . . right before."

He pauses with a slice of bread balanced on his palm, and looks up at her. "Oh."

"Then my dad handed out Sol to each of us," she says. "And he poured us each a full glass of water. And that's what gets to me now—that he filled the whole glass when all any of us was going to need was a sip." She laughs a little. "I mean, Sol starts working pretty much right away, and I'm sure he knew that. It's funny, right? How logic fails us, all the time."

Alexander's brow furrows. She looks away, into the trees. The sky is so dark now that she can't see the outline of the branches against it. The moon is a hazy crescent above them.

"Sol doesn't kill right away," she goes on. "It induces euphoria. So after they swallowed it, they all started *laughing*. I didn't know what to do, so I just sat there. Every second that passed, I almost took it, I *almost* . . ." A shudder works its way down her spine. "But then they kind of just . . . slumped."

Remembering it is like looking at something through a glass of water. It has all the wrong shapes.

"I kept sitting there," she says. "Until the uprising came."

She looks at him again, and she's surprised to find his eyes sparkling with tears.

"You asked me if I ever thought about what kind of man it made him, that he gave us poison," she says. "The answer is no. I never do. I'm pretty sure I know what I'd see, if I looked that closely at it. And it's easier to just remember them all . . . fuzzily."

"What stopped you from taking it?" he says, softly.

"I'm not sure," she says. "But I think . . . I didn't know what I would be dying for."

The flames wrap around the NeverFail log, blue and orange and yellow. Their eyes meet above them. His look black at night. They focus on her like there's nothing else to see.

"You know," he says to her, "you never rattle just because the wind blows. It's a little unnerving, Sonya."

The firelight throws his features into sharp relief, the long line of a nose, the ridge of a brow. He sits cross-legged, a hand balanced on one knee, long fingers dangling. She looks at him, carefully. She wants to put her hands in his hair. She wants to peel back the layers around him. She wants to taste the dip in his collarbone.

She wants him.

She knows it now, and it's as if she's always known it and only just discovered it, at the same time. Her hands tremble with it. She gets up, moving around the fire to stand in front of him. He looks up at her, firelit and patient. He doesn't ask her what she's doing. She doesn't ask herself what she's doing, either.

"I feel," she says, "like this is a betrayal. Of all of them . . . but mostly of him."

"Of Aaron, you mean."

She nods.

"Only," she says, "it's too late."

He shifts forward, onto his knees. The fire is warm at her back. He slips his hands under her coat and rests them on her hips, his touch gentle, careful. He tips his head back and looks up at her.

"So betray him, then," he says.

He makes it sound easy, and maybe it is.

Easy—

She lifts the hem of her sweater over his hands, so his fingers are on her bare skin. His hands are cold and steady. She leans down and slides her fingers into his hair, all the way to the back of his head.

Easy—

Her hand tightens, holding him still as she kisses him. He surges up against her. He feels his way around her rib cage, to her back. He tastes like peanut butter. His breath stutters when she straddles him, sinking into his lap. It was never like this, before, before she let herself want things just to want them. No tally of right and wrong, good and bad, desirable and undesirable, only *this,* unwatched and uncounted, the taste of him, the warmth of him. How careful his hands are as he takes off her coat, tugs her sweater over her head. How he pants against her throat like he can't stop even to breathe.

She's bare, and the night is cold, but not the fire and not him. His hands clutch at her thighs. His head tips back against the pile of clothes they left behind, exposing the marked expanse of his throat. The end is near here, too, the all-too-breakable skin dotted with bruises from what might have been a tragedy. She touches them, lightly, as the two of them move together.

For the first time, she doesn't think of what came before.

She's only here. Only now.

SHE surfaces from sleep and, for a moment, before she opens her eyes, she forgets that she killed a man the day before.

Then she feels Alexander's hot breath against her face and the weight of him against her, and she jerks awake. Alexander is crawling out of bed and tripping, naked, across the dirt as he tries to put his pants on. She snorts with laughter, and he turns to look at her, eyes narrow.

"You laugh now," he says, "but when I refuse to hand you your clothes, it won't be half as funny."

She sticks a foot out from the sleeping bag they used as a blanket, and grabs her pants with her toes.

She dresses under the blanket for warmth, then wanders into the trees to find a stream that looks clean enough to wash in. The sound of moving water isn't far. She crouches beside a brook nearby and splashes her face; she wets her fingers and rakes them through her hair. She sits back on her heels and looks up, into the spiny branches of the Douglas firs and the pale clouds beyond them. She thinks of the man from the Army lying in the dirt with arms outstretched. She shudders, once, and then she can't stop shuddering, sinking to her knees in the dirt, her palms flat in the water.

When she returns to camp, her hands red from cold water and the hair at her temples damp, she doesn't say anything about the episode.

Alexander has a peanut butter sandwich ready for her. They eat sitting side by side, their shoulders brushing when they move.

"I hate peanut butter," she says. "We get it all the time in the Aperture—nonperishable, doesn't need to be refrigerated. I'm so tired of it."

"Were you just fucking with me when you said you missed Arf's?" he says.

"I was definitely fucking with you," she says. "But no, I love those cookies."

He reaches into his bag and takes out a bundle of tinfoil about the size of his fist. Inside it is a stack of butter cookies shaped like cartoon bones.

"Oh my God," she says.

"I think that was the first time I've ever heard you curse," he says, as she takes the cookies from him. "Also, these are the most boring cookies you could have chosen."

"Susanna and I used to break them in half," she says, demonstrating by snapping one of the cookies down the middle. "And whoever got the bigger half made a wish. Of course, she knew where to hold them so she always got the bigger half—"

"Oldest trick in the book."

"But sometimes she let me have it."

They pack up and bury the ash of the NeverFail log. The sun is out. Grace Ward is ahead of them, the bait on the end of a hook. Sonya ignores the sting of her blisters and the deep ache in her legs and tries to keep up with Alexander's long stride.

The Triumvirate has likely accessed her Insight footage by now, and can piece together where they are from what she sees. Sonya and Alexander got a head start yesterday, since her Aperture pass was good for twelve hours, but the faster they move, the better.

"I keep trying to figure it out," Alexander says, after a while. "Why the Army would be involved in any of this. And I keep coming up with nothing."

"I don't think we'll know until we find out where Grace is being held, and by whom."

"It's a good thing we have your Insight footage," Alexander says. "Simple enough to prove you acted in self-defense."

She looks up at him. "I'm going to be in the Aperture for the rest of my life. I've accepted that."

"Well," he says, just as evenly. "I haven't."

She thinks, *Idiot,* but with warmth she didn't expect. She puts her hand in his.

The road leads them through the ruins of old civilizations: parking lots with vegetation bursting through the pavement—so huge Sonya tries to imagine all the automobiles that would fill it, and she can't. Charging stations for electric vehicles that look like spindles with many threads, the cables now eroded. Stores for external ocular devices, the precursors to the Insight, with names like ClearVision and Secretary (OUTPATIENT PROCEDURE! GO HOME WITH THE ONLY HELPER YOU'LL EVER NEED TODAY! one sign reads, in bright pink letters). Spacious complexes for virtual reality gaming, the dated helmets lined up in the windows, covered in dust.

The businesses were abandoned with no one bothering to pack them up. The Delegation promised rewards for those who left the old in favor of the new. People vacated their homes and relocated to city apartments with wide windows; they traded cameras, phones, game consoles, personal computers for Insights, and the government paid them for it.

After one of these stretches of the civilization-that-was, Alexander stops to consult the map. Ahead of them, the road bends to the right. A sign somewhere behind them read TANNER.

"Time to leave the road," he says. "Where we're headed is close to that mountain."

He points at a hump of land in the distance. Sonya unzips the front pocket of his bag to take out his Elicit. He turned it off yesterday to conserve its battery—now they'll need it for its compass.

She lets him turn the Elicit on, since she still doesn't know how to use it, and steers them into the trees.

They don't talk as much in the woods. They're getting close to Grace Ward, and she feels it—in the clench of her jaw, the tightness of her shoulders. She ducks under low branches, waxy needles brushing her cheeks. She takes his hand as they climb over fallen branches or wet slopes. She doesn't need to ask him to slow down now—she's content to be breathless, panting into the wet air, if it gets them to their destination faster.

The scrambling of squirrels and birds accompanies their footsteps, the creak of trees in the wind, the chattering of water. The mountain is up ahead, itself a compass drawing them inexorably north. They stop near a pond for water, a bathroom break, a snack—she eats two slices of plain bread, instead of more peanut butter—and they sit on a log by the shore as they chew, looking out over the water.

"I just realized," he says, his voice sharp and sudden in the quiet. "You changed your mind when you saw her name."

"What?"

"You were adamant about not doing this whole mission. Up until the second you agreed to it, I thought you were going to tell me to go fuck myself and that would be the last time I ever saw you," he says. "But then I gave you the piece of paper with Grace Ward's name on it."

Sonya doesn't dare look at him. She watches the wind ripple the water.

"It wasn't the offer that changed your mind, it was *her.*" He furrows his eyebrows. "Why? Did you know her?"

"Not really," she says.

"But I'm not wrong. You're not doing this for your freedom, you're doing it for *her,* specifically."

She hesitates with a word between her teeth. But the moment has a certain inevitability in it.

"Yes," she says.

Sonya—sixteen years old, her hair curled just so—sits on the Hi-Train, near the window, and tries not to groan. *Minor disruption of the peace, minus three DesCoin,* she thinks. She stays quiet and waits for the train to start again. It stalls here, at almost the same place, every day.

She's just two stops away from home, on her way back from school.

Her backpack—green and gray, patriotic colors—is tucked between her feet. Her knees are together, and her hands are folded in her lap. She ignores the man dozing beside her and looks out the window.

A little girl swings in the side yard of the brick building next to the raised tracks. In another one of these stalled periods, she watched the father of the family construct the swing set, his face red and his forehead shiny with sweat. Now the girl pumps her legs back and forth, seeking height. The swing set bounces every time she reaches her apex. She has worn the grass away beneath her, probably from dragging her feet to stop herself when the swinging gets out of control.

It's dusk, later than Sonya usually goes home. She stayed after school to practice with her vocal ensemble group. She's a first alto, never a soloist, but a reliable keeper of the pitch. The concert is just a week away, and they're struggling with maintaining the rhythm between the sections. When Sonya tried to complain about some of the girls' inability to read music the other night, Susanna rolled her eyes and reminded her that she doesn't know how to read music either. *I don't need to,* Sonya replied, petulant. *I can hear the rhythm just fine.* Minus ten DesCoin for bragging.

The lights are on in the first-floor apartment, right by the swing set. Sonya can only see silhouettes in them, since all the curtains are drawn. Movement in a room toward the front of the house catches her eye, the busy shuffling and stepping of someone in the kitchen—the mother, probably. She sees the blue rectangular glow of a homescreen—the father, maybe, resting after work. She invents a family just like her own, but with one daughter instead of two, of course—these people, with their little apartment, their worn grass, their ragged curtains, would never be permitted to have two children.

Then something shifts near the back of the apartment. Sonya frowns, and leans closer to the window, until her nose is almost touching it. The curtains in the back room open just a few inches. The room is dark, but Sonya sees a small white circle between folds of fabric.

An Insight, shining in the dark.

Her heart races. Sonya's eyes stay locked on the Insight, and she thinks she can see, by its light, the curve of a small cheek, the point of a chin. Then the train starts moving, a calm voice apologizing for the delay. But Sonya can't stop staring out the window. She knows what she just saw: an illegal second child.

She sets up the equation in her mind, the same way she always does. There's a risk of a penalty here. She doesn't know the family in that apartment—maybe their daughter is the one hiding in the dark, and the girl on the swings is someone else in the building. She'll lose DesCoin for telling tales if the information isn't accurate. But no, she's seen the girl on the swings before, and she knows it was the girl's father who built the swing set.

No, she knows what she saw.

I WENT home," Sonya says, her voice flat, "and I told my father. I told him what I saw, and I told him where the building was. I was proud afterward. I was up all night waiting for my DesCoin count to increase. I bragged to Susanna when it did. I even told Aaron. All that green. Look how useful I can be."

She picks up a small rock near her feet, draws her elbow back, and throws it into the water. It drops in with a *thunk.*

"A few days later, the Wards were arrested, and the Delegation took Grace from them."

Alexander was quiet for the whole story, just sitting there next to her.

"You didn't know," he says, his voice creaking.

She replies, "I knew enough."

She's never been to church—there were no DesCoin rewards or penalties for religious practice, the Delegation said, and there's no church in the Aperture—but she imagines this is what it feels like. Seated, wishing you were someone else. Wishing you could walk backward through time.

He puts an arm around her, and she pushes him away and gets to her feet.

"I knew enough," she repeats, firm this time. "Come on. I owe her the truth."

THEY see the smoke from the house's chimney before they see the house itself. It stretches toward the sky in a single gray column, the mountain veiled in mist behind it.

The tire tracks come next. They're deep grooves, curving around a path that Sonya didn't recognize as a path until she saw them. Plants have sprung up in the depressions, suggesting that whoever drove here hasn't done so in a long time.

Then—the dark shape of a building through the trees. Their pace slows as they approach it. It's a cabin, though that word is too small for its size. Its front door is painted blue. There's a garden in front that reminds her, with a twinge of pain, of the seedlings growing in the greenhouse on Building 4's roof. It's caged in chicken wire, presumably to keep wild animals from eating the leaves.

Alexander stops her when they're still far enough away from the house not to be overheard.

"What if they attack us, whoever they are?" he says.

She looks up at him.

"Have you really come all this way without thinking about how the people holding Grace Ward might be dangerous?" she says.

"Well," he says. "Yes, actually."

She smiles, and takes off the backpack. Zipped into the side pocket is the knife she took from Alexander's kitchen. The knife she killed the man with. It's clean now, washed in a stream. About the length of her palm, with a plastic handle. She turns it so the blade is up against her arm, hidden by her sleeve, and touches Alexander's arm.

"I look harmless, so I'll go in alone," she says. "I'll signal you when it's safe."

She moves toward the house, ignoring his hissed objections. He won't risk her safety by coming after her now. She's in the open, in view of the blue door. She limps a little, playing up the soreness in her legs to appear even less threatening. She's a few feet from the bottom of the steps when the blue door opens and a woman steps out. She's holding something familiar.

A gun, she thinks, held up to the woman's eye, her hands wrapped around the body of it. Bigger than the one the man from the Army brought to kill Sonya and Alexander, with a long wooden handle. For a moment it's all Sonya can see, and then the woman herself—tall and gray-haired, wearing a sweater the color of oatmeal and a pair of blue jeans. There's a pencil tucked behind her ear.

"Who the hell are you?" the woman says to her. Her voice is like ice water.

"I just need some help," Sonya says. "I don't mean any harm."

"That why you're holding a knife?"

The woman nods to Sonya's right hand. Sonya reaches out to the side and lets the knife slip from her grasp. It tumbles into the leaves at her feet. She turns her hands so her palms are facing the woman.

"Just didn't want to be caught in a bad situation," Sonya says.

"Guess that plan backfired, didn't it?"

"Yeah, I guess so."

"Don't think you really answered my 'who are you' question," the woman says. "Though I guess the Insight kind of narrows down the options."

Sonya knows what guns do—that they shorten the distance between people. She can't turn and run now. The Insight's bright halo feels strange here, nestled in all these trees. Only moonlight shines like this, out here.

The woman lowers the gun a few inches. Her eyes are dark and creased at the corners. Her mouth is drawn and puckered. There's something familiar about her.

"You come from the Aperture," the woman says.

"I'm on the run," Sonya says. "With a friend. We want to get away from the city. If I tell him to come here, will you hurt him with that . . . thing?"

"Not unless he gives me a reason."

Sonya looks over her shoulder. She can't see Alexander from here, but she knows where she left him. She calls out, "Sasha!" and hears his footsteps on the fallen leaves. He carries her backpack with him, and his eyes flick between Sonya and the woman and the gun in the woman's hand, as long as her arm.

"I see," the woman says, raising an eyebrow. "Star-crossed lovers on the run?"

"Something like that," Sonya says, because if this woman is keeping Grace Ward captive somewhere in her house, it's better for her to have romantic notions than to suspect the truth. "We had to leave in a hurry, and we didn't pack enough supplies. We saw the smoke from the house from a ways off."

"So the question is," the woman says, "am I feeling generous?"

Sonya tips her head up and waits. The woman rolls her eyes and beckons for them to follow her inside.

The house smells like wood smoke and baking bread. There's no entryway to speak of, just a narrow, wood-paneled hallway that reminds Sonya of a coffin. To the right is a living room piled with cushions and sofas with no backs. The walls are lined with bookshelves, but only a few of them are full of books. On the others are bits of old tech. It's a combination, Sonya thinks, of Knox's apartment and the Analog Army building full of hair dryers and record players. Old tossed together with even older like a salad. Wires spill over the shelves like vines. This woman would know how to fix her radio.

She leads them straight back to the kitchen. The ceiling is high, with unfinished wood beams stretching across it. The cabinets, too, are wood, unvarnished and rough. But the counters are pristine white, like in a laboratory. Windows make up the wall opposite, displaying the forest, the edge of a lake, and in the distance, the rise of the mountain that was Sonya and Alexander's North Star.

"Can I wash up somewhere?" Alexander says.

"Not until you give me your names," she says.

Sonya hesitates. She doesn't know whether to give her real name or a fake one, doesn't know anything about this woman's allegiances.

"I'm not an enemy of those in the Aperture," the woman says. "Not an enemy of the Triumvirate, either, I suppose."

She adjusts something on the gun and sets it down, leaning it up against the wall. Sonya's jaw unclenches by a fraction.

“Then my name is Sonya Kantor,” she says. “And this is Alexander Price.”

The woman—now putting on green oven mitts—lets out a low whistle.

“Kantor. Now, that’s a familiar name,” she says. “I knew your father, Sonya. Did you leave him behind in the Aperture?”

“No,” Sonya says. “He’s dead.”

“Sorry to hear that,” she says. She opens the oven and takes out a loaf of bread with both hands. The smell makes Sonya’s mouth water. The woman sets it on the stovetop and takes off her oven mitts, then leans a hip into the counter. “Well, I guess fair’s fair. My name is Naomi.” She tilts her head. “I invented that thing in your brain.”

SIXTEEN

"YOU ARE NAOMI Proctor?" Alexander says.

"You don't need to sound so surprised," she says. "A gal could take offense."

"I'm sorry, it's just—you're *dead.*"

Naomi glances at Sonya. "I take it you keep him around for his looks, not his brains."

Sonya tries to remember the image of Naomi Proctor from the unit on the history of the Insight. The memories are hazy. Only the vague impression of a severe-looking woman with blond hair comes to mind. This Naomi, her gray hair so fair it's almost white, her nose straight and narrow, fits that memory well enough. The day of her death, too, surfaces in memory—not just the procession of the coffin through the street, but the service playing on their homescreens all day. Sitting in the living room together, listening to a somber speech given by the head of Insight Regulation, whose name has slipped from her mind. Every gesture of respect for the dead earned DesCoin, so the Kantors performed them all, even the ancillary ones. The day after, with her unfocused eyes scanning all the DesCoin they'd reaped, Julia told Sonya to buy herself a treat.

"They pretended you were dead," Sonya says, "and exiled you?"

"Not quite," Naomi says. "Sit down, I'll get you something to eat."

They sit on the far end of the sturdy table that stands before the windows. Alexander clenches his hands around the edge of it. It's a reminder: don't trust a woman who threatens you with a gun. Don't trust a woman who came back from the dead. Don't trust a woman whose house is the source of Grace Ward's UIA signal.

Naomi assembles food like someone accustomed to hosting, putting on the water for coffee; slicing bread and apples; pouring nuts into tiny bowls; arranging strips of dried meat. A few minutes later, she sits across from them with a mug of coffee gripped in both hands, the spread of food between them. Alexander is already busy with it; Sonya is more hesitant, breathing in the coffee smell and considering her next move.

"So," she says.

"So," Naomi replies. "They didn't exile me. After Regulation 82 passed, I wanted to leave, and I agreed they could tell people I was dead if it was advantageous to them."

"Regulation 82 made Insights mandatory," Alexander says, after swallowing a mouthful of apple and bread. "That was your technology, and it was about to be everywhere. Why would you want to leave?"

"You'll notice I don't have an Insight of my own," Naomi says, tapping the skin under her right eye. "That's not because I've had it disabled. It's because I never had one put in to begin with. I knew that if I bent to that particular rule, I would be submitting to constant observation, and that was something I didn't want. Nor was I interested in spending the rest of my life playing a game with every decision I made."

"I don't understand," Sonya says. "A game?"

"What do you think DesCoin is?" Naomi says. "Use a crosswalk, earn ten points. Jaywalk, lose ten points. Eat a healthy breakfast, earn five points. Indulge in a donut, lose five points. It's a game that assigns moral value to even the smallest decisions of your life. Do you know the term 'operant conditioning'?"

Sonya shakes her head.

"It simply describes how human beings learn," Naomi says. "That particular behaviors are shaped by their consequences. If you're a child and you grab a knife by its blade, for example, the resultant pain will train you not to touch blades again. If you're a parent and you'd like your child to learn how to pick up after themselves, you might offer them a reward for doing so. The Insight system made use of this psychological reality—it defined desirable behaviors and shaped people by offering either penalties or rewards. In effect, it treated you all as its children. It molded you into exactly who it wanted you to be."

Naomi picks up a piece of bread, breaks off some crust, and eats it. "Only," she says, "who gets to define what is and is not desirable? There are some things we can all agree on—we don't want people to murder or fight each other, we'd like them to feed and care for their children, we would prefer that they don't urinate in public. But things like humming on the subway, eating a chocolate, pointing out when someone is unkind to you . . . A relatively small, relatively homogeneous group of people decided that those things had moral value, too. And that certain things were suitable for some, but not all. You, for example, would be docked more DesCoin for raising your voice to a stranger than, say, your sister. Why do you think that is?"

Sonya glances at Alexander. Naomi Proctor seems to know Sonya's family better than she let on.

"Because *you* were being shaped, not for political power or influence, like her, but to be a supportive spouse and devoted mother," Naomi says. "Each of you quite literally lived in a different system under the Delegation, developed to cultivate particular qualities. For you, patience and passivity. For your friend . . ." She narrows her eyes at Alexander. "My guess would be, loyalty, a high tolerance for tedium, suppressed curiosity."

"I . . . Wouldn't we have noticed if we were losing more DesCoin for a given act than other people?" Alexander says.

"Those discrepancies can always be explained away by context. No one was privy to the exact algorithm that quantified behavior, and the differences for individual acts were relatively minor," Naomi says. "And even if you had realized, at the time, that you were being treated differently—who would you have taken your complaints to?" She smiles. "August Kantor?"

"He did have a system for taking suggestions," Sonya says, softly.

"Ah yes. Slip your complaints into this little box and we *swear*"—here Naomi lays a hand over her heart—"we will address them as soon as we are able."

Sonya sits back in her chair. She remembers, too well, the description of her person as laid out by the Delegation. Moderately intelligent, moody, and not interested in her studies—those must have been the qualities that determined her future. Compliant, though; trusting easily; lack of curiosity—those made her well-suited for the future they had offered her. They presented it like a reward: *Congratulations, darling. You've been assigned a special role.* Her mother was the one to tell her about it. *You're to marry Aaron Price when you turn eighteen.* Aaron, her friend since childhood, the two of them put together at every opportunity. *Isn't that exciting?* And it was. Everyone knew Aaron was poised to become someone important. And Sonya would get to be at his side when he became it, whatever it was, which meant she was important, too.

How early, exactly, had they decided who she was, and what she might be? Was she a teenager, when they put a cap on her usefulness to society?

Was she a child?

Thinking of it now, she wonders how it was presented to Aaron. Had they told him that because he would be someone important, he had earned himself a good wife? Sonya Kantor, beautiful, smart enough to be an interesting conversationalist, obedient enough not to cause trouble? *Congratulations, we've given you a special treat.* Bile rises in the back of Sonya's throat. She realizes that she is squeezing the edge of her chair so hard it's hurting her palms.

Alexander touches her shoulder, gently. She looks at him, her face hot. He nods a little.

"So you wanted to opt out," Alexander says, continuing in Sonya's place. "But they couldn't allow you to do that, could they?"

"No, there were to be no exceptions to Regulation 82," Naomi says, and it's as if she can't see the turmoil in Sonya, has no idea what kind of wreckage she's left behind. She sips her coffee casually. "They offered me a choice: get the implant and join the game, or leave. They were generous with me. Gave me a hero's death. Gave me this beautiful house. They arranged regular shipments of food and special goods. I always liked to be alone."

"And the Triumvirate, what? Just continued sending you things at no cost?"

"Indeed." Naomi smiles a little. "Don't underestimate the power I wield, boy. Do you know what kind of trouble I could cause if I came back from the dead and told everyone that their Insights hadn't actually been removed, and could be reactivated at any time? It's been said before, of course, but never by anyone as credible as I would be."

"What are you talking about, *reactivated?*" he says, heated.

Naomi tilts her head, looks at the scar running along Alexander's temple, a shade darker than the rest of his skin. "That scar is just for effect. Deactivating the Insight is not a surgical procedure, since the Insight cannot be removed without severely damaging the brain. You can only take them out after a person is dead. The Triumvirate consulted with me about this extensively. You can dismantle the system, turn off the lights—but the hardware must remain in place. The Triumvirate thought people would react violently to having dormant technology buried in their brains that couldn't be removed. They thought there would be mass panic. So they made a big performance of the deactivation process—give people a nice little scar to reassure them. The fact is, I could reactivate your Insight right now, Mr. Price. All I have to do is hook you up to a computer."

"How could you *do* this?" Sonya is surprised by the force of the question. Her lungs heave, desperate for air. "How could you make technology that does something you find so *evil,* so *repulsive,* that you won't even use it for yourself?"

Naomi looks at her like she's a child. Sonya feels like a child, too, about to throw herself on the ground and scream.

"It didn't begin that way, of course," Naomi says, flatly. "I was asked to come up with something more convenient than the Elicit. No one wanted to carry those things around all the time. We tried glasses—but people didn't want to wear glasses all the time, either. The implant was a marvel. Elegant. Injected into the eye, and then it used the body's own tissues to self-replicate and grow, like . . ." She laughs a little. "Like a living thing. It's not some foreign body that your brain has simply developed around; it's *you,* it's comprised of your cells, it's technology and flesh in perfect unity."

She sighs.

"It was *that* technology that I was most interested in," Naomi says. "Think what we could do if we could marry the synthetic and the organic so perfectly in other ways! We could give people back their missing limbs; we could replace their malfunctioning organs with perfectly operational new ones. We could extend life for decades. Wear out one heart, one spine, one pancreas—get another. It would be a world without the ailments that so often divide us or limit our potential." Her eyes sparkle. This is the warmest she's sounded since they arrived, and she's talking about replacing spines. "It's unfortunate that our government was so unambitious. All they wanted to do with this marvel of science, this *miracle,* was to peep into your bedroom window."

Naomi was never in government, Sonya remembers. She taught at the university. She taught *Knox.*

"What I'm trying to say to you," Naomi says, "is that I never really intended for the Insight to become a surveillance device. I made the technology I was asked to make because I had my own goals, and those goals were ignored in favor of the Delegation's goals."

They sit, Sonya catching her breath; Naomi finishing her coffee, hands trembling slightly; Alexander staring out the window at the forest beyond the house.

"I need to use the bathroom," Alexander says, suddenly.

"Down the hall, to the right," Naomi says. "Don't go wandering."

Sonya meets Alexander's eyes for just a moment, just long enough to register that Naomi Proctor seems to be hiding something. Or someone. The longer they stay here, the longer they give the Triumvirate to catch up to them, or Naomi to warn them. She just isn't sure that's something Naomi will want to do.

Alexander disappears down the hallway. Naomi moves her—now empty—coffee cup to the side and folds her hands in front of her. There are no rings on her fingers. She examines Sonya's face like she's trying to read it. Sonya wonders if she sees the blank canvas Marie saw, or the sharp edges Knox did. She seems to *know* Sonya's father, enough to know about his daughters. What else does she know?

"I really am sorry to hear about your father," Naomi says. "He was a kind man. Very proud of both his girls—but he had a special fondness for you, I believe. His poster girl."

Something cold spills into her chest. *His poster girl,* Naomi called her. But Naomi Proctor died—or seemed to die—when Sonya was a child, long before she ever posed for that poster.

"How did you know him?" Sonya says.

"We sometimes moved in the same social circles."

"It's just," Sonya says, frowning, "you'd think he would have mentioned meeting Naomi Proctor, famous inventor of the Insight. But he never did."

Naomi shrugs a little. It isn't an answer. She asks, "Did they kill him in the uprising?"

"He killed himself, actually," Sonya says. "My whole family did. With Sol. Rather than be arrested."

"Ah, Sol. The mercy drug."

"Is that what they called it?"

"The company that developed it, Beake and Bell, had a real knack for marketing terrifying things as if they were nice and friendly," Naomi says, with a small smile. She affects a high-pitched, gentle voice: "'Don't let your loved ones suffer another moment of pain. Sol: the mercy drug. Give them peace.'"

"To be fair," Sonya says, flatly, "it did look like they were having fun, in the end."

"So you were there."

Sonya nods.

"I wonder," Naomi says, "where he got it."

"The Sol?"

"Yes. It was a highly controlled substance. Not easy to get your hands on. Every single dose was tracked by the government . . . or so I thought." Naomi tilts her head, studies Sonya. "You know, you still remind me of a Delegation girl. The way you sit, the way you speak. You still act like you are under surveillance."

"I still am," Sonya says, gesturing to her right eye.

"I suppose that's true," Naomi says. "But I have to wonder, if you weren't anymore, how you would act. Who you would be."

"The Insight used to feel like a friend," Sonya says. "Like it was watching over me. You don't feel threatened by a parent checking on you when you're a kid, sleeping, do you?" She shrugs, and looks out the window. "But lately, it feels . . . it feels like it must have felt for everyone else, back then. Like someone's waiting for me to fuck up. Like they're looking for a reason to come after me."

Outside, a squirrel leaps from one branch to another. The branch bows under the creature's weight, and it scrambles toward the trunk, undeterred.

"Are you going to send them after me?" she says to Naomi.

"I may prefer the Triumvirate to the Delegation," Naomi says. "But I really have no interest in governments, in general." She reaches across the table and lays a hand on Sonya's arm. Her touch is gentle, but Sonya still jerks her arm away, startled. Still, Naomi says, arm outstretched, palm flat on the table, "Some unsolicited advice for you, my dear. When you leave this place, keep walking until you come to a place where no one knows you. That's the only way you can figure out who you are when no one is watching."

Sonya notes, in the back of her mind, that Alexander has been gone a long time. She gets up, and moves toward the kitchen.

"Can I have some water?" she says.

"Let me," Naomi says, coming to her feet. But Sonya is already standing in the kitchen, between Naomi and the gun that's leaning against the wall. Naomi frowns at her. Sonya frowns back.

Alexander steps into the doorway.

"There is a room upstairs with a very heavy, very locked door," he says. "Maybe you could give us a tour?"

Sonya and Naomi both move at the same time. Sonya gets to the gun first, grabbing it by the barrel. Naomi gets a hand on it and tries to wrench it from her grasp, but Sonya is young and strong; she holds on to it, swinging the other woman around so her shoulder slams into the wall. Naomi lets go, grabbing her shoulder in pain, and Sonya turns the gun around to hold it the way Naomi did. She points it at Naomi, holding it up to her eye so the other woman is staring down the barrel.

"You don't know how to use that," Naomi says.

"You know, it's really not that hard to figure out," Sonya says. "Worse comes to worse, I can still bash you over the head with it."

It's startling, actually, how easy it is. How her finger slides into place over the trigger, how the weight balances on her hand.

She says, "We came here looking for a girl. Her UIA led us here. Grace Ward is her name."

Naomi's face contorts. "I don't know anyone by that name."

"Don't lie to me. You told us yourself, Insights need hardware to function. Her Insight would have stopped broadcasting a signal if she wasn't physically here."

"If I show you what's in that room, will you believe me?" Naomi says. Her hands are up, palms facing Sonya.

Sonya jerks her chin. "We'll see."

THE gun warms in Sonya's hands as she follows Naomi Proctor down the narrow hallway to the front door, and then around the bend and up the flight of stairs that leads to the second level of the house. Alexander is close at her back. She can hear his breaths, coming in sharp bursts.

The weapon is heavier than she thought it would be, and more cumbersome. After a day of walking—or after a few minutes of struggling with every ounce of strength against a man much larger than she is—her muscles are sore and she wants to set the gun down. But she doesn't. Won't.

At the top of the stairs is another hallway that stretches in both directions. The walls here, like the ones downstairs, are wood paneled. There are no pictures hanging, no tapestries. There were no flowers downstairs, no vases, no little figurines. No sense of this woman beyond her fondness for wires. She takes them to the right, and the door

Alexander noticed is obvious: white, unlike the wooden doors in the rest of the house, with a substantial handle and a keypad lock.

Naomi types in a seven-digit code, and then looks back at Sonya with her hand on the handle. She doesn't look frightened, or ashamed.

Her eyes are full of pity.

She opens the door, and beyond her is a long, bright room. Everything in it is white. A white countertop wraps around the edge of the room, and there are machines positioned on top of it, black or red or gray blocks, as big as a torso, that Sonya doesn't understand. There are racks of vials labeled in spiky script. Screens stick out of the walls here and there, dark now. At the back of the room are metal racks stacked with supplies: boxes of rubber gloves, an array of beakers and glass flasks, pipettes, syringes, boxes with labels she can't read from here, an old centrifuge, a scale.

In the center of the room is a table, rectangular, with two rows of glass cylinders atop it, positioned two feet apart. They're lit from beneath. The solution inside them is faintly blue. Suspended in the solution, in each one, is something small and silvery that winks in the light.

Sonya draws closer. Whatever the thing is, it's about as big as her thumb, with tendrils hanging on the back, like the lappet of a jellyfish. At its head is something round and convex, like the lens of a human eye. She would have thought this was some kind of sea creature, if not for the circle of light at the top of the container, projected from the almost-iris.

The same circle of light burns in her own eye. These are Insights.

"You followed a UIA here," Naomi says, "because these Insights are suspended in a solution that tricks them into thinking they're still inside a body. I have kept them that way, for my research. I'm still determined to use this technology to grow organs that are half-synthetic, half-organic."

An Insight, Sonya thinks to herself, as she stares at the thing floating in the liquid. Naomi said that her Insight was *her,* injected as a kind of tadpole into her body as an infant, where it cobbled together a larger, more mature body from the minerals in her blood. This is its adult state, organic in shape but synthetic in color, like a child that inherited something different from each parent. It floats unmoving, as if it's waiting—but maybe she's the one waiting, waiting for the dread of the truth to settle into her body.

"So you're telling me," she says, "one of these Insights is Grace's."

"Yes."

The only way to remove an Insight from a person's brain is if they're dead. Knox told her so. Naomi told her so.

"Where the *fuck,*" Sonya says, "did you get it?"

"I think you know the answer to that already," Naomi says, in hardly more than a whisper.

Sonya lifts up the gun, though it feels so heavy it might topple her, and holds it up to her eye, the way she saw Naomi do, when she first arrived. *This is your Alice,* she thinks, and she has to swallow a laugh. Alice is Alice Gleissner, the woman whose Insight became Grace Ward's—but Alice is also the girl in Wonderland, and this is what's at the bottom of the rabbit hole.

"Tell me," Sonya says, staring down the barrel at her. "Tell me all of it."

Naomi pulls up straight and purses her lips.

"I harvested it from Grace Ward's body a little over ten years ago."

Sonya nods. She doesn't dare look at Alexander. She knows she'll find something soft and sympathetic in his eyes, and she can't bear it, because this isn't over, this isn't over yet.

She needs to hear the rest.

"You knew my father," Sonya says. "You knew him from after you died, after you left the city. You knew him because he came here, didn't he?"

Naomi's eyes are dark and cool, like earth firmed by frost. They meet Sonya's without expression. It doesn't matter. Sonya's hands shudder around the gun.

"Tell me," she says again.

"Your father took Grace Ward from her family and drove her out of the city with him," Naomi says. "He gave her Sol. She died on the trip. He brought her body to me, and I removed her Insight. Then he buried her."

Alexander says, "There are six Insights here."

"Yes," Naomi says. "Grace was the last one he brought to me, but there were others before her."

"Children." Sonya chokes on the word. "My father killed children."

Naomi only stares.

Sonya charges toward her, and pushes the barrel of the gun into Naomi's forehead, hard enough to jerk her head back, hard enough to leave a mark.

"Yes, or no?"

"Yes," Naomi says.

Sonya lowers the gun, nodding again.

Grace Ward is dead. She's been dead for over a decade.

She swings the gun like a baseball bat at one of the Insight cylinders, shattering it. Blueish liquid spreads over the tabletop. She swings again, and again, her arms aching, until every cylinder is in fragments. Underpinning the sound of glass shattering is a low moan that she knows is coming from her, but can't seem to feel.

Strong arms wrap around her entire body and hold her tight. She drops the gun with a clatter. Alexander's chin hooks over her shoulder and he holds her until she starts to sob, and even after.

AFTER some time—

Some length of time that Sonya doesn't feel at all—

After some time, Naomi takes her outside, behind the cabin, where there's a path worn into the ground, with greenery creeping inward to fill the space. They pass through an archway of Douglas fir branches, heavy with needles, and reach a mossy clearing. Arranged in a neat row there are stones, six of them, smooth, each one the size of a melon. They're streaked with beautiful colors, shades of tan, gray, and the teal of stormy water.

"Grace's?" Sonya says.

"I don't know," Naomi answers.

Of course she doesn't.

"Who are the others?" she asks.

"Older," Naomi says. "Too old now for the Triumvirate to look into."

Naomi leaves her there. Maybe she's going back to salvage her precious Insights, Sonya thinks. The image of Naomi Proctor in white gloves leaning over the still-warm body of a child to take a piece of technology from her head makes her want to vomit.

Faced with the array of stones that are placed too close together to be headstones for adult bodies, Sonya kneels. The ground is cold beneath her knees, and wet, and this place is too quiet, too lovely for what is buried beneath the surface. If the word *sacred* really means "set apart," then she supposes this place is sacred, in that it can only be a place for *this.* This horror.

And she belongs here with it.

SEVENTEEN

LATER, SONYA SITS at the kitchen table again, a mug of tea in front of her that she hasn't touched. She watches a spider outside pick a careful path across its web, and she thinks about sitting next to her father on the Flicker, his shoulder brushing hers as he took a plastic comb from his pocket along with a square of parchment paper. She saw him standing by an open drawer in the kitchen earlier that morning and didn't think to question it, but he must have been preparing the paper just for her, just for that. He wrapped the paper around the comb and held it up to his mouth, his eyes crinkling at the corners from a smile.

He breathed a single note into the comb. The sound was *loud,* squeaky. Everyone else on the train turned to look. A man across the aisle from them scowled at her with bushy eyebrows. August sang "Our Hollows"—another Delegation song—into the comb, and she let out a high giggle.

She remembers that his hands were gentle as he tipped the Sol into his palm, and he didn't fumble with the cap on the bottle. There was such ease in him, even at the end. Even as he gave his daughters poison to swallow.

The string from the tea bag is wet, and sticks to the mug. She leaves it there and walks through the living room, running her fingers over the wire-vines dangling over the shelves, the multicolored plugs with multipronged ends. She goes upstairs, and at the end of the hallway that feels like a coffin, she can hear Alexander and Naomi sweeping up glass in the laboratory.

". . . tell you why?" Alexander is saying.

"I was interested in the Insights. Not in anything else. And I needed ones that weren't fully developed, so it was—a mutually beneficial arrangement. He brought them to me, and I . . . cleaned up afterward."

Alexander makes some kind of pressed-lip sound.

"I just don't understand," he says. "Why kill them? All the other illegal second children were placed with adoptive parents. Why not just do that?"

"These children were older. Between three and five years old when he brought them to me."

"What difference does that make?"

Naomi sighs a little.

"You're asking the wrong question," she says. "You want to know 'why not just adopt them?' but the Delegation's question was 'why not just get rid of them?' The Delegation got rid of a lot of people. People who were outspoken about the Delegation's offenses, people who were undeterred by DesCoin penalties. Lawbreakers, upstarts, revolutionaries. People who were disruptive, disloyal. They just disappeared. Pruned from society to make a nicer hedge. After all, population control was also one of their priorities."

"This is different," he says. "These weren't people who violated the rules, they were *children.*"

"What is a child but a future dissenter?" Naomi says. "This isn't my logic, it's the Delegation's. Imagine, if you will, being old enough to remember when the government ripped you away from your parents. Imagine remembering their names, and where they lived. Would you be able to adjust to your new reality? Would you require counseling so as not to erupt into disruptive behavior in public? Would someone have to watch you constantly to make sure you didn't return to your old home? Would you grow up into someone who was an obedient, loyal servant to your government?"

"No," Alexander says. "I guess not."

The glass tinkles as he takes up his sweeping again.

Sonya shifts her weight, just a little, and the floorboards creak under her feet. She walks toward the laboratory, her cover broken. The table in the center of the room is clean and dry now. Alexander sweeps the last of the glass shards into a tray. The Insights themselves seem to be gone. If Naomi was able to recover them, Sonya doesn't want to know.

Naomi looks her over. Blank. The same way Sonya looks at her. They're equals, the two of them—not purveyors of suicide drugs or thieves of children, perhaps, but they're the ones who make it possible, who make it easy.

"Naomi says she can disable your Insight pretty easily," Alexander says. "If you want."

As a child, she thought it was part of her body, grown from infancy just like her hands or her feet. She learned about it when she was in second grade. The teacher described it like a recipe—a dollop of anesthesia and the pinch of a thick needle, the tiny machine compressed inside it only to unfold, umbrella-like, inside Sonya's brain; and voila, the Insight, her lifelong friend and companion, there to support her every need.

And it was that. It taught her why the sky was blue, how babies were made, what "dammit" meant, how to make cookies. When Susanna tried to trick her with a lie, the Insight made sure she didn't stay tricked for long. It gave her music that pulsed and pounded in her head, movies that made her laugh until her belly ached. It layered history and artistry over everything she looked at.

But these days it hounds her every footstep. It was a passive observer to the attack she fought off in the Aperture, and to the end that David chose without telling anyone, and to every Aperture overdose, assault, and neglected health condition. It watched as her father stole children from their parents and orchestrated their endings. The Triumvirate could be lying in wait outside the city, planning her arrest. The Insight is now a heartless thing, a creeping feeling at the back of her neck and a constant reminder that no matter where she is or how much trouble she's in, she's on her own.

"Yes," she says. "Turn it off."

She sits on a laboratory stool against the windows. Alexander leans against the counter nearby, watching as Naomi pieces together some equipment. Sticky tabs to attach wires to Sonya's temple and cheek and the place behind her ear. Hair-fine wires that tangle together and then bury themselves in a little white box. The little white box has a few buttons, none of them labeled with words, so Sonya has no idea what they do. Naomi attaches the box to a screen in the wall with a blue cable.

Sonya doesn't watch as she taps away at the screen. She looks at Alexander, and tries to remember him this way, at the exact center of the Insight's halo. She remembers running a palm down his body, fitting it around his hip. She feels like it happened years ago, instead of last night.

"Ready," Naomi says. She picks up a different device, this one not unlike the flashlight that a doctor uses to check pupil responsiveness. At the end of it is an open circle, like the halo, as big as Sonya's eye socket. Naomi stands in front of Sonya with it.

"Are you sure?" she says.

Sonya nods, and Naomi bends at the waist, then holds the device over Sonya's eye. She clicks a button on the handle, and there is a pulse of red light.

The halo disappears. Sonya startles, and brings a hand up to her eye to rub it, like she does to get rid of the bleariness of morning. Only the bleary feeling doesn't go away.

"It will take some time to adjust, but you will," Naomi says.

Sonya blinks rapidly. She's heavy on one side, and light on the other. Naomi puts her hands on Sonya's shoulders to steady her, and says, in a low voice:

"Remember what I said. Go to a place where no one knows you. Find out who you are when no one is watching."

SONYA sits on the back porch. The house faces northeast. The sun hasn't managed to burn through the clouds yet today, so she knows it's setting only by the blueish hue that blankets the tree trunks around her. The forest is quiet and still, a carpet of brown needles and moss undisturbed except by the occasional bird landing to peck at the ground.

Sonya covers her right eye with her palm, hoping it will ease the odd sensation of emptiness that now dominates her vision. It feels like there's something *there,* lodged in her eye, making it harder to see.

"It took me a few weeks," Alexander says. The door squeaks as he closes it behind him. He stands beside her, folding his arms as he looks into the trees. "But eventually it does get better. The weirdest part was missing it. I didn't expect to miss it."

"I don't miss it," she says. "I lost it ten years ago, when it stopped responding to me."

He nods. He's just stepped out of the shower. His hair, so much thicker than hers, is still wet in places—around his ears, in the wavy mass at the top of his head.

"Naomi says she'll drive us where we want to go. She has a truck in the shed." He points to the far end of the property, where a wooden structure stands, partly camouflaged by trees. "But we need to decide where that is."

He turns toward her, and takes her hands. His are warm, and strong. She remembers them grabbing her, eager, almost frantic, like he thought she would never let him touch her again, so he'd better get his fill. Wrapping around her thigh, knitting in her hair. She thinks, with the absurdity of someone laughing at a funeral, that she *will* let him touch her again.

"If we go back to the city, you'll be arrested and put back in the Aperture," he says. "Or worse. Maybe we should keep going—try to claim refugee status in the next sector. It might be your best chance at a real life."

She looks at their hands, linked. The cut from the scalpel in the Analog Army's building is still healing. Her nails are bitten to the quick. Her cuticles are splitting. She bears the effects of the last few weeks on her body.

"No one's watching," she says, softly—not to him, not to anyone.

"Naomi could send a message to the Wards," he says. "Telling them what happened to their daughter. She didn't offer, but—I bet I can persuade her."

A bird lands on the porch railing, brown and fat.

"Sonya, you can't change what happened, no matter what you do. You can try to move forward instead. Let all this go."

She nods. The bird pecks at the wood, shuffles back and forth, and then takes off.

"That sounds lovely," she says, in almost a whisper. She squeezes his hands. "But there's no such thing as starting over. There's only running away from something, or facing it. Those are the only options we get."

He looks down at her, brow knitted with concern, and then he nods. He lifts a hand to her neck, using his thumb to tilt her head up. He kisses her, slowly.

IT took a day to walk from the Gilman Flicker stop to Naomi Proctor's house. It takes a little over an hour to drive. Naomi spends the time clucking in disapproval. She wanted to drive them in the opposite direction.

When they drive past the jut of forest where they left their attacker's body, Sonya tastes bile. The memories are still there, though they now feel like they happened to someone else. The Sonya from before, the one who didn't know Grace Ward was already dead.

Naomi drops them off just outside of town. They walk in silence to the train station to wait for the next Flicker to arrive. There's only one other person on the platform: an old woman who doesn't give Sonya a second glance. The beacon of the Insight, which drew everyone's focus, is gone. Maybe, she thinks, they'll finally stop calling her Poster Girl.

The Flicker slides into place, whisper-quiet, and they board. Sonya leans into Alexander's shoulder once it's moving.

"Who do you think left the message?" she says. "The Wards' message, I mean."

"I don't know." He worries at his lower lip with his teeth. "Could it have been a prank? Some sick person who read the article about you?"

"They wouldn't know to call her Alice. It had to be someone the Wards knew."

He nods, but he doesn't have an answer, and neither does she. The air compresses around Sonya's ears as they pick up speed.

"Is there anywhere you want to go?" he says. "Before you go back. Just in case."

She thinks. Closes her eyes. "The waterfront. Suza took me there after school once. She bought me a sticky bun and we ate it on the embankment wall."

"And the smell didn't ruin the experience?" he says, laughing. "Always smells like dead fish up there."

"I mean, the bun was terrible," she says. "But Suza didn't hang out with me very often, so I loved it." She sighs. "I don't think I should take any detours right now, though. The Triumvirate will be looking for me."

"Yeah, you're probably right."

They watch the advertisements play—for Chill Water, a beverage laced with calming medication; for a book subscription service that carries only titles banned by the Delegation; for FaceMelt, a cream that makes scars disappear. Eventually the music, the crisp metallic voices, melt into the background.

"I keep thinking about you," she says, suddenly.

"What?"

"Remembering you, I mean," she says. "Sitting at your desk with those negatives."

"Oh, right." He ducks his head a little. "I tried to develop some of them, a couple years after the uprising, when the chemicals were available again. It wasn't quite the same."

"No?"

He shakes his head. "Under the Delegation, those negatives were almost contraband. Photographs, people think they just record whatever you see, but all those little adjustments the photographer can make—what you focus on, how bright it is, whether it's off center or not, those all affect what you see and how you see it. They're a language, only you don't need to speak it to understand it. So the negatives—they were people talking in a way the Delegation couldn't monitor. Looking at them was like hearing secret messages."

Each one is a world, she said to him, at the time. A nonsense thing to say.

She nods. "So after the Delegation fell—when anyone could say anything they liked . . ."

"I didn't need them anymore," he says. "I could think about what I wanted to say, instead of what I needed to say. Wanting things instead of just needing them—that's a gift." He shrugs. "I know you—maybe you don't see it that way."

Maybe she does, she thinks. But all that's in front of her is necessity. The advertisement for glowing vodka appears on the wall, eerie blue bottles against a black background. A man across the aisle folds his newspaper in half and sets it on the seat next to him; she resolves to pick it up before getting off the train.

"Listen," she says. "Don't come with me to the Wards'."

"What? Why not?"

"Go back to work, get your things. Make a copy of my Insight footage from the last week. And then—go stay with a friend. That woman from the beach, I don't know." She looks at her fingertips, still raw and red from clawing at the hard ground. "Someone tried to kill us on our way out of the city. They won't like it that you're back."

"What about you?"

"We both know I'm going to get arrested pretty quickly, even without the Insight," she says. "Don't worry about me. I'll be tucked away in the Aperture by nightfall."

ON the HiTrain, Sonya rehearses what she's going to say. How she'll refuse whatever Eugenia Ward offers her, even if it's a seat; how she'll allow her tone to soften, but she won't use any euphemisms. She mouths the words *Grace is dead* at the window, and wonders if this is the exception to Knox's rule against euphemisms, because "dead" sounds so unfeeling. An ill-tended plant is dead, an old packet of yeast is dead, but a little girl—shouldn't she be more than that?

A shiver goes through her as the train passes the Wards' apartment building—the same view she had over a decade ago, when she saw Grace in the window, with Alice Gleissner's Insight glowing around her iris. The brakes kick in and the train pulls to a stop. Sonya steps off, onto the platform. She drinks in the cold, wet air, and descends the steps to the street.

Waiting for her at the bottom of the platform are four peace officers, knights all in white.

Somehow this is not an outcome she anticipated, just a block away from the Wards' house. She assumed that without her Insight to trace her, the Triumvirate would be slow to find her; how did they know where she would go when she returned to the city?

"Please," she says to one of them, it doesn't matter which one—they're faceless, in their white helmets with the shimmering Veils. "I just need ten minutes. I just need to talk to someone."

"Prisoner 537 of the Aperture, we have been dispatched to ensure your safe and prompt return," one of them says. The voice is high-pitched and airy, but the person it is attached to is no less intimidating for it. She hasn't heard her number since she was first put in the Aperture.

"I know," Sonya says, frowning. "I know that, I just—I need to tell them what happened to their daughter."

"If you do not cooperate, we will be forced to restrain you," the peace officer says.

"I'm not *not cooperating,*" she says, frustrated. She is so close, she can see the corner of the Wards' building, red brick made dull by cloud cover. "I just—"

One of the peace officers grabs her arm, and she jerks away from him by instinct. This turns out to be a mistake. One of the others grabs her instead, and twists her arm behind her back, making her cry out. They pin her up against one of the platform supports, so the side of her face scrapes the gritty metal, and squeeze her wrists into a zip tie.

That's how she enters the Aperture, not ten minutes later. They pull her out of the car with no attempt at gentleness, and a bright floodlight goes on outside the gate in response to their movement. The twisting circle of the Aperture entrance opens to admit them, and the peace officers march her in. The group of prisoners drinking in the middle of Gray Street falls silent at the sight.

"You will be summoned for a disciplinary hearing," the peace officer closest to her says. "Check at the guard station tomorrow for the date and time."

"A disciplinary hearing resulting in *what?*" Sonya snaps. "I already have a life sentence."

"I assure you, things can always get worse."

The peace officer cuts the zip tie, and they file out of the Aperture, leaving Sonya standing there alone. She looks at the men standing silent a few hundred yards away. In the dark, they are just a cluster of white rings, Insights shining in the dusk. One of them, she recognizes from Building 1.

"Eddie!" she says. "Is Graham Carter at home? Do you know?"

He's forty, maybe, but the swig he takes from a bottle of moonshine belongs to a younger man. He taps the lip of the bottle against his cheek as he looks at her, without hunger, without interest.

"Why?" A quick smile. "Looking for a good time?"

Everyone around him laughs. Sonya turns away and starts walking toward Building 1. He calls after her: "Pretty sure he is, yeah!"

The tunnel surrounds her. Someone lit a candle and set it on the ground under one of the names, Margaret Schulte. It's been burning for a while, the wick surrounded by a pool of red wax. In the courtyard beyond, she sees dark shapes rustling the overgrown grass—rats, out for their nightly scavenge.

She climbs to the third floor, where the first apartment on the left is having a party. The door is open, cigarette smoke and laughter spilling into the hallway. When she passes, she sees a group of people sitting around a table made of packing crates, playing cards. She goes to 3B and knocks.

Graham Carter answers the door in his bathrobe. It's maroon, with a matching rope trim that has separated from the cuffs and now hangs around his hands.

"Ms. Kantor!" he says, and he wraps the bathrobe more tightly across his chest, belting it firmly. "What are you—"

His apartment is even more cluttered than the last time she was here, the corner stacked with old blankets and towels, the empty glass bottle collection expanded. A bottle of moonshine sits open on the kitchen counter, cloudy and yellowish, likely an ingredient in Graham's evening tea, left steaming on a nearby side table.

"You said my father was your friend," she says to him. "That he came by your office just to have lunch."

"What is this about, dear? I'm quite tired, and—"

She moves deeper into the apartment. Graham's bed is in the center of the room, with a crease in the middle of the mattress where it can be folded up into a couch. She runs her fingers over the deck of cards on his side table.

"The thing about that is, he never mentioned you," she says. "He told us all kinds of stories about all his friends growing up, and somehow you just never came up."

Graham looks puzzled.

"Surely you're not suggesting that I was *lying* about that," he says.

"No," she replies. "I'm not. There are two potential explanations for him not talking about you. One is that he didn't know you. The other is that he was ashamed of something."

"I don't—"

"Stop," Sonya says, coldly. "Stop lying to me. I already know what my father did. He killed people. He killed *children.*"

"Don't say such a thing," Graham says. His face, his soft-skinned throat—so like a bullfrog's—are splotched red. "Your father was a good man."

"No, he wasn't." She steps closer. "Stop being a coward."

Graham's chin wobbles. She thinks maybe he'll collapse like an underbaked cake.

"He came to play euchre," Graham says dully. He sits on the edge of his bed, sending a few small feathers soaring from his down comforter. "You remember what I told you, about the codes? Hearts meant Insights, gin rummy meant Blitz . . ."

"Euchre meant Sol," Sonya says.

Graham nods.

"How many times?" Her voice breaks over the question.

He looks at her the same way Naomi Proctor did when she let Sonya into her laboratory. With pity.

"Just," she says, "tell me."

"The truth is, I didn't keep count," Graham says.

It's worse than hearing a number, she thinks. There were six children buried in the woods behind Naomi Proctor's home; not enough to lose track of. This means there are other graves out there. Marked with stones, perhaps; not marked at all, maybe, the underbrush growing over them, well fertilized.

"Where did you get it from?" she asks.

"I didn't have it myself—Sol is highly regulated," he says. "But I facilitated the connection between him and someone who worked at the drug company, Beake and Bell. I didn't know his real name when I arranged contact, and I was never present for any of their meetings." He rubs a hand over his forehead, roughly.

"Great," she says, coldly. "Useful as ever, Mr. Carter."

Sonya turns to go. She can't stand to be here anymore, in this apartment that stinks of stale coffee and moonshine and the smoke from the party next door seeping through the walls. But Graham's voice stops her.

"I did overhear one of his conversations," he says. "He called the man by his name, and the man scolded him for it. It was an odd one—it sounded like a cardinal point. West . . . no, that isn't right—"

Sonya's hand is on the doorknob. She turns back, eyes wide.

"Easton?" she says. "As in, Easton Turner?"

"Yes, that's the one," Graham says. "Easton."

EIGHTEEN

SHE PACES BACK and forth down Green Street, ignoring the shouted commentary of the men nearby.

Easton Turner is one of the three most powerful people in the city. Someone who has reached the limits of what they can gain, and has everything to lose. His political career would be destroyed if anyone discovered he had given Sol to her father—and by extension, to the Delegation—to help him kill children. So while Easton might not have been able to stop the investigation into Grace Ward's disappearance without arousing suspicion, he likely didn't count on Sonya Kantor, spoiled brat of the Delegation elite, making any headway. It was, as she had thought from the beginning, a deliberately impossible task.

But he hadn't counted on her desperation. And she *had* made headway, thanks to Emily Knox, so he first tried to get in her way through Alexander, sending his assistant to imply that it would be better if Grace Ward wasn't found. Then, as she inched closer to the truth, he ended the mission completely, thinking that if she was trapped in the Aperture, she couldn't do any damage.

Maybe he's right about that, she thinks. What can she possibly do to him now? Everything she knows comes from criminals and liars, and she's never getting out of here. And she hasn't answered one of the most important questions: what does Easton Turner have to do with the Analog Army? They're the ones who came after her with a gun. Surely it wasn't a coincidence.

She stands by the gate for a while. The interlocking plates are squeezed tightly shut now. They will open again tomorrow, to admit the monthly supply delivery. A truck will steer into the middle of the Aperture, and peace officers will unload food, fresh and canned; cleaning supplies, toiletries, and clothes, donated by people in the city; and other household goods, lightbulbs and sponges and writing utensils. It's a desperate scramble every month. She usually sits down with Nikhil the night before to outline their priorities. They work better as a duo.

She goes back to Building 4. She's wearing clothing she borrowed from Naomi Proctor. There are pine needles sticking out of her coat, and there's dirt splattered on her shoes. She smells like the woman's soap—sharp, lemon and lavender.

She sidesteps a sheet hanging from the clothesline—it must be Wednesday, the only day Mrs. Pritchard allows "unsightly obstructions." She climbs the steps to her apartment, and pauses just outside, her hand hovering over the knob.

The rules of euchre are hazy in her mind. She played only a few times as a child. There's only one choice in the game: which suit will be the trump suit. It's made with limited information, as you can't know what hand your partner is holding. And after it's made, the rest of the hand plays out the only way it can. Mostly, she remembers the moment of tension as the trump suit is decided, and the moment of relief after all the choices are gone and only the hand remains.

She feels like she still has one choice left to make before she can surrender to circumstance.

She flips on the lights in her apartment and goes straight to the crate next to the bed. She takes out an old notepad with only a few sheets of paper on it, and a pencil, and sits at her kitchen table where little Babs carved her name.

Sasha,

I need you to send a message to Easton Turner's office on my behalf. Tell him I want to play a game of euchre at his earliest convenience.

—Sonya

After a moment of thought, she adds:

P.S. Thank you.

She folds it and leaves the apartment with the lights still on. In the courtyard she waves to Charlotte, taking her sheet off the line, who calls out, "Where have you been?"

"Be right back!" she calls back. She walks through the tunnel to Gray Street and around the corner to Green Street, past the tunnel to Building 1 and up to the guard station, where Williams sits with his hands folded over his stomach, dozing.

She taps on the glass. He startles awake, then nudges the door open with his foot.

"Your security pass has been revoked," he says. "What the heck did you do?"

"Good evening," she says. This is the last choice she has. After this, everything will play out the only way it can. "I came to ask you for a favor."

Williams crosses his arms and waits.

"You know Alexander Price, the tall, gangly one who's been passing through here?" she says. "There's something I left unfinished out there. I need him to finish it for me, only I have no way of getting to him. I was hoping . . ." She clears her throat. "I was hoping you would deliver this for me."

She holds up the note she wrote, folded in half with a sharp crease. Williams sighs.

"You know I can't do that," he says.

"I know you're not supposed to," she says. "I also know I have nothing to offer you. I'm hoping you'll do it anyway."

She holds her breath. The paper quivers a little in her hands. He looks at her, considering. She knows what many guards would ask for, if faced with a young woman of the Aperture in a desperate position. She doesn't know him well enough to know if he's one of them.

"Please," she says. "This is my last chance. Please."

His eyes are blue-gray, so pale they're unearthly rather than appealing.

"All right, all right," he says, and he holds out his hand for the note. "You happen to know where he lives?"

THE next morning she stays in her apartment. She doesn't want to answer questions about her blank right eye, or the bruises on her fingertips, or Grace Ward. She knows that she's clinging to something with all her strength, though she doesn't know what it is, and she knows she will falter eventually, and she'll free-fall. But not yet.

She drifts in and out of sleep until the afternoon. Then she drags herself out of bed and showers. She doesn't look down at her body, battered by the journey and the struggle with the gunman and the time she spent kneeling on the hard ground before Grace Ward's grave.

When she steps out of the spray, she hears the distant grinding of the Aperture gate opening. She runs to her windows and pulls the tapestry aside to see who's coming in—or going out. Waiting for the gate to open is a white personal-use vehicle with three blue, interlinked stars on the hood. Peace officers.

Whether they're here at Easton Turner's behest or here to take Sonya to some kind of trial, she knows they're here for her. She dresses in a hurry, her pants sticking to her legs because they aren't quite dry. She flattens her hair in front of the mirror and then pauses to stare at her right eye, no longer lit by its white halo.

She feels a pang deep in her gut. She doesn't look like herself.

Sonya pinches her cheeks to bring color to them and puts on her shoes. She runs down the stairs, passing Charlotte, who gapes at her, and calls out, "Sonya!"

When she reaches Green Street, she slows to catch her breath. Everyone is moving toward the gate, as they do every time someone comes into the Aperture. They don't pay attention to Sonya, weaving a path through them, until she reaches the gate. A peace officer stands with the guard—not Williams, this time—his hand balanced on his baton. His Veiled helmet turns toward Sonya.

"There. Ms. Kantor, we've been trying to reach you via your Insight."

"Well," Sonya says, and she sounds louder than she wants to, with everyone falling silent around her. "My Insight's not on anymore. So."

"I can see that," the peace officer says. "We've been asked to escort you to Representative Turner's office."

She puts on a good performance of confidence as she walks across the gap that separates the white vehicle from the residents of the Aperture that have gathered to see what all the fuss is about. The peace officer opens the back door for her, and she eases herself in, bringing her feet in last, as her mother taught her to. Ladylike in her bleach-stained pants and pilling sweater.

The Aperture gate opens again, and the vehicle reverses out through the widening pupil without waiting for it to fully dilate. She looks out the window at Renee in her housedress, and the vehicle speeds down the street.

The city looks strange from behind glass, like a dream. The car is moving too quickly for her to notice the cracks in the pavement or the trash stuck to the drains or the graffiti painting the walls with competing messages. From here it looks just as polished and serene as it did under the Delegation. But she no longer feels that the veneer adds anything of value.

The car pulls up to the Triumvirate building, which stands across the street from the diamond-patterned structure where Alexander worked up until a few days ago. This one is polished glass and smooth white stone, the seams between materials hidden so it looks like one solid mass. A grand staircase spills into the street. The Triumvirate's flag—teal, with three narrow white stripes across it—hangs over the entrance, snapping in a gust of wind.

The peace officer escorts her up the steps at a brisk pace that she struggles to match. He tries to grab her elbow, but she jerks it away from him, and he doesn't try to take it again.

The lobby is all glass, like the exterior. Matte floor tiles the same color as the flag; reflective walls that show Sonya herself from every angle. A woman in a sharp gray uniform stops them near the entrance. "Identification?"

The peace officer hands the woman Sonya's Aperture badge. The woman stares at it for a long moment, glances at Sonya, and hands the badge back to him.

"Carry on," she says.

They walk down a few short, dizzying glass hallways. Sonya sometimes mistakes her own reflection for an oncoming stranger, her own empty eyes unfamiliar to her. She loses track of which direction she's going. They step into an elevator and glide up two floors, and the hallway beyond splits off in three directions. They follow the center path to Easton Turner's door.

She clasps her hands behind her back to disguise their trembling. Sending a peace officer to pick her up in the Aperture is a declaration: Easton Turner has power, and he's willing to use it against her. A peace officer sent to escort her can just as easily become a peace officer sent to interrogate her, to disappear her.

A voice within the office calls out, "Come in!"

The office is a sprawl of space with nothing to fill it, a stretch of seamless windows, a wide desk, a neat row of filing cabinets, a bookshelf that hangs from the ceiling like a swing, and a chair for visitors. A man she recognizes as John Clark stands talking to Easton Turner; when she walks in, he takes an Elicit from Easton and, as he passes her, looks her up and down like she's less than he was expecting. The peace officer doesn't follow her in.

Easton's crisp white shirt is rolled up to his elbows, his top button unbuttoned. He smiles at her.

"Hello, Sonya," he says, like they're old friends. "Please, have a seat."

Her body winds up tight, but if he's going to pretend, so is she. She sits in the chair across from him—with crossed ankles, tucked back, her hands folded in her lap.

"Representative Turner," she says. "Thank you for agreeing to meet me."

She understands Easton's part in all this, how he used diplomatic means to suppress her investigation into Grace Ward. What confuses her is Knox's death, and the man who attacked Sonya in the woods—both crimes attributable to the Analog Army, not to Easton Turner. As far as she knows, the Army has nothing to do with the Triumvirate—if anything, they're a threat to the Triumvirate's stability.

"I trust you brought your own deck of cards?" Easton says. "Since we're playing euchre."

"Euchre is played with four people," she says. "Would you like to ask your fellow representatives to join us?"

She considers the tin of pens on his desk, closer to her than it is to him. There's a letter opener in it, with a slim metal handle.

"I'm sure they're quite busy." Easton Turner is still smiling at her. She's never seen him without a smile on his face. Always shaking hands, making speeches about tech regulation, about restrained progress, about opening up trade with the other sectors. *Wouldn't it be nice,* she remembers him saying, a few years ago, in a newspaper article that found its way into the Aperture, *if we could all eat bananas once a month, instead of once a year?*

Sonya, at that time, had not eaten a banana since she was a teenager, but she could still feel the dryness in her mouth as she swallowed it.

"Won't you stay awhile?" he says, and her hands go to her zipper automatically to take off her jacket. She freezes there, an odd echoing feeling in her chest like someone struck a bell behind her rib cage.

"I thought it was time that you and I had a chat," he goes on. "I heard about your little adventure in the woods. Oddly enough, your Insight seems to be malfunctioning—I'm sure I have Ms. Proctor to thank for that—so I wasn't able to watch it all firsthand, but I let the peace officers know where you would go upon your return."

"Naomi was very helpful," Sonya says.

"She's a very interesting woman," he says. "What did you two talk about?"

He looks harmless. The crinkling around his eyes. His white, straight teeth. But it's harmlessness that comes with effort. He leans forward, and at this distance, she can see that his eyes are a warm brown, like light shining through maple syrup. It's not a typical shade, and it reminds her of something.

"Well, she pointed me toward Grace Ward's grave, for one thing,"

Sonya says, as airily as she can manage, with a sour taste at the back of her mouth. "And she told me a little bit more about my father."

"Oh?" Easton says. "Such as?"

"He had a fondness for euchre, evidently." She plucks the letter opener from the cup of pens and lays it on its side across her palm. The dulled blade is etched with Easton's name, in delicate script. "And he used to play with you, didn't he?"

His smile doesn't fade.

"Your father and I met several times, enough for me to get an impression of him," he says. "It's a shame you were deprived of getting to know him as an adult. It might have been illuminating."

His voice is like the computerized one that announced her name in Knox's apartment, its pitch and pace predetermined regardless of subject matter. But it tightens when he says "illuminating," and she wonders about it.

"Sounds like you have some experience with that," she says.

"Most people have, Ms. Kantor."

Sonya nods, but she is thinking about his eyes. Warm brown. Just like the eye she caught a glimpse of behind Myth's Veil.

Myth, who also asked if she would stay awhile.

"You know, I figured out it was the Analog Army behind Emily Knox's death," she says. "And I know it was an Army member who attacked me in the woods. I just couldn't figure out how they were connected to you. I guess I just did."

"I'm not sure what you mean."

"Myth is your father," she says.

Easton's smile finally falters.

She goes on: "You clearly aren't in agreement with the Army's philosophy. But Myth still went to great lengths to ensure that his son's name wasn't sullied by whatever I found out when I traced Grace Ward's UIA," she says. "He must love you a great deal."

She feels something sharp in her chest, something aching. She's not sure that her father, who was so ready to take his wife and daughters with him during the uprising, would do such a thing for her.

"I'm sure he does," Easton says, at last.

"He seems brilliant," she says. "But a bit off balance, you know what I mean? I'm sure it's difficult for you to be related to someone like that, given your choice of profession."

"What are you getting at?"

"What I'm getting at," she says, "is that I'd like to stop this whole game you're trying to play with me." She waves her hand between them. "I reached out to you because I had information that could ruin you. You knew I had it, so you brought me here. Let's start there."

"It's interesting to me that you think you could 'ruin me,'" he says. "From inside the Aperture, and without proof."

"If I was so harmless, I wouldn't warrant a face-to-face meeting with you."

"Perhaps I brought you here to demonstrate how simple it would be to reach you, if that was something I wished to do."

Sonya forces herself to laugh. She sets the letter opener down on the desk.

"But you're a politician," she says, "and you know that it's silly to threaten someone who has nothing to lose—much better to bargain with them."

His eyes narrow by a fraction. She wonders how he expected this meeting to go. She knows that she's pretty, and as Marie reminded her, has a kind of natural blankness that causes people to project whatever they want onto her. Perhaps he expected to find what he read in the Delegation files. A girl with not much to offer.

But that girl—the poster girl—was never actually her.

"What is it that you want?" Easton asks, finally.

"To get out of the Aperture, obviously," she says. "And for you to leave Alexander Price alone. He wasn't responsible for this."

"And what kind of guarantee will I get in return that you will not share any information you have?"

"My sincere oath?" She smiles a little. "I assume that if I break it, I'll be found dead somewhere. It seems to be a simple task for your associates to accomplish. Is that not guarantee enough?"

He purses his lips, adjusts his shirt collar.

"You realize I could just do that anyway," he says.

"I wouldn't do that if I were you," she replies. "My untimely death might trigger the release of material you don't want to be made public."

It is not exactly a lie; she said "might." Let him wonder what that means. Let him wonder who she's talked to, what damage they can do.

Easton's chair creaks as he shifts his weight. Somewhere down the hall, or perhaps in the office next to his, someone is listening to opera. The soprano's solo is just finishing when Easton makes his decision.

"Congratulations, Ms. Kantor," he says. He smiles as if she only just arrived, the camouflage painted on again. "You completed your mission, and as promised, you will be granted your freedom from the Aperture under the Children of the Delegation Act. I suggest you take the evening to say your goodbyes."

"Goodbye, Representative Turner," she says.

NINETEEN

SHE DOESN'T RELAX until she's back in the Aperture. The gate closes behind her, and she leans against the exterior wall of Building 4 to catch her breath. Where the two streets cross, Gabe, Seby, Logan, and Dylan are playing soccer, the goals just soup cans set six feet apart on the pavement, on either end of the square. Logan kicks the ball to Seby, dirt spraying behind it, and Seby scores a goal. Frustrated, Gabe kicks over one of the empty soup cans.

She walks around the corner to Building 4's tunnel, and passes through the courtyard, where Mrs. Pritchard is weeding again. She looks up at Sonya and then does a double take, eyes wide.

"Your Insight, dear," she says. "Did you succeed in your investigation?"

Sonya's throat tightens. She nods.

Mrs. Pritchard gives a small smile. She can't remember the last time Mrs. Pritchard smiled at her. She's wearing her pearls, tucked under her shirt collar, and her hair is pinned back in a neat knot, but there's dirt under her trim fingernails.

"Have a good evening, Mary," she says, and by the time she makes it to the stairwell, there are tears in her eyes. She doesn't understand why.

A can of soup waits for her on her kitchen counter. Chicken noodle, the side dented—a grocery store donation. She stares at it for a long time. It's a gift, obviously, from Nikhil—the only person who goes in her apartment when she isn't home. Which must mean it's also an apology.

She takes out her can opener, and turns the can upside down to open it, avoiding the dent. She dumps the gluey soup into a pot, and laughs, breathy. Earlier she begged the peace officers for ten minutes of freedom. Now she has all the freedom she could ask for, and she's still in the Aperture making soup.

When the soup is hot, she carries it to Nikhil's door, oven mitts still on her hands. She knocks with her elbow. He answers in his second favorite sweater, mustard yellow, with patches in places where it has worn thin over the years. The radio plays in the background.

The place smells like bread, which must mean Nikhil had Charlotte over to teach him how to make it.

"I see you got my apology," Nikhil says to her, nodding to the pot in her hands.

"I'm going to be released," she says. "Tomorrow."

His eyes water a little, as they always do. He dabs at one of them with a handkerchief, and steps back to let her in. She sets the pot down on his table, and opens his kitchen cupboard to get bowls for them.

"We should summon the others, have a proper send-off," Nikhil says.

Sonya shakes her head. She sets the bowls down, then goes back for the spoons.

"I have a lot to tell you," she says.

Her hands tremble as she sorts through the spoons, looking for the big ones they use for soup. The clatter of the silverware is louder even than the radio. Nikhil sets his hand on her shoulder, in a gesture that reminds her of Alexander—how he is so careful not to startle her.

"I hate goodbyes," she says, and her breath catches.

"So let's not say them," he says. "Let's pretend absolutely nothing is going to change."

She nods, and sits down at the table in her usual place. She takes off the pot lid and Nikhil hands her a ladle.

It's possible Nikhil knows the truth about her father, that he always has. It's possible he's lied to her hundreds of times over the last ten years. The last few days have taught her that there's no clarity in love, no honesty—that a person doesn't become better than they are just because you love them.

She remembers, though, that last year Building 4 tried to throw her a surprise birthday party, and the truth seemed to bubble up in Nikhil's throat every time he was around her. When he asked her to go to Charlotte's apartment "for a bit of sugar," he was downright gleeful. He may or may not be willing to lie to her, but he's not particularly good at it.

So she doesn't ask him if he knew what her father was doing, because she doesn't believe he did—but also because she doesn't want to know, not now, not the night before she leaves and won't be permitted to come back. She'll never sit in this apartment at Mr. Nadir's old table, poking around in the back of a radio just because Nikhil says it's a good idea. She'll never rush to the roof in the morning to see if the seedlings have sprouted yet, like a child waking up in the winter to see if the snow forecast was right. Or demand that Charlotte play the Katherine music, even though the rest of Building 4 hates it; or exchange passive-aggressive remarks with Mrs. Pritchard about the state of her hair; or walk to the market with a basket of mint leaves, hoping to exchange them for a new towel or a pair of sneakers.

She closes her eyes, unable to look at Nikhil, suddenly, at this particular angle of his apartment, the warm light, the handkerchief he keeps in one hand to dab away tears, the beat-up table between them. His hand covers hers, and squeezes.

"Just like the life you had before you came here," he says to her, "this life will soon be closed off to you, yes. It's like . . . a cauterized wound. You have to seal it to stop it from killing you. But life is full of this . . . letting things change."

She turns her hand, and holds on to him.

"I will spend the rest of my life here," he says to her. She looks at him, into his bright, watery eyes, the color of an acorn kernel, a moth eyespot. "You can't possibly understand how relieved I am to know you won't have to."

She nods. She doesn't cry, because she hates to cry, but it's a near thing. "Take care of the garden," she says.

AFTER dinner she walks to Building 3. The moon is high and clear. Music with a heavy beat throbs in a distant apartment. The center of the Aperture is empty, the soup cans still left from the game of soccer. Near the corner of Building 1, she sees something shifting in the wind—just a weed, she realizes, when she draws closer. A dandelion, bare of seeds now, collapsing into winter.

She picked a dandelion for David's funeral. When he was alive, he brought them to her whenever he found them—they grew in abundance in the courtyard. Sometimes he made them into crowns for her, or bracelets, by splitting the stems and weaving them together. He told her rarity conferred value, and in the Aperture, even a weed was rare. *Besides,* he said, tucking one of them behind her ear, *what a nice shade of yellow.*

She walks through the tunnel to Building 3, and the names of the lost crowd around her like ghosts. Jack is sitting in the courtyard, reading by flashlight. His Insight is all she can see of his face.

"Hey there, Poster Girl," he says, without looking up. "What's cooking out there?"

"Same old," she says. "Good book?"

"Whoever donated it left notes in the margins," he says. "I like reading those more than the book, to be honest."

She laughs, and opens the door to the stairwell. She climbs up to Renee and Douglas's apartment and knocks on the door.

"Sleeping, Kevin!" Douglas shouts from within the apartment.

"Not Kevin!" Sonya says.

She hears some shuffling, some muttered conversation. A minute or two later, Renee is slipping out of the apartment in an old bathrobe, sandals on her feet. Her hair is knotted on one side where she was sleeping on it.

"Your eye," Renee says.

"Yeah."

Renee frowns at her.

"You're leaving," she says, and Sonya nods.

Renee disappears into the dark apartment and emerges a moment later with a box of matches and a cigarette. She tucks them into the pocket of her robe and leads the way to the stairwell. Together they climb the stairs to the roof, and each floor they pass is silent and still, the residents resting before a day of illusory productivity.

The night tastes wet, and the faint scent of petrichor is in the air, as if it just rained. They lean against the half wall that borders the roof, both looking out at the Aperture gate. Renee passes the cigarette to Sonya, and strikes a match for her; Sonya takes the first breath of smoke. Rarity confers value, she thinks, and she knows she won't smoke another cigarette after she leaves here, because half a dozen brands will be available to her and the allure will be gone.

"You should take my dress, the yellow one," Sonya says. "Go get it in the morning, before Building 4 gets wind that I'm gone. I also have a refrigerator, it's behind the plywood."

"Good looking out, Poster Girl," Renee says, as she takes the cigarette from Sonya with her first two fingers, delicate as tweezers. "They give you a new name?"

"Not yet," Sonya replies. "Not sure I'll bother. Everyone knows my face anyway."

"Wish they'd send you over a sector, so you could actually start again."

Sonya doesn't think about the other sectors much. They were closed off under the Delegation, an impossibility. Even now, travel permits are rare.

"I'm sorry," she says.

"For what?"

"Leaving, I guess." Now Renee will be the youngest person in the Aperture.

"Don't be stupid," Renee says, taking another drag from the cigarette. "I'm happy for you."

Sonya raises an eyebrow.

"A person can be more than one thing at once," Renee says. "I can be so jealous I want to burn my eyes out and happy for you at the same time."

Sonya takes Renee's hand and squeezes. Renee passes the cigarette back to her. They smoke it down to the filter, and don't say goodbye.

ROSE Parker waits for her outside Knox's building, Artemis Tower. She looks more sedate than usual, in black trousers and a white sweater, the only hint of color the scarf she wears in her hair, with its green leaf pattern that matches the vines that cling to the building's entrance. When she sees Sonya approach, she waves and smiles, as if they're friends.

"Wow, no Insight," she says, when Sonya draws near enough to hear her. "What's it like?"

"What was it like for you?" Sonya puts her hands in her pockets. The feeling of wrongness that has dominated the right side of her body since Naomi deactivated the Insight is already beginning to fade.

"When I did it, everyone was doing it," she says. "So we all pretended to be exhilarated by it."

There was a similar charade of happiness in the Aperture, for a time. Everyone pretending to be relieved they hadn't been executed, making plans for a little utopia among the four buildings. *Wouldn't want to be out there anyway,* people said, like this was a choice they had made instead of a prison they were locked in.

"Well," Sonya says, "shall we?"

She leads the way into the building's lobby. There's a different guard here from the one that let her in last time. The woman recognizes her, even without the Insight burning in her iris.

"Here to pay our respects," Sonya says.

"To her door?" the guard says.

"Yes," Sonya replies, tipping her chin up as if daring the woman to call her a fool. The guard gestures to the elevator bank.

They step into the elevator, and as the doors close, Rose looks at her. "You have a real way about you, you know that?"

"I've already been here once since she died."

"I thought they couldn't get her door open," Rose says. "I heard the peace officers applied for a permit to break the wall down."

The elevator rushes up to Knox's floor, making Sonya's ears pop. She's uneasy—the door might not open for her now that she has her Insight disabled—but she has to try. She walks down the hallway and stands in front of Knox's door, just as she did before. The mechanical eyeball swivels, once, before locking on her. The white ring around it flashes. The door opens.

"Guest: Kantor, Sonya," the voice announces. "Clearance level four."

"I didn't know you knew each other so well," Rose says.

"We didn't. But we had a deal."

The apartment looks just as it did when she was last here, maybe with more dust on everything. But it's different, seeing it through Rose Parker's eyes. She touches things, her fingers dancing over the table by the door, the kitchen counter with its coffee rings, the edge of Knox's desk. She disappears into the bedroom, and Sonya hears the squeak of her sitting on the edge of the bed, the jostling of plastic bottles in the shower. Rose comes back, and the look in her eyes is like the whir of a computer fan, everything moving.

Sonya takes the instructions for using the UIA database out of her pocket and unfolds them. She sits in Knox's desk chair and presses the paper flat in front of her, then starts to type. Last time she sat here, she was terrified of what she would find—terrified that it would be nothing. But this time, she knows what's waiting for her on the other side of the program.

"I'm not good with computers, so I was hoping you would help me," she says. She types in the name `Turner, Easton`.

The screen shifts, redrawing the straight lines of roads to reveal that Easton Turner is in an apartment building near the water.

"What is this?" Rose asks, frowning up at the screen. "How are you tracking him?"

"With his Insight," Sonya says.

"He doesn't have an Insight." Rose arches an eyebrow at Sonya. "Does he?"

"We all do," Sonya says, and it feels strange to be on the other end of this conversation. "They can't actually be removed. It's . . . a long story, and I'll tell it, but we don't have time right now. I know this database has kept track of location data for the entire time we've had Insights. I need to extract all Easton Turner's location data from the fall of the Delegation back to about five years before that. Can you figure out how to do that?"

Rose stares up at the screen.

"I mean, I can try," she says. "Let me sit."

Sonya gets up, and walks into Emily Knox's bedroom, where the white blankets are still rumpled. There's a long dark hair on one of the pillows, a dried-up contact lens on the bedside table. She sees a piece of paper sticking out of the drawer. *Violation of privacy, minus two hundred fifty DesCoin,* she thinks, but tugs the paper free anyway.

It's a half sheet, and thick, almost like an index card. There's a grid of black lines and text, recognizable immediately as a government-issued document, overwhelming Sonya with information at first. But the title, stamped in small uppercase, reads PERMIT 249A, FOR TRAVEL TO SECTOR 4C. She thinks of the wallpaper on Knox's computer, the desert sunrise—or sunset, she couldn't tell which. *A girl can dream,* Knox said.

"I think I figured it out!" Rose says from the other room. "What should I do now?"

Sonya tucks the permit into the interior pocket of her coat, and returns to the living room.

"Send it to yourself," Sonya says. "And then do the same thing for August Kantor. Same range of time."

Rose's fingers hesitate on the keys. She turns back to Sonya.

"All right," she says. "I've been pretty patient so far, but you really need to tell me what this is about."

Sonya looks out the window. The city is cloudy, as usual, the water in the bay gray and calm.

"Easton Turner used to work for Beake and Bell, the pharmaceutical company, before the Delegation fell," she says. "Periodically, he met with my father to provide him with Sol, the suicide drug. My father then used that drug to kill people who were inconvenient to the Delegation. On at least six occasions, those people were children."

Whatever Rose Parker was expecting, it obviously wasn't that. She stares up at Sonya, eyes wide.

"Grace Ward?" she says.

Sonya nods.

"What I'm trying to do here is to get Easton Turner's location data, and then my father's location data from the same time frame, to prove they had several meetings," she says. "Combined with my Insight footage from the past few weeks, which Alexander Price has a copy of, it should be enough for you to expose Easton Turner as an accomplice to murder."

"Not enough for a criminal case," Rose says, softly.

"No, but he won't be elected to public office again," she says. "I'm hoping you can also use his location data to prove that he's been working with the Analog Army, but I'm not as sure of that. Emily Knox went to the building they operate out of a couple days before she died. If we find out where it is, Easton Turner's location data might show that he's been there several times. Enough to arouse suspicion, at least."

"This is . . ." Rose waves a hand over the keyboard. "An absurdly useful resource. And a terrifying one."

"That's why I only want to take what we need," Sonya says. "Knox told me to finish up with Grace Ward, and this is how I'm doing it."

"And after that?"

"After that, I wipe it all away," Sonya says.

"You're going to *delete* it?" Rose says. "Do you have any idea how many crimes you could solve, how many people you could help, with all of this information at your fingertips?"

"She asked me to," Sonya says, firmly. "So I'm doing it. What I need to know from you is whether you're going to write this article or not. It's a big risk, but I need someone to take it."

Rose studies her for a moment.

"Of course I will," she says. "I have to tell you, I'm kind of surprised that you're willing to torch your father's name like this just to burn down Easton Turner."

She has it backward, Sonya thinks. It's her father's name she needs to burn.

Comprehension dawns on her as she thinks of what Alexander Price said to her, when she was just beginning this investigation—that he had helped the uprising destroy his childhood home. It had disgusted her then. Now she understands it. It's not something to delight in, something to thirst for, something to relish. It's just what needs to be done.

"These were his choices," Sonya says. "But I'm the one who has to live with them."

AN hour later, Rose Parker leaves the apartment. They spent some time debating exactly what she would need to know in order to implicate Easton Turner fully, and then experimenting with the UIA database to export the data. Once Rose was satisfied, she tied her scarf more firmly around her head, gathered her things, and left Sonya alone in Knox's apartment.

Sonya takes out Knox's instructions for deleting the Delegation data. Scrawled along the top is *DATA PURGE PROTOCOL*. The instructions are written like Knox is talking to a child. Condescending from beyond the grave, Sonya thinks, and she starts to type.

Once the process is set in motion, it takes time. There's so much data that scouring it from Knox's system—impressive though it is—is laborious, and all the machines in the room start to hum, as if the apartment is coming to life. A number in the lower left-hand corner of the terminal reports back the percentage of files deleted.

```
1%
2%
3%
```

Sonya swivels to face the windows, and waits. She falls asleep there, upright in Knox's chair. When she wakes, it's early afternoon, and rain dusts the windows. She turns to discover that the screen reads

```
100%
Thank You.
```

A sputtering sound startles her, and she looks under the desk to see a trail of smoke coming from the computer tower beneath it. She runs to the bathroom to get a towel and wet it in the sink, and by the time she returns, water dripping on her shoes, the entire computer is engulfed in a cloud of dark smoke. The screen above the desk flickers out, and instead of throwing the towel over it, she stands back and breathes in the smell of burned plastic and watches Knox's system self-destruct.

Eventually the smoke dissipates. She hangs the wet towel over the back of the chair, takes one last look at the apartment: stark bedroom, wild tangles of cables, line of pink light around the desk. Then she props the door open—there's no sense in the peace officers breaking it down, after all, since there's nothing left for them to find that matters.

TWENTY

IT'S LATE AFTERNOON when she gets to the Wards' apartment. The curtains are open, the yellow kitchen glowing even on a cloudy day. She stands on the worn welcome mat for a long time, taking deep, slow breaths. Then she knocks.

Trudie Ward answers. She wears a bright pink sweater, and her hair is in a high ponytail.

"Oh," she says, when she sees Sonya standing there. "It's you again." She frowns. "Your Insight's gone. Funny, you don't look like your head's been cut open recently."

"Is your mother home?" Sonya says.

"She went to the market," Trudie says. "She should be back soon." She waits a beat, and then sighs, and holds the door open. "Come in and wait, I guess."

Sonya steps into the house. Trudie goes back to the kitchen counter, where a mixing bowl waits with something chocolatey inside it. She picks up the spatula and skims it around the inside of the bowl in one steady motion, turning the batter over.

"Peace officers came here yesterday looking for you," she says. "They told me you were gone. I figured you ran away for good. To be honest, I was kinda surprised you hadn't done it earlier."

Sonya hears "they told me you were gone" the way she used to hear it when Susanna hit the wrong chord on the guitar—each string's sound crashing into the next. Trudie's voice, lower than average, a little croaky. *They told me you were gone, and I believed them. This is your Alice.*

"*You* left the message," Sonya says. "You pretended to be your sister, and left your mother a message?"

Trudie keeps stirring the batter with the spatula, making three turns around the bowl before setting it down. She sticks her finger in it, tastes the chocolate, and then looks at Sonya.

"It's not like that. I wouldn't do something so cruel," she says, at last. "She asked me to do it."

"Why?"

"Because we were worried you would take your sweet time," Trudie says. "Every day you didn't find Grace was a day you got to spend free. We thought, if you had to hear her voice—if you thought she was in trouble—"

She shrugs. She carries the bowl over to a cake tin waiting on the stove, and spoons the batter into it. She doesn't spill a drop.

Sonya's first attempt at baking was in the Aperture. Charlotte taught her how to make quick bread with flour and oats. Sonya forgot to add the baking powder, and the bread came out like a brick. She ate it anyway, in the morning with her coffee, because wasting flour and oats was almost criminal in the Aperture.

Her mother never taught her—she hadn't known, either. She never had flour on her hands or smudges on her sleeves. She hired help, for dinner parties, and she made a show of domesticity, an apron tied around her waist, a wooden spoon in a stew she hadn't done any of the work for. For Julia Kantor, a dutiful wife was a capable actress. The same isn't true for Eugenia, who taught her daughter to be a capable person.

Sonya's throat tightens. The front door opens, and Eugenia slips her shoes off before even taking her keys out of the lock. She's carrying a loaf of bread wrapped in paper and a bouquet of daisies tied with brown string. Between the flowers and the cake that Trudie is putting in the oven, Sonya wonders if there's a celebration coming up. Her throat gets even tighter.

"Oh!" Eugenia says, when she sees Sonya. "Ms. Kantor. Welcome back. I hope Trudie has offered you something to eat."

"Hello, Ms. Ward," Sonya says. She says it as normally as she can manage, but something in her tone must be off. Eugenia straightens, clutching the bread and the flowers close to her chest. "I need to talk to you. To both of you, if Mr. Ward is home."

"Of course," Eugenia says, and she sets bread and bouquet down on the kitchen counter. She steps into the hallway beyond the kitchen and calls out, "Roger! Come in here a moment."

Sonya stays near the door. She wishes she were on the other side of the wilderness; she wishes she had chosen to leave this behind her. She felt such clarity standing on Naomi's porch, but that clarity is gone now, subsumed by the fear that rattles her spine like an earthquake, buzzes in her teeth.

Roger Ward, who Sonya once watched assemble a swing set in the backyard, shuffles into the kitchen in old slippers. He looks almost the same now as he did then. His beard is grayer, his hair thinner. His shoulders are rounded as if weighed down by a heavy load. He looks at her without recognition, at first, and then with it, like the flare around the spark wheel of a lighter before the flame appears.

"Sonya needs to speak with us," Eugenia says. "Come and sit."

Roger does sit, at the kitchen island. And so does Trudie. Sonya just closes her eyes, briefly, and shakes her head. It's not the elegant refusal she practiced. She can't muster anything more.

The sight of them—Trudie with a chocolate-streaked finger, Roger with his slippers, Eugenia with a key ring still around her finger—is almost more than she can stand.

"I don't want to leave you in suspense," Sonya says. *No euphemisms,* she hears Knox insist, and she says, "Grace is dead."

She hears a sharp intake of air. Not Eugenia's—Roger's. Eugenia's eyes are soft. She isn't surprised. Maybe she always knew. Maybe you can feel it when your child dies, like a piece of your body has withered and fallen off.

"You're sure?" Eugenia says, as Trudie starts to cry. Sonya puts both hands flat against her abdomen and presses down, steadying herself.

"I'm sure," Sonya says. "But that isn't where the story starts." She is aware of her heartbeat, fast and hard in her chest. The pulse in her cheeks. Her next breath catches, but she continues, focusing on Eugenia's soft eyes.

"The story starts with me," Sonya says. "When I was sixteen years old, I was riding the HiTrain after school, and it stalled next to your apartment building. I saw Grace standing at one of your windows while Trudie was playing in the backyard."

Eugenia's hand lifts, hovers near her mouth. The kitchen is silent.

Sonya remembers a splinter she got in the sole of her foot, as a child, running barefoot in the yard. For a day she tried to ignore it, but it was too painful, and she had to confess to her mother that she needed it removed. Julia dug it out of her foot with a sterilized needle. It was deep, and stubborn, and she screamed and sobbed for Julia to stop, but she refused. *It has to come out,* Julia said to her. *All of it.*

"I went home and I told my father, who was the head of the Committee of Order," she says. "He's the one who ordered the raid on your apartment. I don't know the exact details of the story after that. But I know that after he took Grace, he gave her Sol. She died without pain. He brought her body to a house in the woods outside the city to be buried."

Roger takes a horrible, rattling breath. Trudie is still crying, but quiet.

Eugenia only stares.

"A valuable friend of the Delegation—and now the Triumvirate—lives out there. She was able to confirm what happened. I can tell you how to find the place, if you would like to see the grave, and speak to the woman who lives there."

Sonya doesn't want to tell them the woman is Naomi Proctor; it will only sound ridiculous to them.

Sonya rehearsed everything she has said so far, but she never got to this part. The part where she tells them she's sorry. The part where she lets herself soften. All of that feels wrong now. There is nothing that feels right, to take its place. Nothing that makes this easy, or simple, or good.

"I agreed to investigate your daughter's disappearance because I knew I was responsible for it," Sonya says. "I can't . . ." Her breath hitches. Sometime in the last few minutes, she started crying, but she didn't realize it. "I can't apologize to you. I came to tell you the truth. That's all."

She is quiet then. Trudie's and Roger's hands are piled on top of each other on the counter, each of them reaching for the other, comforting each other. But Eugenia has stayed still. Her soft eyes are not so soft anymore. She looks at Sonya, and Sonya wants to cower, but she doesn't. She looks back.

"Do you feel better now?" Eugenia says, in a cold, small voice. "Now that you've made your big confession?"

It would be easy, Sonya thinks, to feel superior to this woman—stripped of her youth, in her faded floral dress, in her ugly yellow kitchen that smells like oil spatter and chocolate cake. But the way she received the devastation that Sonya came to offer her makes that impossible. Sonya could never feel superior to this woman.

"Do you think it makes you noble, that you take responsibility for this?" Eugenia goes on. "You made sure to tell me, didn't you, in your own little way, that you didn't do this in exchange for your freedom, no, you did it for high-minded reasons. You tried *so hard* to make it look like you understand what you did to us. What an elegant manipulation you've brought to our doorstep, Sonya Kantor."

She tips up her chin.

"How did you spend the DesCoin you received as a reward for turning us in? On a new dress, a wild night? Or did you hoard it for the perfect future the Delegation had laid out for you?"

Sonya had, in fact, spent the DesCoin she earned for turning Grace Ward in. She had used it to buy a night with Aaron. Her first time, her virginity lost out of wedlock. A hefty DesCoin penalty.

Sonya flinches at the question. She doesn't answer.

"My daughter is dead," Eugenia says. "Get out of my house."

Cold with sweat, Sonya wipes her cheeks, turns, and leaves. She expected to run into a sea of commuters, coming home from work, but the street is empty, quiet. She crosses it, and then keeps walking, trembling, toward the train.

TWENTY-ONE

THE AIR SMELLS salty and sour. She climbs the steps to the top of the embankment that wraps around most of the city's waterfront, a story high, to protect the city from the rising water level. There are stretches of glass here and there, to give pedestrians a look underwater. She passes one on her way up. Sea foam collects in the upper corners of the window.

The embankment is empty now, likely due to the rain. It taps on her shoulders and the top of her head. It rolls behind her ears and accumulates around her collar. She stands with her hands on the railing, and closes her eyes. All she hears is the splash of the waves beneath her. She wonders what the city sounded like when the streets were full of cars. When the water didn't press up against its edges, fighting to get in.

She doesn't look over her shoulder to find out if Easton Turner sent someone to follow her, to make sure she kept her promise. She never intended to keep it, only wanted to get out of the Aperture for long enough to talk to the Wards, to fulfill Knox's last request. To find the proof Rose needs.

Knox told her at the very beginning, *You don't really understand how much you can find out about a person just based on where they go and when.* She does now. Her father's life had unfurled in front of her when Rose looked up his name, the screen pausing on the last place his Insight emitted a signal: a grave somewhere outside the city, where many of the people killed in the uprising were buried. She could have kept pieces of her family, the ones recorded in the UIA database—could have learned her mother's secrets, as well as her father's, and Susanna's. Ripped the entire family open to see what was inside. She had gone so long with her eyes closed, there was something appealing about prying them open, now, to find out just how foolish she'd been.

In the end, she let them wash away.

The rain gentles to a mist, and she sits down on a bench to watch the water move. It's just starting to get dark. She unzips her coat just enough to reach the interior pocket, where she put the travel permit, but that's not what she's after—instead, she takes out the worn envelope behind it. Until this morning, she kept it in the crate beside her bed. She opens it, and tips a yellow pill into her palm.

Ten years ago, she made the decision not to take her life in a single moment, when she tilted her head back along with her parents and sister but never opened her mouth. But as she watched them descend into euphoric giggles, she thought about it again. And as they slumped over the table, all the life drained from them, she thought about it *again.* She considered the pill in her hand for a long time before the uprising burst through the door to the cabin. Eventually, she hid it, in case she needed it later.

She considers it now. She doesn't feel desperate, or afraid. She feels like someone who leveled everything behind her so she had nothing left to go back to. In a few days or a few weeks, Rose Parker will publish the article that blows up Easton Turner's life, and it will take Sonya's family with it. It doesn't matter that she was a child when her father murdered those people. It doesn't matter whether her mother and sister knew or not. And it doesn't matter if she takes on a new name. Everyone in the city knows her face. She will always be his daughter.

But if she's honest with herself, that isn't why she is considering the Sol now. That honor belongs to Eugenia Ward. *Do you feel better now that you've made your big confession?*

No, she wants to go back and answer. *No, I feel sick all the time, I feel ready to be gone.*

"Hello." Alexander's callused hands close over the back of the bench, beside her. He looks at her—at her wet hair, her soaked wool coat, the yellow pill in her hand. Then he looks out at the water. The only sign of emotion he wears is in his hands, trembling as he lifts them from the bench. He walks around it, and sits beside her.

"Rose Parker came to ask me for your Insight footage," he says. "She was worried about you. I remembered you saying you wanted to go to the waterfront. Had to rack my brain to remember where they used to sell those sticky buns."

"It's the sound," she says. "I like the sound, here."

"Right." He looks at the pill again, chewing the inside of his lip. "You kept it all this time?"

She kept it in her fist, hidden from the peace officers, until they made it back to the city. Then she bent to tie her shoes, and tucked it into the cup of her bra, hoping they wouldn't find it. But they didn't seem to care what she wore into the Aperture, what she brought with her. It's how Mary Pritchard kept her pearls, how Nikhil kept the photograph of Nora, Aaron, and Alexander that lived in his wallet.

All Sonya brought in was her Sol.

"I didn't know what the uprising would do to me, after they arrested me," she says. "It seemed like a good idea to have a way out. And then it just kept seeming like a good idea to have a way out."

"That," he says, "is a terrifying thing for a girl of seventeen to have to consider."

She nods.

"So what's this about?" he says, nodding to her hand. "Shame?"

"I talked to the Wards," she says, looking across the water at the faint bumps of hills on the horizon, gray and fuzzy from the distance and the cloud layer. "Grace Ward's mother asked me what I spent my DesCoin on, after getting her daughter killed. You know what it was?" She laughs, and somehow the laugh turns into a sob. "I slept with Aaron. He'd been trying to convince me it was worth it, but I wasn't willing to do it unless I had an unexpected windfall." She pushes her free hand through her hair, knots her fingers in the fine strands. "God, it's so vile. I can't . . ." She chokes. "I can't stand it. I can't stand what I did to them. I can't stand to know *why.*"

She closes both hands into fists, and digs them into her legs.

"I'll always know what I did, and what came of it," she says. "I will never be rid of it."

Alexander lays a hand on her fist, gentle, to get her to relax it. Then he sits forward, resting his elbows on his spread knees, and stares at the ground between his feet.

"You were trying to earn absolution for what you did," he says. He rubs a hand over the back of his neck. "Well, so was I."

He's always moving, Alexander Price, fidgeting with something in his pocket, playing with his food at the dinner table, tossing a coin as he waits for the HiTrain, chewing his fingernails in the middle of conversations. Every memory she has of him, he's moving. He turns toward her now, lifting his eyes to hers, and he finally goes still.

"I didn't betray my family," he says. "I know you think I did, but I didn't need to—my father surrendered himself right away. And I hadn't done much for the resistance movement, you know? I had joined up a few months before, but hadn't made much progress, and during the uprising, I was just terrified it wouldn't be enough—terrified they would arrest me, too, maybe kill me. I should have hated them, after Mom and Aaron died in the rioting, but I was just afraid of them. So when they asked me where they might find your father . . ." His throat clicks as he swallows. "I told them. I didn't think about what would happen to you, or your sister, I just . . ."

Sonya keeps her eyes steady on his. He shakes his head.

"Ten years later, I found out from a friend that the Triumvirate were evaluating your case—you were right on the line for release," he says. "They thought it was too much of a risk to release you, you were too well known, too much of a symbol for the Delegation. So I barged into the hearing and I suggested they give you something to do, instead. Some way to earn your way out. I said I had some unresolved matters that might be suitable, and they agreed. I thought—if I can get her out of there, if I can get her freedom, it'll undo what I did to her."

He shakes his head.

"It doesn't," he says. "I know that. I know there's *nothing*—"

Sonya reaches out. She sets her hand on his arm, drawing his eyes to hers again.

"Sasha," she says. "I've known this since the Delegation fell."

His eyes look so dark, in this light. A cold, dark brown turned black by a cloudy day.

"There were only so many people who knew where that cabin was," she says. "And most of them were dead before the uprising found us. Why do you think I hated you so much when you turned up in my apartment?" She tilts her head a little. "Well, I guess there were a few reasons to choose from."

"You knew," he says.

She nods. "I tried to keep hating you. But you were young and scared. I know what it's like to be young and scared." She shrugs a little. "You didn't earn it. At some point—I don't even remember when—I just . . . swallowed it."

She looks out at the water again. It crashes against the embankment wall in an imperfect rhythm.

"I guess," she says, "I can't make the Wards swallow it for me."

"No," he says, softly. "You can't. Not even by dying for it."

She nods. She gets up, and stands at the railing.

Deciding to live is as easy as tipping her hand so the pill falls into the water and sinks to the bottom.

SHE's sitting in a social worker's office when she comes to a decision. The office is buried in the back of the administration building that Susanna once described as the most depressing place on Earth. The carpet beneath her feet is speckled gray and blue, worn in all the places where feet commonly tread. A beat-up metal desk stands between her and Agatha Sherman, lifetime bureaucrat, who has an ink stain at the corner of her mouth from chewing on a pen. There are no windows.

She is staring at a piece of paper certifying Sonya's release from the Aperture—not issued by Easton Turner, this time, but by the other two members of the Triumvirate, Petra Novak and Amy Archer.

Agatha's desk is covered with little figurines shaped like frogs and toads. Some are clear glass, and some are painted. One wears a ceramic crown. One has eyes that shift back and forth every second, like a clock. One is the size of Sonya's fist. She can't help but stare at them.

"Okay, Ms. Kantor," Agatha Sherman says. She rubs the corner of her mouth. The ink only smears into her cheek. "Per the terms of the Children of the Delegation Act, your Insight will be deactivated . . ." She pauses, looking up at Sonya. "I suppose you don't require that—but you are entitled to transitional housing and a new identity, if you want it. Most of our Aperture releases have embraced the opportunity to begin anew—"

"No," Sonya says. "No, thank you."

Agatha frowns. She sets the paper down, and folds her hands on her desk. Her elbow nudges one of the frogs—a tropical one, its underside painted blue and black—askew.

"Can I make a personal recommendation?" she says. "You are too well known to do very well with your current name. I encourage you to reconsider. There is no reason to work against yourself here."

"Thank you," Sonya says. "But I don't think I'm going to be in the city for long, and . . ." She shrugs. "For better or worse, this is my name."

Agatha looks faintly annoyed. She is not used to people not taking her personal recommendations, maybe.

"Fine," she says. "I take it you won't be requiring temporary housing?"

"No," Sonya says.

Agatha purses her lips, then stamps the paper with a giant ink seal of the Triumvirate. She passes it to Sonya, who takes it, folds it, and comes to her feet. She reaches across Agatha's desk and restores the tropical frog to his original position, then leaves the office.

SHE spends the next few weeks tangled together with Alexander Price. Her mornings, padding into the kitchen in one of his sweaters, barefoot, to heat up the water for coffee. Her afternoons, reading the books he keeps stacked here and there all over his little apartment. Her nights, waking with a start, only to put her hand on his chest and make sure he's still breathing. She doesn't meet his friends; she doesn't make eye contact with his neighbors. She's waiting, and they both know it.

On the day Rose Parker's special issue of the *Chronicle* shows up at their door, with a note from Rose herself attached to it, Sonya sits down at the kitchen table and reads the paper front to back. The first page reads EASTON TURNER ACCOMPLICE TO DELEGATION MURDERS, by Rose Parker. Then, TURNER LOCATION DATA REVEALS CONNECTIONS TO EXTREMIST GROUP. Then AUGUST KANTOR, DELEGATION KILLER.

That night, she crumples it in the bottom of a trash can and goes out to the balcony with Alexander to burn it. She watches it curl in the flames and turn to ash. Then she stands on her tiptoes to kiss him, and it's a kind of goodbye.

When he drops her off at the airport, so she can catch a rare flight out of the sector, he gives her the dish she made for her father, glued back together, her old house key, and Susanna's guitar pick.

EPILOGUE

Sonya drags a handkerchief across her forehead and tucks it in her pocket before getting on the bike. She kicks the solar motor on, then speeds down the dirt road to the highway. The sun is setting behind the mountains, jagged in the distance, but everything is flat where she is now, and she can see for miles in every direction.

The road is smooth and unbroken, for the most part. Where there's no moisture, Ellie says, there's no need for road maintenance. Dust curls around her bare ankles. It will stain her socks by the time she gets back to the dormitory where she lives with all the other Desert Eden laborers. Dust creeps in every crack there, too—wipe it away in the morning, and it's back by evening. She pulls her kerchief up to cover her mouth as she reaches the highway.

Joshua trees stand on either side of the road like people waiting in line. When she first arrived, she couldn't stop staring at them. She's used to the heavy branches of evergreens, bowing beneath the weight of the rain. She's used to the moss that grows on every tree trunk. She doesn't know how to account for the stiff, bare trunks of these trees, the spiky leaves and the bulging white flowers. The first time she touched one, it drew blood. She loved it immediately.

Find out who you are when no one is watching, Naomi Proctor advised, and Sonya has. She likes things that are difficult to love: the misty air of the Desert Eden dome, which makes everyone else's hair go limp; the dust that collects in the creases of her face; the chemical smell of the sunscreen she has to cover herself with every day to keep from frying in the sun; the freckles that spot her legs and arms anyway, no matter how hard she tries to keep the sun at bay.

She likes finishing her days aching, with dirt under her fingernails, falling asleep on top of the book about plants that her supervisor, Ellie, gave her when she arrived. The sector assigned Sonya here, when she told them she knew how to fix old appliances and grow things, her only useful skills. The place has received her neutrally, neither impressed with her nor particularly critical of her. Ellie likes that Sonya is a quick learner and not easily pushed around. The others like that she knows how to roll cigarettes and play cards.

The sun is behind one of the mountains now, and all around it the sky is orange, so brilliant Sonya has to stop. She kicks off the solar motor and stands with the bike between her legs, in the middle of the road that no one calls I-40 anymore, though the signs are still up, here and there, bent and coated in dirt. The mountains are purple, the clouds that drift above them pink. Sonya reaches into the bag at her side and takes out a camera, an old one she borrowed from one of the other gardeners, Lily. Lily will teach her to develop the film the old-fashioned way. People are like that, here. They want to walk backward through time, just like the Analog Army. For the most part, Sonya doesn't mind.

She adjusts the settings, hesitating with her finger over the wheel that adjusts the aperture. She promised Sasha she would send him photographs with her next letter. He's agreed to forward some of them to Nikhil. Travel restrictions are supposed to loosen soon, he tells her, as the Triumvirate stabilizes. She has never promised to go back, but one day, maybe, she will.

Still, she doesn't lift the camera to her eye. Instead, she just stands there with it in her hands, and looks around.

She's a speck of dust here, unobserved and unremarked upon. Everywhere, in every direction, is emptiness.

Everywhere, in every direction, is freedom.

ACKNOWLEDGMENTS

I WROTE THIS BOOK during one of the hardest parts of the pandemic: about six months in, no vaccine in sight, quarantine fatigue in full swing. There were a lot of people who quietly kept us all going during that time. Thank you to them, especially.

Thank you also to John Joseph Adams and Joanna Volpe for helping me to shape and polish this book. A special acknowledgment to Jordan Hill for your spectacular notes when I needed them most. Thank you to Jaime Levine for your hard work and insights.

Thank you to everyone at William Morrow: the editorial team; the design and art departments for their efforts on this beautiful package, with a shout out to Mark Robinson; the publicity, marketing, and sales departments, particularly Emily Fisher, Tavia Kowalchuk, and Deanna Bailey; and thank you to the unsung heroes in production, particularly my diligent copyeditor Ana Deboo.

Kristin Dwyer, for your enthusiasm and creativity. Elisabeth Sanders, for keeping me on track.

Everyone at New Leaf, especially Meredith Barnes, Jenniea Carter, Katherine Curtis, Veronica Grijalva, Victoria Hendersen, Hilary Pecheone, and Pouya Shahbazian, for your hard work and consistency even through challenging times.

Writers and friends Sarah Enni, Maurene Goo, Amy Lukavics, Michelle Krys, Kaitlin Ward, Kate Hart, Zan Romanoff, Jennifer Smith, Morgan Matson, Margaret Stohl, S. G. Demciri, and Laurie Devore, for keeping me steady and supported and helping me brainstorm for this book on numerous occasions. Kara Thomas, for applying her mystery wizardry to my rough draft. Courtney Summers, for encouraging me early on to be brave and do what this book really needed.

Nelson, husband, friend, early reader, road-trip chauffeur, photographer, confidante, quarantine buddy, for all of it, the whole damn thing.

Roths and Rosses, for your constant support, but also for bearing with me when I was sixteen and needed patience and understanding.

Fitches, for the same, minus the sixteen part.

All the friends who joined me on Zooms and various TV-watching chat platforms and outdoor walks in the dead of winter and frigid porch hangs over the last couple years.

Pink Floyd's "Wish You Were Here," which helped me find Sonya's grief whenever I lost touch with it.

DISCUSSION QUESTIONS

1. The Aperture is a prison made up of four apartment blocks set in the middle of a city neighborhood, where the prisoners are constantly under observation but are also left to themselves to create and enforce any kind of social order. Why did the Triumvirate decide this was the appropriate prison for people who were once important members of the Delegation?

2. Seattle's Pike Place Market is famous (or perhaps infamous) for its Gum Wall, a brick wall where for decades people have been applying their used chewing gum to create an enormous interactive art exhibit. Sonya remembers volunteering to scrape gum off that wall, which despite Delegation rules was constantly being reapplied. She thinks to herself, "People love their small rebellions" (74). Is she right? And if so, what are some small rebellions people practice in today's society? Do they focus on certain current events or issues? Do you have any small rebellions of your own?

3. Several pairs of siblings appear in this story, including Charlotte and Graham, Sonya and Susanna, and Aaron and Alexander. Sonya admits that one of the reasons she agreed to model for the Delegation poster was to set herself apart from her sister. If you have siblings, how did your childhood rela-

tionship affect your self-identity? Did that change in adulthood? If you are an only child, do you think your lack of siblings affected your sense of self?

4. Sonya concedes that under the Delegation's system, she did a careful cost-benefit analysis before taking an action. Are people more likely to do a good deed if other people will know about it?

5. The Analog Army maintains that "Elicits Are a Slippery Slope That Lead Back to the Insight" (75). In logic, a "slippery slope argument" is one that claims a specific small step will cause a chain reaction leading an enormous effect. Is the Analog Army making an effective slippery slope argument? Is there a difference between using technology that is constantly and easily available and using technology that has been integrated into the body?

6. Sonya says to Alexander, "I wonder how you ever knew that what your family was doing was wrong, when everything around you said it was right" (191). Are there any values your family taught you as a child that you've changed your mind about as an adult?

7. The DesCoin system was set up to reward people for desirable behavior. But how should society determine what that behavior looks like? Who gets to choose what is desirable, and how do we decide when those standards should be re-evaluated?

8. Sonya is horrified to learn from Naomi Proctor that the algorithms behind DesCoin were customized for each individual, to shape them into the person the Delegation wanted them to become. Sonya wonders at what age the system made up its mind about a person's future, and what led the system to

sort people into their destined occupations and lifestyles. If you were evaluated by the Delegation at age ten, what role in society do you think they would have assigned to you? How different would their evaluation be if they made it today?

9. Alexander explained to Sonya that he loved looking at old photographs because the decisions the photographer made—the subject, how and at what angle the subject is presented, the lighting—communicate a tremendous amount of information without using words. Think about the last photo you took: what decisions did you make when you were taking it? What did that photo communicate about you and your point of view vis-à-vis the subject of the photo?

10. Naomi Proctor tells Sonya to "find out who you are when no one is watching" (226). Do you find that it's more difficult to discover or be yourself now that we are so connected by social media and telecommunications?